PRAISE FOR DAVID S. BRODY

"Better than Grisham. A fabulous work."
  — Gary Chafetz, BOSTON GLOBE 2-time Pulitzer Prize Nominee
    (review of *Unlawful Deeds*)

"A compelling suspense story and a searing murder mystery."
  — THE BOSTON PHOENIX
    (review of *Blood of the Tribe*)

"An enormously fun read, exceedingly hard to put down."
  — The BOOKBROWSER
    (review of *Unlawful Deeds*)

"A feast."
  — ARTS AROUND BOSTON
    (review of *Unlawful Deeds*)

Early Praise for Cabal of the Westford Knight

"Cutting-edge research and top-notch storytelling. Prepare to be blown away!"
  — Scott Wolter, author of *The Kensington Rune Stone: Compelling New Evidence*

"A wonderful mixture of *The Da Vinci Code* and *National Treasure*. A must read for those who love history and adventure!"
  — Richard Lynch, past President of the New England Antiquities Research Association (NEARA)

"A book I could not lay down. Strongly recommended."
  — Judge David Sinclair Bouschor, past President of the Clan Sinclair USA and former Grand Master of the Masonic Grand Lodge of Minnesota

CABAL OF THE WESTFORD KNIGHT

Templars at the Newport Tower

A novel by **David S. Brody**

Martin and Lawrence Press
Groton, Massachusetts

The Westford Knight
Templars at the Newport Tower

Published by
Martin and Lawrence Press
P.O. Box 682
Groton, MA 01450

ISBN 978-0-9773898-7-2
Library of Congress Control Number 2008941285

Cabal of the Westford Knight/by David S. Brody 1st ed.

Printed in Canada.

Also by David S. Brody

Unlawful Deeds
Blood of the Tribe
The Wrong Abraham

This novel is dedicated to the hundreds of members of the New England Antiquities Research Association (NEARA) who are willing to scratch beneath the polished surface of reported history in search of the hidden truth beneath.

A portion of the proceeds from the sale of this book will be donated to NEARA to support further research in the field of pre-Columbian exploration of North America.

AUTHOR'S NOTE

This is a work of fiction based on fact and reality. All the historical figures, sites, artifacts and archeological findings referenced in the story (excepting the tunnel and crypt in the second-to-last chapter) are genuine, including:

Prince Henry Sinclair

Sir James Gunn

Bernard de Clairvaux (Saint Bernard)

Judge Samuel Sewell and the passages quoted from his diary

The Touro Family of Newport, RI

The Biblical figure, Enoch

Niven Sinclair

Henry Wadsworth Longfellow and his familial relations

The Knights Templar and their history

The Newport Tower

The Westford Knight effigy

The Westford Boat Stone carving

The Westford "Encampment Site" foundation ruins

The Oak Island Money Pit

The Kensington Rune Stone

The Spirit Pond Rune Stones

The Narragansett Rune Stone

The Nomans Land Rune Stone

America's Stonehenge, including the Sacrificial Stone

The "starburst" pattern visible from an aerial view of America's Stonehenge

The Bourne Stone

The Tyngsboro Map Stone

The Machias petroglyphs

The Trois-Rivieres artifacts

The Lake Memphremagog artifacts

The various "stone holes" referenced in the story

Roslyn Chapel, including its maize and aloe carvings

The Sir William St. Clair tombstone at Roslyn Chapel

The Kilmore Church stained glass window depicting Jesus and Mary Magdalene

Touro Synagogue

Touro Cemetery

Royston Cave

The Zeno Narrative and Zeno Map

The Delta of Enoch symbol in Freemasonry, including the Tetragrammaton

To aid the reader, I have included pictures and images of many of these sites and artifacts within the text. The historical references in the book likewise are supported by outside sources — see the notes section printed at the end of the story. All modern-day characters in the story are fictional except for the Scott Wolter character, who is a fictional version of a forensic geologist and researcher of that name.

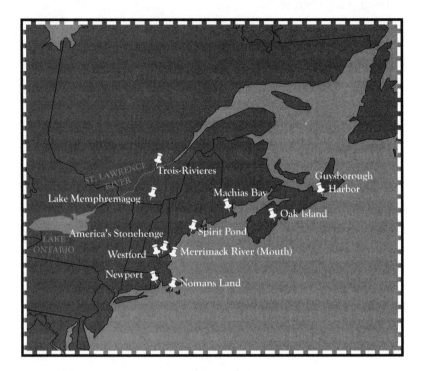

Map of Sites Referenced in Book

PROLOGUE

Many people discovered America before Columbus, but most of them had the good sense to keep quiet about it.
                                                  — **Oscar Wilde**

[May, 1399]

Henry Sinclair brushed the sweat off his forehead with the sleeve of his tunic and swatted at a swarm of black flies buzzing around his beard. "It is a beautiful land, for sure. But the insects are enough to make a man mad." His wealth, his nobility, his titles — nature cared not a damn for any of them. Not here in this new world and not at home in Scotland. The pests were just as happy to alight on the neck of a prince as on a stable boy. It was a good lesson.

His companion grunted a response. "Curse the fool who dragged us across the ocean, I say. We should be home hunting boar. Not dragging our old bones up this hill." He spat. "If God had meant for us to walk, he would not have given us horses, I wager."

Sinclair laughed. James Gunn would never question him in front of the men but with the others out of earshot behind them on the trail, his old friend could call him a fool without fear of retribution. "What's wrong, Gunn, getting too old for a bit of adventure? Should I send you home to sit by the fire? You can gossip with the women."

Gunn straightened in response. His usually pale face was pink from exertion and his thick chest heaved beneath his chain mail armor. Grinning, he rested his meaty hand on the pommel of his battle sword. "Not too old to teach a whelp like you a lesson."

Sinclair towered over his lieutenant by almost a full head but Gunn was as thick as an oak tree and nearly as hard as one. For almost 50 years, since they were old enough to walk, they had wrestled and jousted — sometimes for fun or in anger, sometimes side by side on the battlefield.

Laughing, he raised a hand. "Easy, old friend. Save your strength for when the natives come attacking."

Following a route his mother's Viking ancestors had mapped across the North Atlantic, Sinclair's party — 220 sailors and craftsmen spread over 12 boats — made land in a place he christened Nova Scotia, after the homeland of his father's people. Native legend here told of a tall, yellow-haired god appearing from the east on a one-winged canoe. Fortunately for Sinclair, he arrived with his sail billowing. The natives, who called themselves Mi'kmaq, were not convinced he was that god, but neither were they certain otherwise. They allowed him and his men to explore for the summer and encamp over winter. When spring arrived most of his party returned to Scotland. But he and 23 of his men, including Gunn, remained to continue their exploration. And hopefully complete their mission.

Gunn grunted and used his sword to hack his way along the trail, his eyes peering into the woods for hostile natives. Sinclair couldn't resist. "Gunn, ahead there! Is that a native? With bow and arrow?" Crouching, Gunn squinted for a few seconds before Sinclair guffawed and slapped him on the back. "A mere jest, my friend. Having a bit of fun at your expense."

Gunn shook his sword an inch from his nose. "Your ancestors rutted with donkeys. Just look at their line."

Pushing the tip away, Sinclair leaned back and laughed. He and Gunn were second cousins. "Yes, I'm looking at it now. An ugly lot, for sure."

They waited for the rest of the men to join them and resumed climbing, single file behind Gunn. He set a brisk pace which Sinclair easily matched. It was good to be on the move again after a winter of inactivity. They had left Nova Scotia a week ago and sailed southwest, their galley pushed by a gale from the northeast. On the fifth day they spotted land and took shelter at the mouth of a river. When the storm abated they spotted smoke rising from a distant hill. Their Mi'kmaq guide, Kitpu, believed the hill marked the land of the Penacook, a tribe friendly with the Mi'kmaq that occupied the land just to the northwest of the coastal Massachuset tribe.

The hill was the highest in the region and as good a place as any to explore; they rowed inland, following the river and a tributary to the base of the rise. He took Gunn and five men as well as Kitpu—a lean, leather-skinned man with an uncanny ability to move silently through the woods—to climb the hill and determine whether the land might make a suitable settlement site. He left the other men to guard the galley. And its priceless cargo.

They neared the top of the hill. Kitpu had explained this land was called 'Nashoba,' meaning 'Hill that Shakes.' Sinclair had not shared this information with the men—they were already skittish at being so far inland in unknown territory. They didn't need the added worry of shaking hills.

"Why come we so far inland, my Lord?" Gunn asked. With the men within earshot, he now addressed Sinclair in a manner befitting his status as Prince of Orkney and Earl of Roslyn. Gunn asked the question on behalf of the men, who did not dare question their leader directly.

Sinclair spoke so all could hear. "If we aim to make a settlement, we need to be able to defend ourselves, both from the natives and, perhaps someday, from those at home who might do us harm. It is an unexplored world, this land. But it is only a matter of time before others discover it as we have. God willing, by then, we will have laid a solid claim to it by building villages and fortifications."

He allowed his words to sink in. Others would lust after the natural riches of this new world—timber to build boats, fur and fish to trade, lands to clear and farm. And the Pope would surely send men in search of the treasures he carried. "To properly defend ourselves, our settlement best be inland and it best be high on a hill."

Gunn kicked at the dirt. "Then this might not be a bad spot. Plenty of fresh water and game, a river to take us to the ocean and power a mill and already the flowers are blooming." The rivers and lakes were still frozen in Nova Scotia. "Hopefully the natives are friendly—"

A muffled cough escaped Gunn's mouth, interrupting his words. Sinclair chuckled. "What's wrong, Gunn, did you swallow an insect?" But even as he spoke, his instincts told him something was wrong.

Gunn turned wide-eyed toward Sinclair, reached up slowly and closed his thick hand on the shaft of an arrow protruding from the side of his neck. "Curse it," he sputtered, dropping to a knee.

"Get down, men!" Sinclair bellowed as another arrow hissed by his ear, thudding into a tree. He wrapped an arm around his friend's side and dragged him quickly behind a thick oak on the side of the trail. "James, do not pull out the arrow. Easy, now." He gently moved Gunn's hand away. Blood spurted from the wound. Only the arrowhead itself kept the blood from escaping in a torrent. A pit formed in his gut and spread as an anvil on his chest. He had seen many similar wounds. All had been fatal.

He took a deep breath. Resting a hand on Gunn's shoulder, he called to Kitpu. "Tell them we come in peace. Tell them your chief, their ally, guaranteed us safe passage."

The guide had already begun yelling into the woods. The low murmur of the natives conversing with each other, debating their response, cascaded down the hill.

Sinclair took another deep breath and fought to control his emotions. Gunn would die, it was just a question of how quickly. Only God could help him now; Sinclair said a quick prayer to the Virgin Mother. "Stay down, men," he whispered. "We will wait to hear what the natives offer by way of explanation."

"I pray you release us to pursue the savages, my Lord," one of his men implored.

"Easy now. Remember, we are in their lands." And vastly outnumbered.

A few seconds passed, then a resonant voice from deep in the woods called out a lengthy response. Kitpu translated, his English surprisingly good.

"He say any friend of Mi'kmaq chief is welcome on this land. He say he regret arrow in your man's neck. And he say if your man dead, you may bury him on this hill and they will honor his spirit."

Sinclair exhaled. At least Gunn would be today's only casualty.

Coughing, Gunn spit out a mouthful of blood and shook his head. "I can taste the blood, Henry. It pours down my throat." He forced a bloody smile. "If only it were ale." He reached for Sinclair's hand. "Take care of the little ones, won't you?"

"Of course, old friend." Leaning closer, he smiled. "This is a sign from God, James. I am sure of it. This is the spot God has chosen for us. We will bury you here, on this hill that shakes, next to this mighty oak, and you will be our sentry in this new land. You will guard it for us, for the true soldiers of God, even as the world around you shakes with turmoil and evil." He smiled again, again rested a hand on Gunn's shoulder. His eyes moistened. "And a better sentry Christ himself could not have chosen." He kissed his friend on the cheek.

"You can depend on me, Henry," Gunn whispered. "In this world and in the next." His eyes fluttering, he squeezed Sinclair's hand. "God be with you, Henry."

Sinclair bowed his head and crossed himself.

✝   ✝   ✝

Studying the rough map Kitpu had drawn on a scrap of sailcloth, Sinclair turned away from the men and tried to blink his eyes dry. He would mourn Gunn later, once they were back in camp and safe.

Taking a deep breath, he refocused on the map. They were about three-quarters of the way up the hill—he had hoped to reach the top and leave a marker in stone at its peak. But Gunn's death changed that. He checked the sun, noting its position in the southwestern sky. Perhaps four hours of daylight left. They were a two-hour march back to camp; he would not ask his men to spend the night in these woods.

Just ahead, to the left of the trail, lay an outcropping of rock blown clean of leaves and dirt and pine needles by the summer wind. He examined it and returned to the men gathered around Gunn's body, now wrapped in a brown blanket. "We will bury Sir James just ahead, up the trail a bit." He motioned to four of the larger men. "Carry him, then."

He led the way, already feeling a bit naked without James alongside. Who would he confide in? Who could he trust to do the right thing? Most of all, who would he laugh with after a long day in the field? He sighed and rubbed his tunic roughly over his eyes. In many ways it was a miracle either of them was still alive after decades on the battlefields. They reached the site and he motioned to Murdoch, the armorist. "You have your tools, do you not?"

Murdoch, a tall, lean, quiet man with a red beard and sad blue eyes, nodded. "I do, but I brought but a single punch. And my mallet."

"That will have to do."

As the men took turns digging a grave, Sinclair huddled with Murdoch over the rock ledge. Unfortunately his two expert stone-masons, along with the other artisans in his expedition, were back at camp guarding the ship — he had taken fighting men with him to explore the hillside. Normally Murdoch repaired their fighting armor and other weaponry but he also had experience working with stone. He had been studying the outcrop and pointed out its natural grains and striations to his lord. "I will carve his sword here, using the features of the rock."

Sinclair checked his compass and pointed. "The sword must point north. It will be a signpost for those that follow us to this land."

The armorist nodded. "It shall. The lines in the rock run north and south."

"Good."

The armorist set to work. Holding an iron-tipped punch at a steep angle to the bedrock, he raised a heavy mallet and pounded the punch, his aim strong and true. A chip flew from the ledge, leaving a pea-size indentation in the stone. He examined the punch and looked up to Sinclair. "The rock is hard. Hard as any in Scotland."

"Will you be able to finish the effigy?"

Murdoch studied the punch a second time. "I believe I shall. But as the punch dulls, the marks will become faint."

"The sword is the most important thing. Complete that first. Then turn to the effigy and shield." No knight should be buried without a sword marking his grave. Especially a warrior like Gunn. Were they back in Scotland, he would have commissioned a full carving, life-size, of his comrade. But here in the wilderness this would have to do. Gunn would understand. He knew what was at stake.

"Murdoch, I want to be certain you understand."

The artisan looked up, his blue eyes on Sinclair's.

Sinclair lowered his voice. "This is a memorial to Sir James but it is also much, much more. His effigy and his shield are of small matter. But it is crucial that the sword markings be clear. It is crucial that no one doubt that this is the sword of a Templar knight."

CHAPTER 1

[September, Present Day]

Legend is more historical than fact, because fact tells us about one man but legend tells us about a million men.

Cameron Thorne read the words on a promotional flier taped to the library's book return box, reflecting on them as he jogged up the granite stairs of the yellow brick building. Not bad. A history professor once told him that the historical record was often no more than the product of a single scribe's take on events, shaped by his or her experiences and values. And often slanted by a particular agenda. But the memories of an entire culture created legend.

He darted ahead of a mother and young daughter to hold the library's mahogany door. A pair of blue eyes peered up at him from underneath a pink hooded Red Sox sweatshirt. "Are you coming to hear the story about Prince Henry too?" the girl asked.

He smiled. "Um, no. I'm just here to return some books."

"You should come listen. People think Christopher Columbus discovered Westford. But it was really Prince Henry."

"Discovered America," the girl's mother corrected. "Westford is just one town in our big country. He discovered America — or didn't."

Cam cocked his head. "So did he or didn't he?"

The mother shrugged, smiling one of those smiles meant to be friendly but not flirtatious; as a single guy in a town full of soccer moms, Cam knew the difference. "Apparently not. I'll know more in an hour." She pointed to another copy of the same 'legend' flier, this one hanging in the foyer — that afternoon a local storyteller was presenting 'Prince Henry and the Westford Knight,' the tale of a Scottish expedition exploring the hills of Westford, Massachusetts in 1398. As the girl skipped ahead, the mother turned and smiled again. "I could go either way on Columbus. But they're going to have a fight on their hands if they try to debunk Santa Claus."

"Enjoy," he laughed.

In addition to returning books, he needed to research some old land records for a client who wanted to put some property into a conservation trust. Not as earth-shattering as a legend that debunked Columbus' accomplishments, but Cam enjoyed traveling back through the centuries, tracking the history of New England's settlers through yellowed maps and feather-pen-written deeds. Which is why he became a real estate lawyer in the first place.

He strolled into the library's reference section, breathing in the air of a century's worth of leather bindings and worn cloth and dust and furniture polish. A librarian helped him find some old maps and he spread them on one of the oak tables in the center of the high-ceilinged public room. As he studied them, activity at an adjacent table drew his attention.

An elderly couple was sitting opposite a burly, orange-haired man with large hands and nicotine-stained fingers. The man shoved a document across the table at the couple, the words 'Quitclaim Deed' in large type across the top. An odd place for a real estate closing, but not unheard of. But something about the elderly couple's body language didn't seem right. Most real estate closings were boring affairs, a stack of papers pushed back and forth across the table. Occasionally the parties argued over a stain on the carpet or the lawyers tried to justify their fee by haggling over the language of some document that would never see the outside of a file cabinet again. But in Cam's 11 years of practice, he had never seen anyone recoil in fear.

"Just sign at the bottom." The Scottish accent surprised him but not as much as the menacing tone.

"Emily and I have no interest in selling." With his bug eyes and oversized blue cardigan, the man reminded Cam of Don Knotts in the old *Andy Griffith* shows. His wife, a thick woman with a round, sun-burnt face wearing a floral house dress, nodded in agreement.

"We have an accord, Mr. Gendron," the Scotsman snarled, lifting his bulk from his seat. "You'd be wise to honor it." A few other patrons glanced over at the outburst.

Mrs. Gendron raised her chin but kept her voice low. "We never agreed to sell, Mr. McLovick."

McLovick slapped his thigh, the sleeve of his white dress shirt protruding from beneath a frayed blue blazer. "Of course you did. Why else would we be sitting here today?"

"W-we came because you said you had important business to discuss with us," Mr. Gendron responded.

"Exactly." McLovick's face reddened. "Now I will not be asking you a third time." Still standing, he shoved the document further across the table, grabbing Mr. Gendron by the wrist as he did so. "I'm paying you more than a fair price. Now sign the bloody deed."

Cam took a deep breath, stood and turned slowly toward the trio. "I couldn't help overhearing. I'm a lawyer—can I be of any help here?" He smiled at the older couple, then turned to meet McLovick's hostile stare while balancing on the balls of his feet with his arms loose by his side. He had been sucker-punched in an elevator once by an angry landlord in an eviction case. Fortunately an off-duty policeman witnessed the altercation and Cam was never charged for pummeling the man. But one sucker punch was enough.

"We're fine here. No need for your services," McLovick snarled.

Mrs. Gendron spoke after a short pause. She, too, stared at McLovick. "Actually, I do think it's time we found ourselves a lawyer."

✝   ✝   ✝

An hour later Cam left the library, the Gendrons having left safely while McLovick stewed in his seat. Cam took the stone stairs two at a time, ignoring the pain in his knee still bruised and swollen from a rough sky-diving landing over the weekend. It would loosen up eventually, though not as quickly as it did when he was in his twenties. Or even his early thirties.

He checked his watch. Still time to race over to Wilmington to watch the Bruins training camp practice for an hour before his softball game. He jogged left into the library driveway toward his Harley parked along a line of trees; one of the few good things about practicing law in the suburbs was he didn't have to worry about some lowlife carting his bike away. As he dug in his jacket pocket for his keys, a thick man stepped into his path from behind a tree. McLovick.

Averting his eyes, Cam changed his path to avoid the larger man. McLovick moved with him, his arms folded across his chest. Cam adjusted his course a second time, again mirrored by the Scotsman. Okay then. Stopping, Cam lowered his briefcase to the ground. "You want to dance, McLovick?" The man was half a head taller and perhaps 60 pounds heavier.

"I grew up on the docks of Glasgow. It's not dancing I have in mind." McLovick unfolded his arms, freeing his fists. "Where I come from, a man minds his own business."

"Then I suggest you go home. Around here, we don't bully our senior citizens."

McLovick took a step closer. Cam would rather not have been so close — in a fight, he would need to keep his distance and rely on speed. Plus McLovick smelled like he hadn't showered in a few days. But he couldn't back away. Tilting his head back, he met the man's glare.

They were alone on the side of the building. If McLovick was going to throw a punch, he would do so now. Instead he leered and jerked his thumb toward the Harley. "Nice bike. Next time you might want to put some air in the tires." The words hit Cam in an acrid fog of stale cigarettes and coffee. The bastard had slashed his tires.

"Next time you do something stupid you might want to make sure there's no security camera around." Cam tilted his chin toward the device mounted on the side of the library. "I can see why a sharp guy like you left the docks." He stepped around the bully. "Maybe you should have tried the dancing thing."

⁘ ⁘ ⁘

Cam met with the Gendrons a couple of days later at the Senior Center in Westford, where he provided free legal advice a few days every month.

"Let's start at the beginning, Mr. Gendron. Do you want to sell your house?" He was supposed to meet his mountain-biking buddies in a half-hour. They wouldn't wait, not with the September daylight fading. He settled back in his chair — he'd catch them on the trail if necessary.

Marvin Gendron looked to his wife before answering. "No, no. We've lived in that house since I returned from duty in Vietnam, in 1968. Paid $7,000 for it. A lot of money back then. We have no desire to sell it."

Cam set his pen down; it rolled toward the edge of the laminated banquet table. They were seated in metal folding chairs in a small room of what had originally been a Colonial-style school. "Obviously, Mr. McLovick believes otherwise." He hadn't told them about the encounter outside the library. No reason to alarm them further.

Emily fumbled in a canvas tote bag, pulled out a single sheet of paper and pushed it across the table, her hands marked by dirt caked under her fingernails and calluses on her palms. Probably a gardener. "Why don't we let Mr. Thorne look at the paper. It might help explain things."

As Cam perused the document, he pulled on the whiskers of his goatee. The beard was new to his face; he often found himself plucking hairs, some of them tinting toward gray, from his chin. The document was the standard Massachusetts form for making an offer to purchase real estate. A year ago Cam relocated from Boston and joined his uncle Peter's suburban law firm in the Nashoba Valley a half-hour northwest of Boston. In that time he had seen scores of documents just like it. He skipped to the bottom of the page. The offer was signed by McLovick. "You didn't sign this, did you?"

"No." Emily reached back into her canvas bag, pulled out three more sheets of paper and slid them to Cam.

He scanned them as well. They were identical to the first except for the purchase price. The original offer was for $325,000. By the fourth offer, the price had climbed to $410,000. "You have gold buried in your backyard?" The real estate market, after years of steady increases, had slumped. These increasing offers made no sense, unless the first offer had been a low-ball. "What do you think your house is worth?"

Emily turned to Marvin. "The tax assessment is for $286,500," he said. "Another house in our neighborhood, a Cape like ours, just sold for $315,000."

Odd. "How much land do you have? Is it possible that this McLovick guy is a developer and he thinks he can subdivide your lot?"

Marvin shifted in his seat and played with his wedding ring. "I don't see how. We only have a quarter acre. The house is in the front of the lot, Emily's garden is in the back, a driveway is on the side."

Cam nodded and asked the obvious question. "Don't take this wrong but if he's offering you $100,000 more than the house is worth, why don't you take it?"

"Mr. Thorne," Emily said in a low voice, "as my husband stated, we do not wish to move. We have lived our whole lives in Westford. Our friends are here. Our church is here. Marvin comes here to the senior center for card games. I have my garden. When we die, the house will go to our church." Marvin nodded.

"Okay then. But I thought McLovick said something about a signed agreement."

"He somehow forged Marvin's signature. A young lady came to the door a week or so ago collecting signatures for a senior citizen property tax refund. Marvin signed that—perhaps he was tricked."

"You're certain there's nothing else?"

"Nothing."

"Well, he could always file a lawsuit against you and try to force you to sell. If he does, we'll fight it, of course. But until then, just don't sign any documents without showing them to me first." He smiled as he clicked his pen closed. "Even petitions." More than a legal problem, this was a mystery—why was McLovick willing to pay $100,000 more than the house was worth? And then get so angry that he resorted to near-fisticuffs when Cam interfered?

Cam continued. "But you do have some legal options. You could file an assault case against him for grabbing Mr. Gendron's wrist. Or we could get a restraining order against him."

Marvin sat tall in his chair. "He frightened my wife, Mr. Thorne, and Emily does not frighten easily. We do not want this McLovick fellow near us or our property again."

"All right. Meet me back here tomorrow morning at 11:00. By late afternoon you should have your restraining order."

✦   ✦   ✦

[Thursday]

Cam obtained the temporary restraining order for Mr. and Mrs. Gendron the morning after their first meeting. The order prohibited McLovick from contacting the older couple and from going within 100 feet of their property. But due process demanded that McLovick be given his day in court as well. Today, a week later, he would have the chance to give his side of the story and try to convince the judge to vacate the order.

What was McLovick's angle? When people tossed around $100,000 like a Frisbee, there was usually a good reason. Cam himself was a case in point—he took a $120,000 pay cut to come work for his uncle. Not that he had much choice. At 36, he had been working for one of those mega-firms in Boston where everyone drove a Lexus; the firm was defending the local archdiocese in a batch of priest sexual abuse cases and Cam was assigned to the case. Part of the defense strategy developed by the lead attorney involved intimidating abuse victims with embarrassing information culled from their medical records. One afternoon Cam watched a grown man sob during a particularly ugly deposition session. On the verge of making partner, Cam reached one of those fork-in-the-road moments and made a phone call leaking details of the sordid defense strategy to the press.

A week later he got caught.

Lawyers are nothing if not self-important and in the legal world few sins are considered more grave than disloyalty to a client. Instead of a piece of the partnership pie, he ended up with a temporary suspension of his law license and an exile to the suburbs.

That was the story behind Cam's six-figure folly. What was McLovick's?

Cam met Mr. and Mrs. Gendron a few minutes before 10:00 at the Lowell Superior Court. The commanding stone structure harkened to Lowell's glory days. Few people knew that Lowell, not Boston, had been Massachusetts' leading city in the late 19th and early 20th centuries, a world leader in textile manufacturing. Today it was a struggling mill city trying to reinvent itself through high tech industry and a revitalized downtown.

They climbed the long marble staircase to the second floor, the treads grayed and worn from decades of use. Cam was not surprised to see McLovick standing next to the courtroom door—the injunction itself was not a hardship for him but he would want it removed to protect his reputation. Cam approached. McLovick wore the same tattered blue blazer and a poorly-knotted solid red tie. Cam reached out his hand to shake, a test to see how McLovick would react.

"I have a cold," he said tightly. "Wouldn't want you to get sick." He leered. "Or anything."

"Or anything," Cam repeated, dropping his hand to his side and taking a large step back. "Are you represented by an attorney?"

McLovick, his small eyes darting and shifting beneath puffy lids, exhaled another acrid gust of stale coffee and cigarettes. Cam edged away further. "No, I don't have a lawyer." He thrust his chin forward. "I haven't done anything wrong so I don't need one, right?"

Ten minutes later they stepped in front of the judge, a middle-aged woman with a thin face and short, graying hair. She disposed of some formalities and offered McLovick the opportunity to explain his side of the case. "Your Honor, I honestly don't know why we are here today. All I did was offer to buy their house. In fact, I offered substantially more than it is worth." He smiled, spread his hands. "If that's a crime, I wish someone would victimize me."

The judge nodded and turned to Cam, who stood. "My clients are elderly, Your Honor. And they have absolutely no desire to sell their home, to Mr. McLovick or anybody else. As you can see by their affidavits, they are frightened by Mr. McLovick. He forged Mr. Gendron's signature. He has been acting in a menacing manner. And they are concerned he will not take no for an answer. I personally witnessed him grab Mr. Gendron by the wrist. And he vandalized my motorcycle—I have security camera video to prove it."

"You may serve as either witness or counsel, Mr. Thorne," the judge admonished. "Not both. Which is it?"

"Counsel, your Honor." Of course his testimony about the wrist grab and tire slashing would not be admissible. But he wanted the judge to hear it anyway.

The judge studied Mr. and Mrs. Gendron, then eyed McLovick. "I must say, this seems like flimsy grounds for a restraining order. But I do wonder why you persist in this, Mr. McLovick. What is it about this property that makes it so important to you?"

He offered a wet smile. "To be honest, Your Honor, it reminds me a bit of my own childhood home." He shook his head sadly, his play for youthful innocence undermined by his menacing bulk. "I spent many happy years there." He raised his chin. "And as much as I'd like to purchase it, I must reiterate that I did not threaten these people."

She peered down. "You can't give me more information about your interest in the property? Beyond its sentimental attraction, that is?"

"I am afraid not, Your Honor."

"Well, then, I am afraid the order stands."

McLovick leaned forward, his face flushed. "But, Your Honor—"

She banged her gavel. "Next case."

+   +   +

Cam returned to the office, a nondescript cluster of white-walled rooms in a strip mall on the town's commercial highway. At his old law firm, the other tenants in the office tower included Fortune 500 companies and Fidelity Investments. Here, he shared an entryway with a bakery, a weight loss center and a dentist.

He shook his head — adjacent to a bakery was a hell of a place for a diabetic to find himself, especially one who loved pastries and who didn't always abide by his doctor's orders. He had always believed what he read when first diagnosed at age 10 — that the odds were pretty good he would be dead by 35, that his age would never exceed his waist size. So what difference would a candy bar or a beer make? Now he was 37, his waist measured 33 and the odds had swung in his favor due to recent medical breakthroughs. For the first time in his life he started thinking about unthinkable things. Like his future.

After thumbing through a small stack of messages he typed the name Alistair McLovick in a Google search. He scrolled through a series of random matches, then his fingers froze — McLovick was a treasure hunter. Perhaps Westford wasn't such a sleepy suburb after all.

He picked up the phone and called his cousin, Brandon. His uncle Peter, now his boss, had always hoped Brandon would go to law school and take over the practice. And Brandon had the brains for it. But he loved working with his hands. He had no interest, as he bluntly put it, in sitting in an office arguing on the phone all day. Which was essentially what his father did — Peter was one of those people who liked to argue, who gave life to that old joke about putting two lawyers in the room and getting three opinions. Brandon had worked on a landscaping crew after high school, then saved a few bucks and bought his own truck. Taking advantage of the seasonal nature of the work, he went back to school and got a degree in landscape architecture. He now had a crew of six guys and more than enough work designing and building stone walls and patios and 'outdoor entertainment centers' in increasingly-affluent Westford.

"Hey, I want to bounce something off you. You free for lunch?"

"You pick up sandwiches," Brandon said. "I'll get some gas for the boat. Be on your dock in a half hour. And bring your ski."

Because Cam was seven years older than Brandon, the cousins had never been close growing up. But in the past year the two had become almost inseparable. Partly that was because most of Cam's friends and peers were already on their second or third kid. Some were even on their second or third wives. Cam didn't even have a girlfriend. At least not one he ever saw — Heidi was fun and attractive and passionate; she also happened to be a professional ski racer, which meant she made it back to Boston about as often as he found himself in the Swiss Alps. Great company for a yearly back-country ski trip. Not so great for a weekly dinner and movie.

But he did take some small steps into grown-up land when he moved to Westford. He bought a house. And also got a dog. Hardly a 401(k) or a set of matching china but still a significant psychological step. Friends had advised against Golden Retrievers because they had health problems that shortened their life expectancy. That sealed the deal. Pegasus, a purebred, cost him almost as much as the down payment on his house, a true mutt. A rundown summer cottage with a leaky roof and no heating system, the property had been vacant for years. But it was lakefront, just a few houses up from Brandon's, and Brandon promised to help him fix it up. At the time Cam had three months to kill while he served his bar suspension. Of course, 15 months later the house was still only half-finished. But at least Pegasus had chased away the squirrels nesting in it.

Thirty minutes later, Pegasus at his side, he stood on his dock in his swim trunks. Same size he wore in college. And same kid-like anticipation at the prospect of hitting the water. If he lived to be as old as the Gendrons, he expected to still be skiing.

Brandon nosed in with his Ski Nautique. Cam tossed his slalom ski and ski vest into the boat and hopped in as Brandon reversed the engine and pulled out. Pegasus leapt in behind him. Brandon rubbed Pegasus' head. "Glad you called, the lake is like glass." Physically, it was hard to believe the cousins came from the same stock—Cam was lithe and wiry like a baseball middle infielder, while Brandon was tall and broad and muscular like a linebacker. But they both had an easy smile and a thick mane of wavy brown hair. Everyone liked Brandon. Cam had lived in town for over a year and never heard anyone say a bad word about his cousin.

"What about a spotter?" Cam asked. State law required one; usually Brandon brought one of his workers along.

Brandon scanned the lake. No other boats. "Don't be such a lawyer." He smiled. "Besides, isn't that why you brought Pegasus? You're up first."

Cam removed his insulin pump and put on a ski vest. Sitting on the stern, he slathered some baby oil on his right foot and tugged the tight-fitting slalom ski boot on. He grabbed the ski line with one hand and pushed himself off the back of the boat with the other, gasping as he hit the water. The air was warm but the cold September nights had chilled the water. Brandon gently throttled forward, tightening the ski rope. "You say when," he yelled back.

Cam took a deep breath as he grasped the rope handle tightly. "Hit it."

The boat jerked him out of the water like an angler snatching a trout. He cut to the left, across the boat's wake, and found the smooth water. Leaning hard against the line, he used the ski's edge to slice through the orange and yellow trees reflected in the still surface of the lake. As he approached a 90-degree angle with the boat's path, the line began to slacken and he tucked his knee and spun back to his right, leaning hard now on the opposite edge of the ski. In his wake, a rooster tail of water arced high above him. The sun filtered through the water drops, glistening and refracting and sparkling like the finest chandelier.

He cut back toward the boat's wake, fighting to keep his edge from wobbling as he sliced through the water churned white by the propeller. Leaning even harder against the rope, he burst through to the smooth water on the far side of the wake, trusting his edge to hold him even as his shoulder and hip practically kissed the glass-like surface. He cut back again, slicing across the wake, now in rhythm — lean, cut, slice, lean, cut. A wave bounced his ski slightly; it was enough. The ski edge lost contact with the water. Gravity did the rest. He fell and slapped against the water, bouncing like a skipping stone across the surface — at 50 MPH the lake felt like hard-packed snow. The world slowed down as he tumbled and skidded, remembering to keep himself in a tight ball so he didn't pull a groin muscle or separate a shoulder by catching a limb under the water's surface.

He bounced a total of four times. On what would have been the fifth bounce, he broke beneath the water's surface, a cannonball now rather than a skipping stone. He descended a few feet before the life vest jettisoned him back to the surface like a beach ball slipping out from between a child's knees. After coughing out some water, he waved at Brandon to let him know he was okay. At least it didn't hurt as much as when he fell on his mountain bike.

Brandon grinned as he circled back. "Thanks for the show, Cuz. Thought you were going to bounce all the way to shore." Pegasus stood on the stern seat and offered a bark of concern.

"Hey, if you don't fall you're not skiing hard enough."

"Or it just means you can't ski for shit."

Grinning, Cam climbed into the boat and allowed Pegasus to rub against him. He stretched his neck side to side.

Brandon slapped him on the shoulder. "You looked like a barrel going over the falls."

They ate their sandwiches; Brandon would ski after the waves from Cam's run subsided. He reattached his insulin pump and, after checking his blood glucose level and mentally calculating the number of carbs in his meal, entered the information into the pump's program so the device could deliver the appropriate amount of insulin. He broke a chunk of turkey off for Pegasus and spoke between bites. "Can I run something by you?" He described McLovick's efforts to buy the Gendrons' property. "Turns out he's a treasure hunter—underwater salvage from shipwrecks and stuff."

"Sounds like he's not a very good one. Last I checked, the only shipwrecks in Westford are a couple of old rowboats and a rubber raft."

"No, he knows something. Why else would he offer $100,000 extra to buy some piece of property?"

"You think there's something buried in your clients' backyard?"

"I don't know. But I know one way to find out. Can you lend me a Bobcat for a few days?"

"Sure. You gonna dig?"

"Maybe a little."

"I don't know. I've seen you drive this boat and I'm not sure I trust you in the Cat."

Cam sipped his Diet Coke. "I've been thinking about my wipe-out. You must have been goosing the throttle."

"Yeah, right. No chance Mr. Perfect just fell down and went boom all by himself." Brandon squished his Sprite can. "Start the boat. I'll show you how it's done."

✛   ✛   ✛

An hour later, back in his office, Cam dialed the Gendrons' number. He explained to Emily what he had learned about McLovick.

"We've lived here almost 40 years and I've never heard anything about any treasure."

"Well, if you're curious about this, I have a plan."

"Okay, what is it?"

"The judge specifically said Mr. McLovick can use the road to drive by your house. Knowing him, he'll want to keep an eye on things. One possibility is to get a Bobcat and start digging in your backyard. Nothing major, just a couple of small piles of dirt."

Emily laughed. "I see what you're doing. If he thinks there's a treasure buried and he sees us digging, he might tip his hand."

Cam wasn't sure about this. Was it wise to provoke McLovick? What if he overreacted? His clients were already afraid of him. "You know, Mrs. Gendron, you could also just drop this whole thing, forget the Bobcat. There's no need to do anything—I think eventually McLovick will go away."

"No, I think you're wrong about that. If there is a treasure there, as crazy as it sounds, Mr. McLovick is not going to give up until he finds it. So let's try this dig and see what happens."

Cam nodded. It did sound crazy.

CHAPTER 2

[Friday]

Cam got a call in his office late the next morning from Brandon. "I've got some time now if you want me to bring that Bobcat over."

"Great. Meet you there in a half hour."

After finishing up some work he jumped on his Harley. He sped north, through the town center, noticed again how Westford Center was something right off a Hollywood set—white steeple church, plush town Common with requisite black iron cannon, yellow brick library and stately historical homes all flanking tree-lined country roads. He veered northwest at the triangular town common, angling toward the Graniteville section of town. Here the homes became smaller, befitting their history as residences for the town's mill and granite quarry workers of the early 1900s. He turned onto North Street, a fairly major connecting road, and a half-minute later pulled into the driveway of a neatly-kept light blue Cape with white shutters. A white Bobcat excavator with backhoe sat in front of him, squeezed onto the edge of the driveway next to the Gendrons' red Taurus.

Emily and Marvin came out to greet him. She gestured at the Bobcat. "Your cousin just dropped it off but then he got a call and had to run. He said he'll come back later and put it where we want. Maybe dig up some ground if we want."

Cam nodded. "Wherever we put it, it should be visible from the street."

They walked toward the back yard, a square area about half the size of a tennis court with some woods in the back. Most of the yard was filled with Emily's garden, enclosed by a low stone wall on all four sides. It looked a bit odd because the lines of the stone walls didn't parallel the lines of the lot — it was as if someone rotated the enclosure five or ten degrees counterclockwise and then dropped it back down. "Did you build the stone wall?" Cam asked.

"No," Marvin said, "it was here when we bought the house. Probably an old holding pen for animals."

Emily shook her head. "I'm sorry, Marvin, but I don't agree. I grew up on a farm, and walls that high wouldn't hold anything. I think it's an old foundation of some kind." She pointed to a pile of stones amassed along one of the long walls. "And those are from an old fireplace or cooking area that collapsed."

It was Marvin's turn to shake his head. "How could it be a foundation when it's above ground?"

Cam smiled. This was obviously an argument that had been going on for close to 40 years. "Maybe it's neither a holding pen or a foundation."

Emily turned toward him, the thick, earthy woman's eyes conveying a common sense borne of living off the land. "Well, what else could it be? People around here didn't just build these things for fun — life was too hard, time too precious. Always has been in these parts, ever since the first settlers came. These stones are heavy and there's a lot of them. If they were just trying to clear the fields, they would have made a single wall, not a rectangle. Whoever did this had a purpose in mind."

Odd. And possibly important. "Are there any other rectangular enclosures like this around?"

Emily and Marvin exchanged glances and shrugged. "Not that we've seen," she answered. "I've lived in Westford all my life. There are plenty of stone walls, and even some abandoned foundations and cellar holes but nothing else like this."

Cam waited for Emily to reflect on her own statement, to allow the words to echo back to her. After a few seconds, she looked up and met Cam's eyes. He nodded. "I don't believe in coincidence. I think we might have an idea why McLovick is so obsessed with your property."

✛ ✛ ✛

[Saturday]

The next day Cam grabbed Brandon and together they returned to the Gendrons' house. Brandon did a lot of work with stone walls and Cam wanted his opinion on the enclosure. Nobody had disturbed the Bobcat in the driveway.

They walked to the backyard and Brandon paced around the outside of the garden. "Here, come take a look at this." Cam and the Gendrons gathered around him in the back corner of the lot. "These stones are dressed, which means they were cut." He pointed to stones in a 2-foot-wide opening, an opening Cam had not noticed before. "If you see a stone wall in the woods, the stones are in their natural shape and stacked haphazardly. The farmer picked them up from his fields and piled them on the property line to get them out of the way. But these stones are flat on one side and they line up perfectly, like someone wanted to make a neat entryway."

Emily challenged him. "Well, it may be an entryway but it wasn't built by any farmer. It's too narrow to get a cart in and out. If you had animals in there, you'd need to bring them feed and then cart out the manure."

"I agree." Brandon said. He looked at the sun and turned back to the enclosure. He, too, was wondering why the enclosure walls didn't parallel the lot lines. "Do you have a local map?"

"Yes. And, Marvin, get the lantern also." Marvin ambled toward the house. "I forgot to tell you yesterday," she said to Cam. "About twenty years ago I found a clay lantern buried in the garden. It was wrapped in some kind of cloth. I'm only showing it to you because it came from inside the stone wall."

Marvin returned and handed the map to Brandon and the lantern to Cam. It was dark gray, the size and shape of a beer mug, with eight arched legs and a half dozen square windows carved out haphazardly. Cam turned it over. "I wonder why there's no base."

"I wondered the same thing. Maybe the base piece is separate. Or maybe you're holding it upside down and there's no top."

Cam flipped it. "Now it looks like a rook in a chess game." He held it up to the light and handed it back to her. "It looks old. Have you ever had an expert look at it?"

"We brought it to an antique shop and they didn't know what to make of it."

Brandon had opened the map to Westford, found North Street and turned the map to align with the Gendrons' property. "I have some clients interested in feng shui so I notice this stuff now. The walls of this enclosure are built exactly on the axes of the compass, north-south and east-west."

"What does that mean?" Cam asked.

Brandon shrugged. "I have no idea. It's just odd, that's all."

He grabbed a stick and dug away some of the dirt piled against the outside of the stone enclosure. "The organic material has built up pretty good around these stones. You didn't do that, did you Mrs. Gendron?"

She shook her head. "No but I noticed that too. For most of those stones you see on the bottom row, there's actually another stone underneath it."

"That level of soil buildup means they've been here for a while," Brandon said.

"You think it's Native American?" Cam asked.

Brandon shook his head. "I don't think so. From what I know, they didn't build stone structures."

"Well, if a farmer didn't build it and the Indians didn't build it, who did?"

Shrugging, Brandon studied the map again and pointed toward the woods in the back of the property. "Is there water back there?"

"Yes," Marvin answered. "A small stream that leads right down to the Stonybrook River. That's why the Colonists first settled this area — it had a good supply of fresh water, and we're pretty much standing at an intersection of two old Indian trails. Prospect Hill, in the center of town, used to be a gathering point for the Indians. Highest point in eastern Massachusetts, visible from Boston Harbor. They used to send smoke signals from up there."

Interesting history but it didn't really tell them who built the enclosure. "Well, where do you think we should put the Bobcat?"

Brandon responded. "I'll put it right next to the enclosure but near the driveway so you can see it from the street." He turned to Emily. "Is that okay?"

She nodded. "You can put it on the mulch pile."

While she and Marvin walked back to the garden to direct them, Brandon jogged over to the Bobcat and hopped into the cab, swinging himself into the seat. For a big guy, he moved well.

Brandon's right shoulder twitched as he turned the key, the muscles rippling beneath his t-shirt. Instead of an engine turning over, a flash of light jumped from the Bobcat followed by a thunderous explosion. Cam's brain rejected the information his eyes and ears were sending. The twitch of Brandon's shoulder was such a subtle movement, such a common, ordinary task. Somehow the ramifications seemed disproportionate. Obscenely so. Like a gentle breeze felling an oak tree. Or a pebble tripping a horse....

Cam flew through the air, a hot, blazing gust lifting him and tossing him aside like an ember exhaled by a campfire. He hit the ground, skidded along the grass. Even before he stopped sliding, a pit formed in his stomach. *Brandon.*

He rolled onto his stomach, opened his eyes and tried to locate his cousin. But the explosion had burned the fire into his retinas and the world looked like a giant sun. There was an echo of a loud explosion in his ears but all he could hear now was a sharp ringing, like the shriek of a tea pot announcing its boil. Or was someone screaming? He struggled to his hands and knees, staggering toward the Bobcat.

He shielded his eyes with his hand, fought to blink some sight back into them. A body lay twisted like a rag doll on the ground a few feet from the smoking, twisted piece of machinery. He rushed toward it, toward Brandon and stopped short—Brandon's leg was a mangled mass of blood and bones and blue jeans. The smell of burnt flesh and gasoline assaulted him.

He dropped to his knees, cradled his cousin's head in his hands. "Call 911!" he yelled to Emily, who had staggered over from the garden. "And get me a blanket!"

Cam forced himself to look at Brandon's leg, gushing blood from just below the knee. Brandon moaned. "It's okay, Cuz," Cam said, "you'll be okay. Just hang in there." He ripped off his cloth belt and looped it in a tourniquet around Brandon's right thigh. The blood continued to stream out; he pulled the belt tighter and tied it off. He examined Brandon's torso. No visible wounds but who knew what was going on internally. He racked his brain—was there anything else he could do?

As the ringing in his ears faded, Brandon's moans became louder. Emily appeared with an old comforter and draped it over Brandon's body. The movement fanned the smell of burnt skin. Cam swallowed back his vomit. "The ambulance is on its way," Emily said.

"Cameron," she gasped, "what happened?"

A Bobcat didn't just blow up like that. Taking a deep breath, he looked up and met Emily's eyes. "I think it was a bomb."

Tears filled the woman's round face. "This is my fault," she sobbed.

Cam shook his head. The Bobcat was his idea, not Emily's. This was his fault.

+   +   +

The paramedics arrived quickly to attend to Brandon, concern in their eyes as they gently placed him on a gurney and sped away. Cam had already called Brandon's parents — they were racing to the hospital. He stayed to tell the police about McLovick.

A thick, middle-aged policeman approached. "I'm Lieutenant Poulos. I used to coach Brandon in Pop Warner." He sighed as he shook his head. "Any idea what happened here?"

Cam described the accident and recounted the Gendrons' history with the treasure hunter. He lost the narrative a couple of times — he was having trouble shaking the vision of Brandon's ravaged body from his mind. "McLovick booby-trapped the Bobcat."

Poulos glanced over at one of the bomb squad guys examining the skeleton of the Bobcat. The investigator pursed his lips and nodded to the lieutenant in response.

"Looks like somebody did," Poulos said.

"I know it's not standard procedure but when you arrest him, I'd like to be there."

"Well, hold on. You're getting a bit ahead of the game."

Cam shrugged. His first thought was that the bastard had probably already fled the country. But he quickly reconsidered — McLovick wouldn't have bothered trying to scare them off the property if he wasn't planning to stick around and dig for the treasure. In all likelihood McLovick had paid some low-life to place the bomb. No doubt he had an alibi.

Poulos looked down at his notebook, studied it for a few seconds, then shook his head. "You're a lawyer, right?" Cam nodded. "Then you understand how this works. We'll definitely investigate this McLovick fellow. But, without more evidence, we're a long way from making an arrest."

Cam started to argue the point but caught himself—the police officer was right.

Poulos studied him; his eyes drifted down and settled on Cam's clenched fist. "I know how you feel, son. But don't do anything stupid, okay?"

Holding his gaze, Cam offered a small shrug.

Poulos nodded. "Well, then at least be careful."

The ringing in his ears had yet to subside; he barely heard a man behind him clearing his throat as the policeman walked away. Turning, he looked up to see a tall priest. "Pardon me for interrupting. My name is Monsignor Marcotte. I am the pastor of Saint Catherine's, the church up the street." *Monsignor.* That explained the violet velvet trim on the front of his black priestly robes. Cam had driven by the large stone church on his first visit to the Gendrons and he knew they planned to leave their property to the church when they died. "I heard about the explosion and I ran right over." Which explained why he was still wearing his robes. "I thought I might be of some comfort to Mr. and Mrs. Gendron, once they are finished speaking with the police." He rested his blue eyes on Cam. "Of course, I am very sorry to hear about your cousin. I will pray for his recovery."

Cam nodded. "Thank you. We could all use some comforting." He was not particularly observant—his Jewish mother and Catholic father raised him in both faiths, stressing the common messages and themes in the Judeo-Christian culture, but he could never quite make that leap of blind faith necessary to believe the words of the Old and New Testament were truly the words of God. In fact, as a historian—he majored in American history in college—he came to attribute many of the conflicts in the world to religious intolerance and bigotry. He had read once that God was like a mirror—the mirror never changed but the people who looked into it all saw something different. Unfortunately most people looked in and viewed their own face, confident it had been created in God's own image.

Despite his ambivalence toward organized religion, Cam recognized its many good works and the comfort it gave to billions. Just as the Monsignor was trying to comfort him now. And there was no denying the spirituality of the Monsignor—something soothing, an air of serenity and self-assuredness, poured out from his clear blue eyes. With his neat gray hair and easy manner, he reminded Cam of a Belgian diplomat who taught political science at Boston College Cam's senior year.

"Let me ask you, do you think this might be related to Mr. McLovick?"

The McLovick situation was not the type of problem people normally discussed with their priest. Perhaps the Monsignor was not a normal type of priest. "They told you about that?"

"Yes. They were tempted to take the money and make a gift of it to the parish now rather than when they died." He smiled. "I told them to stay in their home—the church could wait for its money."

Good advice. "I do think it's related," Cam said. "But I'm still not sure why."

The Monsignor nodded and stared toward the tree-covered hill in the distance as if looking for divine guidance. "Do you have a theory?"

An odd question. But Cam needed an ally and the Gendrons had apparently confided in Marcotte already. "Sort of. I know he has a history as a treasure hunter—salvaging shipwrecks and stuff like that. He must think something is buried in their back yard." He paused. "Something worth killing for."

The Monsignor crossed himself and bowed his head in a quick, silent prayer. He lifted his head and nodded, a nod that indicated agreement rather than merely understanding. "I need to be careful here — you and I, as attorney and priest, we are required to keep certain communications in strict confidence. So please excuse my oblique approach to this conversation." He took a deep breath. "In the event you intend to continue to represent Mr. and Mrs. Gendron in this matter...." He paused and raised an eyebrow, offering Cam the opportunity to respond.

"Yes, I do. They need my help, and I'm responsible for what happened to Brandon — "

The Monsignor lifted a hand to stop him, the silk robe rustling. "Nonsense. You did not plant the bomb. Whoever did so will have to answer to the proper authorities. In this world and the next."

"Well, that may be but the Bobcat idea was mine." He shivered, remembering Brandon's bloodied body. "I'll continue to represent them as long as they want me to. And I'm going to find out who did this to Brandon."

"Good. I think they still need you. But I will suggest that you are only scratching the surface of this mystery, Mr. Thorne."

"Wait. How do you know my name?"

The priest smiled. "I am familiar with your work in the sex abuse scandal cases."

He appreciated Marcotte's candor. In all the months he worked on the case, nobody from the Church had ever referred to the case as a sex abuse scandal. It was always 'the allegations' or 'the incident' or 'the unfortunate conduct.'

"It took a lot of courage for you to do what you did. Leaking that testimony forced the Church to confront its crimes, to deal with its victims. Not many lawyers would have done what you did, risking your career like that."

Cam smiled wryly. "Priests and lawyers. Not exactly the most popular members of society right now, are we?"

"And to think, mothers used to dream of their children becoming lawyers or clergymen." The Monsignor took a deep breath. "But, getting back to the matter at hand, my recommendation is that you make an appointment with a young woman named Amanda Spencer. You can reach her through the Westford library. Do so soon. I've never met her personally but I believe she can shed some light on this matter." He lifted his hand and stroked his chin. "But be careful. As you have seen, this is a volatile situation."

Cam looked back toward the driveway. "I doubt McLovick will try anything else. He knows the police will be watching him."

"Regarding Mr. McLovick, consider this: If he planted the bomb, it means he is certain there is a treasure buried here, which makes him — whether in jail or not — a continuing danger." The Monsignor raised his index finger. "But perhaps he had nothing to do with the bomb. And if that is the case, then I think the danger is even greater."

"I don't follow." Perhaps because his head was still ringing like a church bell.

"Well, if Mr. McLovick didn't plant the bomb, then someone else did. Someone who saw the Bobcat and wants to keep both the Gendrons and Mr. McLovick from digging. Someone who probably knows for certain what is buried in the back yard."

"Well, then, who?"

The Monsignor shrugged. If he knew, he wasn't telling.

Cam eyed the priest. Marcotte held his gaze without blinking, a steady, kind half-smile on his face. The words the bailiff used in the courtroom while swearing in witnesses popped into Cam's head: "The truth, the whole truth and nothing but the truth." He believed the priest was telling the truth and also probably nothing but the truth. But the *whole truth*, now that might be a different story.

The police finished questioning the Gendrons and Emily immediately broke away and moved toward Cam and Father Marcotte. The Monsignor turned to embrace her before glancing back at Cam.

"Make sure you contact Ms. Spencer. I think you'll be fascinated by what you learn."

+   +   +

Cam spent the early part of the afternoon at Massachusetts General Hospital. Brandon had been airlifted there and the surgeons were trying to save his life and, if possible, also his leg. Uncle Peter, his dark blue tie knotted tightly against his Adam's apple and his thin brown hair combed neatly to the side like something out of an IBM training manual, sat tall in a chair and stared blankly at a wall through horn-rimmed glasses. He and Brandon were about as opposite as two people could be yet they had somehow found common ground. Perhaps he admired, even envied, Brandon's ability to squeeze so much joy from life — other than a wedding photo, the only picture in his office was of his son grinning triumphantly after scoring a touchdown in the annual "Mud Bowl" football game he organized every spring. Every once in a while he turned to Cam and asked him to recount, again, how the Bobcat blew. Cam left out the part about it being his idea to use the Bobcat to bait McLovick.

Aunt Peggy alternately wept and twisted rosary beads in her hands, praying. She had apparently come straight from a power walk with her friends — her gray-blond hair was tucked under a pink Red Sox cap and she was still wearing one of those baby blue, matching sweatpants and top outfits that had been popular in the 1970s and were now making a comeback. Cam paced back and forth, unable to offer any comfort to Brandon's parents and unable to do anything about Brandon's attackers.

After an hour, he had had enough. He hated hospitals, probably because every time he went to one as a kid he had some doctor telling him he would go blind or have to have his feet amputated or even die if he didn't take better care of himself. Now it was Brandon facing amputation and perhaps even death, while Cam seemed to have skated by death's door. At his last visit to Boston's Joslin Diabetes Clinic — he spent three days there during his bar suspension — they told him he was in fine health; with recent breakthroughs in diabetes treatment he would probably live to see his hair fall out and his chest sag to his belly and his erections wilt. It was the first time the doctors hadn't hedged their bets. The welcome news, sagging and wilting aside, forced him to face a whole new question: What did he want to do with his life? He had coasted through law school and his professional career on talent alone — he seemed to have an innate ability to dig in and ferret out the key issue or fact that would turn a complex case. But he had never really had to work hard at it, never really had to fight to attain a lifelong dream. The question of what he wanted to do with his life was one he had never really pondered before — and he hadn't gotten very far with it in the past year. But he knew what he needed to do right now.

"Uncle Peter, I'm going to see if I can find out anything about who did this." Cam's parents were flying up from their vacation home in North Carolina and Brandon's sister was driving down from Vermont so there would be plenty of family support.

He said his goodbyes and pulled out his cell phone as he followed signs back to the parking garage. He called information, then dialed the Westford library number and asked to speak with Amanda Spencer. A woman took his name and number; ten minutes later his cell phone rang, 'Unavailable' flashing on the Caller ID display.

"This is Amanda Spencer. You telephoned me?" A British accent.

"Yes, Monsignor Marcotte suggested I contact you. This is regarding a situation involving Emily and Marvin Gendron, who are my clients." Cam began to describe recent events.

Ms. Spencer cut him off. "I am aware of today's ... accident." Word sure traveled fast in this town. "If you wish me to discuss these matters with you, you will need to provide me with your full name and social security number, your date and place of birth, and three professional references."

"I'm sorry, what?"

She repeated the terms, her tone patient but unyielding.

"Look, lady, I don't have time for this—"

"Very well then. I wish you a good day, Mr. Thorne—"

"Wait, wait." He took a deep breath, squeezed the irritation out of his voice. He had no other leads in this case and he was becoming increasingly curious about what Ms. Spencer might be able to tell him. And how was it she already knew about the accident? He supplied the information, using law colleagues as references.

"Very well. Meet me at noon tomorrow at the library. If I am not there, it is because your references were not satisfactory. In the meantime, I suggest that you familiarize yourself with the legend of the Westford Knight."

Again with the Westford Knight. After his encounter with the little girl at the library, he had Googled Prince Henry and the Westford Knight and learned of a stone carving commemorating the death of a medieval knight exploring the Westford area in 1398. Apparently a stone plaque marked the site. "Okay," he said. "Tomorrow at noon. How will I find you?"

"You will not. I will find you, Mr. Thorne." The line went dead.

CHAPTER 3

[Sunday]

Cam woke up before five the next morning, his sleep tormented by visions of Brandon's carefree face just before he turned the key of the Bobcat. When Uncle Peter had called a little before midnight, Brandon was still holding on. Doctors had amputated part of one leg.

He lifted his legs from under the covers, flexed them. What would life be like without the ability to walk or run? He rolled out of bed, threw on some biking shorts, a t-shirt and his running shoes and, after checking his blood sugar, wolfed down a frozen waffle. He also grabbed a small digital camera and slipped it into an inner pocket on his shorts.

The morning air was cool and dry. The sun illuminated the tree-tops, a rainbow of leaves fluttering on the oaks as October began to sneak up on September. After stretching quickly he jogged to the end of his street, Pegasus by his side.

Normally he ran around the lake, about a five mile loop. Today, instead, he turned away from the lake and headed out of the Nabnasset section of town toward the town center. He ran hard, eager to get a sweat going. He focused on the trees and the squirrels and the mist rising from the wetland areas bordering the road, trying to clear his head, to push the anger and outrage out of the front of his mind. He would call upon those emotions later, to fuel him and energize him. But for now he needed his analytical skills if he hoped to find Brandon's attacker. Or attackers.

As the sweat poured out of him and his breathing settled into an easy rhythm, he was finally able to focus on yesterday's events in a semi-detached manner. It would be foolish to conclude Brandon was the intended target of the bomb. It was just as likely, perhaps more so, that the attacker had targeted Cam. After all, he had obtained the restraining order and advised the Gendrons not to sell the property. Which meant he could still be a target. And here he was, jogging along like an idiot, totally unaware of what or who might be targeting him. And totally unprepared. He veered into a wooded area and grabbed a thick branch about the size and heft of a baseball bat. Not much, but better than nothing. He watched for idling cars and out-of-place pedestrians and movements in the woods.

At the bottom of a hill, where the Stonybrook River meandered through a lowland area, he crossed a narrow bridge and began climbing again on the opposite side of the slow-moving river. The incline up Depot Street led to the town center. But before he got there he would make a stop to do his homework.

He made good time up the steep hill, his legs still fresh and strong, Pegasus keeping pace. About a mile up the hill, on the left just past an elementary school, five granite pillars, arranged in a pentagon and linked by a thick black chain, outlined the Westford Knight carving. He sprinted the last 50 yards and darted across the street, his hands behind his head to help fill his lungs after the long climb. The pillar and chain, only a few feet from the curb of the road, framed a ledge of flat, gray bedrock.

"Stay," he said to Pegasus.

He read from a granite tombstone-like plaque marking the site:

**PRINCE HENRY FIRST SINCLAIR OF ORKNEY
BORN IN SCOTLAND MADE A VOYAGE OF DISCOVERY
TO NORTH AMERICA IN 1398. AFTER WINTERING
IN NOVA SCOTIA HE SAILED TO MASSACHUSETTS
AND ON AN INLAND EXPEDITION IN 1399
TO PROSPECT HILL TO VIEW THE SURROUNDING
COUNTRYSIDE ONE OF THE PARTY DIED. THE
PUNCH-HOLE ARMORIAL EFFIGY WHICH ADORNS
THIS LEDGE IS A MEMORIAL TO THIS KNIGHT.**

He had read about the Portuguese ruler, Prince Henry the Navigator. But this was a different Prince Henry. He snapped a picture of the marker.

He dropped to a knee and studied the stone outcropping. He easily identified a series of closely-spaced, pea-size indentations engraved in the shape of a medieval battle sword, approximately three feet in length, complete with pommel, hilt and guard. Part of the blade itself was comprised of the glacial striations of the rock but the other features were clearly man-made. Fighting the morning shadows, he focused in with his camera on the sword image.

THE SWORD OF THE WESTFORD KNIGHT

Adjacent to the sword, faint chalk markings depicted the Knight's shield. He turned his head, trying to ignore the chalk and focus on the markings in the rock. These markings were far less evident than the punch-holes that formed the sword, perhaps nothing more than natural imperfections in the bedrock. Above the sword's oval-shaped pommel he made out the faint image of the Knight's head in the rock's surface but, again, the markings were far less clear than the sword. He stood up and tried to view the effigy as a whole but remained uncertain whether what he saw was a medieval knight with sword and shield or just a medieval sword. Either way it was a fascinating artifact.

Dropping back to a knee, he ran his fingers along the sword carving, imagined the ancient carver pecking at the rock in the hot sun, forcing the hard surface to yield to his tool. Was the legend true, was the ledge really carved by Scottish explorers a century before Columbus? If so, why were Prince Henry and his men wandering through Westford? Did they just happen upon it, exploring the land, or did they have more specific plans?

He stood and gazed around, wondering if the body of a medieval knight was buried in the yard of one of the neighboring Colonial-style homes. Would one of the homeowners someday discover an armor-clad skeleton while digging a hole for a fencepost? He snapped a couple more pictures and reread the granite plaque before resuming his run.

Monsignor Marcotte had referred him to Amanda Spencer, who had directed him to the Westford Knight. Apparently, therefore, the Monsignor believed the Knight was somehow related to the Gendrons' property and the treasure. Was the Prince Henry party looking for some kind of treasure in Westford? Or had they buried one while here?

He crossed the road to the sidewalk and continued his jog up the hill toward the town center, Pegasus still at his side and the club-like branch still in his right hand. The early Sunday morning traffic was light and what there was of it moved at a leisurely pace. It was hard to be in a rush at 6:00 on a Sunday morning. Which was why the roar of a car engine sent a wave of panic through him.

He spun his head. A black, older-model Cadillac jumped the curb and barreled toward him, two tires on the sidewalk. Had they been following him and seen him studying the Knight carving? He sprinted ahead, Pegasus at his side, but a picket fence blocked his escape from the sidewalk. Remembering his training from the high school track team, he pumped his arms and raced along the fence line toward the shelter of a large oak tree where the fence ended. As Pegasus barked in warning, the car closed on him, now only feet away, the engine so loud that it sounded like it was coming from in front of him as well as behind. He forced his legs and arms to pump harder, his body to ignore the sharp pain in his lungs, his brain to resist the urge to spin and check the progress of the hurtling mass of steel. The heat of the car's grill warmed the back of his legs like the hot breath of a monster at his heels. He fought back the panic. Vaulting the fence was a possibility but that would leave him splayed on the other side with only wooden slats between him and tons of careening vehicle. The engine roared even louder as the car downshifted on the steep incline, accelerating toward him. *Now or never.*

He took one more long stride to clear the fence line and dove for the tree, his body soaring forward and to the right. As he neared the ground, he tucked his chin and rolled, making a ball of himself just as he had done during the water-ski fall. He popped back to his feet and spun in time to see the Cadillac go careening by, less than a body length away, its tires tearing up the same green lawn that had cushioned his fall.

The car screeched to a halt, its chassis still straddling the sidewalk, smoke steaming from its tires. Pegasus stood in front of Cam and barked at the vehicle. "Easy, fella. Stay." The thick branch lay on the grass, near where he had rolled, and he considered charging at the car and confronting the driver. But McLovick, or whoever it was, surely carried a more formidable arsenal than a stick. Cam tensed, ready to flee into the nearby woods as the driver revved the engine. The white reverse lights flashed at him menacingly, then the driver shifted into gear and sped off.

Cam made a mental note of the license plate and plopped down on the cool, dew-covered grass, his heart pounding in his chest. And began to shiver. Not from the cold, or a sugar imbalance, or even from fear but from an almost numbing sense of foreboding.

+   +   +

Cam spent a good part of the rest of the morning answering questions from the police. No, he didn't get a good look at the driver—he was wearing a hat and sunglasses and the car's sun visor shielded his face. Yes, he was sure it hadn't been accidental or sun glare or a flat tire. Yes, he thought it was related to the attack on Brandon. The police made a quick call—the license plate was a dead end, the Cadillac having been stolen from a mall parking lot the night before.

Lieutenant Poulos offered Cam a ride home. "How's Brandon doing?"

"Still hanging in there." Cam had phoned his uncle between answering questions from the police. "He was sort of lucky he got thrown out of the Bobcat. Otherwise he would have got burned even worse than he was." He swallowed. "But they couldn't save his leg." A jolt of guilt rushed through Cam like an electrical charge, as if saying the words made the whole surreal series of events somehow more real, more concrete. He had come up with the stupid Bobcat plan—Brandon was just doing him a favor, just being a good guy.

Poulos glanced sideways. "You can't beat yourself up over it. You were trying to do the right thing. The guilty party here is the guy who planted that bomb."

Cam shrugged and forced a half smile. "Thanks."

"You know, one of the best field goal kicking coaches around is a guy with cerebral palsy, spent his whole life in a wheelchair. Coaches now for the Miami Dolphins."

Cam tried to rally. "Yeah. And the guy they call the grandfather of hockey goalie coaches just had a foot amputated and rides around in a cart on the ice. He's still coaching." He had followed the story because the coach lost his foot due to complications from diabetes. He tried to picture Brandon with a prosthetic leg. It just didn't fit. Brandon was always jumping around, hyper almost. But, then again, he was one of those glass is half-full people. He might give thanks to be alive and make the best of things.

They drove in silence for a few minutes. "Think that bomb was meant for you?"

"It was meant for whoever was planning on digging up that yard. Brandon just happened to be the one who jumped into the driver's seat." He tried to fill his lungs with oxygen, to squeeze the heaviness out of his chest.

"I remember how I felt the first time someone took a shot at me. Quite a wake-up call. All of a sudden, you look at life a bit different."

Cam nodded.

"We got a warrant and searched McLovick's house. Nothing."

"Alibi?"

"Yup. Pretty good one."

"McLovick's a scumbag but he's not stupid. He's the obvious suspect so he'd be careful."

"Like I said, we've got nothing."

"How about forensics?" On those TV shows, they were always catching the bomber by tracing the duct tape or the battery or the friggin' dental floss he used. Always something mundane.

Poulos let out a long sigh. "You're a lawyer so you know how this works. There's only so much money to go around. If Brandon lives, no matter how bad he's hurt, the case isn't going to get the same scrutiny as a fatality."

The irony was that lawyers always said a dead client was a bad client. Personal injury attorneys wanted their clients to live anguished lives, the better to maximize pain and suffering damages. Suffer greatly but don't die. The police, on the other hand, were saying that it would be easier to solve Brandon's case if he were dead, that somehow the attack was more offensive if Brandon happened to stop breathing. The civil courts valued Brandon more if he lived, the criminal courts more if he died. Cam had too much on his mind to try to decide which point of view was more screwed up.

⁃⊹ ⊹ ⊹

Cam walked into Westford's J.V. Fletcher library an hour later for his scheduled meeting with Amanda Spencer. He had showered and thrown on a pair of old jeans and a green golf shirt. Normally he would have put Pegasus on a leash and roller-bladed the few miles into town center. Or at least taken the Harley. As he drove, he remembered lying awake at night as a kid on a Boy Scout camping trip after being told a bear had been spotted nearby. He hadn't slept, knowing that at any minute the bear might crash through the tent wall. In the end, the bear had wandered away in the night. He doubted he would be so lucky this time.

Ten minutes early, he drifted over to browse the Westford Knight collection in the reference area. Maybe he should have stayed and listened to the storyteller with the little girl and her mother. A photograph of a rubbing of the Knight caught his eye and he pulled it out of its plastic sleeve to examine. He had seen only the sword when examining the carving; the rubbing showed the Knight in more detail.

WESTFORD KNIGHT RUBBING

"You know, you can make a rubbing look like pretty much anything you want."

He turned to see Uncle Peter, red-eyed through his horn-rimmed glasses, standing behind him in a pair of khakis and a wrinkled dress shirt. He had never seen him unshaven before. "What are you doing here?"

Peter shrugged. "Trying to be useful. Nothing I can do for Brandon. And Peggy's driving me crazy. I thought I'd see what this Westford Knight nonsense is all about."

Cam had called him and recounted his visit to the Knight site and subsequent joust with the Cadillac. "Glad to hear you have an open mind about it."

"Come on, Cameron. There's a reason it's called a legend."

"All right." He held up a hand. "We're both stressed out. I don't want to argue."

Together they thumbed through the plastic-sleeved collection of photos. A number of older photographs taken in the 1940s and 1950s, like the rubbing, showed the Knight more vividly. Apparently the accumulation of rock salt and sand from passing snow plows, along with the elements and passage of time, had eroded many of the Knight's details.

"Maybe it's a knight, maybe it's not," Peter said.

A young woman with white-blond hair and fair skin glided toward them, a brown soft leather briefcase swinging at her side. She halted a few feet away, feet together, and straightened her back. A pair of deep, shamrock-green eyes studied Cam. "I am Amanda Spencer." Her eyes practically jumped off her cream-colored skin like green sparkles on a Christmas sugar cookie. He had expected someone plain and dowdy and older. Instead he found himself staring at a face that belonged locked in a medieval tower, waiting to be rescued by the Knights of the Round Table.

She held his eyes. "I see you are not hurt," she declared in the same British accent he had noticed during their phone call.

How did she know about his footrace with the Cadillac this morning? "I'm fine." Normally he read people easily but she was a wall to him. "By the way, I'm Cameron Thorne." He held out his hand, smiled.

She offered the most perfunctory of handshakes, a quick touch with the tips of her fingers. "Of course you are. You may follow me."

He shook his head. So much for his boyish charm. "Oh, and this is Peter Thorne, my uncle. It was his son who was ... injured. I hope it's all right that he joins us."

She studied him for a few seconds — he had not undergone a background check. Finally she sighed and nodded. "I hope your son makes a full recovery."

She had that kind of blemish-free skin that made it difficult to guess her age but Cam ball-parked it at late twenties. Of average height, she strode gracefully, like a dancer or gymnast. She wore a long, shale-colored blazer over a floral blouse and a beige skirt that swung loosely at her knees. The look reminded him of a friend from his old law firm who, though she knew the firm expected her to dress in proper business attire, insisted on doing so as fashionably as possible. Her hair was shoulder-length, except for a single, braided lock that protruded an extra five or six inches down her back, swinging irreverently like a golden pendulum as she walked.

They headed down a long staircase toward the rear exit of the library before circling back underneath the stairs and stopping at a small display. A thick stone, about the size of the seat of an office chair, rested on a metal pedestal. She stepped aside, leaving a clean, floral perfume in her wake, and motioned for Cam and Peter to examine the artifact. "This is called the Boat Stone."

Carved onto the light gray face of the stone were three distinct designs: an old-style sailing boat, an arrow, and the numbers 184. The impressions appeared to have been made by a series of holes punched into the stone, much like the carving on the Westford Knight rock ledge but at closer intervals.

BOAT STONE

"How old is it?" Cam asked.

She shrugged. "I was not present when it was engraved so I do not know for certain."

No, but presumably you're the expert on this stuff. "Perhaps you could indulge us and hazard a guess."

Instead of responding, she nodded and straightened herself. "Please pardon me for a bit." She walked down the hall, pulled out her cell phone and whispered her way through a quick conversation. While he waited, he snapped a picture of the stone.

She returned, her tone softer. "I apologize if I have been rude. Let's begin again. Please call me Amanda." She held out her hand, this time shook his firmly. "Lately," she continued, "most of the people I show these sites to are only interested in clues to some buried treasure. Or they believe aliens carved the Knight." She offered a half-smile. "It can be a bit trying. Which is why I asked for your background information."

That's what her phone call was for. "And I checked out okay?"

"Well, you are a solicitor." This time a full smile. "But otherwise you seem acceptable."

He held her eyes for a second, thankful to have finally broken through. He lowered his voice. "Look, someone blew off my cousin's leg because of this buried treasure. He could have died. Then I almost got turned into road kill myself. And some priest tells me I need to talk to you, presumably because you can help me figure all this out." He gestured toward the Boat Stone. "Please? We really need some help here."

She nodded, took him by the arm and spun him gently back toward the display. This time the floral scent mixed with the warmth of her breath and body. Peter stood behind them, his arms crossed. He sighed audibly. She ignored him and spoke. "The boat depicted in the stone is a medieval knorr and the arrow is a medieval crossbow arrow. Many experts believe the Knight effigy and this stone were carved by the same people. The Boat Stone may have been some kind of directional marker, pointing the way to an encampment site or ship—"

"Which way was the arrow pointing?" Peter interrupted.

"It was found by a farmer when the town was widening the road near his home and moved many times, so nobody knows. The road followed an old trail, used by your Native Americans."

Cam wasn't sure why they were *his* Native Americans but he let the comment pass. "Close to the Knight?"

"No, not particularly. A bit of a hike. But the Stonybrook River connects the Knight and the Boat Stone sites. Prince Henry and his mates could well have come up the Merrimack River from the coast, then found their way to Westford on the Stonybrook."

"Impossible," Peter countered. "It's not navigable."

"Not entirely. But it is with a bit of portaging." She paused. "What you might find interesting is that the Boat Stone was found in the western part of town on Route 40."

Cam's stomach tightened. "Route 40, where it intersects North Street?"

"Spot on. In close proximity to the Gendrons' home. I assume that's why Monsignor Marcotte suggested you contact me. He must fancy that your Mr. McLovick's interest in the property is related to the Knight and the Boat Stone."

"Look, if they're *my* Native Americans, then he's *your* Mr. McLovick. He's Scottish, not American. I want nothing to do with him."

"Touché." She smiled and nodded. "From what I know of Mr. McLovick, I would not want to lay claim to him either."

He answered her smile and found himself staring at her mouth. But the memory of Brandon's bloodied body intruded. He refocused on the Boat Stone. Medieval ships, arrows, knights, swords, the numerals 184, stone enclosures — they were all somehow related but they didn't fit together in any neat pattern. "You said the boat and the arrow are medieval. How about the numbers? When did Europeans begin using Arabic numerals?"

"I'm not certain of the exact date but they were definitely in use by the late 14th century."

"So you think this Prince Henry Sinclair legend is true, that he sailed over from Scotland a hundred years before Columbus and ended up in Westford and that his men carved the Westford Knight and this stone?"

She stared at Cam for a long time, her green eyes boring in like drill bits. There was an intensity in her gaze that disquieted him. He wanted to turn away but sensed she was testing him, probing for weaknesses, questioning whether she could trust him. It was an incredibly effective technique — he had nothing to hide but after five seconds under her gaze, he began searching his conscience for something he had done wrong, some lie he had told. Finally she allowed her eyes to soften, took Cam by the elbow and walked him toward the door. "Come, it is best that we speak outside."

✝ ✝ ✝

Cam and Amanda exited the library, Uncle Peter on their heels, and crossed the street to a shaded wooden bench on the triangular town common. He wished he could ask Peter to leave—Amanda might be less guarded without his sullen, stalking presence.

Shifting his weight forward on the park bench, Cam eyed the passing traffic. Amanda smiled at him. "I understand you are jittery. But I don't think they will try anything out here in the open."

Again with the pronouns. "Who, exactly, is 'they'?"

"My bosses are wondering the same thing; we're bothered also." She lifted her head. "Do you see that house across the way, the yellow one?"

He peered across the common at a sprawling yellow Victorian with white trim and a single turret. "Yes."

"My office is on the second floor. When folks come to the library and want to view the Knight, the staff phones me and I amble over and escort them down the hill to view the effigy." It was an odd way to make a living, or even spend your free time, but he had too much on his mind to bother questioning it. "I also am in charge of maintaining the entire Westford Knight collection. It is the largest collection of Westford Knight-related material in the world."

He had a friend who collected old lighthouse postcards, claimed he had the largest collection in the world. He resisted making the comparison. "But that's not why we're sitting in this park right now." Or in Peter's case, pacing.

"I fancy not. But it should indicate to you that there are folks who place great value on the Westford Knight and its history—enough to pay me a full-time wage and hire an office and pay my expenses." She paused. "And also, when necessary, take the appropriate security precautions."

"Such as?"

"Such as there are two pairs of security operatives watching us now."

He sat forward, studying the cars surrounding the triangular common. "Obviously, the security is not for Peter's or my benefit."

"It is for mine. We are not certain who is targeting you, or why. But since it apparently relates to the Knight, we are taking extra precautions."

He was beginning to understand why she had been so guarded early in their meeting. "What other precautions might you be taking?"

"You are being videotaped through my office window. And this conversation is being recorded." She glanced at her briefcase, which presumably held the recording device. "Later, our people will have a go with it — body language and voice patterns and such — to determine whether you are being truthful. We believe your story is true but, again, we also believe in taking necessary precautions."

Precautions were one thing. This was borderline paranoia. But he needed Amanda's help. "Whatever help you can give us, I'd appreciate."

Clearing her throat, she began. "I am going to begin in the year 1118, when Christian forces had recently retaken Jerusalem. I know for some Americans that seems prehistoric — you picture folks living in caves and just learning about fire."

"Assume I know nothing. I only took one semester of European history. I took a lot of American history but that only takes me back to 1492."

Peter lifted his chin. "Well, I know a bit about European history."

"Good," she smiled. "Well, during the Crusades all families of noble birth were expected to do their part in the war against the Muslims. So a Frenchman named Hughes de Payen and eight other French noblemen founded an order of warrior monks dedicated to protecting Christian pilgrims journeying to Jerusalem. They were given quarters above the ruins of the old Temple of Solomon and thus took the name, the Knights Templar. You've surely heard of them."

"There was a special on TV about them last week."

"One of the noblemen who financed de Payen's mission to Jerusalem was his Scottish father-in-law, St. Clair, the Baron of Roslyn. Over the generations, the St. Clair clan continued to be closely affiliated with the Templars in France and they continued to govern Roslyn, in Scotland. By way of example, the grave of Sir William St. Clair, who died in 1330, is marked with a tombstone inscribed with 'Knight Templar' in letters as large as his name." She pulled a loose-leaf notebook out of her briefcase and opened to a photo of the tombstone. "The family name was later Anglicized to Sinclair." She waited until Cam looked up from the photo. "Our explorer, Prince Henry, was Sir William's grandson."

THE TOMBSTONE OF SIR WILLIAM ST. CLAIR, ROSLYN CHAPEL

"So Prince Henry was a Templar knight?" Cam asked.

"Impossible," Peter interjected. "The Templars were long disbanded by then."

Amanda nodded. "Most historians concur with you, Peter. And I'll revisit your point. But first let's go back to the early 1100s. Once in Jerusalem, the Templars didn't patrol the highways or protect pilgrims as was their mission. Instead they spent nine years excavating a series of tunnels under their quarters, near the old stables of the Temple."

"I've heard this hogwash before. There's no evidence support-ing it." In the best of times, Peter possessed the social skills of a snapping turtle.

Amanda remained impassive. "But there is. In the 1860s, a British archeological team led by Sir Charles Warren excavated under the old Temple. They failed to uncover any treasures or artifacts from Biblical times. But they did find Templar relics."

"Well, I've never heard of it."

"I can give you a reference if you'd like to have a go with the research yourself," Amanda said as she turned back to Cam. "In any event, after nine years the Templar knights returned straight away to Europe, where they were received by royalty all over the continent. Now, nobody is certain what they found in the Temple ruins. But whatever it was, it was the springboard for this small order of monks to become the most powerful and wealthy force in Europe, even more so than the Church. At one point, they owned a third of the land in Europe."

"Isn't there some record of what they found?" Cam asked.

Amanda shook her head. "No, the Templars were a secret society."

Peter raised a finger. "I've found that usually when there's no evidence for something, it's because the something didn't exist."

"That is one possibility. But the facts here are indisputable: The Templars were the most powerful force in Europe for almost two centuries. There must be some explanation. It did not occur by accident."

"So there's no direct evidence," Cam interjected. "But we build cases on circumstantial evidence all the time. Can we figure out what they found based on their actions?"

Amanda leaned forward. "Indeed, many have tried. Here's what we know. First, soon after returning to Europe, the Templars oversaw the building of a vast number of stone cathedrals and abbeys across Europe, soaring structures supported by flying buttresses." This design freed the internal walls from weight-bearing responsibility and allowed for large, ornate, stained-glass windows. Before that, churches were simple and plain and dark. "From this, we can deduce that the Templars somehow acquired secrets of geometry and architecture that had been lost after Roman times. Perhaps in the Temple ruins, perhaps from some other source in the area around Jerusalem."

She paused, looked to Cam and Peter for argument or rebuttal before continuing. "Second, and related to this, is the fact that the Templars built a large fleet of ships and became experts in navigating them far beyond normal travel routes. It is possible they rediscovered ancient navigational and astronomical secrets of the Phoenicians, perhaps even ancient maps."

"You're not one of those people who believe the Phoenicians sailed to America, are you?" Peter rolled his eyes.

"Indeed, I am. But that is a discussion for another day. You will not dispute, I trust, that the Phoenicians were master sailors."

Peter grunted his assent as Cam spoke. "So what you're saying is that the Templars acquired knowledge."

"Yes, either buried in the ruins of the Temple or through interaction and trading with others in the Levant, the Middle East. This was knowledge that had been lost to Europe, secrets that gave the Templars the means to accumulate tremendous wealth. Eventually they used that wealth to build a large, fierce army of warrior monks. And they possessed enough land and livestock to support the whole operation."

"Guns *and* butter, a tough combination to beat. So what happened to them?"

"First I want to continue to talk about what they found buried in the ruins of King Solomon's Temple. I trust you have heard of the Ark of the Covenant?"

Cam nodded as Peter guffawed. Most Americans were familiar with it because of the movie, *Raiders of the Lost Ark*. The ark was the sacred container that housed the Ten Commandments. In the movie, the Nazis craved it because they believed it possessed supernatural powers.

"Well," Amanda continued, "many believe the Templars found the ark and carried it with them to Europe. Others think they found or traded for other artifacts in Jerusalem, like the Holy Grail or fragments from the cross Jesus was crucified on or even the head of John the Baptist. All of these, obviously, would have been extraordinarily important discoveries."

"All right, this is getting ridiculous now. There's no evidence for any of this." Peter folded his arms across his chest and stared down at Amanda.

Amanda held his eyes. "Perhaps you are correct. But often myth is more powerful than reality. Over the centuries, thousands have suffered and even died because of religious artifacts that may or may not have been found by the Templars in Jerusalem. I do not wish to be crass but your son Brandon is a perfect example of my point. Whether something of value is buried beneath the Gendrons' backyard is really not relevant. What is relevant is that someone *believes* something is buried there. It is that belief, not the reality, that put Brandon in the hospital." She turned to Cam. "There is an expression on Wall Street: 'Buy on the rumor, sell on the news.' In the case of the Temple of Jerusalem artifacts, people have been buying on the rumor for centuries."

This was not the version of European history Cam had learned at Boston College. "I could see how finding these artifacts, or even people thinking they found stuff, would make the Templars pretty important in Europe. Especially during the Crusades."

"Precisely. Again, the Muslims controlled the lands surrounding Jerusalem and the Christian world was intent on ensuring that religious artifacts not be lost."

"Okay, so that answers my question about what the Templars found in Jerusalem." Either ancient knowledge or some important religious artifacts. Maybe both.

Amanda shifted on the bench so her face remained shaded as she waited for a loud truck to pass. "There is, of course, one other possibility, which I am sure you can guess."

Cam thought about McLovick. "There's always a treasure, right?"

Peter groaned audibly. "You're kidding, right?" He typically used sarcasm when trying to turn a witness. It was usually a sign he was losing the case.

Amanda remained steadfast. "Recall that the Templars accumulated a tremendous amount of wealth and power in a remarkably short period of time. It is entirely possible they bankrolled themselves using the lost treasures of the Jewish people. You've heard of the Dead Sea scrolls?" Cam and Peter nodded. "Well, according to the Copper Scroll over a hundred tons of silver and gold were hidden just before the Temple of Solomon was destroyed by Roman forces in 70 A.D. Some scholars believe it was secreted in the tunnels beneath the Temple."

"Did you say one hundred tons?"

She nodded. "And nobody has ever found an ounce of it."

"Except maybe the Templars."

"Correct. The 1860s British excavation confirms the Templars were digging. Why dig for nine years unless you've found something?" She took a deep breath. "As I said, for 200 years during the 12th and 13th centuries the Templars were the most powerful military force in Europe. In fact, in the eyes of the Pope, too powerful. And too rich. The Church itself was heavily indebted to the Templars, largely due to the cost of the Crusades. As was the French royal family. Finally, on Friday, the thirteenth of October, 1307, the French king, Philip, arrested 15,000 French Templars and charged them with heresy and sodomy and a whole list of crimes against the Church. Similar arrests occurred all over Europe."

"That's one way to deal with debt collectors," Peter said.

Amanda smiled politely but her hands were clenched tightly in her lap. "King Philip tortured and murdered thousands of Templar leaders and the Church officially disbanded the Order. The Church and Philip divided the Templar lands and other assets."

Cam had read about this. "That's the origin of Friday the thirteenth being bad luck, right?"

"Precisely," she said, her hands unclenching. "But the Templars had advance notice of Philip's plan. A group of them boarded the Templar fleet, loaded the boats with their treasures and sailed to Scotland, which was at that time outside the control of the Pope. Most people believe they ended up in Roslyn. With the Sinclairs."

"Most people?" Peter challenged.

"Allow me to reword that. Most people who believe the fleet escaped believe it went to Scotland."

"Put me down as a non-believer."

"That's fine, Peter, but then you must answer one question: What happened to the Templar wealth? All historians agree it existed and all agree that neither Philip nor the Pope recovered more than a few morsels. It must have gone somewhere, don't you agree?"

"Well, I suppose so."

"What treasures were supposedly on the ships?" Cam asked.

Amanda shrugged. "Again, this is the mystery. Perhaps it was the secrets of ancient knowledge, perhaps religious artifacts, perhaps gold and jewels, perhaps all three."

Cam pictured the ships sailing under the cloak of darkness, the French authorities raiding empty piers at daybreak. "And the Pope just left them alone after that?"

"Well, the Pope had ordered the arrests of the Templars all across Europe. Some monarchs complied with the demand, some did not, but the torture and killings were essentially limited to France. For example, in Portugal the Templars merely changed their names to the Knights of Christ and continued on merrily as before. And the Pope knew not to push his advantage too far. He had succeeded in erasing an enormous amount of Church debt, he had appropriated valuable lands and buildings and he had eliminated a powerful check on his power. But many in Europe had strong ties to the Templars so the Church, wisely, did not pursue the Templars to Scotland. At least not right away."

"What about later?"

Amanda focused on a large oak tree across the common, as if looking for guidance in its gnarled roots and branches. "This circles back to your question about the Templars being disbanded. Nothing was heard from the Templars for the next couple of generations. Around Europe, many of the Templars joined sister orders like the Teutonic Knights and the Knights of Christ. But in Scotland the Order moved underground and reconstituted itself as the Freemasons, purportedly a stoneworkers guild."

"You're dead wrong," Peter said. "I happen to be a Freemason myself." Cam had no idea his uncle was a Mason. It made sense—he was always joining one group or another as a way to network and mine for clients. Still, he had trouble picturing him wearing one of those funny hats. "Any connection between the Templars and the Masons is a myth."

"With all due respect, sir, it is you that is wrong. I can show you."

He rocked back and forth on the balls of his feet. "Go ahead. Let's just say I'm skeptical."

She dug through her bag, pulled out a book and turned to the index. "Ah, here it is." She opened to a page with a photo of an image carved in stone. The carving displayed a blindfolded man with a noose around his neck being led forward by a bearded companion. "What does this look like to you?"

ROSLYN CHAPEL "INITIATION" CARVING

Peter studied the image. "A candidate being prepared for initiation into Freemasonry."

"Any doubt in your mind?"

"No. It's not like a cross or a rose or something—a blindfolded man being led by a noose is a pretty specific image. We still use the ritual today."

"And how old is Freemasonry?"

"It was founded around the year 1600, give or take."

"Well, this carving is from Roslyn Chapel, built in the mid-1400s. How could it depict a Masonic ritual if Masonry did not yet exist?"

Peter gazed back at her, blinking. He stopped rocking.

"In fact, Roslyn Chapel, built by Prince Henry Sinclair's grandson, is full of Masonic symbolism and imagery. Any Mason who has visited will tell you it is a veritable shrine to Freemasonry. Again, how could a shrine exist to something that had not yet been established? The answer, of course, is that the Masonic order was active in the 1400s, and probably even earlier, as a secret successor group to the Knights Templar. Documents as old as 1390 exist establishing this fact."

She waited a second to see if Peter would respond before turning back to Cam and continuing matter-of-factly. "After being outlawed, the next time the Templar order appeared publicly was during the Peasants Revolt in England in 1391. Peasants rioted and looted churches and manors, beheading noblemen and church leaders. The peasants seemed to especially target members and property of the Knights Hospitallers. Many believe the Hospitallers — you may know them as the Knights of Malta — were complicit in the Friday-the-thirteenth arrests. The Templars may have organized the revolt as revenge against the Hospitallers. Or as a preemptive strike before the Church came after them, aided by the Hospitallers."

Cam watched the cars go by, many of them SUVs loaded with kids on the way to soccer games or church or the shopping mall. It was hard to believe that the tale that began in Jerusalem almost 900 years ago would end here, today, in suburban Westford. Yet apparently the dots somehow connected. He took a deep breath. "So you think the Templar treasures made it up to Scotland — to Roslyn — to the Sinclair family. And from there, Prince Henry sailed with them to America?" From Jerusalem to France to Roslyn to Westford, the Sinclair family seemed to be tethered to the treasure, whatever it was, like the man guiding the blindfolded apprentice in the Roslyn Chapel carving.

"Prince Henry's mother was a Norsewoman so he was half-Viking as well as half-Scottish. He was both the baron of Roslyn and the prince of the Orkney and other islands, which were then Norwegian holdings. From his mother's side of the family he knew stories of Vikings sailing to lands west of Greenland. He probably had some old Viking maps. And he also had Templar maps and navigation charts through his father's side of the family."

Assuming all this was true, one way or another it seemed like Prince Henry was destined to find his way to North America. "So these Templar treasures are what people like McLovick are searching for here in Westford?"

"There's more to the story than that but, essentially, yes. He believes the stone foundation in the Gendrons' yard served as an encampment site for Prince Henry's expedition. It may very well contain clues to help find the treasure, perhaps even the treasure itself."

"Now hold on a second," Peter said. "If this is all true, why doesn't anyone know about it?"

She shrugged. "Not the treasure, perhaps, but many people know about Prince Henry. Tourists from all around the world come to Westford almost every day to visit the Knight."

"Getting back to this foundation," Cam said. "Has anyone tried to dig it up?"

"No. In the 1960s an archeologist conducted a preliminary survey—he concluded the stone enclosure was at least a few hundred years old, probably older. But nobody's done a full dig."

Cam asked the obvious. "Why not?"

"Fair question. I honestly don't know."

"Okay, well here's another question: Why did Sinclair come to America in the first place? And why would he bring the treasure if he did come?"

"I believe that's two questions," she smiled.

"I'm feeling lucky."

"Odd comment from a bloke almost killed twice in two days." She arched her eyebrow. "I'll answer your second question first. Prince Henry brought the treasure here to keep it away from the Pope. Since few people in medieval Europe knew how to get to North America, it was an ideal hiding spot."

Peter rocked forward. "But people don't cross an ocean just to hide something. Even a treasure. There are easier ways to hide things."

"Valid point. In fact evidence exists that the treasures were hidden in Iceland before being transported to America—80 Templar Knights arrived in Iceland in 1217 and an Icelandic researcher believes he has located the cave where the treasure was buried. Later the Templars retrieved the bounty and brought it to America."

"So back to my first question: Why come to America?"

"There are many possible reasons. From his mother's family Prince Henry surely heard tales of rich fishing grounds and abundant ship-building timber far to the west." Her tone had flattened, as if she were reciting words memorized from a textbook. "He ruled a large area and Scotland was a poor country being strangled by a trade embargo and recovering from the Black Plague, so there were compelling economic reasons for him to explore new territories."

Cam studied her. "But you don't think that's why he came."

She raised her eyes to his. "You read people well. No doubt you are an effective solicitor."

"Enough to know when someone is ducking my question. So I ask again: Why do *you* think he came?" Her manner toward him had warmed but he still could not count on her full candor.

For the first time she was off script. Pink colored her pale cheeks—perhaps from the hour spent in the sun, perhaps from unease at his question. "It does not really matter why." She shrugged.

"Either Prince Henry came or he did not. If he did, either he buried a treasure or he did not."

Again ducking the question. "Well, I'll ask the question this way then. Do you think he came? Do you think the legend is true?"

She straightened her back as the pink on her pale cheeks darkened. "In fact, I do. But, again, for your purposes, it does not matter what I think. It is as I explained earlier: What matters is not whether the legend of Prince Henry is *true* but that it is *relevant*. Folks are being blown up and run down because someone is convinced that Prince Henry Sinclair buried something here. What that is, and why he might have brought it here, is not particularly important. People have a way of believing what they want to believe. And someone believes in the Prince Henry treasure." She stood. The history lesson was over.

As far as it went, Amanda's observation was correct. But her line of reasoning revealed something else: Only one type of person expressed no interest in the mystery of a buried treasure and that was a person trying to keep others from digging for it.

✛   ✛   ✛

Amanda watched Cameron Thorne stroll away, his athletic build carrying him effortlessly across the common. She had been tempted — sorely tempted — to answer his final inquiry candidly. He had a right to know why he was in danger. But her orders were clear: Reveal to him only the basics of the Sinclair history. If he was worthy, he would uncover the hidden secrets himself.

Of course, most folks did not die as a result of their unworthiness. They made some inquiries, ran a handful of Google searches, perhaps read a few of the fringe publications discussing pre-Columbus exploration of America. But eventually they reached a dead end in their research and moved on. Unfortunately for Cam, someone was trying to bump him off — his dead end could leave him, well, dead.

She strode through the common and across the street to the yellow Victorian which bore a small brass sign, 'WKRC,' an abbreviation for Westford Knight Research Consortium. The Consortium was comprised of a group of Northern European families that boasted Prince Henry Sinclair and his expedition companions as their ancestors. The group did not receive visitors at its offices, which was why there was no doorbell.

She entered the alarm code password, unlocked a heavy dead-bolt and climbed a set of stairs that turned back on themselves a few times — the old servants staircase. Halfway up she stopped to inspect her face in the mirror. "Damn it." Even in the shade the sunlight had turned her face pink. She hadn't expected the meeting to go so long. It was a careless, and soon-to-be painful, miscalculation for someone with a sun allergy. She would have been safe in England in September but Boston, despite its colder winters, was significantly closer to the equator — it was only slightly further north than Rome and Barcelona. Tomorrow she would awaken with red, hive-like rashes and blisters.

At the top of the stairs, she placed her chin on a rubber platform, stared into a camera-like lens embedded in the wall and counted to four while the device scanned her retina. A green light flashed and another thick deadbolt retracted automatically. Today, for the first time in her year on the job, the security measures seemed warranted.

She entered the outer of the two rooms that comprised her office; her living quarters were on the third floor. The office resembled a men's club — leather and dark wood and nautical paintings. She could swear she smelled cigar smoke every time she entered.

The female security operative who had been operating the video camera had departed. Amanda sighed. She had no need for a house full of sorority sisters but she did fancy a mate to catch a movie or go for a cocktail with once in a while. Not that her bosses in London hadn't been candid with her when they first recruited her based on the recommendation of one of her professors who happened also to be a Consortium member. They informed her this would be a lonely assignment that required weekend hours. It paid twice what she could have made working in London but she hadn't been prepared for life as a twenty-something single woman living in American suburbia, with no family and no real friends.

Walking through the outer room, she hung her blazer on the back of the chair in front of her computer. She lowered herself into the chair and faced the screen, holding her head still while the face recognition software scanned her visage. After a few seconds, the keyboard unlocked and she skimmed her emails — a couple of personal messages from old university friends but mostly inquiries from researchers around the world asking for background information on the Knight. Answering emails from strangers and walking tourists up and down Depot Street from the library to visit the Knight occupied most of her time. Her employers were intent on preserving the Knight and related artifacts and on promoting historical research that supported the Prince Henry legend, but beyond that she had no idea what their ultimate mission was. Or why the stakes seemed so high.

She picked up the cordless phone to ring Beatrice Yarborough, her predecessor and current boss, then reconsidered. For important calls she had been instructed to use the satellite phone. Her computer monitor read 2:34 P.M. — she had spent over two hours with Cameron Thorne. It hadn't seemed that long. Shrugging the thought away, she dialed the London number using the satellite phone. It was 8:30 P.M. London time. Hopefully Beatrice hadn't gone out.

"Amanda, darling. Thank you for the lovely note."

"And thank you again for the jams." Now retired, Beatrice had too much time on her hands. And no family to help fill it. Almost weekly a package arrived for Amanda, filled with small gifts or crafts or food items.

"Not at all. But obviously you have important information. What is it, dear?"

Amanda pictured the woman, short and round and bubbly, her cheerfulness masking a sharp mind and near-compulsive nature and also making her seem younger than her 72 years. Amanda sometimes watched the old television show, *Murder She Wrote* – Beatrice could have played Angela Lansbury's Jessica Fletcher character, a small-town amateur detective. Like the character, Beatrice was a retired teacher, in her case a professor of medieval history. Amanda didn't have all the details but apparently a love affair with another professor had turned bad and Beatrice left the university under a cloud. It must have turned fairly ugly because she not only left academia, she left England altogether, landing in Westford. For 22 years she kept watch over the Knight. For the past year she mentored Amanda from London, though she made it clear she would have preferred to remain in Westford, as she put it, "watching over and protecting the Knight" – thankfully, she did not blame Amanda for her forced retirement. When Beatrice had first arrived in Westford few people knew of Prince Henry's journey. But she introduced the Knight to the town fathers and schoolchildren and promoted his story in the press. Tourists from Scotland visited the site as did weekenders from Nova Scotia, where Prince Henry and Sir James first made landfall in Guysborough Harbor. History buffs, too, made a point of visiting Westford, intrigued by the possibility of European exploration in America a century before Columbus. But Beatrice had not achieved her goal of seeing the Prince Henry legend become accepted as historical fact.

Amanda began to describe her conversation with Cameron Thorne.

"Remember, dear, every detail. Nothing is too unimportant." Which wasn't entirely true. During Amanda's first month in Westford, a visitor to the Knight site had asked to view any evidence that aliens had carved the figure. Resisting the urge to roll her eyes, Amanda dutifully transcribed the request in her log, as was her charge. Later, Beatrice chided her. "Amanda, darling, the Consortium is interested in history, not histrionics." To this day, Amanda sensed Beatrice wondered if she herself believed in extra-terrestrials.

"Our entire meeting was videotaped—you may download it if you wish. At the conclusion, Mr. Thorne asked why I believed Prince Henry made his voyage. I answered as I was trained—he did so for economic reasons. But he sensed I was withholding information. I want permission to tell him more, tell him about the other reasons—"

"Impossible." Beatrice interjected. "You know the protocol."

Beatrice inhaled on one of her French-made cigarettes. No doubt Orkney, her Siamese cat, was curled in her lap. Amanda had once visited the woman's flat in London's Kensington district, her devotion to her job evidenced by a life-size plaster mold of the Westford Knight carving displayed in the center of her living room. "Yes, but this is different. Lives are at stake. I believe we should make an exception."

"It seems to me that if lives are at stake it is because this Mr. Thorne put them there with his ridiculous plan—what was he thinking, bringing heavy machinery to the encampment site?"

"He was thinking he did not want a treasure hunter to nick valuables from his clients' backyard."

"Amanda, our mission is to protect the Knight. Not to help some solicitor protect his clients' vegetable patch. Treasure hunter or not, at least this McLovick fellow is a professional. He would have documented his find, would have followed established archeological protocols to ensure the value of his discovery. But Thorne has no training. He almost destroyed the encampment site—God forbid he actually stumbles upon an artifact and tries to pull it from the ground. The professional archeologists would discredit the find immediately."

"I suppose you are correct." There was a history of the archeological community discrediting amateur discoveries across New England and Quebec.

"Of course I am." Beatrice softened her tone. "We need to be very careful, Amanda. From what I know of Mr. Thorne he seems to be one of these American cowboys — out for vengeance and armed with the arrogance of a lawyer. Hardly the type of man suited to pulling delicate artifacts from the ground."

Cowboy was not the word Amanda would have chosen to describe Cam. Nor was arrogant. But she let it pass. "Well, that's even more reason for me to assist him. To make certain he doesn't do anything foolhardy."

"These protocols have been in place for centuries, Amanda. The answer is no. And I assure you, this is not the first time lives have been at stake. Nor will it be the last."

Amanda took a deep breath, tried a different tack. "Did you know Mr. Thorne is of the blood line?"

"I most certainly did not."

"I ran his genealogy through the computer this morning. His mother's maiden name is Kahn. She is a Cohen."

Beatrice exhaled. "The fact that Mr. Thorne is part of the *Rex Deus* line is interesting but ultimately irrelevant." Amanda first heard the term during her Consortium training. *Rex Deus* described the group of families — mostly European — who believed they descended directly from the 24 High Priests of the Temple of Jerusalem at the time of Jesus. They claimed to be the protectors of the true teachings of Jesus. The Cohen line — Jews and, later, Christians — were the royalty of this priest class, descended from Moses' brother Aaron. Amanda was not quite sure how *Rex Deus* factored into the Consortium's mission but she knew it was important to them, knew they tracked the bloodlines of everyone they came into contact with. Europeans tended to care about this stuff much more than Americans but this went beyond even that.

Beatrice continued in her professorial voice. "As you are aware, the knowledge we possess is shared on a self-selecting basis — it is one of our most fundamental tenets. Those who are worthy prove themselves by discovering our secrets. Only the wise and open-minded succeed. It has always been thus, and must always be." She paused. "I am hopeful that you, Amanda, will soon be privy to these secrets."

"Really, if I am not yet privy to them, then it doesn't really matter what I tell Cameron Thorne, does it?"

"Of course it does, dear. He must make the journey, starting from the beginning, himself. As I said, if Mr. Thorne can piece everything together, then he may be worthy of sharing our secrets. If not, well, then he is not. *Rex Deus* or not, the answer is no. You may not violate the protocols."

"But that's illogical," Amanda countered, trying to suppress her frustration. "He cannot prove he's worthy if he's already dead."

"Exactly. I do not mean to be critical, dear, but it is you who are being illogical. If he is truly worthy he will prove himself by staying alive."

+ + +

After leaving Amanda in the common, Cam walked to his SUV in the library lot. Suddenly even the act of starting his car seemed potentially life-terminating. Knees weak and a bit light-headed — whether from fear or lack of food, he wasn't sure — he dropped to the ground and slid under the Jeep. He knew enough about cars to know what belonged on a chassis and what did not.

Seeing nothing, he popped the hood and released it gently, exhaling as it opened without incident. Nothing on the engine block either. This time.

The memory of Brandon's bloodied leg fresh in his mind, he slowly turned the ignition and waited for his world to end. The engine roared but did not attack. Exhaling, he drove across the street to the white clapboard police station abutting the Colonial-style Town Hall. He parked next to a cruiser near the front entrance to the station, leaned against his door and pulled out his cell phone. But he felt far from safe even here.

He replayed in his mind the past 24 hours. The Bobcat had obviously hit a nerve — someone didn't want him digging in the yard. McLovick, or whoever it was, probably figured the bomb would scare him away. When he made an appointment with Amanda Spencer and visited the Knight site, it led to his close encounter with the Cadillac grille. They had probably decided he was a threat to them and had been following him. But who "they" were was still unclear.

Pacing in the police station parking lot, he phoned an old friend from law school, Claude Blank. Claude and his family had lived in Paris for a few years when Claude was in high school and he liked to mock Americans and their lack of culture. But he was more interesting than the other lawyers Cam knew and they had lunch in Boston a couple of times a year.

Cam got right to the point. "Isn't your sister an archeologist for the state or something?"

"Actually, she was just promoted last year. She's head of the state archeology department." Claude had a habit of closing his eyes — almost like extended blinks — as he spoke, especially when he wanted to make a point. "Why do you ask?"

"It's for a client. I need someone with some archeological expertise. Any chance she might be able to spare five minutes for a quick call today?"

"I don't see why not. Give me your number."

A couple of minutes later his cell phone rang. "This is Rhonda Blank."

"Hi. Thanks so much for calling. I'm sorry to bother you on a Sunday."

He waited for a response; getting none, he plowed ahead. "I'm looking for some information on the Westford Knight, it's a carving on—"

"Bunk," she interrupted.

"I'm sorry, what?"

"It's bunk. It was carved by some boys in the late 1800s as a prank."

He hadn't expected such a definitive response. He wondered if she, like Claude, closed her eyes when she spoke. "Oh, so you've studied it?"

"I don't need to waste my time studying it."

She made the cheerless Claude seem downright affable. "Well, what about the Boat Stone, in the town library?"

She snorted a response. "Also bunk."

"I'm sorry. I don't mean to question your expertise but my cousin is clinging to life in a hospital room because someone thinks there's something to this legend. And I almost got run down by a car today for the same reason."

"You've asked for my opinion and I've given it. There is absolutely no credible evidence, in Massachusetts or elsewhere, of any pre-Columbus exploration of America other than the Viking settlement in Newfoundland." He imagined a long, dismissive blink. "I'm sorry you were taken in by all this. Goodbye, Mr. Thorne."

+   +   +

Instead of driving all the way home after Rhonda Blank hung up on him, Cam stopped a block from his house and left the car on the side of the street. He cut through a neighbor's lawn and descended the slope to the lake's edge. After tying his sneakers together and draping them around his neck, he rolled up his jeans and slogged through the knee-deep water. He crouched low as he approached his house, listening for Pegasus. The wind was at his back—the dog should smell him as he approached and run to greet him.

He climbed over a dock and hugged the shoreline. Nothing from Pegasus, not even a short bark of inquiry. Sweat dripped down from his underarms even as the lake water numbed his toes. He moved some branches aside and peered through the brush toward the cottage. No dog, no movement of any kind. He had left Pegasus in the fenced yard, free to chase squirrels and nap in the sun. He gave a low whistle. Nothing.

Ignoring the rocks and twigs jabbing at his bare feet, he scrambled over the sandy beach area and sprinted toward the house. "Pegasus, where are you boy?" Hearing a faint whimper, he tore around the corner and spotted Pegasus curled in a golden ball near the front step, a thin gray archery arrow protruding from his shoulder. He slid to the dog's side. Pegasus whimpered a greeting, shakily lifted his head toward Cam's face.

He hugged the dog and gently stroked his forehead. "It's okay, fella." He yanked his cell phone from his jeans pocket and punched 9-1-1 into the pad, giving his name and the address as he pulled back Pegasus' fur thickened by warm, sticky blood. "My dog's been shot. Please send an ambulance."

"Um, I'm sorry, sir but we don't respond to veterinary emergencies." A woman's voice, kind but firm. "You'll need to bring the animal to an animal hospital."

He swallowed a curse as he looked into Pegasus' eyes — the dog was barely conscious. "Come on fella, hold on." He lifted him, the dog resting his head on Cam's neck. As he did so, he noticed a piece of paper wound tightly around the arrow just below the feathers, secured by clear tape. He set Pegasus back down, ripped the tape off and unwound the bubble gum-wrapper-size scroll. "Last Warning," it read.

Shaking with fury, he lifted Pegasus again and staggered a block toward his SUV. He groped for the passenger side door handle, tears clouding his vision, and gently lay Pegasus on the seat. The dog was now shivering, his breathing fast and shallow, his eyes closed.

He ran around to the driver's side, grabbed a blanket from the back seat and covered Pegasus with it. It didn't seem to help — there was simply not enough blood left in the dog's body to keep it warm. Cranking the heat, he aimed the vents at Pegasus and sped down the street. At the corner he stopped, resting his hand on Pegasus' head. The dog stared up and offered a single last whimper before sinking deep into the seat. Cam shifted into Park, closed his eyes and dropped his head on the steering wheel.

✝   ✝   ✝

A soft rap on the window jarred Cam back to reality. He lifted his head off the steering wheel and opened his eyes. Lieutenant Poulos stood in the street, his eyes averted from Cam's tear-strewn face. Cam took a deep breath, wiped his face with his sleeve and opened the window.

"I heard there was a 9-1-1 call from your address. Something about a dog being shot. Thought I should check it out." Poulos glanced at Pegasus' dead body. "I'm sorry about the dog."

Cam nodded, careful not to let his eyes follow the policeman's.

"Listen," Poulos continued, "how about we go back to your place."

Cam was in the middle of the street, his SUV still running. He needed to clear his head, to try to act rationally. Poulos could probably help in that regard. "Okay."

They drove up the street and pulled into Cam's driveway. Poulos pulled a shovel from his trunk. "Might be a nice idea to bury the dog in your backyard."

"Okay."

Poulos opened the passenger door. "I'm just gonna grab the arrow first. It's evidence. Maybe we can grab a print from it, or trace it."

Cam fumbled in his pocket for the piece of paper. "This was taped to the arrow."

Poulos scowled. "Guess there wasn't much chance this was random." He tucked the note and the arrow into an evidence bag. Another squad car had arrived and Poulos directed an officer to search the woods across the street for evidence. Poulos gently lifted Pegasus out of the car and waited for Cam to lead him to a spot in the backyard.

"This was his favorite spot, in the shade under that tree."

Poulos set Pegasus down and stuck the shovel deep into the ground, the man's strength evident in the thrust. Cam reached for the shovel. "Thanks but I'll do it." The officer surrendered the shovel and Cam threw himself into digging the grave. He dug angrily, fiercely, deeper and deeper into the ground. The sweat dripped into his eyes, stinging, and the tears flowed. It was odd. He felt terrible about Brandon's injuries — he had put his cousin in harm's way — but there was no way he could have seen it coming. To leave Pegasus home alone was just plain stupid. The tears were of frustration as much as sadness.

After about 20 minutes, Poulos put a hand on his sweat-stained shoulder. "That's deep enough, son."

Nodding, he stepped out of the thigh-high hole. He lifted Pegasus off the blood-stained blanket, gently lowering the dog into the hole. Lying on his stomach, he reached down and arranged Pegasus's paws and head into what he thought was a comfortable position, then removed his collar and slipped it into his pocket. He kissed his hand and touched the dog's nose. "I'm sorry, fella."

Poulos filled the hole with dirt while Cam stared out at the lake. The policeman cleared his throat. "My guy found some broken branches in those woods across the street. Probably where the arrow was shot from. But nothing else, no debris or nothing." He paused. "Any idea what's going on here, Cameron?"

He trusted the old football coach but didn't really have much to tell him. "Not really. Someone's pissed that I'm poking around the Gendrons' property. But I don't know why."

"Somebody said this might have something to do with the Westford Knight."

"Yeah, it seems like it. That's why I was talking to this woman at the library today. There's a legend that the people who carved the Knight might also have buried some treasure here."

"Look, I've lived here my whole life and I've never heard boo about any treasure. In fact, I don't even think that whole Knight story is legit. Anybody could've carved that rock."

Amanda's comment echoed in Cam's head. "But that almost doesn't matter. Whether the Knight is real or not, or whether there's a treasure buried here or not, the fact is that some people around here believe the legends and they're getting pretty pissed off we're getting in their way."

"You're right." Poulos hitched his pants up over his bulging waist. "Because of that, I figured we should go dig up the Gendrons' yard, see what all the fuss is about. But it's a crime scene so first I had to run it by the District Attorney's office. Pretty basic stuff, happens all the time. But they vetoed it. Some mumbo jumbo about it being a potentially historically significant site that can only be dug up by a licensed archeologist."

"What makes them think it's historically significant?" They obviously hadn't been talking to Rhonda Blank.

"That's what I said. Their answer was that if this McLovick fellow, who apparently is some kind of famous treasure hunter, was interested in it, then it must be significant."

"Sort of circular reasoning if you ask me."

"I agree. But the bottom line is we can't dig over there. Not without more evidence to justify it." They both looked down at Pegasus. "So, what are you going to do?"

"Well, I can't just stay here and wait for these assholes to take me out. I'm going to disappear for a while, try to figure this all out on the run."

Poulos shifted. "I like the idea of you getting out of town for a while. For your own safety. But you should drop it. Let us do our job."

"You know I can't do that." He locked his eyes onto the officer's.

While Poulos waited, Cam packed his camping gear in a large backpack along with road maps and a couple dozen packets of freeze-dried food and trail mix. He devoted a side pocket to his blood sugar monitor, test strips, pump supplies and insulin, plus an insulated lunch bag and some freezer packs to keep the insulin cold. He also grabbed a roll of cash he stashed in an old sneaker for emergencies along with his digital camera and laptop computer with portable charger. It would be the laptop's first camping trip.

He left the pack on the floor of the cottage's living area and pushed through the front door to where Poulos was finishing a call. Cam stuck out his hand. "I wanted to thank you for your help. And your concern. I appreciate it."

"Nothing to thank me for. I'll keep an eye on Brandon while you're gone." He handed Cam a slip of paper. "Here's my cell number. Use it if you need it." He pulled another cell phone from his trousers' pocket. "We have a few of these we use for domestic violence cases. You can use it in an emergency."

"You think my cell is being tapped?"

Poulos pursed his lips. "Probably. At least you should assume it is."

"Sounds like this McLovick is pretty sophisticated." As an underwater treasure hunter, he would have the latest technology.

"Him, or someone else." Poulos walked slowly to his squad car, opened the door and leaned his chest on the window. He wiped the sweat from his face. "You seem like you're on the right track with this Westford Knight stuff. Just check in with me once in a while — I'll keep looking from my end, try to piece some stuff together." He kicked at the ground. "And be careful."

The officer drove away. They both knew it would be best if he didn't ask where Cam was going.

+ + +

Hunched a bit under the weight of his pack, Cam walked stiff-kneed down the slope to the tired wooden dock secured to his beach area by a couple of fraying metal cables. After a final glance back to Pegasus' grave, he tossed the pack onto the deck of his aluminum fishing boat and yanked the ripcord on the small outboard engine. Anybody following him would expect him to travel by car.

He puttered along the shoreline toward the swamp area at the end of the lake. Once in the swamp he veered into a sheltered, shallow area, cut the engine and listened for any sound of a trailing boat. A few boaters in the main part of the lake enjoyed the fall warmth but nobody approached the swamp. After a half-minute he restarted the engine and navigated his way deeper into the marshy wetlands.

Recent rain had raised the water level and he was able to wind his way along with only an occasional thud of the boat bottom against a submerged rock or tree stump. He passed another fishing boat — two teenage boys — and waved politely. An old railroad track bordered the swamp and he angled toward a sandbar near the tracks. After gunning the throttle, he cut the engine and lifted the prop out of the water, allowing the boat to coast onto the bar. He hopped out the front, dragged the boat under an overhanging tree and covered it with some brush. He didn't plan on needing it again soon. But that didn't mean he didn't plan to return to some type of normal life again either.

He threw the pack over his shoulders, pulled himself up the embankment and began hiking along the rail line. After a few hundred yards he came to a main road, crossed it quickly and trudged into a wooded area on the far side. He ducked behind a cluster of trees, covered himself with leaves and twigs and pulled some binoculars from his pack. If he had been followed, his pursuers would need to show themselves to cross the road.

He waited almost an hour, scanning the road and the rail line. Nothing. Unless they were tracking him from above, he had lost any tails. At least for now.

He pulled himself to his feet, stretched his legs and moved away from the road in the fading daylight. He was now in the East Boston Camps area of town, a 300-acre preservation area the town recently purchased to prevent development. It would be fairly empty on a Sunday night in September, especially away from the main trails. Hopefully the weather forecasts were correct and it would remain dry and temperate. Interestingly, the Stonybrook River ran through the site, connecting the Westford Knight site to the Boat Stone discovery site. If Cam was going to figure this whole Prince Henry mystery out, maybe it wouldn't hurt to follow his trail a bit, to camp where he had camped, to see the land as he had seen it.

He followed a trail deeper into the woods until he reached Burge's pond. There were a few buildings on the north side of the pond that housed a summer camp for children; he rounded the pond to its more deserted southern shore, found a flat, dry area sheltered by a large oak tree and made camp. This would be home. For however long it took.

✝   ✝   ✝

Jacob Whitewolf Salazar lay on his stomach in a small wooded area and studied the rear of the box-shaped house through his night vision goggles. In some ways he welcomed the mosquitoes buzzing around him, the bites a small penance for the dog's suffering. The idiot he had been working with — some hothead from Mexico named Felipe — missed the animal's heart. Salazar should have taken the shot himself—as much as he abhorred the order, at least he would have done it right. Hours later, the sound of the dog's whimpering still echoed in his head. He located Mars, the warrior star, and offered a quick prayer for the animal's soul. Death was part of his job. In many ways, in fact, death was his entire job. But there did not have to be suffering. The Bobcat explosion was another example—Felipe should have killed the man, or not planted the bomb at all. Leaving a man crippled dishonored him. The spirits of the man's ancestors would haunt Felipe.

He rolled into a sitting position, thankful he was working alone now. Security work, they called it. Mercenary work was more like it. All he knew about his employers was that they were from Argentina, had close ties to the Catholic church and often needed people intimidated or killed. He took orders from a guy named Reichmann.

Almost three o'clock in the morning and no movement in the house. The treasure hunter had turned the lights off two hours ago. Salazar broke off a piece of Slim Jim and offered it to a cat—Minerva, according to her tag—that had befriended him. Wherever he found himself—Asia, Europe, Latin America—a cat soon appeared. As a youth he had saved a tabby from torture at the hands of a neighborhood bully and nursed it back to health. The cat died a few years later but its spirit remained, guiding and protecting him ever since. He had explained it all to his mother before she died, perhaps a decade ago:

"So now the cat's soul stays with me, like a guardian spirit."

"You shouldn't say things like that, Jacob." He still remembered how her brown eyes had grown wide in worry, how she clutched her rosary beads. "There is no such thing as animal spirits. Only Jesus can save you."

"You shouldn't have married daddy, mama."

"Your father was not the problem. It is your grandfather who put these crazy ideas in your head." He loved her too much to point out the Narragansett legends were no more crazy than the story of a virgin birth.

A leaf crunched beneath him. It was odd to be home in New England — normally he was deployed in Latin America or Europe. Not that it mattered; the assignments were all the same — interminable stretches of inaction interrupted by a few minutes of intense, often fatal, activity. Because he was well-trained, fit and meticulous, the risks were minimal. And the pay was decent, enough to send money to his mother-in-law every month to care for Rosalita. Her seventh birthday was in two weeks; hopefully he'd be off-duty and still in New England — she deserved at least one parent to celebrate with her. Christina's weekend in Miami with her girlfriends six years ago turned into a three week bender followed by 90 days in rehab. A week later she went out to grab some coffee and never came back. No goodbye, no postcard, nothing. Just a little girl missing her mommy. And a $30,000 bill for the rehab.

His parents were dead and he couldn't exactly drag Rosalita around the world with him on paramilitary assignments so she moved in with Christina's mother in Providence. He finished a room above her garage and stayed there when he was in town. It was unconventional but it actually worked out okay. The only problem was Gloria's insistence on immersing the girl in Catholicism. No doubt his own mother's spirit was pleased.

He ducked deeper into the woods and dialed the special phone line they set up at Gloria's house. "Good morning little flower." Rosalita would check the answering machine when she awoke. "I was wondering if the Tooth Fairy came last night? I hope so. Maybe you can use the money to buy Daddy a gift, huh? Maybe a new fishing pole?" He laughed, muffling his voice with his hand. "Speaking of gifts, I got a special one for your birthday." Over the past few months he had assembled and painted a true-to-scale, ginger-bread-style doll house from a kit; refinishing the room above Gloria's garage had required less work. "Only 15 days 'til you're seven! I bet you're growing bigger every day. And I bet you can give Daddy a big, strong hug! Well, okay, I need to go now. I love you very much. I'll try to call when you get home from school today. Oh, and don't forget to feed your kitty and brush her hair."

The Scotsman lived alone. Not even any pets, which said a lot about the man. Salazar rubbed Minerva's neck a final time, threw his satchel over his shoulder and, staying in the shadows, edged across the back yard toward the house. He decided against cutting the electricity — things like cordless phones started beeping when power failed, which might wake the man. McLovick was his name. Bigger than Salazar, a few inches taller than six feet but soft. No military training. But strange things sometimes happened when men collided in battle. A lucky blow, an unexpected weapon, a slip — any of these could negate his special forces training.

He removed a crowbar from his bag, wedged it between the basement door and the jamb and, with a quick twist, snapped the door open, splintering the wood. The smell of heating oil and dank air filled his nostrils as he padded into the cellar, reminding him of the triple-decker he grew up in New Bedford, an old fishing and whaling city south of Boston. His grandparents lived on the first floor, he lived on the second with his parents and two sisters and his uncle lived alone at the top. Most of the time his dad and uncle were at sea, fishing. His grandfather was a stonemason but he also loved to work with wood; Salazar spent a lot of his childhood with him making furniture in the basement workshop. One time they made a dugout canoe out of a single tree trunk, just as his Narragansett ancestors had done.

He ducked beneath the pipes and listened for the sound of movement upstairs. Hearing nothing, he unclipped the taser gun from his belt and continued to the staircase. He climbed the stairs four at a time, using his arms on the railing to support his weight so the stairs did not creak. A small tin of oil from his pack served to lubricate the door hinges at the top of the stairs and he slowly pushed the door open.

The last light McLovick had turned off was in the rear of the second floor. Salazar crept up another set of stairs, the goggles turning his world a monochromatic green. As he approached the top stair he heard loud snoring from the back bedroom. Good. The Scotsman was likely in the deeper stages of non-REM sleep. Even so, he palmed the revolver-shaped taser and readied it. He edged toward the bedroom, testing each step before putting weight on a potentially creaky floorboard, the snoring serving as a beacon in the night. Peering into the room, he saw the large man's form splayed diagonally atop the mattress in a white T-shirt and boxers, his open mouth and closed eyes facing the doorway.

Salazar took three quick strides and pounced. He pushed the taser deep into the treasure hunter's flabby midsection, squeezing the trigger as the man's eyes opened in surprise. McLovick screamed, his body jolting off the bed, and convulsed as his muscles spasmed. Salazar moved with the victim, riding him, thankful McLovick wasn't naked, holding the weapon against the thin fabric of his T-shirt for a five-count. At four, the screams quieted as he began to lose consciousness.

Ignoring the stench of urine and feces, he grabbed McLovick under his arms and, bracing himself against the wall, gently lowered him to the floor beside the bed. He bound his hands and feet together, then looped the rope around a heavy dresser. McLovick barely stirred. He found a bathroom down the hall and returned with a glass of water. He splashed the water in the treasure hunter's face, then slapped him lightly a couple of times on the cheeks until he awoke.

"W-what the fuck is going on?" McLovick sputtered, straining at the ropes. "Who the fuck are you?"

"Sorry for the intrusion," Salazar said quietly, his voice even and controlled. He didn't like people who cursed; Christina used to swear in front of the baby. "But you can't be surprised. You were warned plenty of times to leave Westford."

The treasure hunter began to stammer a response but Salazar held up his palm to stop him. "Now, tell me about this treasure." Reichmann's orders had been specific: Kill McLovick. Nothing about the treasure, no instruction to question the treasure hunter or look for maps or documents that might reveal what he was digging for. Salazar would comply with his orders. But he also needed to consider Rosalita's future.

He waved the taser in front of McLovick's face. From somewhere in the woods, the cat meowed up to him. "Imagine how this would feel on your balls, on your anus, maybe on your tongue." McLovick's eyes grew wide. From what he had observed, the treasure hunter was a nasty, selfish man. It was a good thing he was not a parent. Even so, no man deserved to suffer before dying. "Okay, I have some simple questions for you. Don't make this difficult for either one of us."

Ten minutes later, the questioning complete, Salazar gently placed a blindfold over McLovick's face. "We're done now. Thanks for cooperating. You got nothing more to fear from me."

He stood and took two loud steps toward the door. As McLovick relaxed at the sound of his assailant departing, Salazar silently spun back and, cobra-like, whipped his steel flashlight into the man's temple. The single, fierce blow crushed the thin bone and ruptured McLovick's middle meningeal artery. He died instantly, without fear or pain.

CHAPTER 4

[Monday]

Cam awoke the next morning before dawn, less than 48 hours since Brandon's leg had been turned into hamburger meat.

He pulled out the cell phone Poulos lent him and called Brandon's hospital room. Dependent on intermittent WIFI service, he would often be running blind. Maybe Uncle Peter could help him out a bit.

"Hello?"

"Brandon, that you?" He had expected Brandon's mom or dad to answer.

"Yup. Back from the dead." The voice was groggy, thick, flat.

Shifting the phone to his other ear, he began to pace. "Brandon, I'm really sorry." Brandon didn't respond so he plowed ahead. "I'll never forgive myself for doing this to you. You were doing me a favor and you end up ... well, almost dead."

A pause, then a mumbled response. "Not your fault."

Of course it was his fault. And of course Brandon would harbor some resentment toward him. But he wasn't the only casualty. "They killed Pegasus." He thumbed the dog's collar, still in the pocket of his jeans.

"Pegasus? Shit. I'm sorry, man." The words were still thick but at least there was some life behind them. "What the fuck is going on?"

Cam told him about his belief this was related to the Westford Knight and some kind of treasure. "I figured it'd be best to drop out of sight for a while. I'm on the run."

"Where are you?"

Were they monitoring Brandon's calls? Maybe he could buy himself some time. "Drove all night. Upstate New York." He took a deep breath, afraid of the answer to the obvious question. "What are the doctors saying?"

Brandon forced the words out. "Plan is wait for the wound to heal and swelling to go down. Should take about a month." He swallowed. "Then fit me for a prosthetic leg."

"You actually sound pretty good."

He snorted. "Drugs, cute nurses. Could be worse."

Cam smiled. "You know, I was calling to talk to your dad, hoping he could do some internet surfing for me. I need to learn more about these guys, about the Westford Knight, about this treasure. But do you feel up to it?" It might be good therapy for him to feel like he was doing something productive.

"No problem. Dad can bring me a laptop. I want to catch these motherfuckers."

"Okay, good. Do a Google search for the Westford Knight. Also try using words like 'treasure' and 'map' and 'secret' in the search string. If you come across any books that look interesting, get your parents to bring them in from the library. We're trying to figure out what kind of treasure might be buried here, and why. Your dad knows most of the story—he can help you out."

"Got it."

"Great, get better buddy. I'll call you later."

+   +   +

The conversation with Brandon vitalized Cam. His cousin, barely out of life-saving surgery and facing months of rehab and a lifetime of hardship, was willing to do whatever he could to catch the bastards. Cam owed it to him to do the same.

He scooped some pond water into a pot and checked his blood sugar level while he waited for the water to boil for a few minutes to kill the pond bacteria. He then added the water to a bag of dehydrated scrambled eggs with ham and hash browns. Normally he would have tried to watch his fat intake but today he needed the protein.

While he ate, he studied the map in the early morning light. McLovick lived a couple of miles away, in the Graniteville section of town. Maybe it was time to have another talk with the treasure hunter.

He washed up, stuffed a few essentials in a fanny pack and set off on a slow jog along a trail that followed the banks of the Stonybrook. After about a mile, the river, now no wider than a stream, took a hairpin turn to the south while a tributary continued northwesterly toward the Gendrons' property. He turned with the main river and jogged underneath some power lines, the sun just peeking above the tree line to his left. It wasn't the most direct route but it kept him on high ground and cut trails.

When he reached a residential neighborhood he crouched behind some thickets and pulled out his map before crossing a main street and jogging up a dead end lined with small Colonial homes. He surveyed the numbers — McLovick's house was the third on the left, yellow with black shutters. And a lawn that needed mowing. He retraced his steps and circled back to the Stonybrook River running behind the property.

He edged along the river bank until he was directly behind McLovick's house. Climbing through some brush, he found a comfortable position face down next to a tree and studied the house. No movement inside. A white sedan — the same one McLovick drove to court — was parked in the gravel driveway. What time did treasure hunters wake in the morning? Cam glanced at his watch.

Damn – his hand was shaking. The two-mile jog may have messed up his blood sugar. He rolled to his side and pulled his blood glucose meter from his pack. A small lancet from the device pricked his finger and he squeezed a drop of blood onto the shiny gold, inch-long plastic test strip he had inserted into the meter. Five seconds later the meter confirmed his blood sugar was low. He grabbed a granola bar from his pack and refocused on McLovick's house.

Just after 7:00 but still no movement. Using binoculars, he studied the rear of the house. The paint was peeling, the gutters were loose and the basement door jamb was splintered as if someone had forced it open. He pulled Poulos' cell phone out of his pack and dialed McLovick's number, the ringing audible through an open window on the second floor. On the fourth ring McLovick's Scottish accent curtly instructed callers to leave a message. He hung up and redialed using his own cell phone — maybe McLovick would see Cam's name on the caller I.D. and answer. Still nothing.

He was tempted to peer through a window, maybe check the water meter to see if McLovick might be running the shower. But voices from next door — a mother sending a child off to the bus stop — stopped him. He ducked lower, peered out. A dog, out on a walk with its owner, barked his way and pulled at its leash. The neighborhood was waking up. Time to get out of here before someone saw him and called the cops.

As if on cue, a police cruiser pulled up in front of McLovick's house. Good. Maybe here to question him about the Bobcat explosion. Or about Pegasus' death. A tall, thin officer strolled to the front door, where Cam lost sight of him. The policeman knocked loudly. "Mr. McLovick, hello? Anyone home? Hello?" The officer returned to his car and made a call on his radio before walking toward the rear of the property.

Cam would have liked to stick around and see if the police found McLovick — and if so, what they wanted with him — but he was not likely to be able to learn much from the woods anyway. And it wouldn't be good to be found hiding in them.

✛ ✛ ✛

Cam needed a set of wheels. If the whole Sinclair legend was true, there was more to it than just the Knight and Boat Stone in Westford. He had read briefly about other New England sites that indicated pre-Columbus visits by Europeans. If even half of what he read was true, Columbus had arrived fashionably late to the New World's Grand Opening party and it was time to do some serious rewriting of history books. In any event, he would need to visit these sites, learn all he could about them, figure out if any of them were pieces of the Prince Henry puzzle he was trying to fit together.

He phoned Brandon at the hospital with the cell phone Poulos gave him. Uncle Peter answered.

"Do you have your cell phone?" Cam asked.

"Yes."

"I'll call you right back on that." It was unlikely Cam's pursuers had tapped Peter's number. Yet.

"How's Brandon doing?"

Peter exhaled a long sigh. "All right, I suppose. Other than his leg, physically he should be fine. His doctor's a bit worried about his psychological state — it's almost like he's in a state of denial. He's acting like nothing happened. You know Brandon; he prides himself on not letting anything get to him. He's actually too upbeat."

"Well, denial is the first stage of grief. So it makes sense." Anger would be next.

"I suppose so. Anyway, I'm glad you called, Cameron. This Westford Knight stuff is bullshit. I'm disappointed in you, wasting your time with it."

Apparently Peter had already moved on to the anger stage. Cam took a deep breath. His uncle was one of those people who lived in a black and white world — there was no room for legends or myths or possibilities. Either something was true or it was false. Either someone was guilty or he was innocent. One of his favorite sayings was that a girl couldn't be a little bit pregnant. It was a quality that made him a tenacious, though sometimes not overly effective, advocate for his clients. "It may not be bullshit, Peter. In fact, it's why Brandon got his leg blown off."

"I've been reading up on it. Despite what that pretty librarian says, there's not a single reputable historian who buys the story."

"Well, look for a non-reputable historian then."

"Come on, Cameron, use your brain. We're supposed to believe that all the history books are wrong, that these Scottish explorers landed in Westford of all places? We're 30 miles from the goddamn coast. And some of these kooks think they buried the Holy Grail over here. You might as well go searching for aliens. You're wasting your time."

Cam counted to three. "Look, forget the whole Holy Grail thing. The point is that someone out there thinks the Prince Henry legend is real. So real that they put a bomb in a Bobcat and then tried to run me down and then killed my dog. So if we want to figure this all out, we have to educate ourselves."

"There's nothing to educate ourselves on! This is all a bunch of hogwash. You're on the wrong track, Cameron. And if you're not, you're dealing with people who are truly delusional. Either way, you're putting yourself in danger. It's time to stop this nonsense. Let the police do their jobs before you get hurt also."

He didn't have time for this. "I really need to talk to Brandon, Peter. Please."

"Sorry," Brandon said weakly after a few seconds. "Dad's a bit upset."

"No problem, I understand. You got a minute?"

"Yeah, doc just left."

"I need wheels. Something they won't trace to me. But be careful, this line might be tapped."

"I hear you." He paused. "I introduced you to a guy a few weeks ago, over at the 99 Restaurant. An Orioles fan."

"Right." The guy played on Brandon's softball team and owned a small used car lot.

"He'll help you out. Tell him I sent you. And he'll keep his mouth shut."

"Thanks. Get some rest, Cuz."

He hiked back through the woods. By mid-morning he was behind the wheel of a dark blue, 12-year-old Subaru wagon with 155,000 miles on it. But Brandon's buddy swore by the engine. One exit south on Route 3 he found the Wal-Mart in Chelmsford. He purchased a couple of boxes of power bars, three cases of bottled water, another dozen freeze-dried meals and two TracFones — disposable, prepaid cell phones that didn't require any credit information and therefore couldn't be traced. He put 400 minutes on each phone, paid cash for everything and turned his face away from the security camera as he left the store.

As he loaded the Subaru, he spotted a Starbucks across the parking lot — most Starbucks offered WiFi service. Before driving he needed to know where he was going. He grabbed his laptop and a legal pad, paid for the service and found an empty table toward the back of the restaurant. After testing his blood sugar and delivering his insulin, he treated himself to a cup of hot chocolate and a corn muffin while his laptop booted. He typed 'Westford Knight' and 'Sinclair' into a Google search string.

Most of the sites related the same general story: In 1398, Prince Henry Sinclair, the Baron of Roslyn, sailed westward from the Orkney Islands north of Scotland. The fleet of a dozen boats carrying a few hundred men 'island-hopped' across the Atlantic from the Faeroe Islands to Iceland to Greenland to Newfoundland (where they were driven off by hostile natives) and eventually to Guysborough Harbor in Nova Scotia.

Details of the journey were recounted in the Zeno Narrative, a mid-16th century Venetian family nautical history outlining a journey undertaken in the late 14th century by a Zeno ancestor serving as navigator on a fleet led by a Scottish prince traveling to lands west of Greenland. The Narrative identified the Scottish prince as Zichmi, a deviation from the name Sinclair that later scholars ascribed to a simple penmanship error. The Narrative also identified unique topographical landmarks of Nova Scotia, most specifically an open tar pit about 50 miles from Guysborough Harbor.

As Cam surfed, jumping from site to site, he uncovered other pieces of evidence substantiating the Zeno Narrative account. One site recounted fishermen pulling a 14th-century Venetian cannon from Nova Scotia's Louisburg harbor and concluded it was likely from one of Admiral Zeno's Venetian ships. Another discussed a farmer in Nova Scotia stumbling upon the ruins of a medieval fortress in his fields. A third showed photos from Roslyn Chapel, constructed decades before Columbus sailed, featuring carvings of American maize and aloe—crops which were unknown to Europeans before Columbus' voyage. A Native American history site recounted the legend of Glooscap, a fire-haired deity arriving from the east on a floating, one-winged bird (that is, a single-sailed vessel) who taught the natives how to fish with nets. There was too much here to be dismissed as mere coincidence. He kept reading.

After arriving in Nova Scotia, the legend continued, Prince Henry and his group befriended the natives and spent the winter. Cam, himself a hockey player, especially appreciated the report from British soldiers at the time of the founding of Halifax, Nova Scotia in 1749 to the effect that the Mi'kmaq natives played shinny, an early form of ice hockey, and that their oral history said that it was taught to their ancestors by blond-haired visitors from the east.

Most of the expedition returned to Scotland in the spring while Prince Henry remained with a few boats and a score of men to continue their explorations. Guided by natives, he traveled south along the New England coastline, eventually moving inland via the Merrimack River to the highest point in eastern Massachusetts, an Indian gathering spot that is now known as Prospect Hill in Westford. While on Prospect Hill his loyal lieutenant and friend, Sir James Gunn, died and Prince Henry ordered his armorist to inscribe an appropriate funereal effigy for the fallen knight on an outcropping of bedrock.

Cam continued surfing, following the links, adding new search words and jotting down other New England sites related to Prince Henry's expedition. He uncovered other significant evidence supporting some type of pre-Columbus, post-Viking European contact, despite Rhonda Blank's assertions to the contrary: stones with runic inscriptions (runes being a medieval Scandinavian alphabet still in use in Iceland) found in northern Maine, Cape Cod and Narragansett Bay, Rhode Island; a stone tower in Newport, Rhode Island; a stone dam and medieval gargoyle on a lake on the Vermont-Quebec border; extensive Native American oral history; linguistic similarities between the Algonquin and Scottish languages; and even DNA evidence hinting at a genetic link between Native Americans and Northern Europeans.

Cam pointed the Subaru south toward the Newport Tower, it being the most easily-accessible of the sites as well as the most prominent. He cut through Boston rather than skirting the city on the outer highways; he was pretty sure he wasn't being followed but he was also pretty sure he was playing out of his league right now. A pro football coach had once explained what it was like to be a rookie quarterback in the NFL — the player didn't know enough to know what he didn't know. Cam was the rookie quarterback. Would he even know if he was being followed?

He made good time in the midday traffic and crossed the Zakim Bridge into Boston, exiting the Central Artery and winding his way toward his old office building in the Financial District. Periodically he checked his rearview mirror but he really didn't expect to be able to pick out a tail. But he also didn't expect a tail to have a parking pass to the Center Plaza parking garage — he had kept his after being fired and the firm forgot to disable it. After making sure nobody slid through the gate with him, he accelerated down the ramp and sped through the garage toward a second egress. He laid on the horn as he drove, warning cars and pedestrians away, before racing back up a ramp to an exit gate. He reinserted his card, the gate rose in front of him and he wheeled out onto a side street. Any tail would have had to drive slowly through the garage to avoid giving themselves away and then lose more time by stopping and paying the cashier. He didn't waste any time pushing his advantage: He cut left out of the parking lot and climbed Beacon Hill, darting through the maze of one-way streets and narrow alleys that comprised the city's oldest neighborhood, thankful for the years he spent living in the city. Seven or eight turns later, he cut downhill on Beacon Street, took a left on Arlington Street just past the Cheers bar and raced through a yellow light in front of the old Armory building. A block later he turned onto the Mass Pike on-ramp, confident that he had not been followed.

He made good time to Newport, still ahead of the afternoon rush hour. As he distanced himself from Westford, the tension seeped out of his neck and shoulders. It had been, what, two days since Brandon turned the key to the Bobcat and changed their lives? He shook his head — the Cam who woke up Saturday morning would barely recognize the Cam on his way to Newport on Monday afternoon. It was like one of those alternate-universe science fiction shows. The characters were the same but their lives were totally different. In any event, the Monday Cam was happy to be out of peril-filled Westford, a place the Saturday Cam had always considered sleepy and sheltered.

Just before five o'clock, he pulled into the parking lot of the Newport visitor's center. "I'm looking for the Newport Tower."

"Hmm, never heard of that one," a college-age clerk at the information kiosk answered politely.

"How about an old stone windmill?" Some people believed that's what it was.

The worker shrugged again. "Hold on, let me ask someone else." He called an older woman over. Cam repeated the inquiry. Another shrug.

How could this be? The stuff he read made it sound like the Newport Tower was the biggest historical mystery on the East Coast. How could the tourist bureau not know anything about it?

"Is it part of the mansions?" the woman asked. Newport was famous for its industrial-era summer "cottages" — mammoth, opulent residences built as summer playgrounds for the titans of American industry and finance.

"No, it's a round stone tower, probably in the oldest part of town."

The woman pulled out a tourist map, a hand-drawn schematic displaying restaurants, hotels and tourist attractions. She drew a circle around a ten-block area east of Newport Harbor. "That's the oldest part of town."

"What's that?" He pointed to a round gray thimble-like object marked 'Old Stone Mill.'

"Gee, I don't know." She drew a line on the map. "But it's easy to find — just go up Touro Street, then bear right onto Bellevue."

He found Touro Street and slowed as he passed the Touro Synagogue, the oldest synagogue in the country. Roger Williams, an early proponent of religious freedom, founded Rhode Island; the plaque out front related how Jewish settlers established a congregation soon after in 1658. A block further on, still climbing a hill, he stopped at a traffic light in front of the curiously-named Viking Hotel. Across the street a granite arch marked the entrance to the wrought iron-enclosed Touro Cemetery. According to the map the Newport Tower, assuming that's what was on the map, was located in Touro Park. *Touro Street, Touro Synagogue, Touro Cemetery, Touro Park.* More than a coincidence, probably, but what was the connection? His problem was he didn't know enough about any of this to be able to make the proper inquiries, to understand a clue even when he stumbled upon one.

The light turned and he continued another couple of blocks to a park on his right. He turned onto Mill Street and there it was: a round stone tower, maybe 30 feet high, rising majestically off the lawn on eight cylindrical pillars, each pillar joined to its neighbor by a stone arch. He shook his head: Who had taken the time to piece together the thousands of stones, and why? A single square window, twenty feet in the air, winked at him as the setting sun played off a piece of quartz; the Tower, like an aging but still-skilled seductress, was attempting to reel in a fresh admirer.

THE NEWPORT TOWER

Cam had visited every Colonial historic site on the East Coast — most notably Colonial Williamsburg and Plimouth Plantation — and not a single other structure resembled the tower in front of him. Jamestown boasted the remains of a 1690 church tower but it was built of brick, not stone, and it was square. And Plimouth Plantation depicted a Plymouth colony constructed totally of wooden structures. A row of 18th-century stone houses existed on Huguenot Street in the Hudson Valley town of New Paltz, New York but they were built by French settlers, not English. And even these settlers built their original houses in the late 1600s with wood.

He shook his head at the memory of his encounter in the tourist center. How could anyone, never mind someone working in a tourist center, not know about this tower? It was so clearly unique among the Colonial architecture, so flagrantly inconsistent with the clapboard and brick construction of every other nearby structure, so obviously out of place on this side of the Atlantic. It reminded him of a wedding he once attended where a guest entered the church wearing a kilt. Nobody doubted that the man was Scottish even though the wedding was in New York. Similarly, how could anyone think this tower was anything but European?

He approached a sign at the edge of the park. "The Old Stone Mill's past is clouded by historical uncertainty," the sign read. "No direct proof exists confirming the date of its construction but there is considerable evidence suggesting it was built sometime between 1653 and 1677 by Benedict Arnold, the first Colonial governor of Rhode Island and the great-grandfather of the famous Revolutionary War traitor."

American history was Cam's area of expertise. This made no sense. Life for Colonists in the late 1600s in Rhode Island was marked by frequent and sometimes fierce battles with the Indians. In fact, only a few hundred households existed in all of Rhode Island at that time. It wasn't until the end of King Phillip's War in 1676 that New England Colonists began to feel safe enough to settle outside the main cities. Why go to the considerable effort of building a stone structure that was of no defensive use? And if the structure was indeed a mill, why invite collapse by building it on stone pillars rather than a solid foundation? Most fundamentally, who could have afforded to employ dozens of laborers at a time when the settlers were barely able to eke out a sustenance lifestyle? American settlers built in stone only once hostilities with the natives had ended and they had stabilized their existence. He had no idea who built the Tower. But he was pretty sure it wasn't early Rhode Island Colonists.

He glanced around the park — an older couple inspecting the Tower, some college kids sharing a picnic lunch on a bench, a woman walking her dog. He stared at the dog for a few seconds and sighed sadly before refocusing on his park companions. All typical park activities. But all also good covers for a trained operative.

He followed a paved path toward the Tower and snapped a couple of pictures. A few trees and statues dotted the park but the Tower was clearly the focal point. There was also something familiar about the Tower and yet not familiar. He relaxed his eyes, stared past the Tower but not at it. The trick worked — the Tower looked like a chess rook, cut off at its base and turned upside down. In other words, like a medieval castle on its head. He thought about a recent Harry Potter book, where the characters joined the game and became live chess pieces in order to defeat an evil enemy. He had a knight in Westford and now a rook in Newport. He, himself, felt like a pawn, a foot soldier in some larger game going on around him.

He studied the Tower from a different angle. There was something else familiar, in addition to the rook shape, something more recent....

He jumped and turned, reflexively, even before his brain registered the tap on his shoulder. "What?" he exclaimed. He backed away, ready to defend himself, surprised to see a woman's face a couple of feet from his. Behind the sunglasses, under the Red Sox cap pulled low, there was, like the Tower, something familiar about the face.

She took a single step toward him. "It's okay. It's just me." She raised her hand slowly, pulled the cap from her head. A cascade of flaxen hair fell past her shoulders.

"A-Amanda." Her china doll complexion of yesterday was gone, replaced by a pinkish, bubbling rash on her cheeks and chin.

"I know, I look hideous," she sighed. "I'm allergic to the sun, like a werewolf or something—soon I'll be fancying Piña Coladas at Trader Vic's."

He smiled—he too was a Warren Zevon fan. And for some reason he didn't find the rash particularly unattractive. "It's just a rash, no big deal. But what are you doing here? How did you find me?"

She removed her sunglasses, her green eyes probing his. "You don't know, do you?"

"Know what?"

She waited half a beat. "Alistair McLovick is dead."

"What?" He rested his hand on the wrought iron fence surrounding the Tower. "I was just over at his house this morning—"

"I know," she interrupted, studying him. "And so do the coppers. At first they thought it might be a random home invasion. But then they found a blood glucose test strip in the woods behind his house. And they know you're diabetic."

He closed his eyes. His blood on the test strip tied him directly to the crime scene. "They think I did it."

She nodded. "They're trying to locate you."

He replayed the morning in his mind. "They probably also found my cell number on his caller ID. Nobody answered so I figured he was out."

"He was out all right. Somebody tied him up and clubbed him over the head. A mate found him—he was bothered when McLovick missed a meeting and didn't answer his telephone."

"How do you know all this?"

She shrugged. "It's what we do."

"So who would want to kill McLovick?" He offered a wan smile. "Beside me, I mean."

"Likely the same people who placed the bomb in the Bobcat, and who tried to turn you into a bumper ornament for their car, and who killed your dog."

This made no sense. He had been sure that McLovick was the bad guy here. Now he was dead, killed by a different bad guy. Or bad guys.

She continued. "Whoever popped McLovick's clogs probably didn't want him digging any more than they wanted you digging." She paused. "And there's a secondary benefit to killing McLovick—you getting arrested. You can't dig if you're in the clink."

"Benefit to who?"

She took his elbow. "Look, we can discuss all this later. For now, I think we should move on. It's not safe."

"Why? I'm pretty sure nobody followed me." Then the obvious hit him. "But how did you find me?" He scanned the park.

"I knew if you were intent on solving this mystery, sooner or later you'd come have a look at the Tower. Probably sooner—this is the granddad of all the New England sites. Practically everyone who visits the Knight either just came from, or is journeying to, the Tower. Of course, if you killed McLovick there would be no reason for you to bother. Really, why try to solve the mystery when you've already avenged the crime?"

"Good point. You can be my defense lawyer." He turned toward the Tower. "Just give me a couple minutes to check it out."

"Okay, but quickly." She gestured. "There's a fireplace high on that wall, with two flues that vent to the outside. Opposite the fireplace is a window—a boat out in Narragansett Bay could see the fire through the window. Some folks believe the Tower was a navigational beacon."

"What are those notches in the stone above each of the pillars inside?"

"Joists probably rested in them to support a second floor." She pulled him away from the Tower. "Please, Cameron, we can chat later. It may be that they didn't track you, but they tracked me."

"What do you mean?"

"They know I met with you yesterday; it is possible I led them to you. I'm sorry." She glanced at a black BMW idling along the edge of the park. The driver, alone in the car, shielded his face from them as he spoke into a cell phone. "I don't fancy the looks of that car over there."

He tensed as he analyzed the situation. "If they followed you, then they haven't seen my car yet. Let's see if we can lose them on foot, then get my car later. I'd rather not be without wheels." He glanced at her feet; she was wearing tennis sneakers. "Feeling fast?"

She slipped her baseball cap back on. "I can bloody well outrun you."

He laughed. "It's not me you have to worry about. It's our friend in the BMW."

"Actually, you are incorrect. It's like the bear in the woods. I don't have to outrun the bear, I just have to outrun you. Once he catches you, he won't give a damn about me."

"I see. All for one and one for all, huh?"

"Absolutely not. The Musketeers were French. We Brits are much more practical." They continued slowly, around the Tower but away from the BMW. "You lead the way."

"Okay. Hopefully he's alone." He tightened his fanny pack as she draped her oversized leather carrying bag over her shoulder and clenched it to her side. "I think we're on the highest hill in town." He remembered the map. "There's a bunch of one-way streets and small alleys between here and the harbor — let's head downhill and see if we can lose him."

They began to walk down the slope. Within seconds, the BMW's ignition roared to life.

They ran, Amanda matching his pace, their sneakers slapping rhythmically against the pavement. At the first intersecting street they cut right; the BMW followed, squealing around the corner, closing on them. He had a fresh memory of his encounter with the Cadillac — no doubt the driver would run them down if given the chance. He pulled Amanda to the left, down a long, narrow driveway separating two boxy, Colonial-style homes.

A chest-high stone wall, covered in ivy, blocked their path at the end of the drive. "Be ready to climb," he yelled. He raced ahead a few strides, preparing to stop short of the fence to aid Amanda over the top. As he slowed, Amanda flew by, leapt into the air, pushed off the top of the wall with her hands like a gymnast on a vaulting horse and propelled herself over the top.

She landed and found her balance, turning back to smile at him. "Please hurry, won't you? I believe the bear is in pursuit."

He spun his head — a man in black pants and a gray sweatshirt jumped from the car and sprinted toward them. He seemed calm, like this was a normal part of his day and he would chase them all night if need be. Cam pushed himself up, slung his legs over the wall and they raced off again, her stride and breathing mirroring his. They scampered through the yard, up another driveway which exited on the parallel street.

"Follow me." He pulled her left; a few houses later they turned left again, now heading back up the hill toward the park. At the end of a short block they turned left a third time, returning to the street where the foot chase began. The BMW, its headlights on, loomed ahead. He looked back; their pursuer had gained on them but he would not catch them before they reached the car.

Cam didn't envy him explaining to his superiors that he had left the keys in the car.

"Jump in the passenger side." She nodded and he sprinted ahead, skidding to a stop and sliding behind the wheel of the idling auto. As she hopped in, he reversed back a few feet and spun the wheel, gunning the engine and racing away just as their pursuer closed to within a few yards. "Duck," he gasped. "This guy might be so desperate he takes a shot at us."

"Or so embarrassed," she laughed.

"Do you think he's alone?" He exhaled as they turned onto an intersecting street.

With her face flush from exertion, her rash was barely noticeable. "Yes. Likely they wouldn't have wasted more than one bloke trailing me. But he's probably calling for aid now. And this car may have a tracking device. We should abandon it quick as we can."

"Any back-up would be coming from Westford, right?"

She shrugged. "Or perhaps Boston. The license plates are Massachusetts."

"Either way, we have at least an hour. I have an idea."

As he drove, she searched the glove compartment. She pulled out a pack of mint gum and a couple of maps. "No registration. And nothing personal."

He drove to a park near where he had seen a bunch of teenagers playing roller hockey on a tennis court earlier in the day. He skidded to a stop just short of the fence. "Hey, any of you guys know how to drive?"

"Yeah," the tallest one responded.

"Okay, I have a deal for you. This is my buddy's car and we're playing a joke on him. I'll give you a hundred bucks if you drive this car over to the police station and just leave it there. But you gotta go right now."

"A hundred bucks?"

"There's another hundred in it for your buddy to go with you." Cam pulled two $100 bills from his wallet, waved them in the air. "Make sure you leave the car at the police station." He flipped the boy the keys, dropping the bills on the hood. "And don't worry if you ding it up a bit. It's a company car."

✛   ✛   ✛

As the BMW tore away, Salazar's mind was already at work on an explanation that might portray the incident in a positive light: He had followed the blond woman. She led him to Thorne. Salazar gave chase. They evaded him. When he returned, the police, called to the scene by bystanders, had surrounded the BMW. He abandoned the vehicle rather than risk being apprehended.

A believable story. But hardly a shining moment in his career. Probably not enough to get him fired, especially because he had succeeded in finding Thorne. But enough to remind him of the tenuousness of his position. One unfortunate screw-up and he would be done, tossed aside by his employers in favor of a younger, stronger man. He needed to ensure his landing would be cushioned, preferably by a small pile of gold and jewels.

Fearing the taser gun, McLovick had directed him to a file containing maps and drawings, insisting he did not know where the treasure was or even what it might be, the fear in his eyes confirmation that he was not holding anything back. But he did confirm the obvious: There was a treasure, buried somewhere, and the property in Westford was somehow related. Salazar had photographed the contents of the file with a digital camera and replaced the file; removing the papers would have been inconsistent with a random home invasion and robbery gone bad.

Using his cell, he phoned in his report to Reichmann. As he waited for his new orders, he scrolled through the photos on his digital camera: maps and drawings of something called the Oak Island Money Pit in Nova Scotia; a map of Westford showing the

Gendrons' property and the Westford Knight, along with the river system connecting the two sites, highlighted in yellow; and a map of New England and southern Canada with a hatched line connecting a series of inland and coastline sites, presumably marking someone's journey. Important information, but only to someone who had an ability to decipher it. He still had no idea where the treasure was located, or even what it was. And the police were keeping a close watch on the old couple's property so it wasn't as if he could just sneak over there one day with a shovel.

His eyes followed the path of the BMW's escape. Perhaps it wasn't such a bad thing that Thorne and the girl possessed the wits and the cleverness to evade him. Somebody needed to lead him to the treasure.

CHAPTER 5

Cam and Amanda separated after ditching the BMW. He hiked back to the Touro Park area while Amanda ducked into the tourist shops. They arranged to meet in just over an hour, at 7:00.

He hailed a cab at the nearby Viking Hotel and asked the cabbie to circle the park so he could view the Tower. He slumped in the seat and peered out the window searching for any signs of surveillance. Nothing. As he glanced back at the Tower, it hit him: The Tower resembled the Gendrons' clay lantern. He had missed the connection the first time because he was thinking about Harry Potter and the real-life chess game. Was the lantern a model, or a replica, of the Tower? Perhaps a clue of some kind? Or maybe it was just a lantern.

He paid the cabbie and found the Subaru. After circling the park one last time, he followed Bellevue Avenue south toward the mansions. He turned into a couple of mansion parking lots and reversed his direction, and even backed down a one way street. Nothing suspicious.

Still ten minutes before he was supposed to pick up Amanda. He dialed Brandon's hospital room with his TracFone.

"Hey, how you feeling?"

Brandon ignored the question. "Shit, Cam." He seemed more alert, more energized. "The cops are looking all over for you."

"McLovick?"

"Yeah. If he's dead it means he probably didn't plant that bomb, right? Somebody else was trying to stop him and us from digging."

"Right. I think someone's trying to hide something. Or keep something hidden. And they got pissed when we started digging around."

"Well, I Googled the stuff you asked about and found a couple of books that talk about the Westford Knight and treasures and stuff. One of them even said this Prince Henry guy may have buried Jesus' bones over here."

"I haven't heard that one yet."

"Most of what I read talks about a place up in Nova Scotia called the Money Pit, on Oak Island. That's where McLovick was digging before he came down here. Every time someone tries to get to the bottom of the pit it fills with water, like it was booby-trapped or something. There's some elaborate tunnel system going all the way to the ocean. A bunch of people have died trying to get to it. FDR even tried digging for it."

"The President?"

"Yup."

"So is this pit related to Prince Henry?"

"Could be. One possibility is he brought the treasure with him in 1398—remember, he made landfall in Nova Scotia. But here's an interesting little fact: When his grandson built Roslyn Chapel in the mid-1400s, he brought dozens of stonemasons and other laborers to Roslyn for the job. And check this out—work didn't begin on the chapel for five years. Why pay all these guys to sit around and do nothing?"

"That's how you run a job site, right?"

"Yeah. Guys sit around for five minutes and I'm ready to explode. Five years? Just not gonna happen, even back then. The theory is they weren't sitting around. They were in Nova Scotia building the Money Pit."

"So then why'd McLovick come down here if the treasure is on Oak Island?"

"Don't know. Maybe he thinks there's something here that will help him figure out the Pit. Or maybe they split the treasure up and some of it is in Westford. My mom is bringing me more books tonight. I'll dive in."

"You have energy for this?"

"Yeah, enough. I read, then I nap, then I read some more. Doc says it's fine. Probably good for me to keep my mind off ... things." He paused. "Hey, how can I reach you?"

Cam explained the TracFone. "I don't want to give you the whole number on this line, in case it's tapped." He gave the first six numbers. "The last four digits are O'Reilly, and Wendy's age." O'Reilly referred to Terry O'Reilly, Brandon's favorite hockey player as a kid, number 24. And Wendy was Brandon's ex-girlfriend, who recently lamented her 30th birthday. So 2430 were the last four digits.

"Got it. A TracFone? Does that mean they can track you on it?"

"I think just the opposite. That's why the terrorists and drug dealers use them."

"Sounds like you're in good company there, Cam. I'm sure your parents are very proud of you."

It was good to hear him joking a bit. "You should get one too in case they're tapping your phone. Tell your dad to grab one."

A few minutes later, as arranged, he picked Amanda up in front of the Brick Alley restaurant just as the sunlight was fading. She skipped across the cobblestoned Thames Street to the car, slid into the front seat and offered him a small package wrapped in gift paper. "I happened upon a gift for you," she said, smiling.

He had taken a course in body language while in law school; it had been invaluable both in the courtroom and at the poker table. Scientists said smiles that wrinkled the skin next to your eyes couldn't be faked. He took some extra time with the paper as he pondered both the gesture and her smiling eyes. His attraction to Amanda, the pain from his loss of Pegasus, his rage at the assault on Brandon, the constant fear that someone was trying to kill him — everything festered inside him. It was as if he was full and the next drop of emotion would cause him to overflow, to bawl like a baby in front of Amanda.

Unable to prolong the unwrapping any longer, he pulled a navy blue t-shirt out of a gift box. He held it up and read the inscription on the front: 'I Outrun Cars and Bears.' Laughing, he looked at Amanda. "That's a hell of a thing to be known for."

Her eyes twinkled. "Well, it seems you have an affinity for it. But I must say, you Americans take sport in some odd activities."

The water-skiing with Brendan was, what, four days ago? It felt like four months.

"Well then, what next?" she asked.

"Well, first of all, let's get you to a bus station or something so you can get home."

She scowled. "Home? Not bloody likely."

"Look, this is my ... problem. There's no reason to get both of us killed."

"Bollocks to that. I've spent a year on this job. All I do is answer posts and walk tourists up and down the hill. Now that something exciting is happening, I fancy to be part of it. Besides, what makes you think they're just going to leave me be?" He didn't have a good answer. "I reckon I'm better off here with you, trying to figure this all out."

Cam thought about Brandon and Pegasus and McLovick, did some reckoning — which was a term apparently common in England as well as the southern U.S. — of his own. "You may be right. They probably would come after you. Maybe you should go back to London."

"What, these folks don't know about planes?"

"Good point." He could use her help. And if she was working against him, she would have already turned on him when the thug from the BMW was chasing them. "All right, I suppose I'm stuck with you."

"Indeed you are." She winked, a lightning-quick gesture that had him wondering if he'd imagined it.

Face flushing, he cleared his throat. "All right. First thing, we need to get out of Newport." He pulled out into traffic. "I think we lost our tail in the BMW, for now. But I don't want to push our luck. Any idea who these guys are?"

She stared out the window. "I've been having a go with that. I agree that it must be somehow related to the treasure. But that's as far as I've managed." She shrugged. "I'm sorry but the Consortium is very clandestine, very segmented. It's really a cabal — a secretive, exclusive, mysterious club — more than anything else. Folks assume that I know all there is about the Knight, and in some ways I do. But I'm really just a glorified intern. There's a whole separate layer to this, a world of secrets and legends and mysteries that I'm not privy to. I know many *facts* about the Knight — and about other sites like the Newport Tower — but I don't necessarily know what these facts *mean*."

Terrorist cells worked the same way — the field operatives knew very little about the overall operation, often not even knowing the ultimate target or means of attack. Only the inner core of senior commanders understood how the disparate pieces fit together. "Well, what do you know about this cabal you work for, other than their interest in Prince Henry?"

"Near as I can tell, it's comprised of two groups — families who descend from Prince Henry or other members of his expedition, and families who are part of the *Rex Deus* line."

"I'm sorry, *Rex Deus?* Is that like a secret cabal within the cabal?" He resisted making the *Animal House* double-secret probation comparison — the Brits had Shakespeare, the Americans John Belushi.

Actually, Amanda seemed like the type who might appreciate both.

She explained the blood line tracing back to the high priests of Jerusalem. "They believe they are the guardians of the true teachings of Jesus. Many of the Consortium families are in both categories — they descend from Sinclair and they are also *Rex Deus*. One of the reasons I was recruited for this job is because I descend from a Templar family."

"Wait, I thought the Templars were celibate."

"Apparently some of them joined the order later in life."

"Apparently. Back to this Consortium — so what's their agenda?"

"It almost feels funny saying it. Especially in the States, where you folks scoff at the whole concept of royal blood. But I reckon they want to prove their worthiness through their ancestry. They want to show Prince Henry, not Columbus, discovered America. Somehow it validates them, enhances their family name."

"What about the Vikings? They were here before Columbus or Prince Henry."

"Fair point. But the Columbus supporters say the Vikings weren't exploring, they were merely out fishing and lost their way. So they don't really matter. Not that it's much of a distinction if you ask me. Again, this is more important in Europe than it is here."

He shook his head. "Does anyone really care what your ancestors did 600 years ago?"

"In Europe, yes."

"Then could it be that the Consortium is trying to find this treasure, whatever it is? I mean, isn't that the type of things cabals do?"

Amanda stared out the window again for a few seconds. "I suppose it's possible. For one thing, it would definitely prove Sinclair was here. And it would explain many things about the Consortium, about their secrecy and the resources they commit to the Knight.

But I wouldn't jump to any conclusions — I've never heard anyone from the Consortium even mention the word treasure."

"Well, if the Consortium is after the treasure, could they also be behind all the violence?"

"Again, it's possible." She turned in her seat, studied his face as if weighing a difficult decision. "Do you recall when you queried why Prince Henry came to America and I told you it was for economic reasons like timber and fishing?"

"Yeah, and I thought you were hiding something from me."

"I know you did." She reached over and touched his arm. He noticed the car drifting right, realized he had leaned slightly toward her to meet her hand. He quickly adjusted as she continued speaking. "And you were spot on. I'm sorry."

"Look, Amanda, you barely knew me then. Heck, you still barely know me now."

"I know. But for some reason I trust you. I trusted you then, also, but I didn't have the courage to violate the protocols."

"Protocols?"

"A set of rules that have been passed down for centuries. One of the primary protocols is that the secrets of Prince Henry and his expedition are never to be revealed, only discovered. As I said, the Consortium is comprised of families who either descend from Sinclair or other Templars, or are otherwise *Rex Deus*. But its inner circle is a self-selecting group comprised of the most knowledgeable members — the cream rises to the top, as it were."

"What secrets?"

"I don't know. Apparently I'm just the milk," she laughed.

"Wait. I'm confused. If you don't know the secrets, what was it you were hiding from me?"

"Sorry, I'm nattering but not being clear. In your case, you asked a question and I gave the cursory response. But the information I withheld from you was only the first or second step of what would be a long journey."

"So are you willing to give me this information now?"

"And violate the protocols?"

He squeezed the wheel. "Yeah."

"Well, of course." She grinned. "I'm here, am I not? I was just waiting for you to ask."

"I can tell this is going to be a long car ride," he said, shaking his head. "But won't you get in trouble?"

"Doing research is part of my job. And if they sack me for trying to save your life, well, then it was probably time for me to move on anyway."

"Speaking of moving on, any ideas where I should be headed?"

"As a matter of fact, yes. Go north, toward the Maine coast. There's something I want to show you."

"Okay."

"But back to the Sinclair expedition. The information I withheld from you is this: One of the main reasons he journeyed to America was to map out the New World for future settlement. They were coming to stay, not merely trade and fish and explore, which is why they brought artisans and clergymen along with soldiers." The revelation was really not that surprising. "And if they planned to stay, they needed accurate maps."

He remembered something she had pointed out about the Newport Tower. "You said the Tower functioned as some kind of lighthouse or beacon."

"Exactly. That was part of its use. But one thing you'll begin to notice, a theme that will continue to repeat itself, is that these structures and artifacts have multiple uses. Without modern tools, it was extremely difficult to carve an effigy in a rock or, of course, build a stone tower. What I mean is the Westford Knight effigy was not just an effigy but also a directional marker — the Knight's sword points due north. And the Tower was not just a beacon but also many other things as well."

"Such as?" He felt like a kindergarten kid trying to learn algebra. Even worse, Amanda knew algebra but had no knowledge of calculus. In order to figure all this out, they were going to need to learn calculus on their own. And on the run.

"For one thing, the eight pillars line up on the eight compass points. And the windows are placed in the Tower to not only aid in navigation but also perfectly sight to events such as the winter and summer solstices, as well as other astronomical occurrences which I do not understand well enough to explain to you. Recall that there were no calendars during medieval times. Yet one needed to ascertain exact dates for religious observances and also for day-to-day life."

"So you're not buying the whole Colonial windmill theory?"

"Not a bit of it. An archeologist just completed a dig of the Tower. She couldn't say for certain who built the Tower but she was clear on one thing: It was not your Colonial settlers. If you want to view a Colonial windmill, there's one straight across the bay in Jamestown. It's wooden, its shape is tapered and there are no pillars blocking the windmill's blades. And it's built on a firm base." She paused. "The Tower may have been built by someone other than Prince Henry. Perhaps the Vikings, perhaps the Portuguese. But it wasn't built by Benedict Arnold." She explained that the unit of measurement used to build the Tower was the Scottish ell, not the English foot which was used on every other Colonial structure. "The Narragansett Indians have a legend that the Tower was built by 'fire-haired men with green eyes who sailed up river in a ship like a gull with a broken wing.'"

Cam smiled. "Gull with a broken wing. I like that — it's exactly the way someone would describe a sailboat if they had never seen one. So you think Sinclair built the Tower?"

"No. I happen to believe it was built as a memorial to him. He was a phenomenally important chap during his time — a baron of

Scotland and a prince of Norway—yet there is no tombstone or marker or even record of his death in Europe."

"Nothing?"

"No. In fact, his lands and title never passed to his son; after a number of decades they eventually passed directly to his grandson. It's as if his family didn't know if he was still alive or not. That makes me surmise he died in America. The Tower would be an appropriate monument to a man of his importance."

"Why would his family not have known of his death? I mean, once he found his way over, didn't others go back and forth as well?"

"Soon after Prince Henry left for America, England attacked Scotland. Any ships that may have been used to explore were needed for the war. Or were lost in battle."

He drummed his hands on the steering wheel. "Remember when I asked you whether you believed in the Prince Henry legend and you told me it didn't matter whether it was true or not, only that people *believed* it was true?"

"Rather brilliant of me, was it not?" She fluffed her white-blond hair.

He couldn't help but grin. "Yes, brilliant. So brilliant that I'm going to steal it and argue that it doesn't really matter if Sinclair built the Tower, or if it's a monument to him, or if he had nothing to do with it at all. What matters is that someone *believes* the Knight and the Tower and the Boat Stone and who knows what else are related to some kind of treasure. In order to understand what they're after, and figure out who they are, we need to know all we can about all these sites. Both fact and myth."

She settled back in her seat. "As I said, drive toward Maine." She held up a plastic shopping bag. "I'm ready to go—I picked up some clothes and a toothbrush while I was waiting for you."

Smiling at the prospect of a day or two alone in the car with Amanda, he shifted to the left lane and accelerated. "How far up in Maine?"

"Near Augusta."

"Easy enough. Straight up the turnpike."

"I want to show you the Spirit Pond Rune Stones. Here's a surprise — the experts believe they are fake."

"Speaking of the experts, did I tell you I spoke to the Massachusetts state archeologist?"

"How fortunate."

"I guess you know her, huh?"

"Rhonda Blank. I've had my own history with her. We call her Blinky Blank. Whenever she is asked to consider a pre-Columbus artifact, she closes her eyes — you know, those long blinks that make you think she might be napping — and shakes her head. As if she doesn't want to see the evidence."

He smiled, remembering Claude's eye-closing tendency. Apparently it did run in the family. "Well, she said the Knight was carved by some neighborhood boys in the late 1800s as a prank."

"The Fisher lads. It's a fine story — there were four of them and they lived nearby. But the facts don't add up. There's a reference to the carving in a town history publication that dates back to the year the oldest boy was born. It's impossible for them to have carved the effigy."

"As we say in the law, why let the facts get in the way of a perfectly good story?"

"The Fisher lads did add a peace pipe to the carving, which is how the story began. But it's a simple matter to distinguish between the pipe and the rest of the Knight. Unless you close your eyes like Blinky Blank."

"So what's her problem?"

"Many archeologists have staked their professional reputations on certain truisms. For example, that Columbus discovered America.

She got her job with the state because she's a protégé of some old Harvard professor who scoffs at talk of contact before Columbus. The last thing they want is for new evidence to appear that contradicts them. So they just stick their heads in the sand."

"Speaking of new evidence, the Gendrons found a clay lantern in their backyard that looks a lot like the Newport Tower. I just noticed the resemblance when I went to pick up the car."

"It resembles the Tower? Do you reckon that's what McLovick was looking for?"

"I did." He smiled. "But then I thought I'd been watching too many movies."

"Well, either way, I'd fancy having it carbon-dated. But even if the testing dated it circa 1400, the mainstream archeologists would argue it was brought over from Europe by the Colonists. It's tragic, really. They're supposed to be academics. Yet they refuse to even consider that some of these artifacts might be more than hoaxes."

"Tell that to Brandon. Someone thinks this stuff is pretty real."

"Yes, poor Brandon. You can judge the Spirit Pond Rune Stones for yourself. I've only seen them once. Looked pretty bloody authentic to me."

He made sure there was plenty of room between the Subaru and the car in front of them before turning to her. "Thanks for your help. I want to figure this all out and catch those S.O.B.s."

He dialed Brandon's cell, explaining to her that Brandon was helping with internet research. "And this phone is untraceable."

On the third ring Brandon picked up. "Hello Cameron." But it wasn't Brandon.

He considered hanging up; instead he signaled Amanda to stay quiet. "Lieutenant Poulos. Guess I shouldn't be surprised to hear your voice."

"Call me back on the cell number I gave you."

He redialed, appreciative of the policeman's caution. "Listen, Cam, you need to come back to Westford. You need to answer some questions."

"Look, Lieutenant. I had nothing to do with McLovick's death. I think you know that." No response. "Anyway, I can't come back until I figure this all out."

"That's our job."

"With all due respect, we've got one guy maimed and another one dead. Plus a dead dog and I've almost been killed myself. Twice."

"Twice?"

"Yeah, I had another footrace with a car today. It's getting a little tiring, to be honest."

"That's why you need to come in."

He took a deep breath. "Look, there's some really strange, complicated stuff going on. And I don't mean to say I'm smarter than you guys. But we need to figure out the motive here before we have any chance of catching these guys and I'm starting to put it all together. But I can't do that if I'm holed up in some police station giving statements and answering questions."

"I told my captain you'd probably say something like that. He said it sounded like O.J. Simpson."

"You know, that's bullshit. I'm not out on some golf course. I'm out here, now, dodging cars and trying to figure this all out. So cut the O.J. crap, all right?"

"Easy, son. It wasn't me that said it."

"That's bullshit also. You'd didn't have to repeat it. You said it to get a reaction out of me."

Poulos remained silent.

Cam took a deep breath; the officer was just doing his job. "What about you guys? You have any leads? Maybe one of McLovick's partners trying to take the treasure for himself?"

More silence.

"All right then. I'm not coming in just so somebody can hold a press conference and say they're making progress on the case."

Cam waited through a long pause. "Officially, I have to tell you that you're making a mistake," Poulos finally said. "Unofficially, I have a message to pass on to you: Monsignor Marcotte says he has some information that will help you." Cam scribbled down Marcotte's contact information on a scrap of paper. "And be careful, Cameron."

"Thanks, Lieutenant." He gave Poulos the license plate number of the BMW. "Maybe that's a lead you can use."

Brandon's voice came over the phone. "I'll call you back."

Five minutes later, Cam's TracFone rang. "I'm calling from my new phone." Brandon gave Cam the number. "Poulos is gone. He was here about an hour, waiting for you to call." Brandon seemed stronger, more energized. "He noticed some of the books lying around here, stuff my parents brought in."

"That's fine — it's no secret this somehow relates to Prince Henry and the Templars. But do me a favor. Every time you're done with an internet search, run the disk cleanup function on your laptop. That'll delete the cookies and the web page history so nobody will know what sites you've been on." That wasn't totally true — the information could still be recovered. But not quickly. "So are you alone?"

"My dad's here. And Poulos left a guy outside my door. For my protection, he said."

"Probably not a bad idea. Anyway, I need to know what you can find about the Spirit Pond Rune Stones, up in Maine."

"Got it. And my dad wants to talk to you."

Peter skipped the pleasantries. "I've been looking into this Westford Knight carving. It's all a hoax, Cameron. Some kids carved it in the late 1800s. The Fisher boys, they lived up the street."

Cam explained the reference in the town history. "Unless they crawled out of their crib with an ice pick, they didn't do it."

"Well, that doesn't make it authentic. And I don't see the Knight and the shield. All I see is a sword. Everything else is worn away."

"You saw the old pictures in the library. But it doesn't really matter — it's still a medieval battle sword punched into a rock ledge. Amanda said they had a weapons expert in England study it — the proportions are perfect. How would some farmer know what a medieval sword looked like? And why would he carve it into the rock even if he did?"

Peter plowed ahead. "And this Boat Stone thing, these numbers 1-8-4, that's just a date. It's a trail marker from 1840-something."

"Nice theory but where's the fourth number?" He took a deep breath. "If the numbers were 1-3-9 and I told you that meant it was 1390-something but they forgot the last number, you'd tell me I was full of shit. And you'd be right. More to the point, why would someone in the 1840s carve a medieval boat and medieval crossbow arrow onto a stone? Why not carve a schooner and a musket?"

"I don't know. People do crazy things."

"I don't know either. But at least I'm trying to figure it out."

"Welcome to my world," Amanda said as he hung up. "Nobody wants to look at this with an open mind. Folks like Rhonda Blank say we have no evidence. Well, what about the artifacts themselves? Aren't they evidence? We shipped the Boat Stone out to a forensic geologist in Minnesota — he concluded that the weathering patterns in the carvings were consistent with a 600-year-old artifact. Isn't that evidence?" She sighed. "Sorry to grizzle — it's just a bit frustrating oftentimes."

"Don't let Peter's opinion bother you. He's not exactly open-minded. My dad really had to strong-arm him into giving me a job — he thinks I'm a loose cannon."

Amanda chewed on her lip as her eyes darkened and narrowed. "Speaking of your job, I have a confession to make. I don't reckon you're going to be too pleased with me." She took a deep breath.

"The Consortium performed a background check on you. Now I feel like I'm privy to private matters about you that I have no right to know."

It wasn't like he was a sex offender or anything. "So you know I'm a diabetic, and you know I got suspended by the Bar Association, and you probably know I used to drink too much." He smiled. "But I'm really not that interesting. So no big deal."

"Thanks. Some folks would be all bothered by it. Actually, there is one other thing I learned: You are part of the *Rex Deus* bloodline."

He turned, expecting to see Amanda's straight white teeth grinning back at him. But her expression was flat. "You serious?"

"Yes. Your mother's maiden name is Kahn. She is a Cohen."

When Cam was a child in the synagogue with his mother and her family, Grandpa Morey was always called to read from the Torah first, before the other men in the congregation. His mother had explained that since Cohens descended from Aaron, who was the brother of Moses and the first high priest, the tradition was to call a Cohen first to the Torah.

"Well, in that case, I take back all that stuff I said about royal bloodlines not mattering. Do I get to wear a crown or something?"

She cuffed him on the shoulder.

"Seriously, what difference does it make?" he asked.

"Well, for one thing, the Consortium is convinced that only someone with *Rex Deus* blood is worthy of figuring out the Prince Henry mystery and finally proving the legend is fact."

"Great. But they also may be the ones trying to kill me."

"I've been pondering that. I don't see why they wouldn't want you to succeed."

"Like you said, there's a lot about this Consortium that you don't know."

"They don't know I'm here with you — I just went off without informing anyone." She fiddled with her cell phone. "I was reckoning I should ring in, perhaps ask for their aid. But I'm hesitant."

He tightened his grip on the steering wheel. "I'm not inclined to trust them." He smiled. "Even if they are my distant cousins."

"All right then, I won't ring them." She dropped her phone in her bag. "Now what's all this about your law license being suspended? From what I read, they should have given you a promotion, not suspended you."

A rest area loomed in the distance. He hadn't eaten dinner yet and he was beginning to feel a bit shaky. "Let's eat first, then I'll tell you the whole story. I hope you like fast food."

"My goodness, Papa Gino's and McDonald's. Fine dining."

"Hey, you can get anything on the menu. Either place. My treat."

They each grabbed a chicken fillet sandwich and a wilted salad and sat at a booth looking out at the gas pumps in front. He was just about to visit the men's room when a BMW sedan — this one gray — pulled to a stop in the fire lane in front of the restaurant. Two muscular, stern-faced men jumped from the car. "Amanda, shield your face but check out those guys."

"They look like they were cut from the same cloth as that bloke in Newport. Think they remembered their keys?"

One of the men circled around to the side door while the other guarded the front. Cam's chest tightened. "Is your cell new?"

"Brand new. Why?"

"The new ones have a built-in tracking device. You know, in case of emergency so they can find you."

She looked down. "But my phone is off."

"Believe it or not, it still tracks." He had just read a law case where the FBI was able to hack into a Mafia cell phone and use it as a transmitter, even when the power was off. If the people tracking them had someone working at the cell phone company, someone with access to the company's computers, they could track them using Amanda's cell. "They know we're here someplace but I think they can only track to a general location." But they would have no trouble spotting Amanda's white-blond hair. "Quick, go to the ladies' room."

"Should I lose the phone?"

"No, not yet."

As she circled away from the front entrance to the restrooms, he positioned himself in the middle of the dining area so that he could see both the front and side doors. Fortunately a tour bus had just pulled in and the restaurant was packed. The henchman at the side door entered and jabbed at his phone. His partner in the front answered on the first ring before hanging up and dialing another number. While he spoke he punched at the controls of what looked like a handheld GPS device. Someone was giving him the coordinates of Amanda's phone. The thug scanned the room, probably looking for Amanda. Or listening for her British accent. Cam knew he didn't have much time.

An employee, probably called suddenly to help at the counter with the tour bus rush, had left a bucket and mop leaning against a wall near a garbage can. Cam ducked his head and strode over to it. Sometimes the best place to hide was in plain view. Pulling the mop out, he began to clean the floor in short, sweeping motions. He took a deep breath and called out in a loud monotone, imitating as best he could the voice of someone with a mental impairment. "Excuse me, excuse me. I need to mop the floors. I need to mop the floors. Excuse me." In his path, customers turned away in embarrassment and discomfort as each stroke brought him closer to the restrooms. He called out loudly again, his head down. "Excuse me. I need to mop the floors. Excuse me." He passed within a few feet of the thug by the side door, resisting the urge to splash the man's shoes. A few seconds later he pulled the wheeled bucket into the small hallway that accessed the restrooms.

Rapping on the ladies' room door, he kept his voice loud and flat. "Excuse me. Excuse me. I need to mop the floors."

He didn't wait for a response, praying that Amanda would not call out. He pushed the door open and closed it quickly behind him. "Damn," he whispered. "No lock."

Amanda poked her head out from inside a stall. "If there had been, don't you think I'd have locked you out?"

"Good point." He liked that she hadn't panicked. "Quick, give me your phone. Stay here." He stuffed the phone into his pocket, wheeled the mop and bucket back into the dining area and continued his charade. "Excuse me. Excuse me. I need to mop the floors." The operatives were now wandering through the restaurant, inspecting the diners, their faces reddening in frustration. It would not be long before they checked the restrooms.

He mopped his way out the front door of the restaurant and, making sure he was out of sight, began sprinting toward the car service area. As he reached the gas pumps a small dump truck began to pull away. He raced aside the truck, tossed the phone onto a pile of bark mulch and watched it nestle itself deep into its new home. He jogged back toward the service garage and crouched low behind a van parked next to the air hose.

His heart pounding in his ears, he peered out. Either the thugs would be monitoring the GPS device and race to follow the now-moving beacon or they were on the verge of crashing through the ladies' room door in search of Amanda. If the latter, there was nothing he could do to help her....

Almost involuntarily, he sprinted back toward the restaurant, grabbing the mop for a weapon. It was a careless move, a stupid move that might draw attention to himself even as the henchmen were set to screech off in pursuit of the mulch truck. But he couldn't help himself. He had made the mistake of allowing his mind to picture the two men roughing up Amanda and now his mutinous heart had overruled his brain. *Run,* the organ commanded his legs, and Cam could no sooner stop his limbs from obeying than he could prevent them from reflexively pulling away from the touch of a hot stove. The best his brain could do was convince his eyes to stay focused on the front door and be prepared to duck and hide if the thugs emerged.

Thankfully, blessedly even, the ruffians burst through the swinging door. Cam leaned on the mop and turned his face toward the wall of the restaurant. The thugs ran right by, ignoring the dimwitted, mop-wielding janitor.

In light of his foolish sprint back to try to save Amanda from the two trained ruffians armed only with a wooden mop, their assessment of him as a dimwit was not far from the truth.

+   +   +

"Honest," Cam pleaded, his brown eyes large and expressive. "I was coming back to help you."

They had returned to the Subaru, heading north. Amanda was enjoying herself—she sensed that Cam wasn't certain if she was peeved at him. Normally she was a clumsy flirt, especially with American guys who didn't seem to appreciate her sarcasm. But the rash on her face liberated her—he wasn't likely to find her attractive in any event so she could just be herself and have some fun with it. "Rubbish," she retorted. "You were probably out looking for some harlot to pair up with. You were going to leave me in that loo forever."

He laughed. "Yeah, like a modern day Rapunzel. After a few years you could throw your golden locks out the bathroom window and hope some prince would rescue you."

She liked his wit, his ability to banter and verbally joust. "It's a shame I don't know any princes."

"Not true." He arched an eyebrow. "You told me I'm part of the *Rex Deus* line."

Turning in her seat, she made a pretense of sizing him up for the first time. Not too shabby. Handsome, fit, sweet, smart. Not to mention the puppy dog eyes and an easy smile. Too bad she looked like a swamp monster. At least she hadn't caught him staring at her pus or blisters. "Well, I suppose you'd do in a pinch."

"Wow, a ringing endorsement," he laughed. "But kidding aside, I think we need to do something about your hair. It makes it too easy to spot you."

She bent over, fished a bottle of hair color out of her shopping bag. "I'm one step ahead of you, just waiting to arrive at a room with a shower."

"I guess no more Rapunzel jokes. What color do you have?"

"Well, it says brunette but my hair is so light it reacts oddly to these dyes. I sported purple hair for a bit in college."

"Great, that will make you blend right in."

She settled back in her seat. "So what's all this about a law suspension?"

They passed a green highway sign — still a couple hundred miles to Augusta. "It actually starts way back when I was a kid growing up in Andover. I was about 12 and I had this friend — his name was Marty, he was my best friend — who lived down the street." She studied him as he spoke. Even with a goatee he had a boyish face — eager eyes and a couple of wisps of brown hair that fell over his eyebrows — so it wasn't difficult to picture him as a youth. Unlike most men in their thirties, he hadn't developed even the hint of jowls or an extra chin. He looked a bit like the boy next door but with an edge. Which made him the boy next door that the girls wanted to sneak into the woods with. "We did all the stuff 12-year-old boys do — played sports, rode our bikes, watched horror movies —"

"Chased girls, no doubt."

"Actually, not. That didn't really start for us until a year or two later."

"That's because I wasn't there."

"No doubt," he smiled. "I would have quit both hockey and baseball for you."

"No doubt."

"So, anyway, the summer after sixth grade, Marty's parents sent him up to a YMCA summer camp up in Maine. When he came back, he was ... different. I guess sullen is the word. This went on for a couple of months and I started hanging out with him less. But on Halloween we went out together. We thought it would be fun to put on monster masks and jump out of the bushes and scare the little kids." He shook his head. "Well, Marty's idea of scaring them was different from mine. He pushed them down, took their candy. He even punched one kid in the stomach. So I told him to stop being a jerk. Well, one thing led to another and we started fighting. He was bigger than me but he wasn't very strong. I put him in a headlock until he calmed down. Then I told him I didn't want to be friends anymore and I ran home."

"And?"

Cam blinked a couple of times, rubbing the back of his hand across his brow. "And the next morning they found him dead, hanging from a belt in his bedroom. No note, no explanation. Just a young kid who was hurting so much that he wanted to die. I had no idea."

She reached over, rested her hand on his shoulder. "What a horrid story. You don't blame yourself, do you?"

"Actually, for years I did. I figured if I had been a better friend...." He paused, took a deep breath. "Anyway, twenty-plus years later, I'm working on this priest sex abuse case, and I'm reading one of the case files, and the guy is talking about being abused at a YMCA summer camp in Maine. And of course it all just made perfect sense. It was the same camp Marty was at."

"And for all that time you blamed yourself for Marty's death," she whispered.

"Right. But that's not what pissed me off. What pissed me off is that some ... animal just sucked Marty's will to live right out of him." He shook his head. "And then these maggots covered it up, let this priest go right on molesting kids even after they knew what was happening. I just don't understand it—I know a lot of good, honest, devoted priests. Why did they allow this to continue?"

"It wasn't those priests who knew about it," she frowned. "Weren't other lawyers at your firm hacked off about representing the Church in these cases?"

"Lawyers have an amazing ability to be self-righteous. They'll spout out stuff about everyone having the Constitutional right to an attorney, blah, blah, blah. Well, they're right, everyone does have that right. And it's important to make sure the poor and the dispossessed and the minorities don't just get railroaded through the court system. But that doesn't mean priests who molest dozens of young kids have the right to have a team of lawyers defend them by attacking the people they molested."

"They did that?"

"It's really the only defense they had. Try to make things so painful and uncomfortable and embarrassing that these guys would just settle. But I couldn't go along with it. Not after what happened to Marty. So I leaked some stuff to the press, internal firm memos that outlined the defense strategy. The judge threatened the reporter with jail time if he didn't give up his source."

She crinkled her nose. "And for this you were punished?"

He laughed. "Well, this goes back to how lawyers take themselves way too seriously. I had one guy say to me in this horrified voice, 'But you violated the attorney-client privilege!' Like it was as bad as what the priests did. Well, yeah, I did. But just because something is against the rules doesn't make it wrong, just like because something is legal doesn't make it right. I mean, everything the Nazis did was technically legal based on the laws they pushed through."

He shook his head. "I had a law professor once who used to quote Dickens, 'Sometimes the law is an ass.'"

She waited for him to continue but apparently that was the entire story. "Well, I'm afraid I was a bit of an ass myself when I first met you."

"Not really," he said, glancing sideways at her. "At least not compared to the guy who tried to run me over."

She grinned. "Most of the solicitors I know are so serious."

He stared at the highway. "I read something once: After God created the world, he made man and woman. Then he invented humor to keep the whole thing from collapsing."

"And I read once that humor is the shortest distance between two people."

"I guess they're really saying the same thing."

They rode in silence for a few seconds, each alone with their thoughts. He spoke first. "One thing I never asked you was what you thought about the enclosure in the Gendrons' back yard."

She didn't think twice about violating the Consortium's protocols again. "That's quite an interesting site. There are reports of the Boat Stone going back to 1900. Nobody paid it much attention until the 1960s when an amateur archeologist by the name of Glynn stumbled upon it. Glynn consulted with an expert in England, who theorized it was a marker for an encampment site. Nobody recalled which way the arrow originally pointed so the expert recommended pacing off 184 paces — remember, the Boat Stone has the number '184' carved on it, though to be fair some folks don't think the 8 is really an 8 because the top isn't closed. In any event, Glynn did his pacing and found the rectangular stone layout in what at the time was a wooded area. When Glynn returned the next summer to excavate the site, he reported that the enclosure was gone, plowed over to build a home. As far as I know, that's what everyone has believed since."

"But it wasn't plowed over. It's still there. I saw it."

"Yes." She raised an eyebrow. "So the question is, why did Glynn report it destroyed?"

He slapped the steering wheel. "Because he found something there and didn't want anyone else to disturb it. Or find it."

Glynn's report had never made sense to her. Until now.

"So what happened to Glynn?" Cam asked.

"He died soon after." She held up her hand. "And before you inquire, I don't know if it was under suspicious circumstances."

"Well, either way, apparently he took his secret with him."

"Yes. Until Alistair McLovick arrived."

"And now McLovick is dead also." He pursed his lips. "And we still don't know anything about any treasure."

"Speaking of treasure, did you ever read *Treasure Island* when you were a lad?"

"Sure. I loved that book."

"Well, I stumbled upon an interesting theory a few months back. Apparently Robert Louis Stevenson grew up in Scotland, close to Roslyn Chapel. What's interesting is he chose the name Gunn for the chap who was the only inhabitant of the island in the story. An island that contained a vast buried treasure. An island which he described as an unknown land far to the west."

He turned. "Gunn. As in Sir James Gunn."

"Spot on. Spelled the same."

"And Ben Gunn was left alone with the treasure, same as Sir James." He drummed on the steering wheel. "When was *Treasure Island* written?"

"Late 1800s. Well before anyone in the States had heard of the Westford Knight."

"So the theory is that Stevenson knew about the Sinclair treasure, that *Treasure Island* was based on the old Sinclair family legends?"

Amanda smiled. "Well, I did some more research. It happens that Robert Louis Stevenson's mother is part of the Sinclair clan."

Shaking his head, Cam grinned. "Why did I just know you were going to say something like that?"

✛ ✛ ✛

As he and Amanda sped north through southern Maine, Cam dialed Brandon's TracFone.

"Hey, Cam."

"So how you doing?"

"It's weird. It hurts where my foot used to be. You know, phantom pain. They say I need more rest; they keep threatening to take away my laptop."

"Well, don't overdo it." He explained who Frank Glynn was. "But if you're up to it, I'd like to know when Glynn died. And how."

"Okay. And I've got a couple of things for you. Poulos called. The BMW is registered to some shell corporation. Nothing but a post office box for an address. He's trying to chase it down."

"No surprise. What else?"

"Monsignor Marcotte called, not sure how he found me. My dad talked to him for a long time. He's still waiting for you to call him."

"Yeah, I've been a bit busy." He explained the incident at the rest area. "So, someone is definitely tracking us."

"Could it be this Amanda chick?" Brandon whispered.

Cam's stomach clenched. "I don't think so." He quickly glanced over, tried to study her expression. If she wanted to set him up, she easily could have done so already. For example, when he picked her up after separating in Newport. "No, that doesn't add up."

"So, who is it then?"

"I don't know."

"Well, I've been looking at this Oak Island Money Pit." Cam held the phone so Amanda could listen. "The two theories are that it's either a pirate treasure or a Templar treasure. But check this out. The skull and crossbones on the pirate flag—"

"The Jolly Roger?" Cam interrupted.

"Yeah. Well, it's actually a Templar symbol. It's still used in Masonic rituals. Anyway, it turns out that after the Pope outlawed the Templars in the 14th century a bunch of them became pirates."

"Pirates? I thought they were religious knights."

"They were," Brandon agreed, "until the Pope arrested and tortured and outlawed them. At that point, what did they have to lose? They had ships and no place to call home. Later, other pirates started using the Jolly Roger because they knew nobody wanted to mess with the Templars."

"Wait until your dad finds out. He'll probably sue them for trademark infringement."

"Brandon's spot on," Amanda said as they laughed. "The Templars definitely possessed the engineering skills to build a booby-trapped pit like on Oak Island. In some ways, the pit is like the pyramids in Egypt with their water traps. Hard to believe any pirates had the skills to build something so elaborate. But if Templar ships, flying the Jolly Roger, sailed in and its crew dug the Money Pit, well, that would be consistent with your Native American oral history of pirates constructing it."

Now the pirates were involved too. Cam heard Uncle Peter's voice asking if the aliens would be arriving on the scene soon. But the crazy thing was, it all made sense.

Cam put the phone back to his ear. "All right, it's just me again."

"Nice accent. She hot?" Brandon asked.

"Yeah, as a matter of fact." He barely noticed her rash and blisters anymore—he always seemed to be staring at her eyes or teeth. "What about the Spirit Pond Rune Stones up in Maine? Learn anything?"

"Not much. Most people think they're fake. Some guy named Eric Forsberg from Minnesota is going to be in Fitchburg this week giving a talk about them. He's an expert on the Kensington Rune Stone out in Minnesota — people have been debating whether that's a hoax or not for over a century. This Forsberg guy thinks the Kensington and Spirit Pond stones are related. It's part of some conference run by the New England Antiquities Research Association, NEARA."

Cam wrote down the conference details. "Thanks, Brandon. Get some rest." He hung up and turned to Amanda. "We were talking about you."

"Really?" She arched an eyebrow. "Mind if I open the window a bit? I suddenly feel quite hot."

✢   ✢   ✢

Cam pulled into the dark parking lot of a Motel 6 outside of Augusta at around 10:30. "I was thinking it might be better if you stayed in the car," he said to Amanda. "They'll remember your hair."

"Be honest. You just don't fancy being seen cavorting with Mrs. Frankenstein."

He chuckled as he walked to the office area. After the day they'd had, most women — and men, for that matter — would be edgy and tense; Amanda was not only making jokes but ones at her own expense. He paid cash for a pair of rooms with a connecting door.

He parked the Subaru around back and handed Amanda a key, shifting awkwardly from one foot to another. What next? A handshake? A wave? Some kind of kiss?

She made the decision for him, stepping forward and wrapping her arms around his chest, squeezing him to her. He breathed her in, the same clean, floral smell he first noticed in the library. "I'd invite you in," she said, pulling back a bit to look in his eyes, "but I must wash my hair." She held up the bottle of hair dye, smiled and kissed him on the cheek. "Good night, Cameron. And thanks for a ... memorable day."

CHAPTER 6

[Tuesday]

Cam woke a bit before 6:00. He wanted to go for a long run but settled for a hundred push-ups and twice as many sit-ups on the floor of the room. After showering, he wrapped a thin white towel from the rack above the toilet around his waist and walked out of the bathroom.

"Good day," a voice sang out, startling him. He held the towel closed with one hand.

Amanda was leaning against the edge of the desk, smiling. Her hair was a dark maroon, almost like a burgundy wine. She tossed her locks with a shake of her neck. "What do you think? I'll wash it out again later and lighten it up."

"Good idea. You look like something out of an eighties music video," he laughed, thankful his muscles were still tight from his workout. Would she even notice? Or care? After grabbing his jeans off the end of the bed, he pulled a navy blue jersey from his pack and retreated to the bathroom. "Give me a minute." He dressed, brushed his teeth and checked his blood sugar level. "Sorry to be a pain," he said as he emerged from the bathroom, "but I need to have some breakfast."

"Of course. I've been known to fancy a few bangers myself."

They found a pancake house near the motel and made small talk while they ate. He learned that she grew up as an only child in a middle class family outside of London. Her father died while she was in high school and as soon as she went off to college her mother took up with an aging drummer in a marginally successful rock band. Eventually her mother sold the family house; most of the time she and the drummer were on tour anyway. "He was on okay bloke but it meant I really had no place — or even family — to come home to on holidays and such. Plus my mother burned through most of what dad left and I was deep in debt from college, just getting on with dead-end jobs. So when the job offer from the Consortium happened by, paying as well as it did, I reckoned why not take it." She looked away. "Not to mention my fiancé thought it was all in good fun to slap me around. I moved out while he was on a business trip. I never said goodbye. And never looked back."

"And now, a year later?"

"I work every weekend and I'm the lone voice in New England complaining about the sun. And I'm bored out of my bloody mind." She smiled. "At least I was until a few days ago."

✟   ✟   ✟

The Spirit Pond Rune Stones were housed in the town of Hallowell, about a mile from the Maine State Museum in Augusta. Amanda directed Cam to a brick warehouse building in an industrial park on the side of a commercial highway that also housed the state lottery and alcoholic beverages commission. He parked next to a tractor trailer and scrunched his face. "Why are they kept here? Shouldn't they be on display someplace?"

"Good question. Some bloke in an office made the decision that they're a hoax. So now they're hidden away."

She led him across a cement-floored loading dock, pushed open a door marked 'Archeology' and entered a large room lined with file cabinets and old display cases. She gave her name to a middle-age man with thick glasses and white hair growing from his nose who guided them to a table tucked amid the clutter in the back of the room.

He pointed to three shoebox-size plastic tubs stacked on the table. "There they are. Take as much time as you need."

THE SPIRIT POND MAP STONE

THE SPIRIT POND INSCRIPTION STONE

THE SPIRIT POND DRAWING STONE

Cam opened the cover of the first tub. "They're smaller than I thought." He pulled out a sandstone-colored, triangular-shaped flat slab with foreign lettering—runes—across the top and a map carved into the main body of the bicycle seat-sized stone. On the reverse side, a series of pictures had been carved—a canoe, a bow and arrow, a fish, a bird, a flower, all apparently depicting objects local to the area. "This is amazing. Why don't more people know about these?"

Amanda opened the other two plastic cases. From one she removed a pentagonal slab with 10 rows of runes on the front and six more on the back. The other contained a slab with yet more runic lettering. Shaking her head, she responded to his question. "It's sad, actually. There's a bunch of these artifacts all across New England. Every time someone finds one, the experts dismiss it as a fake. They say things like, 'If it was authentic, don't you reckon we'd find other evidence?' Well, the fact is that there's plenty of other evidence." She shook her head again. "But it's all stashed away in plastic tubs like this. God forbid we should let the public decide for themselves."

✝   ✝   ✝

Salazar pulled the rim of a brown UPS cap low over his forehead and adjusted the fake mustache and beard. Pushing a two-wheeled trolley through the door marked 'Archeology,' he called out, "I got a bunch of boxes for some guy named Gilbert."

A middle-age man in a wheeled office chair turned toward him. "Just leave 'em there."

Salazar nodded, careful not to turn his face directly toward Thorne and the girl, who was no longer blond. She also had some rash on her face. Thorne didn't seem to care, didn't turn away from her. Salazar touched his own cheeks, still pockmarked from a bad case of acne as a youth. Christina used to make jokes at his expense, especially when she'd been drinking. He wore a beard for a while but shaved it when she left him.

He motioned toward where Thorne was examining three sand-colored, book-size slabs. "I got more of 'em back in the truck and they're heavy. Sure you don't want me to pile them over against that wall?"

"That'd be great, thanks."

Salazar's orders were to use whatever means necessary to prevent them from continuing their research. Not much ambiguity — no more warnings, no more second chances. Too bad; it would have been better if they had simply gone away. They seemed like a nice couple, smiling and laughing together. And they were obviously bright and resourceful — they evaded two of Reichmann's men at a rest area yesterday, which made his own Newport debacle look not so bad by comparison.

An old special ops buddy had once argued that it was immoral to kill outside the battlefield. It was a distinction without a difference — other than in cases of self-defense, all killing was the same, whether on the battlefield or not. War was an attempt by a nation or a tribe or a religious faction to elevate itself at the expense of another. It was about power and wealth; morality rarely played a part. His Narragansett cousins who protested the Thanksgiving holiday were being silly. Christopher Columbus and the Europeans did not slaughter natives because Europeans were evil — they did so because they were mighty, just as Native Americans had attacked and conquered one another for centuries. Salazar had been ordered to kill McLovick for the same reason he killed an opposing combatant on the battle field — because McLovick threatened his employer's wealth and power. McLovick had been warned to abandon his search for the treasure and ignored the warning, just as Thorne and the girl had ignored their warning. They were like villagers who chose not to flee as enemy soldiers approached; they could hardly be surprised to find themselves in the crossfire. As the African proverb stated, when elephants fight, it is the grass that suffers.

Of course, this analysis begged the more fundamental question of the morality of killing itself. As a soldier, he had long struggled with the issue, in the end concluding that humans were no different than animals — some would eat while others starved; some would rule while others perished. The taking of life was no more evil than an eagle making a meal of a field mouse; the evil derived from the infliction of suffering. When a body died, its soul moved on to the next corporeal being. So long as the body did not suffer, the soul remained healthy. A soul that suffered, however, returned in a wicked form to inflict more suffering. When animals killed, they did so quickly, efficiently. The gratuitous infliction of suffering — not the act of killing — was the true sin. A uniquely human one at that.

Thorne and the girl continued to study the artifacts. Just as Salazar had no problem killing to promote his employer's interests, he had no problem disobeying his employer's orders to promote his own. Like Thorne and the girl, he was mere grass under the elephants' feet. Perhaps his little Rosalita could someday be the elephant.

Fumbling with some paperwork as he slowly stacked the boxes, he leaned closer and listened as they discussed the mysterious rune stones.

✝   ✝   ✝

Cam studied the runic letters inscribed neatly on the stone. "If this is a prank, it's pretty elaborate. It's tough to carve stone by hand. Plus, how many people even know what the runic alphabet is?"

"The so-called experts always say that it just takes one prankster." Amanda examined the carvings with a magnifying glass. "But, again, they're ignoring all the other artifacts around New England. It would actually take a dozen pranksters working over a dozen decades in a dozen different places."

"The map and the pictures are self-explanatory. But what does the runic inscription say?"

"Nobody is certain. There are no word separators so the letters all run together. Most folks reckon it's a ship's log describing their journey."

"How do these relate to the Prince Henry voyage?"

"The dates 1401 and 1402 are encoded on the map stone using something called the Easter Table, which is the same way the Kensington Rune Stone was dated. Sinclair left the Orkneys in 1398 and traveled to New England in 1399. So the dates make sense." She pointed to a line on the map stone. "This shows the Maine coast, specifically the Popham Beach area, and the arrow points to Vinland as two days sail to the south."

"Vinland's earlier than Prince Henry, right?"

"Right, that's the Viking settlement from around the year 1000. But it does tie in. Although Prince Henry lived in Scotland, his mother was a Norsewoman, a Viking. He may have possessed some of the old Viking maps of Vinland."

"So is Vinland actually two days' sail to the south?"

"Nobody knows for certain. But there's a small island off of Martha's Vineyard called Noman's Land. It's restricted now—your military used it for years as a bombing range and it's full of unexploded ordnance. There's a stone there with a runic carving on it that reads, 'Leif Eriksson, 1001.' And another line that some experts translate as 'Vinland.' Makes you wonder whether the island's name derives from 'Norman's Land' or 'Norseman's Land.'

Sure seemed possible.

"In any event," she continued, "the stone was originally carved high on a bluff but it slid down to the water's edge in the late 1800s. Some folks are trying to relocate it into a museum but Rhonda Blank wrote a letter on behalf of the state historical commission opposing it. She claimed moving it might 'disturb other cultural resources.'" Amanda rolled her eyes. "The stone is offshore and under water. It's on an island used for decades as target practice for your navy bombers. What other 'cultural resources' could she possibly be bothered about? Missile casings?"

"This goes back to what you said before. She's staked her professional reputation on the absence of pre-Columbus contact. So the last thing she wants is people preserving or studying artifacts that might prove her wrong."

"Right. And there are other rune stones near Cape Cod. The Bourne Stone is of interest because we can trace it back to the 1600s. It sports a carving of a medieval ship similar to the one on the Boat Stone." She dug around inside her leather carrying bag and pulled out a photo. "This is a rubbing."

A RUBBING OF THE BOURNE STONE

The image next to the footprint on the lower left did look like the Boat Stone ship. "What do the experts say about this one?"

"Since it was originally found in a Native American church they say it was carved by your Indians."

He studied it. In the 1600s the Colonists set up Praying Towns and built churches for Native Americans who had converted to Christianity. "Even if they did have the tools to do it, the ship is medieval. They had to see the ship before they could carve it."

"This is what the Consortium has been up against for years." She shook her head. "There's another rune stone in Narragansett Bay in Rhode Island. And of course we have the Newport Tower. As you Americans say, a lot of smoke for there not to be any fire."

And a lot of runes for there not to be any Europeans. He shifted his eyes back to the Spirit Pond stones. "Getting back to this map stone, I thought they found archeological evidence that Vinland was up in Newfoundland, not near Cape Cod." In the 1970s amateur archeologists, ignoring the skepticism of the professionals, uncovered a Viking settlement in L'Anse aux Meadows.

"There's just one problem with that site — there are no grapes growing that far north."

"No grapes, no Vinland. I get it."

"Sort of a fundamental problem seeing as they named the settlement after the grape vines, if you ask me. It may be that L'Anse aux Meadows was only a stopover on the way south to the actual Vinland."

"Getting back to the so-called experts: What do they think of this map?"

"As I said, they ignore it because they assume it must be a hoax. The Blinky Blank syndrome."

"Do they have any evidence it's not legit?"

"Nothing specific, no. But it doesn't fit their theory so they simply dimiss it."

"Hey, this is interesting." He pointed to the map stone with the arrow indicating Vinland was located two days sail away. "If you were drawing a map, today, which way would south be?"

"Along the bottom, of course."

"But this map, based on the contours of the coastline, has south orienting to the right, where you'd expect east to be. Why?"

"Apparently the medieval custom was to put east at the top because east was the direction of both Jerusalem and the Garden of Eden, the world's most important places."

They pondered the information for a few seconds. "Really," Amanda said, "in some ways this helps prove the authenticity of the rune stones. If they were a forgery or a hoax, the prankster would still have used modern mapmaking conventions."

"Right. South would be at the bottom. Even for a hoaxster, it would have been second nature." He continued to study the map. "If it's authentic, Vinland would actually be near Martha's Vineyard. Vinland and Vineyard. Just like any 4th-grader would guess."

"The Vinland-Vineyard connection is actually not that surprising. It's similar to Noman's Land and Norseman's Land. I've learned that these types of coincidences occur so often that they're not really coincidences. The same sites, and the same names, and the same symbols all keep turning up again and again. It can't be just random." She smiled. "In fact, I have a theory about all this if you fancy to hear it."

"Of course. But let's talk in the car. We should get going." He snapped a few pictures with his digital camera, stepped around a UPS delivery man and reluctantly left the warehouse.

✝   ✝   ✝

Salazar didn't bother following Thorne and the girl. The tracking device he had attached to the underside of the Subaru's bumper would do the job for him.

First he phoned Rosalita, left another message. "Hey big girl, I just wanted to wish you luck in your game today. Try your hardest and I'm sure you'll do great. And don't forget to use your left foot." Her coach had told the girls that when they went home and kicked the dog to use their left foot because it was good practice. Rosalita didn't get the humor but Salazar, even as an animal lover, appreciated it. "When I come home, we can practice and you can show me all of your new moves. Oh, and remember to be a good teammate — tell the other girls they played good even if they weren't so great, you know? Okay, bye honey."

Next he phoned Reichmann in Buenos Aires. "I spent the night questioning desk clerks at hotels along the Maine Turnpike. They stayed at a Motel 6 in Bangor, paid cash, checked out this morning."

"You mean you lost them again?" Reichmann spoke English with a thick Spanish accent.

"No. Your guys at the rest area lost them. I just found them for you."

Reichmann sighed. "Yes, you are correct." He pronounced the 's' in 'yes' as a 'z'. "Good work tracking them to the motel. They cannot have gone far."

The display on Salazar's tracking device showed the Subaru heading south on the Maine Turnpike, back toward the Boston area. "The clerk said they were asking for directions to Montreal. My guess is they're heading north."

+   +   +

Back in the Subaru, Amanda took a deep breath. "Seeing that you're such an expert on American History, what was the first English colony in America?"

Cam clutched and shifted. "Why do I think this is going to be a trick question?"

"Your answer, please."

"I thought you were going to tell me about names and sites and symbols repeating themselves."

"Answer the question, solicitor."

"Okay. Jamestown."

"Incorrect." Smiling, she made the sound of a buzzer.

"That was harsh."

"Actually, you are partly correct. Jamestown is tied with another colony in Maine called the Popham Colony, founded by one George Popham in 1607. It lasted only one year before it was abandoned. For perspective, your Pilgrims didn't arrive in Plymouth until 1620, 13 years later."

He turned to her. "Wait. Popham. Didn't you mention something about Popham Beach earlier?"

"Ah, so you were listening. And you are correct. Popham Beach is the area depicted on the map we just viewed. And, yes, they are one and the same."

"So the English settlers just happened to stumble upon Popham Beach, out of the thousands of miles of American coastline?"

"Now we've come again to my theory about too much coincidence. I think a far more likely scenario is that our friend Mr. Popham possessed an old map, one that directed him toward a safe harbor with fresh water and perhaps even friendly natives."

"A map from the Prince Henry voyage." It seemed possible. "Okay, where next?"

"I've been pondering that. Drive back toward Westford. There's something I want you to view in Tyngsboro."

"Works for me. Monsignor Marcotte wants to talk to me and I'd rather do it in person than over the phone. It's not that I don't trust him but—"

"The whole Church thing?"

"I guess maybe it is that I don't totally trust him."

"Really, there's a religious aspect to all of this that I've never looked at very closely. Perhaps he has some insights that'd be helpful. I've never met the man but we've chatted on the phone a few times. He seems to have a keen interest in the Knight, which I've never quite understood."

They drove southwest down the Maine Turnpike, crossed into New Hampshire for a few miles, then entered Massachusetts. "Actually, we need to make a quick detour," she said. "Take this next exit."

He nodded. "Okay. Where to?"

"It always seemed odd to me that Prince Henry came this far inland. Why? Perhaps the answer is that his native hosts wanted to show him something. Something important."

"Okay. The more we can learn about Prince Henry, the better."

They ate energy bars and dried fruit for lunch as Cam drove, crossing back into New Hampshire. "This site is called America's Stonehenge," Amanda said between bites. "It used to be called Mystery Hill but as a tourist site the new name sounds more ... ancient. It's comprised of a series of stone chambers and markers and cairns, dating back a few thousand years. Your Native Americans lived on the site but many experts believe it was built either by ancient Europeans or the Phoenicians."

"Sorry for my ignorance but where did the Phoenicians come from exactly?"

"Near present-day Lebanon, approximately a thousand years before Christ."

She directed him off the highway, where they followed the signs to North Salem and America's Stonehenge. After buying tickets in a wooden building that also housed a gift shop and snack bar, she escorted him along an inclined dirt pathway through the woods to a complex of stone enclosures and formations. They squeezed between neatly-placed stone walls into the heart of the complex. "This is the Sacrificial Stone."

THE SACRIFICIAL STONE, AMERICA'S STONEHENGE

He crouched and studied the flat, trapezoidal stone. About the size of a kitchen table, it sat two feet off the ground on stone supports. "Wow. They think this was used for sacrifices?"

"Yes, perhaps human ones." She pointed to a carved channel in the stone running around the perimeter of the trapezoid. "This is for the blood to flow out."

"Very considerate. Wouldn't want to have a messy sacrifice."

She smiled. "Do you see that stone wall?" The 'head' of the Sacrificial Stone abutted a long, two-foot high wall. "It's actually the exterior wall of an underground chamber called the Oracle Chamber." She gestured toward a grassy mound behind the wall. "A fellow—a priest, probably—would hide in the chamber and speak into a stone-lined tube that runs underneath the Sacrificial Stone, called the Speaking Tube. The voice would then amplify out the tube, under the slab."

"So it sounded like the sacrificed body was talking?"

She nodded. "Or the gods speaking through it. Neat trick, eh?"

They walked quickly through the site, Amanda pointing things out as they went. "Using the main complex as ground zero, that boulder lines up due north, it's called the True North stone ... And that one lines up directly with the sunrise on the summer solstice ... That boulder lines up with the sun on the winter solstice ... This whole site is a massive astronomical calendar."

He shook his head. "What a cool place. I wish we had all day to explore. I can't believe I grew up 20 minutes away and didn't know about it."

"Yes, I'm surprised it's not more popular. Whoever built it—Europeans or Phoenicians or natives—it's a brilliant achievement. That's why I feel so certain the natives would have brought Prince Henry here." Her eyes followed a line of boulders running to the horizon. "And so certain he would have been awestruck by it."

CHAPTER 7

An hour after leaving the America's Stonehenge site, Amanda directed Cam to a quiet country road running parallel to the Merrimack River in Tyngsboro. The river, which once powered scores of mills in northern Massachusetts and southern New Hampshire, flowed south from the New Hampshire lakes, then turned east and north, fishhook-like, before emptying into the ocean along the northern Massachusetts coast. Tyngsboro sat at the southern tip of the river, at the bend of the hook.

"If Prince Henry did come to Westford, he almost certainly traveled along the Merrimack River," she said.

"From the coast?"

"I believe so, from Newburyport. He came to Westford, then followed the Merrimack north to other rivers before reaching Quebec. Others think he came the other way, traveling down from Lake Memphremagog in Quebec and following the rivers in northern Vermont and New Hampshire to the Merrimack. Either way, there are a number of Templar artifacts in Quebec around Lake Memphremagog and along the Saint Lawrence River. An old map shows how the river system used to be different, prior to an earthquake in the late 1600s. Prince Henry could have made the trip without having to portage his boats a great deal."

She leaned across him, peered out the driver's side window. He moved his head just enough to keep an eye on the road but otherwise did not edge away. "Here we are," she said.

They got out of the car. He scanned the street — no black BMWs, no careening Cadillacs. At least not yet.

She pointed across the road. "I want to show you a boulder off in those woods. And please bring your New Hampshire map."

She guided him to a Volkswagen-size boulder, split approximately in half. A shallow trench ringed the boulder like a moat. "Some fifteen years ago an archeologist excavated around the boulder. But he failed to backfill it when he completed his dig and the boulder's own weight caused it to split."

"Another so-called expert?"

She nodded. "He didn't find anything in the ground so he simply left the trench. Archeologists have a saying: 'The ground doesn't lie.' But sometimes they are so intent on their digs that they ignore items in plain sight. Such as the carving on this rock."

She began to brush away the leaves and pine needles, revealing a weathered, half-inch-deep groove carved into the stone's surface.

THE TYNGSBORO MAP STONE

"Open your map, would you? Let's have a look at the Merrimack River." He did so. "Here's its track," she said, "winding south through New Hampshire, then it hooks to the east and north before exiting to the ocean." She handed the map back to him and traced the path of the boulder carving with a stick. "See how they match up?"

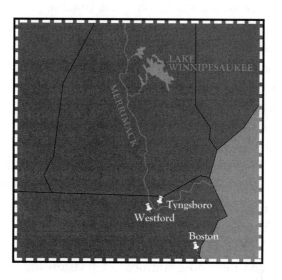

THE MERRIMACK RIVER AND ADJACENT WATER BODIES

"Wow. That's pretty accurate."

"The only detail that's a bit off is that the carving makes it look like the river hooks further north than it really does. But I think that's because the boulder is round and the artist was trying to carve a two-dimensional map, so some of the curves appear exaggerated." She smiled. "Wait until you see this."

Climbing atop the rock, she moved to the part of the boulder furthest from the street and brushed away more debris to expose a lobster-shaped indentation in the stone. At the top, on the northern side, three finger-like grooves — the lobster head and its two claws — protruded from the main part of the hollowed depression.

He joined her atop the boulder. "Hey, that's Lake Winnipesaukee. Those three fingers at the top are the bays. I used to go to summer camp up there."

She pointed to another indentation to the west of Winnipesaukee. "Recognize that?" she asked.

"Newfound Lake, maybe Lake Sunapee?"

"I think Newfound. Look," she said, brushing away a few pine needles, "here's the Pemigewasset River, flowing down to join the Winnipesaukee River to form the Merrimack."

The carving was extraordinarily accurate, especially if it was as old as it looked. Another remarkable artifact. And potentially another piece to the puzzle. He snapped some pictures with his digital camera. "So how does it fit in with Prince Henry?"

"Well, as I said, he almost certainly would have traveled on the Merrimack." She pointed at the bottom of the hook in the river. "This is Tyngsboro, the closest spot to Westford on the Merrimack. I reckon they carved the map in this boulder so they could find their way." She jumped off the boulder, walked around to the side. "Have a look at this."

He followed her and examined a television-size stone on the ground a few feet from the boulder.

"This chunk fell away when the boulder split." She pointed to a notch in the main rock. "See the groove here. It's part of the map."

Rubbing at the groove, his finger slid into a hole where the groove ended. He dug the dirt away. "Any idea what this is?"

They both stared at a triangular shaped hole, rounded at its corners, about the size of a half-dollar. "No. I never noticed that before."

He took out his pocket knife, dropped to his knees and dug out more of the dirt. "It's about three inches deep."

"Might it be just a quarry hole?" She joined him on the ground as he snapped a few pictures.

"I don't think so. It's not the right shape for a modern drill bit and it's rough on the inside. A modern drill bit would leave a smooth surface. But it's definitely manmade. Somebody put it here for a reason."

They studied the hole for a few seconds, considering its import, Cam acutely aware of Amanda's gentle breathing only a few inches from his cheek. He could happily have stayed there all afternoon.

But the world had other ideas.

A beige Crown Victoria cruised slowly up the road toward them, visible through the brush separating them from the street. The car braked before continuing past. The tinted front windows were illegal in Massachusetts without a special permit. Cam tapped Amanda on the arm, gesturing toward the car with his chin. Another car, this one a dark blue Lincoln Town Car, approached from the other direction.

"That's it. Let's get out of here."

"Into the woods?" she asked, scrambling to her feet.

"Yes." They edged away. Something in the back of his mind was bouncing around, forcing itself to the surface of his consciousness like an air bubble on a deep water dive. Something about the Boston University Corporate Center they passed just before arriving at the Map Stone site.

The bubble burst to the surface.

"Follow me." He took her hand and they ran deeper into the woods, up an incline, toward the Boston University site. It was now used for corporate training but the land originally housed the Tyng Mansion, built in the late 1600s. According to local legend the Mansion and four neighboring houses were interconnected by underground tunnels. The tunnels, which ran down to the Merrimack River, were used by the early settlers to escape Indian raids. While mountain biking through the woods a few years earlier a fellow rider had shown him the tunnels and related the legend.

He peered through the trees, elbowing aside branches as he ran. "I think it's back this way, set in a mound."

They pushed deeper into the woods. Amanda grabbed his shoulder and pulled him to a stop. "Listen, I hear something."

They arched their heads, trying to listen between panting breaths. "There's someone up ahead."

She scrunched her face. "Are you certain? I hear them from behind."

"Great." He grimaced. "Guess I better find that tunnel."

He visualized the trail map, oriented himself to the Map Stone, replayed the ride in his mind. Down a long slope, across the fall line, past a pond, then a sharp turn....

"This way. The tunnel opening should be right up here."

They pushed ahead, Cam sprinting to a raised mound covered by leaves and dirt and pine needles. He dropped to his knees and used a large branch to prod along the bottom of the raised earth. He hit a hard object and dug some dirt away with his hands, revealing a fieldstone set into the side of the mound. "Quick, come help me."

They scraped more dirt away, exposing a two-foot-square wall of fieldstones.

"Are they mortared?" she asked.

"No," he grunted, muscling the top one off and rolling it aside. A waft of dank, sulfurous air enveloped them, the flatulence of Mother Earth. "Guess it hasn't been open in a long time."

They pushed a few more stones aside, Amanda surprising him with her strength. He wondered where the tunnel would lead, or even if it was passable.

"We should leave some stones right by to close the hole from the inside," she said.

Nodding, he reached out to retrieve the smallest of the stones before freezing in fear.

"You're a difficult man to find, Mr. Thorne."

Crouching, he spun on his heel and looked up to see Monsignor Marcotte staring down at him, flanked by four twenty-something guys in jeans and rugby shirts. Marcotte wore a long black leather jacket instead of his velvet robe and collar. He looked more like a wise guy than a priest.

Cam shut his eyes. *The Monsignor.* It all made sense. The cleric was the common thread—he had known about the Gendrons' problem with McLovick, he had conveniently appeared on the scene just after the Bobcat blew up, he had recommended that Cam contact Amanda, he had been in contact with Lieutenant Poulos. Now, somehow, he had tracked them here.

Cam played for time, half his mind engaging the Monsignor while the other half searched for an escape plan. "Apparently not difficult enough," he responded, edging closer to Amanda.

The Monsignor smiled at Cam and Amanda, motioned to his posse. "Give them room to stand up." He turned to Amanda. His eyes radiated the same serenity and warmth Cam had noticed during their first meeting. "I am sorry we are meeting under such ... strained circumstances." He held his hands together in front of his crotch, like a mourner at a funeral, and took a deep breath. "I am sure you both are wondering why unknown men are attempting to abduct, or even kill, you. Perhaps I can shed some light on this."

Cam eyed the tunnel opening. They had successfully removed most of the stones. They could dive for it, try to outrun this odious priest and his henchmen. But he had no way to signal Amanda of his plan. And if he went first, there was no way she could fight them off and join him.

He glanced at the tunnel a final time, turned away and reached for Amanda's hand. She squeezed his and smiled bravely. Together they faced the Monsignor.

✝   ✝   ✝

"We are returning to Saint Catherine's Church. We will talk when we get there," the Monsignor announced. Otherwise they rode in silence in the Lincoln Town Car, Cam and Amanda crammed together in the back seat between two of the Monsignor's men.

Cam forced himself to stay patient. The man to his left, who had been tense and alert as they walked back through the woods, had begun to relax. In fact, he looked no older than a college student. The longer Cam remained calm, the longer it appeared he was not a risk to flee or fight, the more likely he would be to have the element of surprise on his side. If he and Amanda could break away from their captors, he was confident they could outrun them. Again. Unless, of course, the Monsignor chose to chase them with bullets this time.

Fifteen minutes later they pulled into the front driveway of a sprawling, multi-gabled, brownstone church. "Please escort our guests to the basement," the Monsignor ordered. "I will join them there shortly."

The two young men from the Town Car ushered them through the massive mahogany front door. As the lead man opened the door with a pair of fingers, its weight perfectly balanced on the hinges, Cam wondered at the audacity of the Monsignor. Not only was he bringing his prisoners to his church, he wasn't even bothering to bring them in a back door.

They wound their way around the sanctuary and down some stairs to a windowless, blue-carpeted meeting room with a series of cheap, religious-themed paintings on the walls. The men motioned for them to take seats around a rectangular mahogany table, closed the door and left them alone. The room smelled of heating oil and was inordinately warm, as if an old furnace was cranking on the other side of one of its walls.

"Any chance they left that door unlocked?" Amanda asked.

"What's that expression? A snowball's in hell."

"Appropriate."

The door opened and Monsignor Marcotte, resplendent again in his green-trimmed velvet robe, entered in and offered a kind smile. "I'm aware of what happened to your dog." He bowed his head in sympathy.

Cam clenched his fists. Would they suffer a similar fate? "Look, cut the bullshit, all right? You found us, you have us, we know we can't escape. But spare us your whole sympathy act."

The Monsignor's brow furrowed, as if he seemed truly surprised by Cam's comment. But Cam wasn't fooled—he had seen the whole lying priest act before. Marcotte stood and paced partway around the table before sitting again opposite them. He shook his head slowly. "I am sorry. Truly sorry. I owe you both a tremendous apology." He focused his serene, clear blue eyes first on Cam, then on Amanda, and ran his fingers through his well-coiffed gray hair. "You are not my … prisoners … here." His mouth contorted as if the word tasted rancid on his tongue. "You are free to go at any time." He stood again, walked over to the door and opened it. "Truly."

They exchanged glances. Something didn't add up. "You mean we can leave? Right now?" Cam challenged.

"Yes," the Monsignor nodded gravely.

"Then why the whole chase through the woods over in Tyngsboro?"

The cleric sighed. "I have left numerous messages for you, both with your cousin and with Lieutenant Poulos. But you have not returned my calls. I have urgent information for you and it seemed like tracking you down was the only way to deliver it. We chased you," he shrugged, turning his palms to the sky in exasperation, "because, well, because you ran from us."

"How do you explain this room?" Amanda swept the room with her arm.

"I thought you would prefer to meet down here, away from windows and prying eyes. I meant the room as a sanctuary, not a prison. Again, you may leave at any time. But I do hope you stay—we have much to discuss."

"So that wasn't you chasing us in Newport? And at the McDonald's?" Cam asked.

The Monsignor shook his head, a distasteful look on his face. "Absolutely not."

He wasn't sure what to believe. But why would the priest lie now that he had them in his custody? "So how did you find us?"

"One of my parishioners lives in Tyngsboro, across the street from the Map Stone. I asked her to call if she saw anyone. When she phoned, I raced over with a few of our youth counselors."

Cam glanced at Amanda. She seemed to be thinking the same thing he was. Either the Monsignor was telling the truth, in which case he had gone to a lot of trouble just to have this conversation with them, or he was lying, in which case they were his captors and really had no choice but to listen to him anyway. "So what's this urgent information?"

Marcotte brought his hands together as if praying, rested his chin on them as he spoke. "First of all, are you aware I am a theology professor at the College of Holy Cross, in Worcester?"

"No."

"I am fortunate to be able to both minister and pursue my interests in education and history. One of the ... uncomfortable ... subjects in academia these days, especially in the theology field, is the study of Templar history." He offered a sheepish shrug. "A colleague of mine likened the study of the Templars to a kind of academic pornography. Everyone is fascinated by the subject but nobody wants to get caught with their nose in the book."

Cam smiled. Not a bad line for a priest.

"Having said that, the Templars are a vital part of medieval history. Their impact can't simply be ignored." He smiled at Amanda, then turned back to Cam. "I'm curious, what did Ms. Spencer tell you was the treasure the Templars may have brought to the New World?"

Cam summarized: Perhaps they brought religious artifacts, perhaps ancient knowledge, perhaps gold and silver. Perhaps all three.

"If you have something to add, please do so." He dropped his hands to the table. "I'm in way over my head here. Everyone but me seems to be an expert in medieval history. I feel like I'm trying to do a crossword puzzle in a language I don't speak."

Marcotte smiled. "In fact, I do have something to add. Do you remember the name of the two families identified in *The Da Vinci Code* as carrying the bloodline of Jesus?" he asked, referring to the popular 2004 novel by Dan Brown theorizing that Mary Magdalene was the wife of Jesus and bore his children.

Amanda shrugged. "I read it when it was first released, before I left London. I don't recall the names." Cam didn't remember either.

"And you haven't reread it since?" the cleric asked.

"No. Why?"

The Monsignor smiled. "That explains it. If you had, you would have immediately recognized one of the names. Remember, the book is fiction but it is based on historical sources. One of the bloodline families was Plantard." He leaned forward in his chair. "The other was St. Clair."

"*Sinclair,*" Amanda whispered, her eyes wide. "Cam, I showed you the picture of Sir William's tombstone, Prince Henry's grandfather, the name spelled *St. Clair*. They Anglicized their name when they moved to Scotland. But it's the same family."

"Wait a second." Cam's neck tingled. "Our Prince Henry, who came to America and carved the Knight, is part of the Jesus bloodline?"

✝   ✝   ✝

Amanda was the first to break the silence that had enveloped the church basement after Cam's comment. "I knew there was something the Consortium wasn't telling me."

The Monsignor smiled kindly. "I have a feeling there are a number of things the Consortium is hiding." His eyes shifted from Amanda to Cam. "From all of us."

She frowned. "I hadn't even heard of Prince Henry when I read *The Da Vinci Code*. But I should have made the connection."

"Don't be hard on yourself. Brown only mentioned the names a couple of times in the book. Most people don't remember them. Without any context, they mean nothing. They're just names."

Cam didn't share Amanda's frustration. He never saw this one coming. He simply didn't have enough experience and background in the subject to make these types of connections. On the other hand, *The Da Vinci Code* was fiction. "How do we know the author didn't just come up with the St. Clair name by happenstance? And are you just assuming this Jesus bloodline theory is true? Last I checked, the Vatican wasn't exactly going along with the idea."

"I think we can all agree that the Vatican responded in the only way it could—denial," Marcotte said. "But for the purposes of understanding the Sinclair family and its history, we need to consider the possibility that the bloodline theory is valid." The Monsignor paused, waiting for disagreement, before continuing. "Brown got his ideas from a book published in the 1980s called *Holy Blood, Holy Grail*. In fact, the authors of that book sued Brown, accused him of stealing their ideas. Anyway, *Holy Blood, Holy Grail* names the Sinclairs, along with a few other families, as carrying the Jesus bloodline. These families descend from the Merovingians, a dynasty that ruled present-day France and Germany in the fifth through eighth centuries, the Dark Ages. The Merovingians trace their ancestry back to Mary Magdalene, to when she arrived in France after fleeing Jerusalem. For those who believe the Jesus bloodline theory, it's pretty much a given that in medieval times the Sinclair clan was a major branch of the Jesus family tree."

"You're talking 12 or 13 centuries," Cam countered. "The family tree by then would have been a forest—there must have been thousands of Jesus heirs. How can you single out the Sinclairs?"

"You're not thinking in ancient terms. In the Dark Ages and medieval times, royal families were very careful to keep their bloodlines pure. Family trees looked more like vines, circling back on themselves, sometimes even at the risk of choking off life." He stood, retrieved a book off a side table and opened to a marked page. "Here's a quote from Niven Sinclair, modern patriarch of the Sinclair clan: 'When I was studying our family history, I reached a point when I could almost predict who was going to marry whom. Just as we returned to root stock with our Aberdeen Angus cattle, the Sinclairs did this every third generation. Many marriages were annulled on the grounds of consanguinity but were 'restored' after paying the Church money.'"

"In other words, they married their cousins," Amanda said.

"Correct. And they did so seemingly for a purpose, even against the laws and norms of the day. So the number of direct heirs would actually have been fairly small. As leader of the entire Sinclair clan, it is safe to conclude that Prince Henry carried as much Jesus blood as any man alive." Marcotte took a deep breath. "So, to sum up, not only do we have the Knights Templars fleeing the Church, escaping to America with their treasures but we have them being led by Prince Henry Sinclair, purportedly heir to the Jesus bloodline."

After allowing his words to sink in, the cleric leaned forward and narrowed his eyes. "Could it be that one of the things Prince Henry transported was a genealogical record, evidence that Jesus' bloodline lived on in the Sinclair line?"

Amanda slapped the table. "Yes. That makes perfect sense. If such a record did exist, of course they would be concerned for its safety. The New World would be a ideal spot for Prince Henry to hide it—"

"Because nobody else knew how to get here," Cam interjected.

The Monsignor nodded. "Exactly. The Church would kill—literally—to suppress such a genealogy, especially during medieval times. And Prince Henry would have gone to great lengths to preserve it because it established his family's holy bloodline."

Cam eyed Marcotte. The lawyer in him wanted to slow this down a bit, make sure they weren't getting ahead of themselves. It was one thing for Dan Brown and others to write that Jesus had heirs. But for a priest to be so matter-of-fact about it seemed odd. "Monsignor, do you believe the bloodline story?"

He pressed his hands together, holding them under his chin as if in prayer. After a few seconds he took a deep breath and pulled a folder from his briefcase on the floor. "In fact, I do. It would have been highly unusual for Jesus, as a Jewish male and a direct descendant of King David, not to marry and have children at an early age — "

"Wait a second," Cam interrupted. "What about the virgin birth? How can Jesus be part of King David's line? How can he be part of *any* line?" Cam himself didn't believe Jesus was the son of God. But he wasn't wearing a priest collar.

"True," the Monsignor smiled. "But at the time Jesus was a young man, it was *believed* he was the son of Mary and Joseph and therefore part of King David's line. Joseph never denied paternity so legally Jesus was his son and part of his line. In fact, the Book of Matthew traces Jesus' Davidic line through Joseph while the Book of Luke traces it through Mary. His dual Davidic lineage, on both his mother's and father's side, played a large part in Jesus' acceptance by the populace as the Savior. And as I said, the norms of the time would have required a male of royal lineage to marry young and continue his line."

"Okay," Cam conceded.

"But you asked me about Jesus' heirs, not his own conception. And I said I believe he did indeed procreate. As a priest, as a man who preaches faith over reason, I would like to believe otherwise. But as a scholar, I have reached a point in my life where I cannot ignore the evidence. For example, Bernard de Clairvaux, a 12th-century Cistercian monk and one of the most powerful men in the history of Christiandom, referred to Mary Magdalene as the 'Bride of Christ' in his Sermon 57."

Amanda interrupted. "Wait a second. When I was in grammar school the nuns all wore wedding rings and referred to themselves as brides of Christ. But nobody took it literally."

The Monsignor spread his hands. "Of course. But please, I have studied these matters for decades. Bernard did not choose his words lightly—when he said bride, he meant bride in the literal sense." He shrugged. "But you are right to be skeptical. Perhaps this will be more convincing."

He slid a photograph across the table. "This is a stained glass window in Kilmore Church in Western Scotland. It was built in 1906 so it's not all that old but, again, it reflects the traditions and beliefs of the people. The window shows Jesus holding hands with a pregnant Mary Magdalene."

KILMORE CHURCH STAINED GLASS WINDOW

Cam studied the window. There was no doubt the bearded, haloed figure was Jesus. "How do you know it's Mary Magdalene with him?" Cam asked.

"Long red hair and a green gown — these are historical attributes of the Magdalene." Marcotte smiled and spread his hands. "Besides, the caption along the bottom says so."

Cam squinted. "So it does."

"She clearly has a bun in the oven," Amanda said. "Not much room for interpretation there."

"And their right hands are clasped in the universal symbol of matrimony," the Monsignor concluded.

"Legend is more historical than fact, because fact tells us about one man and legend tells us about a million men," Cam whispered, recalling the flier promoting the Westford Knight speech at the library.

Amanda looked at him. "What was that?"

"Nothing. Just something I read."

"Those that believe in the bloodline," Marcotte continued, "believe that Mary gave birth to Jesus' daughter, Sarah, and that they lived in southern France. It is there that the bloodline was nurtured and protected. Even today, the cult of Mary Magdalene is strong in the region. For obvious reasons, the Church rejects the whole Sarah legend." Marcotte slid another image across to them. "This is a carving from Royston Cave, in England. The cave was a secret Templar meeting spot and its walls are covered with carvings displaying Templar legend and symbolism. Probably 14th century, after they were outlawed. This one shows Jesus, Mary Magdalene and Sarah — by the way, the name Sarah, fittingly, means 'princess' in Hebrew. The three figures are surrounded by ancient fertility symbolism, in case the message wasn't already clear. It is apparent that the Templars, at least, believed in the bloodline theory."

ROYSTON CAVE CARVING

They studied the image. "How come this stuff never came out before?" Cam asked.

"In fact, it has been debated for centuries among theologians. In the end, I think the local legends and traditions tell the true story. Written history reflects the beliefs or opinions or agenda of the writer. Local legends and tradition are more universal, less malleable — as you said, they tell us the beliefs of millions. They are often the most accurate versions of history."

Marcotte faced Amanda. "Getting back to the matter at hand, my guess is that the Jesus bloodline is why this Consortium of yours is comprised of so many families that descend from Prince Henry. They not only want to prove their ancestor was first to America, they also want evidence that they descend from Jesus himself."

"They want to locate the genealogy," Amanda breathed. "They reckon Prince Henry buried it in America."

"Exactly. And I believe that, as much as the Consortium wants to find this genealogy, the Church even more so wants it to remain buried. They have been able to limit the damage done by *The Da Vinci Code* by dismissing it as pop fiction. But hard evidence — a genealogy, for example — could shake the very foundation of the Church."

"Wow." Cam whistled. "So that's our treasure, that's what somebody doesn't want us to find. The Sinclair genealogy. The Jesus bloodline."

"I would not say for certain but I think it is a strong possibility. I have made a number of calls to colleagues, both here and abroad." The Monsignor smiled. "You may be surprised to learn that priests gossip like a bunch of old women. And based on what I'm hearing, I believe the people who are making life so miserable for you and Ms. Spencer — and who maimed your cousin and killed your dog and murdered Mr. McLovick — are affiliated with an orthodox faction of the Church."

"Opus Dei?" Cam asked.

The cleric smiled again. "Despite recent publicity, Opus Dei is not a militant group. I may not agree with much of their orthodoxy but I don't believe they are capable of this type of paramilitary operation."

"So then, whom?" Amanda pushed.

"Have you ever heard of the Legions of Jesus?" They shook their heads. "They are orthodox Catholic clergy based in Latin America. They played a large role in supporting the right-wing dictatorships of people like Pinochet in the late 20th century and have close ties to many of the paramilitary types still running around Latin America. Mostly they draw support from Catholic business tycoons. Recently they've become active in the U.S." The Monsignor paused. "They also have close ties to certain radical, orthodox factions within the Vatican."

Great — another cabal. Another connection between the Church and fascists. "Didn't the Vatican help a lot of the Nazis get out of Europe at the end of World War II?"

"Exactly, and it's related to this. Historians call it the Rat Line — sort of like a perverted version of the Underground Railroad, with the Church hiding Nazis and helping them get to Latin America. The Vatican was afraid of communism spreading and it thought the Nazis would be a good counter-balance to the Communists in Latin America. A lot of the Nazis became advisors to the Latin dictators, helping them with security and military strategy. The ties between the Vatican and the right-wing groups in South America have been strong ever since. They often do the Vatican's dirty work, sometimes without the Vatican even having to ask."

Cam swallowed. "You mean we're up against the Vatican?" He stared at the Monsignor, his eyes shifting involuntarily to the priest's collar. "And you're on our side?"

"I don't believe the Vatican is directly involved. At least not Vatican leaders. But there are ties between certain Vatican factions and the Legions of Jesus." Marcotte spread his hands. "Regarding the question of my allegiances, I have wrestled with my place in the Church often over the past few years, especially in light of the priest sex abuse cases. It was difficult to maintain my faith in light of such ... un-Christian behavior by both the priests and the Church hierarchy. But in the end, I still believe the Church does more good than harm, still does the work of Jesus in many parts of the world, still offers faith and comfort and peace to millions of people." He smiled. "In many ways, I feel like many Americans disillusioned by our foreign policy. I am embarrassed and disappointed. But I'm not ready to up and move to Canada yet. I feel like I can do more good by staying with the Church, to try to effect change from within."

He continued. "So, regarding things like the possibility of a Jesus bloodline, as a Jesuit and an educator I don't agree with keeping these types of secrets." He explained that the Jesuit order often took liberal positions that didn't align with the strict teachings of the Vatican. "You, Mr. Thorne, saw firsthand in the priest sex abuse scandal what happens when an institution like the Church operates in secret."

The Monsignor sighed. "In any event, I believe in open, honest discourse. If the Church is built on faulty dogma, let us address it head on. If Jesus married and had a child, so what?" He shook his head. "Is the Church so vulnerable, so morally precarious, that it cannot deal honestly with its history? I believe such an exercise would strengthen the Church, allow it to distance itself from the sins of the past and empower it to perform truly Christian works here, today."

Rising to his feet, the Monsignor stared down at them. "However, I also realize that you two have found yourselves in a mess not of your own making. If you wish, I can make some calls, try to get word to this ... paramilitary team ... that you have called off your search, that you are willing to allow these treasures, whatever they are, to remain buried."

Cam studied the Monsignor. Marcotte was a college professor as well as a monsignor. But was he really that well connected? Perhaps they were wrong to trust him.

He seemed to read Cam's thoughts. "I understand your suspicions. Remember that six-degrees-of-separation theory that went around back in the nineties, that every person on earth can be linked together through six others? Well, in the Catholic religious community it's more like three or four degrees. As I said earlier, priests gossip like old women. Everyone knows someone who knows someone. I'm sure I could reach the right people. I think they might be convinced to let you be."

"You *think*? We're just supposed to go back home and hope that nobody sneaks in during the middle of the night and covers our face with a pillow? Even if we wanted to give this up, and I'm not sure I'm willing to just let it go, we'd need a better guarantee than that."

The Monsignor ran a hand through his hair. "Unfortunately, I can make no promises. As I said, this is a sensitive issue for the Church. I am fairly certain that the Vatican does not know where this genealogy is buried, or even if it actually exists. But I do know they are not willing to sit around idly and be surprised by it being found. Before the internet, there was little risk of anyone putting the pieces of this Prince Henry puzzle together, little chance of anyone actually finding anything. Now, anyone with internet and a GPS can try to connect the dots and search for treasures. At some point, someone will stumble upon something the Church would prefer to remain buried, such as the genealogy. Which is why there are certain factions in the Vatican who believe they can't allow any treasure hunting at all. Witness Mr. McLovick and your cousin Brandon."

Cam looked again at Amanda. Her green eyes hardened and she nodded slightly. "Well, even with assurances, which it seems like you can't give," Cam said, "I can't just let this go." He had hoped to track down the maggots that attacked Brandon and killed Pegasus, hopefully send them to jail for the rest of their lives. But he couldn't send 'certain factions in the Vatican' to jail. At least in the sex abuse cases, there had been actual predator priests that could be imprisoned. All he could do here was help expose whatever it was they were trying so hard to keep quiet. Hardly a pound of flesh. But better than just walking away. Especially because just walking away wasn't really an option. He removed Pegasus' collar from his pocket and twined his fingers through it. "These people are out of control; they need to be stopped. And the best way to do it is to expose their dirty little secrets."

"It's not such a little secret, as you know."

What had he gotten himself, and Amanda, into? He was like the dog chasing the mail truck—what would he do once he caught it? They were doing battle with one of the most powerful entities in world history. "Holy crap," he breathed.

"Indeed," said Monsignor Marcotte. "And you need to be very careful not to step in it."

✛   ✛   ✛

Salazar bowed his head in the empty church, crossed himself out of respect for his mother. To be fair, the virgin birth and resurrection stories were no more outlandish than many Native American myths. In both cases it was all about faith. Which was why he did not want Gloria immersing Rosalita, young and impressionable, in the well of Catholicism. His Narragansett ancestors had almost been exterminated by followers of Jesus Christ. He himself had witnessed the suffering his employers inflicted in the name of Catholicism. And the Church was nearly medieval in its treatment of women.

On the other hand, could two billion Christians be wrong? To be safe, he bowed his head and offered a prayer to the Virgin Mary, asking her to intercede and beseech God to forgive his sins. *And if I am not worthy for intercession, I pray you intercede on Rosalita's behalf. She is innocent and pure. Her hands are not stained in blood as mine are.*

Moving to the vestibule, he phoned Reichmann. He had not learned anything in the hour since the priest led Thorne and the girl from the car into the church. Where he took them within the church, and for what purpose, he did not know. But it was best to take credit for this information now, before Reichmann learned of it through other sources. "I found Thorne and the girl. They're at Saint Catherine's Church in Westford, with a priest. He's wearing a robe, like a monsignor."

"With a priest? I thought you said they were heading north toward Montreal."

"They were. Then they turned around."

Reichmann sighed loudly. "Perhaps it is time for me to leave Argentina." He cleared his throat. "Just so we are clear, Señor Salazar. You are to eliminate Thorne and the girl at the first opportunity."

✝   ✝   ✝

Still sitting around the table in the church basement, they debated Cam and Amanda's next move.

"I think it's naïve for us to assume the Legions of Jesus won't find out you were here," Marcotte said. "Too many people saw you. So let's turn it to your advantage a bit."

"You're willing to help us?" Cam asked.

"I've devoted my life to the Church. And I've sworn allegiance to the Holy Father. But I don't believe the Pope knows anything about this. It's like in this country—sometimes the CIA or the military do things the President would never authorize and has no idea is going on. My allegiance is to the Pope, not some extreme faction, some cabal, operating out on the fringe."

"Okay. Thanks."

"So, here's what I propose. I'll send a couple of youth counselors back to the Map Stone site to retrieve your Subaru. Once they return, I'll leave you alone for a moment and you make a show of slipping out and racing away. Then I'll make a couple of calls, calls that will likely be channeled back to whoever is giving orders to the Legions of Jesus."

It was a good plan because it hid the fact the Monsignor was helping them. "What will you tell them?"

The Monsignor spread his hands. "Why, the truth, of course. That I tracked you down because I was concerned for your safety. That I warned you to abandon this quest. That you refused and slipped away." He smiled. "And that you are heading to Nova Scotia because you believe the treasures are buried on Oak Island."

They weren't going to Oak Island. "That might buy us a day or two. Thanks."

"Anything involving Nova Scotia makes the Church nervous. In addition to the Prince Henry connection, in the early 1600s Nova Scotia was called Arcadia, later shortened to Acadia. Mary Magdalene, when she first fled Jerusalem, took refuge in the Greek city of Arcadia before heading to France. So Arcadia, historically, is where the bloodline goes to escape persecution and seek sanctuary. The Church knows there is great meaning in names."

"How do you know the Arcadia name isn't just a coincidence?" Cam asked. Not that he believed it himself.

"The explorer Verrazzano, who coined the Arcadia name, made it clear that it was named after the Greek city."

"But that doesn't mean the Legions of Jesus will just focus all their attention on Nova Scotia," Amanda said.

"Agreed. Even if there's only a small chance this genealogy exists, the extremists will do anything they can to eliminate any risk. The damage to the Church would be cataclysmic. It's not just about doctrine and dogma and Church teachings. It's also about credibility and trust—the Vatican has been insisting that the story of Jesus and Mary Magdalene having a child is bunk. If it blows up in their face, their credibility is shot." He lowered his voice. "Forget the whole infallibility of the Pope thing. They'll have trouble just getting the parishioners to believe he's not a buffoon, advised by a bunch of charlatans."

"That's a pretty harsh assessment."

Marcotte shrugged. "It all goes back to not telling the truth in the first place. You look pretty silly when the world proves you wrong. Especially when you're wearing a cloak of infallibility."

CHAPTER 8

Cam and Amanda 'escaped' from Monsignor Marcotte as planned and raced the Subaru north up Route 3 into New Hampshire. At a rest area south of Manchester they made small talk for a few minutes with a woman working the information desk before asking her for directions to Nova Scotia. Reversing course, they exited the highway and headed south back to Massachusetts on smaller, country roads. If the Legions of Jesus were as diligent as the Monsignor expected, they would find the information desk employee.

Cam sighed. "So, do you trust the Monsignor?"

"I suppose so. He had us in his grasp and let us go. He may have a hidden agenda, but I can't imagine what it might be."

"I agree. For now I'm inclined to trust him."

"Well, here's another question: Has he reached the correct conclusion? Do you really reckon the Vatican, or even a fanatical faction, is so bothered by the possibility of a genealogy that it would resort to murder?"

"You don't?" Cam had no doubt.

"The Monsignor said it would be cataclysmic for the Church if the Sarah legend is proven to be true. I'm not certain I agree. The Catholic Church is built on faith, not reason. None of it — the conception story, Christ's resurrection, the concept of Communion — is rational."

"Yeah, but —"

"Let me finish. Since faith is not rational, why should a piece of hard evidence such as a genealogy change people's faith? It would be like attacking a ghost with a butcher knife. Faith and reason exist on separate spiritual planes."

"I hear what you're saying. And maybe a generation ago you might be right. But the sex abuse scandal really changed things, at least in America. Attendance went way down; more importantly from the Church's perspective, contributions went way down. Some archdioceses had to declare bankruptcy. People are no longer willing to just blindly accept what the Church says."

"I don't know, Cameron. There are still tens of millions of active Catholics in the States."

"Sure there are. But many of them are now questioning the authority of Church leaders for the first time — staging sit-ins to prevent church closings, raising money outside of the Church structure to support local Catholic causes. I really think that's why *The Da Vinci Code* was so popular — if it had come out a generation ago nobody would have paid attention to it. But people today are ready to question institutions like their church and their government."

"I suppose we'll have to agree to disagree then."

"You can disagree with me. But I think you'll agree we should defer to the Monsignor's judgment on something like this. And he thinks this Legions of Jesus group is after us."

She took a deep breath, let it out slowly. "I suppose we have no choice but to assume he's correct. And I will concede that the Church has been known to brutally counter even mild threats."

Relieved to have found some common ground, Cam opened the window and stuck his hand out to check the temperature. Still mild and no sign of rain. At least the weather was cooperating. "Sorry to do this but I don't think we can risk checking into a motel tonight. In order to be credible, Monsignor Marcotte had to give a description of our car and license plate number. How do you feel about camping?"

"It all depends. How many sleeping bags do you have?" She arched an eyebrow.

He smiled, not sure how to respond but pleased she wasn't sulking after their disagreement. He was drawn to her, rash and all. Yet the last few days had been surreal and unique. For both of them. He had participated in a psychology experiment in college in which pairs of people of the opposite sex were placed in stressful, dangerous situations. Many of them developed an intense attraction to one another. Apparently the adrenaline produced by danger caused the same type of physiological changes in body chemistry as did feelings of attraction and love.

A shopping mall appeared ahead, saving him from answering the sleeping bag question directly. "We can grab some supplies here."

A dozen years ago — heck, a couple of years ago — he would have shared his sleeping bag with Amanda without hesitation. But there was something about her that gave him pause, that made him want to make sure whatever relationship they might end up having rested on a stronger foundation than a shared fear of a Vatican-fringe hit squad.

✢ ✢ ✢

While Cam went into the strip mall to purchase supplies, Amanda used his TracFone to ring London on Beatrice's secure satellite phone. If she and Cam were going to battle Vatican factions, they would need some aid. Perhaps the Consortium could offer it. Cam agreed it was now worth a try.

It was early evening here, nearly midnight in England. Beatrice picked up on the first ring.

"Amanda, are you well? Where have you been? I've been worried sick about you."

"I'm fine. Well, other than nearly being killed by a Vatican-fringe paramilitary group."

"Pardon?"

"I know it sounds daft. But it seems we're on the verge of a major discovery involving Prince Henry. And they are intent on stopping us."

Beatrice was silent for a few seconds. "I think, dear, that I need to advise Mr. Babinaux." Leopold Babinaux was the Consortium chief, a grandfatherly type who presided over an international shipping empire with thousands of employees. Amanda had only met him a few times; somehow he always recalled her name.

"Very well. Put him on a three-way. I'll ring you back in five minutes."

She ended the call, took a deep breath and got out of the car to stretch her legs and get some air. She was both exhausted and more alive than she had been in years.

While waiting she gathered the garbage that had accumulated on the floor of the Subaru, mostly wrappings from the energy bars and peanut butter crackers Cam snacked on to maintain his sugar levels. In all likelihood the diabetes accounted for Cam still being single at 37. Most unmarried men at his age either had commitment issues, were ninnies or were queer. Cam's only issue seemed to be his diabetes. He had told her that until recently he never expected to live past his thirties, so naturally he dated women like ski-racer-Heidi who couldn't commit to a serious relationship. It wasn't as if Amanda was intent on hunting down a husband but it was nice to have finally met a fellow worth the chase.

Humming, she returned from the dumpster, checked her watch and pushed the redial button on her phone. Beatrice picked up on the first ring. "Amanda, I have Mr. Babinaux on a three-way."

Leopold Babinaux's tone was kind but grave. "It appears you have been rather engaged, Miss Spencer." He cleared his throat. "Please recount for us your ... adventures."

She began, describing Cam's meeting with the Gendrons, the explosion that injured Brandon and the car that tried to run down

Cam. "That's when he and I met. I assume you've listened to the tape of our conversation?"

"Yes. Mrs. Yarborough has summarized events until that point. But beyond that, we are in the dark."

"Yes, well, sorry about that."

"Not at all," he said kindly. "But, please, do not spare any details."

"First, the phone I have is a device called a TracFone. It's an untraceable mobile we purchased in an electronics store. Is there a possibility they could locate us now via the signal?"

Babinaux consulted with someone in the background and returned to the line. "You are correct to be concerned, but not to worry. You were wise to ring us on the satellite phone. Please continue."

"When I learned that McLovick had been killed, I didn't believe Cameron Thorne did it. And if he did not, I reckoned eventually he would find his way to Newport to view the Tower." She described how someone followed her there, how she and Cam eluded him and escaped again at the highway rest area.

"You are fortunate. I commend your resourcefulness."

"We feared they had tracked us again but it turned out to be Monsignor Marcotte trying to aid us. He believes this all relates to the Jesus bloodline, that some Vatican fanatics fear we're going to uncover evidence that the story of Sarah is true. A genealogy or some such thing. Which is why they're trying to stop us."

Babinaux cleared his throat. "Yes, we have had periodic contact with the Vatican over the years and I would say this Monsignor Marcotte is correct in his assessment. Certain Vatican officials are highly concerned about our efforts to validate the Prince Henry legend. They are not opposed to the legend itself but apparently are afraid of what we might find if we dig too deep — literally and figuratively. I do not know if Prince Henry possessed a genealogy of some kind. But I do know that this is the type of matter the

Vatican does not — in fact, cannot — take any chances on. They have informed us in no uncertain terms that they will take whatever action is necessary to prevent us from excavating around any of the Prince Henry sites."

That explained the Consortium's hesitancy to dig. "So that is why I rang you up — I need to understand this all better. I need the Consortium's assistance. I've been working for you for over a year but there are many secrets that haven't been shared with me, information I need to help unravel this mystery." She took a deep breath. "For example, why did you conceal from me that Prince Henry was the main heir to the Jesus bloodline?"

Beatrice responded. "As we discussed, dear, the protocols are clear on this: We are a self-selecting group. We do not share knowledge; knowledge shares itself with us. We did not conceal anything from you. I have no doubt that at some time you would have made the connections yourself. Be patient — a year really is very little time."

"Mrs. Yarborough," Babinaux interjected, "the current circumstances may call for an exception to be made to the protocols. Miss Spencer is in danger, as apparently are some of the Prince Henry sites themselves. I will consult with our senior council. But I can tell you this: It may very well be that the Vatican has more to fear even than the confirmation of the Jesus bloodline through Sarah."

"*More* to fear?" Amanda repeated.

"Yes." He took a deep breath. "I cannot yet give you specific details. But this much I can tell you: You are in grave danger and you must be extra vigilant and extra careful. When threatened, the Church sometimes forgets the teachings of Jesus Christ."

✢   ✢   ✢

Beatrice stayed on the line with Babinaux after Amanda hung up. "Originally I was concerned about Amanda and the solicitor digging and contaminating an important site. But now I feel the dangers are far more grave."

He cleared his throat. "Are you sure you are not overstating things?"

There it was again — the implication that she was unstable. The incident with Alberto, blown out of proportion by a bunch of do-gooder academic types, had come back to bite her again. Somehow a simple lovers quarrel had been twisted into accusations she had an unhealthy fixation on Alberto, as if somehow *she* was the unstable one in their relationship. He had carried on a six-year affair with her, promising to leave his wife as soon as the children were older, only to instead take up with an archeology student less than half his age. What did they expect her to do, invite them over for tea? The man was a louse, without an ounce of honor or dignity.

She swallowed. "No, I do not believe I am. As you well know, there are certain aspects about Prince Henry's expedition that are best not made public, matters that could sully his reputation forever."

This kind of strategic planning was her strength. It had been a game with Alberto — tracking and tormenting him and his little tartlet on visits to restaurants and theatres and weekend trysts. On one occasion she phoned ahead to cancel their lodging reserva-tions on a busy holiday weekend, forcing them to pass the night in his sedan. On another she snuck into Alberto's office prior to an archeology lecture on the topic of ancient practices of ritual necro-philia. She slipped an image of Alberto and the tramp, *in flagrante delicto*, into the slide projection for mid-lecture display. It was the talk of campus for weeks; students began referring to Alberto as Dr. Death. Harmless shenanigans aside, she was perfectly within her rights to enter his campus flat and retrieve her computer. She could not be blamed for his failure to print out a hard copy of his almost-completed treatise and research notes — the computer was hers, as were the floppy disks he used to back up his work. There was no law against deleting files from one's own computer or eras-ing one's floppies.

"Beatrice, we are a long way away from that scenario. I am more concerned about the safety of Ms. Spencer and her companion. They are on the run, in danger. They may need this information to protect themselves."

He was a businessman, not a historian. He did not understand that history needed to be finessed like a modern political campaign. Few Americans knew that Abraham Lincoln's plan to free the American slaves included exiling all members of what he called the Negro race and resettling them outside United States border. Few Italians were aware that Christopher Columbus was probably Portuguese or Spanish. Few Argentines realized that Evita Peron used money she raised for the poor to fund her lavish lifestyle. History is not truth — it records not what occurred but what is remembered.

"With all respect, sir, I disagree. They are being advised by a monsignor who is well-versed in medieval religious history. Amanda has knowledge of all the sites in and around New England. By all appearances this Cameron Thorne is quite capable. And now they are aware of the bloodline connection. If you agree to her request, if you break the protocols and share more information with them ... well, they could uncover secrets that are best left buried. We dare not risk endangering the legacy of Sir James and Prince Henry." And ruining decades of hard work — her hard work.

Soon after the university strong-armed her into the psychiatric evaluation which yielded the 'unhealthy fixation' diagnosis, a distant cousin offered her a job with the Consortium. She was already a bit of an expert on the exploits of Prince Henry, being a direct descendent on her father's side of Sir James Gunn, Prince Henry's lieutenant and the warrior memorialized by the Knight effigy. The position offered a respite from university life and drama and an opportunity to research Prince Henry — a neglected figure who played a central role in medieval history — from the American side. She took a sabbatical and never returned. In fact, she would be in

Westford today were it not for a follow-up psychiatric evaluation a year-and-a-half ago. A random headshrinker spent a couple of hours with her and concluded she had another 'unhealthy fixation,' this time with the Knight. The Consortium directors, aware of the Alberto episode, recalled her to London. The whole business was nonsense. What did they expect after more than two decades caring for the poor soul, alone and forgotten for centuries on the wrong side of the Atlantic? Of course she would take a personal interest in both his legacy and that of his lord. The truth was they were casting about for an excuse to put her out to pasture in favor of a younger girl who could bat her eyelashes and attract the attention of the simple-minded American news media.

"Wise counsel, Beatrice, much obliged. I will share it with the other directors."

She said goodbye. But Babinaux had already dismissed her.

She strode to the kitchen. Orkney leapt to the counter and watched her expectantly. Someone was in Westford, digging for hard evidence of Prince Henry's voyage while she was stuck an ocean away. The Consortium had for years contemplated archeological digs and excavations but had delayed and dawdled and vacillated. "What if we find nothing, or if the results are unfavorable?" one director asked. "Would that not undermine our cause?" Another argued that barristers never asked a question of a witness to which they do not already know the answer. "We should not dig until we know what we shall find," he counseled. The position reminded her of the simpleton who refused to enter the water until he first learned how to swim. The Consortium had turned conservative, content with the status quo. Well, now, the decision was out of their hands. For better or worse, someone else was trying to dig.

She snatched a clear plastic pharmacy bottle, wrestled the cap open and poured the small red pills down the drain. Sir James and Prince Henry needed *her*, not some chemically-lobotomized shell of her former self.

✝ ✝ ✝

Cam had purchased a sleeping bag for Amanda along with other supplies. They now continued south, following the back roads of New Hampshire.

"Really now," Amanda began, "Mr. Babinaux claims the Vatican may have more to fear than just proof of the Jesus bloodline."

"*More?*" Cam smiled. "What, did Jesus have two wives?"

She laughed. "I don't know what Babinaux was getting at. He said to ring Beatrice tomorrow. Assuming he receives permission from the other council members, she will illuminate the dark corners of this business for us."

He considered Babinaux's statement, tried to imagine what they might have stumbled upon that could be even worse news for the Vatican. He gave up after a few seconds. He simply didn't know enough about religion or Catholicism or medieval history.

"Speaking of tomorrow, what time is Eric Forsberg's lecture?" he asked.

"Brandon said four o'clock."

"You've been to these NEARA conferences before, right? Is it worth getting there early?"

"I reckon so. Most of the important sites in New England were uncovered by these NEARA folks. They are an interesting lot. As in any group, a few members have some rather unique ideas. Of course those are the folks who are most interesting."

"Unique?"

"The pyramids were built by aliens, that type of thing."

"Oh, that's not bad. I thought you were going to tell me there were people who believe this whole Prince Henry legend."

"I said unique," she smirked. "I didn't say they were lunatics."

He kept waiting to find some flaw in this attractive, vivacious woman. But other than the rash, there was nothing. And that was as close to nothing as you could get. He thought about her sleeping bag comment again. At some point tonight there would be that awkward moment when they would either climb into one bag together, or resist doing so. Either way, he didn't expect to get much sleep — he wasn't sure he'd be able to sleep with her resting only a foot or two away. And he definitely wouldn't sleep with her sharing his bag. But the day was beginning to darken and no amount of apprehension could stop the sun from setting. "We only have an hour before dusk so we should probably find a campsite."

He knew of a good mountain biking trail a couple of towns west of Westford that would not take them far out of their way and was accessible via an old logging road. The cops sometimes patrolled the area on the weekends and during the summer but they'd have no reason to check on it on a Tuesday night in September.

He found the trail and pitched the tent in the fading light while Amanda boiled water and pulled out a handful of pouches of freeze-dried food from his pack. "Let's see. Your choices are chicken teriyaki, chicken teriyaki or ... chicken teriyaki."

"I'll have the beef tenderloin."

They sat on a log while they ate, their food spread on a blanket in front of them, thankful that the wind kept the mosquitoes away. After a few bites, Amanda stood and reseated herself on a large rock opposite him. "I feel like I've spent the last two days looking at your profile, sitting in that car. I fancied seeing you head-on for a change."

"Phew. I thought it was because I hadn't showered."

"Actually, you showered this morning. Remember, I barged in on you in your towel. My only regret is that I didn't have a dollar bill to tuck inside."

"Wow, was that this morning? It feels like a month ago."

"Do you realize we've only known each other for three days? We met Sunday and today is Tuesday."

"Let's see. Three days — that's the acorn anniversary, right?" Smiling, he dropped to a knee, reached across and held out an acorn to her.

She accepted it gingerly, holding it to her heart with a theatrical flourish of her arms. "I'll cherish it forever."

The combination of standing to return to his log and her theatrics brought their faces to within inches of each other. Without thinking, he leaned in and kissed her lightly, his heart nearly exploding in his chest as her lips received his. He held the kiss a few seconds, her scent even more intoxicating than her smile. He pulled back only because he began to feel dizzy.

"Wow," he breathed, dropping back to one knee.

"Can I have seconds, please?" she asked, her neck stretched toward him.

✝   ✝   ✝

Salazar turned away as they kissed.

From his vantage point in a tree a hundred feet away, he could easily take them out with his assault rifle. Instead he slipped from his perch and hiked back to his car. They would have to come out of the woods in the morning the same way they went in. And he wasn't going to kill them yet anyway—the map on the boulder in Tyngsboro was no doubt an important clue but he still had no idea where the treasure was buried. Following Cam and Amanda remained his best strategy for finding it.

He phoned Reichmann, reaching him as he was about to board a plane for Miami en route to Boston. Rosalita had left a message with details about a play she was going to be in. If the mission went well, perhaps Reichmann would reward him with a little extra vacation.

"Have you eliminated them yet, Señor Salazar?"

"No." He was running out of excuses. At some point Reichmann would become suspicious. Then he would have all the vacation he wanted. "They left the church, then snuck back in. I assume you don't want me to kill them there."

A pause. "Very well. You have them under surveillance?"

"Yes."

"Then tomorrow will do."

Salazar reclined the front seat and closed his eyes, pleased with his decision to leave the woods. He didn't care about the comfort factor. But it would have been in poor taste to sit in the tree and gawk.

+   +   +

Cam moved in again, this time steadying himself better, and kissed Amanda hungrily. She slid off the rock into his arms and together they slumped onto the blanket, their bodies grinding against each other.

This is exactly what was not supposed to happen.

He stopped kissing her and instead buried his head in her hair, pulling her close to him, their breaths coming in short, sharp gasps. He needed her help, needed her as a partner to figure this all out and bring Brandon's and Pegasus's attackers to justice. What if their lovemaking was awkward or unfulfilling? How would they deal with it in the morning? It wasn't like they could just say goodbye and be on their way. They were stuck with each other.

Summoning every ounce of willpower, he pulled his body away from hers, kissed her gently on the forehead and took her hands in his. He sat, pulled her up with him, stared deep into her wide green eyes. He began to speak, found his throat was constricted, smiled and tried again. "I'm really, really in trouble here. I think, in my entire life, there's nothing I'd rather do more than just keep on kissing you but—"

She covered his mouth with her hand, gently. "Shush. You don't need to say anything more. I can see it in your eyes." She smiled. "Besides, I'm used to throwing myself at men and being rejected."

"Yeah, right."

She stood up. "We need chocolate."

"Chocolate?"

"Yes. If we're going to starve our libidos, we can at least indulge our appetites." She frowned. "Unless it's a problem with your diabetes."

"No, chocolate's fine. I just have to tweak my insulin." He smiled ruefully. "Actually, diabetes is the least of my problems right now." Standing, he adjusted his jeans and dug a couple of Snickers bars out of his pack. He sat down heavily on the blanket. "Are you sure this is going to work?"

As she tore open the wrapper, she nestled against him. "I'm actually hoping it doesn't."

CHAPTER 9

[Wednesday]

Somehow they made it through the night in separate sleeping bags, though Cam woke up hourly to peer across at Amanda's sleeping form. Just before dawn he awoke for good and found her asleep, facing him, breathing softly, her fingers interlaced with his. He gently removed his hand, splashed some cold water over his face and began to prepare breakfast.

A few minutes later Amanda soundlessly approached and embraced him tightly. Cam handed her a cup of coffee and a bowl of trail mix.

"Hey, your rash is fading."

They dropped to the blanket. "A bit. Now I just look like I have a horrid case of acne."

"That's what you get from eating all that chocolate."

She blew into the cup. "I'd be happy to pass on it tonight."

First they had to make it through the day. "I've been thinking about something. Monsignor Marcotte thinks the Vatican is worried we might find some kind of genealogy that will validate the whole Sarah as daughter of Jesus theory. But if that's the buried treasure, why would McLovick have been looking so hard for it?"

She swirled her coffee, as if looking inside for answers. "Assuming the Monsignor is correct, I suppose the simple answer is that the

Vatican might be mistaken. Marcotte said they feared we would dis-cover a genealogy but I don't reckon even they know for certain what is buried." She paused. "And the other possibility is that McLovick planned to ransom the genealogy back to the Church."

"Makes sense." He stood up. "Either way, we're not going to figure it out sitting in the woods. Once you're done with breakfast, we should hit the road. I want to hear what this Eric Forsberg guy has to say."

Amanda dumped her coffee on the ground. "I'm ready when you are."

+   +   +

Back in the Subaru, back on the road. This time heading to Fitchburg, an old mill town about 50 miles northwest of Boston out Route 2. It was Wednesday, the first day of the NEARA conference.

Cam watched as Amanda pulled down the visor mirror and worked to stuff her now-burgundy-colored hair under a baseball cap. "I attended their conference last year and I've likely escorted a number of the NEARA members to the Knight site."

"You think they'll recognize you?"

"Most folks seem to recall my hair. That and my accent."

"Well, just don't talk."

"Really, I'm planning not to. And the rash might actually be a blessing."

He glanced at a map and made a quick turn, still sticking to the back roads. "What exactly is it this NEARA group does?"

"The acronym stands for New England Antiquities Research Association. The members explore the woods, looking for rock formations and petroglyphs and cairns and stone chambers. They're interested in anything that predates the Colonists."

"I know a lot more about this than I did a few days ago. But I don't really feel any closer to figuring out where this treasure — this genealogy, if that's what it is — might be buried." He grabbed the

TracFone. "Which reminds me. I need to call Brandon, see what he's learned and how he's doing."

Brandon answered on the first ring. "Hey, I don't want to sound like your mother but you didn't call yesterday."

Cam blinked, a wave of guilt washing over him. "I didn't?"

"No, shithead, you didn't."

Brandon was sitting in a hospital bed with nothing to do but seethe about his fate and wait for Cam to call in so he could feel a bit useful. He needed to keep that in mind. "Wow. Sorry about that. I tried once but we were out of range," he fibbed. "Then I was getting chased through the woods."

"You all right?"

"Yeah, fine." Cam related their encounter with Monsignor Marcotte. "He thinks a radical faction of the Vatican is trying to keep us from digging around."

Brandon's voice rose. "Wait, he thinks the Vatican is behind this? They're the mother-fuckers who blew off my leg?"

"Not the Pope himself. Vatican hardliners."

"It was bad enough when I thought some treasure hunter did it." Brandon was Catholic, though not particularly observant. "But the friggin' Church?" His voice tailed off.

"Apparently they're worried we're going to find some kind of genealogy that proves this whole *Da Vinci Code* theory is true."

"So that's what this is all about." He took a deep breath. "Well, whatever they're trying to hide, you need to find it."

"We're trying, buddy."

His tone remained somber. "Did you say *we*? Does that mean that chick is still with you?"

"Yeah."

"Oh."

Driving around with someone like Amanda probably sounded pretty good to Brandon right now. Even with killers in pursuit. He tried to downplay it. "She's pretty much stuck in the car with me until we figure this all out. I think she's getting pretty sick of me. In fact, she may take me out before the Vatican gets another shot at me."

Amanda rolled her eyes.

"Well, whatever," Brandon said, exhaling. "Anyway, I've got some interesting stuff for you. As much as my dad keeps trying to tell me it's all bullshit, it's pretty cool. Even he's starting to come around."

"You mean he thinks we're on the right track?"

"I wouldn't go that far. But he did drive down to check out the Newport Tower yesterday. And he's been carrying around a big book about the Kensington Rune Stone. Anyway, I've been reading these books from the library. I'm a friggin' expert in Templar history now. They're some pretty intense dudes. Did you know they never bathed, never took off their loincloths? And some of these guys were living in the freakin' desert, sweating their balls off all day."

"Maybe that's why they were so feared in battle."

"Good point," Brandon chuckled.

"Good to hear you laughing. I know it must be tough."

"Yeah, well, anyway, do you guys know what this *Rex Deus* thing is?"

"Amanda told me about it. Something about a bloodline of high priests, traced back to Moses' brother. In fact, she tells me I'm part of the line myself."

"You? No way."

"Really. My mother is a Cohen."

"Un-fucking-believable. A couple of days ago you were nothing. Now you've got the hot girl and the royal blood." Cam pictured his cousin shaking his head. "Well," Brandon continued, "did you know that all nine of the original Knights Templar were part of this *Rex Deus* bloodline?"

Amanda leaned into the phone. "I did not. The organization I work for is obsessed with the *Rex Deus* line. A number of the members claim to descend from it. They believe it makes them royalty or something."

Brandon snickered. "Well, the joke's on them. They won't be so happy when they find out they're probably also related to old Cam here."

+   +   +

After stopping for an early lunch, Cam and Amanda reached Fitchburg around noon. They followed Brandon's directions to a hotel just off the highway in a wooded area away from the city's old industrial center.

"I'm not comfortable leaving the car in the parking lot," he said. "They may think we're up in Nova Scotia. But from what the Monsignor said, the Legions of Jesus can afford to have surveillance teams all over New England."

"I agree. I'm not certain it would occur to a group of paramilitary types from Latin America that we'd be at this conference — they probably have never heard of NEARA. But better safe than sorry."

He drove past the hotel and found an old dirt road. Thankful for the all-wheel drive and dry weather, he navigated along the rutted way and hid the Subaru in the brush. After filling a day pack with supplies they hiked back toward the hotel.

"I don't want to miss the Eric Forsberg talk," she said, "but I don't need to be hanging about all day where some bloke might recognize me." She pointed at a small shopping plaza. "Why don't I pick up some supplies. And your TracFone is almost empty of minutes — I'll look for another."

He turned to say goodbye and she met him lip-on-lip, pulling him tight to her. A car honked in approval as it drove by. After a few seconds, she pulled away and looked earnestly into his eyes, her hand still on his cheek. "You will not be rid of me quite that easily, Cameron Thorne." Grinning, she kissed him quickly again. "Very well, then. It's one o'clock now. Shall we meet at, say, three, at the hotel lobby?"

Cam killed the next two hours making small talk with the NEARA members and thumbing through the dozens of books displayed, most of which covered pre-Columbus exploration. Within this crowd, the prospect of Prince Henry exploring New England in the late 1300s seemed perfectly plausible, almost mundane. Sinclair was just one of many European visitors to our shores over the centuries.

One man had an interesting theory that helped explain the unwillingness of people like Rhonda Blank to consider the possibility of pre-Columbus contact. "It's a lot easier to demonize the Europeans when the imperialist Columbus is the target, not some peace-loving explorer from Scotland like Henry Sinclair. So the Politically Correct folks don't want to find evidence of any contact before Columbus. It would ruin their whole message about the evil European imperialists."

Cam once heard a political commentator describe a hot new political figure as a vessel into whom voters poured their hopes and dreams. He was beginning to think of Prince Henry the same way. To the Consortium group and other descendants, his fame and glory ran through their veins, added to their prestige and nobility. To the Scottish people, his explorations were heroic, a source of national pride. To treasure hunters like Alistair McLovick, his travels — and cargo — were the key to untold wealth. To the enemies of the Vatican, the evidence he left behind debunked the teachings of the Church. To the NEARA folks, he was just another link in the chain. And to Cam, he held the answer to the mystery of who maimed his cousin, killed his dog and tried to splatter him across the pavement.

✝   ✝   ✝

From behind the lectern, blond-haired Eric Forsberg commanded the room — tall, broad-shouldered, square-jawed, confident. About 40, Cam guessed. In another era he might have been a Viking chief. Today, according to the program, he was a former star college hockey player who worked with a forensic geologist named Scott

Wolter. Wolter had carved out an expertise for himself in the field of studying and analyzing construction materials — stone, masonry, concrete — to determine structural soundness and integrity. In other words, if a structure failed — for example, when Boston's Big Dig tunnel collapsed — Wolter's company tested it to determine why. As a hobby, Wolter used his state-of-the-art instrumentation to study stone carvings and artifacts. Forsberg had joined Wolter's company out of college, worked his way up to partner in the firm and now shared Wolter's interest in stone artifacts.

THE KENSINGTON RUNE STONE

Forsberg had flown in from Minnesota to discuss the Kensington Rune Stone — specifically, its possible relation to artifacts found in New England. He surveyed his audience, stepped out from behind the lectern and, using a Power Point projection to illustrate his points, explained that the Kensington Rune Stone was a tombstone-size slab inscribed with runic lettering found in Minnesota by a farmer named Olof Ohman in 1898. Long thought to be a hoax, the stone, dated 1362 by the carver, told the tale of a group of Scandinavian explorers who returned from a fishing expedition to their campsite in what is now west-central Minnesota to find 10 of their comrades "red with blood and death."

"Our firm was brought in as an outside expert to study the stone, to render a scientific opinion," he explained. "As most of you probably know, you can't carbon date a stone because it's not organic. But you can, at a microscopic level, study the weathering patterns of any carvings or inscriptions. Different minerals in a stone will weather and fade away at different rates."

He sipped his water. "I won't bore you with the details of our petrographic analysis but we concluded that the Rune Stone was carved before modern-day settlers arrived."

He scanned the room. "Now this becomes a simple question of logic: If the farmer Ohman and his contemporaries — who were the first Europeans on the land — didn't carve the stone, then what are the other possibilities?" He smiled. "Aliens? Divine intervention? Native Americans fluent in the runic language? Of course, the only other possibility, the only logical possibility, is that the stone was carved by a group of Scandinavian explorers just as it says it was."

The audience murmured in agreement as Forsberg pressed on. "In my mind this should have been the end of the debate. But there were still a number of skeptics who questioned our conclusions. Some Scandinavian linguistic experts argued that many of the runes on the stone were not authentic, that they were mistakes made by an amateur hoaxster. Well, I'm a fighter," he grinned, "and so is Scott Wolter. We don't like it when people tell us we're idiots. Especially when we know we're right. So we found our own expert in runology, a guy named Dick Nielsen."

He again sipped his water. "The smoking gun in this mystery was the so-called 'Dotted R' rune found on the Rune Stone — as the name suggests, the rune is shaped like a capital R with a dot in the middle of the closed loop. When the stone was first discovered nobody had ever seen the Dotted R rune before, which skeptics argued proved the stone was a hoax. But in 1935, Scandinavian scholars found the Dotted R on medieval documents. So, the question becomes, if the experts didn't know about the Dotted R until 1935, how did it make its way onto the Kensington Rune Stone in 1898?" He surveyed the audience. "The answer, of course, is that it couldn't have — unless it was put there by a medieval carver. So, rather than proving the rune stone is a hoax, the Dotted R is the smoking gun that proves the carving is a legitimate medieval artifact."

THE 'DOTTED R' RUNE ON THE KENSINGTON RUNE STONE

Forsberg continued. "In addition, the Dotted R provides a crucial clue as to the identity of the carver. Wolter and Nielsen found the Dotted R rune on 14th-century grave slabs in Gotland, an island off the coast of Sweden. This tells us that the stone's carver likely came from the Gotland area." He smiled. "Or that the same aliens who came to Minnesota also made a stop in Gotland."

Forsberg organized his papers, pausing to allow the audience to digest his point. Amanda leaned closer. "I've read his reports on this. To me, it's an airtight argument — the science and the linguistics both prove the stone is real. But you still get experts who call it a hoax."

"Based on what? I mean, is there other evidence he's not sharing?"

"None that I've seen. It reminds me of a comic I read once, I think it was poking fun at the Creationist types, you know, the Bible Belt people. But it applies here as well. It went like this: 'Step 1. Dig hole in ground. Step 2. Insert head into hole. Step 3. Fill hole with sand, covering head. Step 4. Wonder why vision is impaired.'"

Laughing, his thoughts turned to Rhonda 'Blinky' Blank and her refusal to open her eyes to these new discoveries.

Forsberg continued. The reason for his visit to New England, he explained, was that Wolter and Nielsen had identified the same previously-unknown runic letters from the Kensington Rune Stone on the Spirit Pond Rune Stones in Maine. "This is strong evidence linking the two stones to each other and to Gotland." He showed a couple of slides, pointed out the specific runes. Cam understood the gist of the presentation but his brain was now close to full, like a saturated sponge; he pictured droplets of potentially-crucial information dribbling to the ground in his wake as he moved across New England. He turned away from the projection screen for a few seconds and allowed his thoughts to settle and his mind to go blank. The details didn't matter. What mattered was that Forsberg offered hard proof of late-14th century European exploration of North America. And if it happened once, it stood to reason it had happened multiple times, especially since Minnesota was so far inland.

The echo of doubt that had been sounding in the back of his mind over the past few days—the one that sounded a lot like Peter's voice proclaiming there was no hard evidence supporting the Westford Knight legend—had been silenced. Forsberg's case in favor of the Kensington Rune Stone not only opened the door to pre-Columbus exploration, it blew it off the hinges. One of his favorite historical anecdotes was of Paul Revere riding through the Massachusetts countryside pronouncing the British were coming. The Kensington Rune Stone sang a similar song about an earlier group of Europeans.

Forsberg continued. "In addition to the runic symbols, there are two other fascinating things about the Spirit Pond Rune Stones." He showed a slide of the map stone Cam and Amanda had examined in Maine the day before. "First, according to this map, Vinland is along the southern coast of New England, not up in Newfoundland as many believe. I'll let the Vinland experts debate this but it seems pretty significant to me."

Many heads nodded in agreement. "The second interesting thing about these Rune Stones is the dating. Back in the 1970s, archeologists found a campsite, a wooden longhouse, right along the shore of Spirit Pond near where the Rune Stones were found. They carbon-dated the floorboards of the longhouse and came up with a date of 1405, plus or minus a decade or so. But because the Spirit Pond stones were originally thought to be dated as 1010 A.D., nobody got too excited about the 1405 date for the floorboards." He paused here and surveyed the room, a subtle signal that he was about to make a key point. "But we don't think 1010 A.D. is the correct date of the Rune Stones."

Using more projections, Forsberg explained how, during medieval times, only priests were educated enough to compute the Christian calendar, which they did by using a special chart called the Easter Table. Forsberg then demonstrated how certain markings on one of the Rune Stones were actually inscriptions that, when applied to the Easter Table, denoted the year 1401. "We're pretty confident the 1401 date is the correct one. It works with the Easter Table and it's consistent with the grammar and style of the runes. Which means the 1405 carbon dating of the longhouse now becomes incredibly relevant."

He surveyed the audience again and smiled. "What does it all mean? I'll tell you. It means that some expedition from Northern Europe was on the Maine coast in 1401. And they are somehow related to the group that was stranded in Minnesota in 1362."

Which also meant the Minnesota and Maine Rune Stones were consistent with the story told in the Zeno Narrative, the 16th-century Venetian recounting of the Zeno family's navigational exploits — a group of fisherman were lost far to the west of Newfoundland in the 1360s, one of the fisherman escaped and returned to Iceland to tell the tale years later, and in 1398 a Zeno ancestor led Prince Henry Sinclair and his fleet back across the Atlantic using maps provided by this fisherman.

But Forsberg wasn't finished. "And do you know how we are certain our conclusion is correct?" He flashed a new image onto the screen — an 'X' with an extra line branching perpendicularly upward, northwesterly if it were a map, off the midpoint of the upper right limb of the letter. "We call this the Hooked X. The runologists in Scandinavia had never seen it until we showed it to them — at first they thought it was a mistake, more evidence of a hoax. But I can show you three examples of it." He displayed the Kensington Rune Stone, this time with a red arrow Photo-Shopped on to point out the Hooked X letter. "It is here, on the Kensington Stone."

A 'HOOKED X' RUNE

He left the image up for a few seconds before projecting two more images, both with red arrows showing the Hooked X. "And on the Spirit Pond stone. And on a boulder in Narragansett Bay, near Newport, called the Narragansett Stone, which is only visible at low tide on a calm day and even then for only about twenty minutes."

THE NARRAGANSETT RUNE STONE

Cam wished he had a pause button to slow things down and allow him to process the flood of information. But Forsberg marched along, stepping toward the audience and folding his hands behind his back. "So, can anyone tell me how this Hooked X, never seen before in Europe, appears on three separate stones in North America?"

He waited, patiently sweeping the room with his eyes. Cam did the same and noticed the crowd anxiously waiting for Forsberg to continue. "Of course, there can be only one logical answer. The Rune Stones must have been carved by the same people, by which I mean the same group or family or order. Which means the people who carved the Kensington Rune Stone in Minnesota in 1362 are closely related to the people who carved the Spirit Pond stones in 1401 and then also carved the Narragansett Stone." He smiled again. "Unless, of course, as the mainstream archeologists will no doubt tell you, this is all the most elaborate hoax in history."

Amanda leaned in again. "I still reckon it was the aliens." He squeezed her hand.

Flicking off the projector, Forsberg strolled down the center aisle of the meeting room. "So, what does it all mean? I will let you figure that out. But my guess is that it has something to do with the Zeno Narrative, and Prince Henry Sinclair, and the Newport Tower."

He smiled, slapped himself playfully on the side of his head. "Oh, that's right. I forgot. The Zeno Narrative is a forgery. And the Rune Stones — Kensington, Spirit Pond, Narragansett — are all hoaxes. And the Prince Henry voyage is just a legend. And the Westford Knight is just natural rock striations. And the Newport Tower is a Colonial windmill." He paused, surveyed the room. "How could it be otherwise when the archeologists are so certain nobody was here before Columbus?"

Cam had given enough presentations to know the difference between polite clapping and sincere, approving applause. The former was often nothing more than a gesture of appreciation that the presentation had finally ended — similar to a patient's gratitude when the dentist put his drill away. The latter was what you'd often hear at a concert or ball game — an expression of thanks for entertainment or enjoyment or, as was the case today, knowledge. Forsberg had enlightened his audience, including Cam and Amanda, and they were thanking him for it.

There really was little room for debate on much of what Forsberg had presented — the Kensington Rune Stone was comprised of certain minerals and they weathered at certain known rates. Short of some staggering 19th-century conspiracy involving a team of experts in petrography, runology, religion and medieval history operating in Scandinavia, Minnesota and New England, the stone's authenticity was a virtual scientific certainty.

Smiling and making small-talk, Forsberg made his way out of the meeting room, turned a corner and pulled out his cell phone. His shirt was wet with sweat — no doubt he would want to go to his room and change and dump his laptop before returning to the conference. "Do you think it'd be worth it to try to talk to this Forsberg guy?" Cam asked.

"Absolutely. It sounds as if he's been researching these sites like they're pieces of a larger puzzle. He's trying to fit them all together. But it's too dangerous to wait in the lobby for him — I might be seen."

The desk clerk wouldn't give them Forsberg's room number but they learned the NEARA group was all on the third floor. Using the TracFone Amanda called the front desk and asked to be connected to Forsberg's room while Cam wandered the third floor, listening for an unanswered phone. Ten minutes later they met outside of room 332. "This is it," he announced.

After moving to the far side of a fire door Cam peered through the glass at the elevator, waiting for Forsberg. Figuring Forsberg would stick around downstairs to answer questions for a few minutes, Amanda sat on the floor and tried phoning Beatrice and Babinaux; she was unavailable and he was in a meeting and couldn't be disturbed. "Probably discussing with the other Consortium council members how many of their inner secrets they could trust me with."

They waited twenty minutes, taking turns with the books Cam purchased, but Forsberg did not appear. Cam began to pace, his nervous energy trumping his patience. "I don't know how those cops do it, on those stakeouts. I'd go crazy with boredom." He walked past the staircase door, stopped at the ice machine and reversed course. "It's almost six, right?"

"Right, just a few ... Cam, watch out!"

He turned in time to see a body hurdling through the air at him, backlit from the light on the stairway landing. He raised his arm to shield the blow but was too late. The man's shoulder drove into his chest, the impact propelling him through the air like a bowling pin. He crashed to the ground and skidded before crashing a second time into the wall, the weight of his assailant crushing his shoulder into the unyielding surface. His head whiplashed against the wall, his vision momentarily going black. Desperate, he tried to squirm away, ducking low to the ground and spinning, speed his only advantage against the larger, powerfully built man. But his attacker's vice-like grip held tight. The man grunted, hoisting

Cam and flipping him onto his belly before shoving his face into the carpet.

He wrenched Cam's arm behind his back. "Hold still or I'll break your arm."

Cam twisted his head, raised his eyes to see Amanda rushing at the assailant, waving a butter knife. "Leave him be," she ordered, jabbing with the knife.

Her face clouded. "Mr. Forsberg?" She lowered the knife. "What in bloody hell are you doing?"

Cam felt the tension on his arm ease a bit. "Who are you?" Forsberg panted. "What do you want?" Cam sensed a bit of fear in the man, which seemed strange given it was Cam's face mashed against in the carpet.

"What do *we* want?" Her voice raised an octave. "You're the loon who attacked us."

"And you're the ones waiting to ambush me outside my door."

"Oh, what a bloody mess," she snorted. "We just want to talk to you. Now get off of him."

"If you want to talk to me, why do you need to lurk outside my door?"

"We're not *lurking*, we're *hiding*. Someone's following us so we're just being cautious." She sighed. "That's what we want to talk with you about."

Forsberg hesitated, then patted Cam down. Not finding any weapons, he sighed and lifted himself off as Cam rolled to his side. Forsberg reached a large hand down to him. "Sorry about that," he mumbled.

Cam took the hand, allowed himself to be yanked to his feet. "Ex-hockey player, huh?"

"Yup."

"Just my luck." He rubbed his left shoulder, tried to lift his arm but only could raise it to his chest. "Couldn't you have been on the debate team instead?"

Forsberg smiled, gracious in victory. "Well, it wasn't really a fair fight. You never saw me coming." He took a deep breath. "Guess I overreacted a bit. It's just that ... well, someone's been following me, making prank calls, that sort of stuff. My wife just got another threatening call this morning, warning me to abandon my Hooked X research. They actually threatened to kill me. I'm getting a bit paranoid. And then I saw you lurking outside my door...."

Cam decided to trust the man. "Someone's after us also. Like Amanda said, we were trying to stay out of sight."

Forsberg smiled again. "Maybe we should start a club."

Amanda had a better idea. "Maybe we should just go get ourselves a pint."

CHAPTER 10

They met an hour later at the mostly-empty, U-shaped bar of a local Outback Steakhouse. Amanda, seated between Cam and the blond-haired Forsberg, ordered a lemonade and a beer and mixed herself a shandy as she listened to them chat about sports. Men in America were identical to men in England — they seemed to bond quickly, almost intimately, over sports and beer and testosterone. Somehow their violent meeting, coupled with Forsberg downplaying his victory, made the connection even stronger. It was similar to the rugby squads that bashed each other's heads in for an afternoon and then retired to a pub together to drink their pain away.

The specter of sexual intimacy made it rare for women to participate in this male bonding. Not that she was complaining. She enjoyed the flirtation, the mystery, the sense of discovery and wonder and giddiness in her budding romance with Cam. And as she watched the charismatic Forsberg warm to Cam and his earnest, honest manner, she found herself even more attracted to him, as if her choice was being validated by an independent authority.

Forsberg interrupted her musing. "So, Amanda, Cam says you two just met. He must be quite a charmer to convince you to tag along to a conference like this, eh?"

Forsberg smiled, his rugged features enhanced by the scar on his square chin and the small chip on his front tooth. An unspoken question lurked beneath the surface inquiry. Setting down her glass, and a bit surprised she had finished almost half of her shandy already, she met Forsberg's steel blue eyes. "Actually, we came specifically to see you, to hear your speech on the Spirit Pond stones." She turned to Cam, who nodded his assent for her to continue. "As I said before, we're in a bit of trouble. We reckoned perhaps you could help."

She and Cam alternately recounted the events of the past few weeks, beginning with his first meeting with the Gendrons and ending with their realization that Prince Henry was heir to the Jesus bloodline. "Monsignor Marcotte believes Vatican hardliners are trying to prevent us from discovering some type of genealogy that will prove Jesus and Mary Magdalene produced a baby, Sarah — which, by the way, means 'princess' in Hebrew," she concluded.

Forsberg remained silent for a few seconds, sipping his beer. He took a long, deep breath and exhaled slowly. "Wow. What you guys are saying explains a lot, fills in a lot of blanks for me."

When he didn't continue, she tilted her head. "Do you care to explain what you mean by that?"

Forsberg smiled. "Of course. I just need to digest things for a sec." He took another sip of his beer, ordered another round and took another deep breath. "Okay, here we go. The speech I gave a couple of hours ago was science. That's what I am, a scientist. I deal in facts and hard evidence. But part of science is the laws of probability. There's too much going on here for this just to be a series of random occurrences. I can't buy that the Hooked X on the different Rune Stones is just a coincidence. Nature doesn't work that way. The world doesn't work that way."

Cam smiled. "I like that. 'The world doesn't work that way.' That says it all right there."

"Thanks. Anyway, I'm a scientist but I'm also a human being and this whole Hooked X thing keeps me up at night, wondering. What does it mean? Why was it used?" He reached for a cocktail napkin, pulled a pen from his blazer pocket and drew an upside-down V. "Throughout history, this has been the symbol for the phallus, the penis, the male member." He drew another V, on top of the upside down one, forming the letter X. "The V symbol indicates the womb, the vagina, the birth chamber. Together, the two symbols make the X, symbolizing the union between man and woman." He looked up. "You with me so far?"

They nodded.

He added another line perpendicular to the upper right stem of the X. "This line turns a regular X into a Hooked X." He sat back, turning the napkin toward them. "Any idea what the hook might signify?"

Amanda ventured a guess, focusing on the small V inside the larger V. "Could that be a baby in the womb?"

Forsberg grinned. "Exactly." He turned to Cam. "Men hardly ever get that but women all seem to. Scott Wolter's wife, Janet, was the one who first figured it out." He glanced back to Amanda. "Is the baby in the womb a boy or a girl?"

"A lass, I suppose. It's a small V, a female form." Suddenly it hit her. "You mean Sarah? You think the hook in the X represents Sarah?"

He nodded. "That's exactly what we think. We think the Hooked X rune is an embedded code, a message from the carvers that the Jesus bloodline—from Jesus and Mary Magdalene through Sarah and, based on what you've just told me, down to Prince Henry Sinclair—had journeyed to the New World."

She and Cam stared at the Hooked X scribbled on the cocktail napkin. It was an outrageous, outlandish theory. But it was consistent with everything they had learned and seen thus far.

Forsberg shrugged. "So what do I know? I'm just a geologist. But I will say this: You guys tell me the Vatican is maiming and murdering people because they're afraid that Sinclair and his group left some kind of genealogical evidence of Jesus' bloodline here in America. And that explains a lot of what's been happening to Scott

Wolter and me — like I told you we've been followed and have been getting threatening phone calls ever since we started talking about this Sarah stuff. My wife's scared. I'm scared."

"We can relate to that," Cam said.

"I shouldn't complain. It's nothing like what's been happening to you guys. We're not getting run down by cars."

"Heck with the cars." Cam rolled his shoulder. "It's the ex-hockey players I'm afraid of."

Laughing, Forsberg again sipped his beer. "Well, these Vatican folks are a lot smarter than me. Assuming your monsignor friend is right, they think the evidence is out there someplace, otherwise they wouldn't be so intent on stopping you guys. Until I heard your story we had no idea the Vatican gave a damn about any of this." He held up the cocktail napkin, shook his head. "Heck, we were just speculating, playing 'what if' games, doodling on napkins. But based on the Vatican's reaction, now I think our theory may actually be correct."

✝   ✝   ✝

Cam was having trouble accepting what Forsberg had just told them. Sure, Monsignor Marcotte had theorized that the Vatican was worried about some kind of genealogy proving Sarah's birth, but Cam never really thought he and Amanda would actually stumble upon anything so monumental. A week ago, he was just a real estate attorney trying to help an elderly couple keep their house. Now, he was ... well, still a real estate attorney but this time one on the verge of a discovery that could shake one of the pillars of Western civilization. He wanted another beer but gulped some water instead.

"So, wait, let me get this straight. You think all these Hooked X markings are a code of some kind? A signal that the heirs of Jesus were exploring America?" Perhaps Prince Henry was part of the most secret cabal of all.

Forsberg stared absently at the TV monitor above the bar. "You know, Cam, I really don't know what to think. Honestly. This is all so bizarre. When I hear you describe it like that, I just shake my head and think it's all too far-fetched. But then I look at all the evidence and I don't know what else to think." He swigged his beer. "It's frigging mind-boggling."

He was glad to see that Forsberg shared his incredulity, that he did not totally accept even his own theory. The lawyer in him focused on the words 'all the evidence.' "What have you found besides the Hooked X?"

"Good question. The other stuff doesn't really have anything to do with religion or Jesus or Sarah. At least not that I can tell. But there's a lot more going on here than just rock carvings. It looks to me like Prince Henry and his gang were here not just to explore but to make a permanent settlement. Probably for all the Templars who had gone underground early in the 14th century. They knew that at some point the Pope was going to come after them. They were still outlaws, still outcasts. They had to get out of Europe."

"You are correct," Amanda said. "England, which was loyal to the Pope in those days, was constantly attacking, trying to retake Scotland."

"Right. So the Templars packed their treasures and sailed to the New World. I'm simplifying—they probably sent a small fleet over first with others planning to follow later. Which, since no big colony has been found, they probably never did, likely because of war between England and Scotland, or maybe because of another outbreak of Black Plague. Anyway, the first thing they'd likely do when they got here—after making friends with the natives, of course—would be to start mapping the New World and scouting for settlement sites. So the Rune Stones would serve multiple purposes—"

Cam interrupted. "You said something earlier about the stones being carved by people from Gotland."

"Right. Gotland was full of Cistercian monks during that period. The Cistercians happened to be a sister order to the Templars — they were really the only literate people during that time."

"And," Amanda added, "there was a close connection between the Cistercians and the Sinclair clan dating back to the 12th century. It would have made sense for Prince Henry to bring a Cistercian monk or two along to keep records and act as a scribe."

"So, anyway," Forsberg continued, "the Rune Stones would have served multiple purposes. The stone itself would be a marker, like a breadcrumb in the woods. And the Hooked X would be a coded sign that the stone was carved by the Templars, the guys who believed in the Jesus bloodline."

"X marks the spot," Amanda murmured.

"What?" Forsberg asked.

She smiled. "I was just thinking about *Treasure Island* and how X marks the spot of the treasure — that was the first book to do that, to mark the treasure with an X." She explained to Forsberg the *Treasure Island* story's parallels, and possible connection, to the Sinclair treasure. "And now we have another X. And another treasure."

Forsberg grinned. "I like it. The Hooked X marks the spot."

"It fits," she said. "With the Templars, one needs always to think in layers, to look at multiple levels. As you said, a rune stone might serve multiple purposes: the message itself conveyed information, the stone's placement served as some kind of directional marker and the Hooked X identified its author and perhaps indicated the presence of some type of treasure."

"Exactly." Forsberg sipped his beer. "Look at the Newport Tower. It probably served multiple purposes — beacon, baptistery, observation tower, astronomical device, maybe a memorial of some kind. But I also think it was meant as a major navigational marker. Maybe a prime meridian for longitudinal measurements."

"If you're going to go to the trouble of building something like that," Cam said, "you might as well incorporate as many usages as you can."

"Right. I haven't had a chance to take a careful look at the sites out here in New England but I bet you find they line up in some significant way."

"The sword on the Westford Knight points north," Amanda commented.

"Same thing with the foundation in the Gendrons' back yard," Cam added, turning to Forsberg, "the one we believe was Prince Henry's encampment site. Brandon noticed it right away. The sides run exactly north-south and east-west."

"See what I mean. That's the stuff I'm talking about." Forsberg pulled out his laptop from beneath his feet and powered it up. "Check this out." He showed an aerial view of what looked like a farm. "This is the Ohman farm in Minnesota, where the Kensington Rune Stone was found." He hit a button and a red arrow appeared. "This is where the stone itself was buried. What's interesting is that, over the years, the Ohman family has found a number of triangular-shaped holes, about the size of a half-dollar, in the larger boulders on the farm. For years, people in the Midwest have found these holes around the countryside. You can tell they're pretty old because they're not perfectly round, which they would be if made with a modern drill bit. The locals call them mooring holes." Forsberg illustrated with a straw in Cam's soda glass. "You know, put a metal rod in the hole and tie your boat to the rod. The pressure of the boat pulling the rod wedges the rod sideways, tight against the opposite side of the hole, securing the boat. It's simple but effective."

Cam and Amanda exchanged knowing glances, both thinking about the hole on the Tyngsboro Map Stone. They allowed Forsberg to continue.

"Anyway, a colleague of ours, a woman from South Dakota named Judi Rudebusch, started looking at these a little more carefully. And she realized that some of them were nowhere near water. Well, why would you need a mooring hole where you wouldn't have boats? So Judi started theorizing that maybe they were markers of some kind, not just mooring holes. And it turns out she may be on to something — in Iceland during medieval times they used stone holes to map the countryside."

"So did you examine the holes at the Ohman farm?" Amanda asked.

"You're damn right we did," Forsberg smiled, changing the picture on his laptop monitor. "Check this out. Scott Wolter and I made a line through all the stone holes, like kids playing connect the dots. And look what we got." He angled the computer toward Cam and Amanda. The display showed three red lines, each connecting a series of dots. The lines intersected at a single point.

Amanda gasped. Cam just shook his head. This was getting too weird. The lines intersected at the exact spot the Kensington Rune Stone was buried.

✠   ✠   ✠

Still shaking his head, Cam decided to have that second beer after all. He looked at Amanda and raised an eyebrow. She understood him, nodding in agreement.

"This is not as fancy as your laptop but you might find it interesting." He pulled his digital camera out of his daypack and found the picture he was looking for. "Have you ever heard of the Tyngsboro Map Stone?"

Forsberg said he hadn't. Amanda described its location and explained its significance as Cam showed him a picture of the boulder. Next Cam showed the picture of the triangular-shaped hole they found in the broken-off piece. "Does that look like one of your stone holes?"

It was Forsberg's turn to be flabbergasted. "Damn, it sure does." He shook his head. "You said this boulder is near a large river?"

"Yes," Amanda answered. "It sits at the bend of the Merrimack, at its southern point."

"Makes sense. These holes are usually found along major rivers, or on top of high hills, or along trails. And usually on large boulders, especially ones with odd shapes or other prominent features."

"It's a big continent," Cam said. "If you're leaving bread crumbs or whatever for the next guy coming along the trail, you'd better make them easy to find."

"For all we know, they may have put flags or banners in these holes, just so they'd be more visible. But there's no way to know for sure." Forsberg looked down again at the small screen on Cam's digital camera. "Getting back to this Tyngsboro Map Stone, it looks to me like we clearly have a map and we clearly have a bread crumb. I bet that you'll find other holes in the area. And I bet they'll somehow line up with this one."

✦   ✦   ✦

Salazar slid off his bar stool and strode quickly to the parking lot. Could this talk of a Jesus bloodline be true? He didn't buy the virgin birth story but if it was true and God did have a son, why couldn't the son have a child as well? He thought back to the birth of Rosalita — nothing could be more holy than bringing a child into the world. He would open his mind and reflect on the matter. The spirits of his ancestors would guide him to the truth.

Not that the truth was paramount here. What mattered was that Thorne and the girl believed the bloodline theory. More importantly, they believed it to be an important clue leading to the treasure.

He phoned Reichmann and summarized Forsberg's research and conclusions. Blasphemy or not, it was exactly the kind of allegation that enraged the Legions of Jesus. "Forsberg's convinced these artifacts are evidence of the Jesus bloodline. He's a scientist, very persuasive. But so far he only shared his theory with Thorne and the girl." He paused and added a lie — the possibility of Forsberg publicizing his conclusions might be just what Salazar needed to buy some time. "Tomorrow he's planning to tell the others at the conference."

"Then our path is clear. Forsberg is now your number one priority. Disregard Thorne and the girl for now. The scientist must be silenced."

✝   ✝   ✝

They finished their beers. Cam reached for the check with his left hand, recoiling from the stabbing pain in his shoulder. In that instant Forsberg snared the bill. "It's the least I can do after that sneak attack of mine."

Cam smiled. "I can't say I really want to wrestle you for it. Thanks."

They walked outside, stopping in front of Forsberg's rental car. He shook Forsberg's hand and Amanda surprised Forsberg with a hug and kiss on the cheek. "Thanks for your help," she said, stepping back and slipping her arm around Cam's waist.

Forsberg's face clouded. "You two be careful, okay?" He handed them each a business card while Cam scribbled his new TracFone number down on a scrap of paper, absent the last four digits which Forsberg quickly memorized. "If you guys need anything, anything at all, don't hesitate to call."

"He's a good man," Cam said as Forsberg drove off in his rental car. Cam had lost Pegasus and almost lost Brandon. But he had gained Amanda and now Forsberg. He liked to think of the relationships in his life as existing in a series of concentric rings, with himself at the center. The past week had been like a wild game of musical chairs around his inner circles.

He slipped his hand into Amanda's and pulled her close to him. The evening was beginning to chill and they had a couple of miles walk back to the Subaru.

"Well now, what next?" she asked.

He pulled out his TracFone. "Let's see what Brandon's learned. Also I want to tell him about this stone hole stuff. Maybe he knows of others around Westford."

Brandon reported he was feeling better, regaining some of his strength. "The nurses keep threatening to take away my laptop. So I told them I'm just looking at porn. That shut them up."

"I bet it did." Cam summarized Forsberg's Hooked X theory. "He also thinks all these sites—the Newport Tower, the Rune Stones, the Westford Knight—all are part of a mapping system of the New World. He thinks Prince Henry and the Templars, or what was left of them, were coming here to settle, to escape the Pope. So of course they needed somehow to find their way around." He explained the stone holes. "And check this out: We found one of these holes on the Map Stone in Tyngsboro."

"Really? That can't be a coincidence."

"Forsberg thinks there are probably other ones around. Any ideas where to look?"

"I guess it'd make sense to look near the Knight. That's the highest hill in eastern Massachusetts."

"But it's all built up. Whatever might have been there is probably gone."

"Well, the other big hill is Cowdry Hill, where the new Highway Department garage is. Not too far from the Gendrons' property, come to think of it. There used to be some granite quarries up there but otherwise it hasn't been developed."

"Good idea. If that was Prince Henry's campsite on the Gendrons' property, he would have explored that hill."

"Well, before you come back to Westford, I think you should take another drive up to Maine."

"Why?"

Cam turned the phone so Amanda could hear. "I was reading about something called the Machias Bay petroglyphs, up past Bar Harbor."

She leaned in to the speaker. "Aren't they Native American carvings?"

"Yeah. But mixed in with the deer and the teepees and the canoes is a carving of a medieval ship. I think they call it a knorr. Looks a bit like the Boat Stone ship but it's tough to see just from the picture. I think you need to see it in person to be sure."

The headlights of an oncoming car illuminated her face as she responded. "You know, that's interesting. How would the natives know what a medieval ship looked like?"

"They'd know if one was sitting off the coastline," Cam answered.

"Precisely," she said. "And if it was carved during your Colonial times it would be a Colonial ship, not a knorr."

"There's a place that does kayak tours," said Brandon. He gave them the contact number. "That's the best way to see the carvings. But it's a haul to get up there — probably six hours."

Cam thanked him and gave him the new TracFone number. "Hey, you don't write these numbers down, do you?" He didn't want to insult his cousin but it wasn't out of the realm of possibility that someone might come into his hospital room looking for a way to find Cam.

"Shit, Cam, my brains weren't in my foot. I write down the first six numbers and memorize the last four. And even the ones I write down I write on my thigh — only the nurses get to see them."

"Sorry to doubt you, Cuz. Keep getting better. Talk to you soon." Cam turned to Amanda. "He sounds much better, more upbeat, less angry."

"He's probably going to ebb and flow for a bit. It's only natural. He's got a lot to be cross about."

Cam checked his watch. Just after 7:00. "You up for a road trip? We can make it most of the way tonight. And I'd like to keep moving if we can."

Her eyes sparkled in the dusk. "I suppose I could tolerate another few hours with you."

✛   ✛   ✛

Beatrice Yarborough waited until the threesome left before darting over to the bar from her table in the corner. She snatched the cocktail napkin from the bartender just as he was about to clear the empty glasses and debris. "Give me that."

"Whatever." The bartender, a balding, overweight man with a droopy mustache, shrugged. "By the way, no smoking in here."

She exhaled smoke through her nose, staring at the Hooked X scrawled on the napkin. Damn. Things had certainly progressed—in the wrong direction—during her seven-hour flight. She removed a twenty dollar bill from her handbag and placed it in front of the bartender. "Did you hear what the folks sitting here were speaking of?"

He glanced at the twenty and shrugged again. "Nope."

She removed two more twenties and waved them slowly. "Are you certain you recall nothing?"

He edged closer, leaning in. "They were talking about religion, I think. Jesus, the Vatican, stuff like that." He pulled the twenties from her hand.

"Did they mention the name Sarah by chance?"

"Yeah, the lady was all excited about it, said something about some symbol representing Sarah."

She turned away. The sixty dollars was money well spent, though the information it bought was itself potentially catastrophic. Originally she was concerned Amanda and her new friend would stumble onto some site or artifact and contaminate it before the professionals could establish its authenticity. But the stakes had grown much higher. They were on the verge of making a discovery that would sully the reputation of Prince Henry and Sir James forever. Babinaux was a fool for instructing her to share Consortium secrets with them. Not that she had obeyed him.

For decades the Consortium had walked a fine line, promoting the legend of Prince Henry the explorer while suppressing the Templar and Jesus-bloodline back-stories. They championed a simple narrative, one that school children could embrace — a noble, courageous explorer braving the icy northern Atlantic in 1398 to discover the New World, a land rich with timber and fish and fertile ground, so that his impoverished lieges could live in comfort. This was the Prince Henry tale they advanced, whitewashed of any reference to a traitorous enemy of the Church fleeing Europe to escape the Pope, laden with treasure and religious artifacts plundered from the Temple of Solomon. The Church and the American political establishment would never allow the latter version of Prince Henry to be glorified; they would label him a plunderer and heretic and relegate him to a small, ugly footnote in history.

She took a long drag on her cigarette. Somehow Amanda and her lawyer friend had put themselves on a collision course with history. If they were not somehow derailed, Prince Henry — good, brave, noble Prince Henry — would become forever reviled as an enemy of Christianity. A Judas.

She slipped into the ladies room, glared at a young secretary-type applying eyeliner in the mirror. The girl scurried away, leaving Beatrice alone. She dialed a number with an Argentina area code.

"Señora Yarborough. A pleasure to speak with you again." The voice was smooth, syrupy, designed to get bees with honey.

She preferred vinegar. "You have failed. The two ... problems ... are still outstanding." It hadn't been hard to figure they'd find their way to the NEARA conference. Aside from herself and a few other members of the Consortium, nobody knew more about the Prince Henry sites than the NEARA folks.

"Yes. Unfortunately we momentarily lost their trail. But we have located them again."

"The situation is far worse than we believed. They are aware of the Hooked X and its Sarah symbolism."

The man clucked his tongue. "That is most unfortunate." He spoke in a saliva-filled manner, as if his tongue was too big for his mouth. Spanish was a beautiful language as spoken in parts of Spain. In Latin American it often sounded like cows chewing their curd.

"It is beyond unfortunate. They are on the verge of exposing the Roman Catholic Church for the fraud that it is." And, more tragically, taking Prince Henry and Sir James down with it at the same time.

"Now there is no reason to make statements like that, Señora."

"Listen to me. My statements are the least of your problems. I strongly suggest you do what needs to be done."

"My men are on the job. God's will be done. And God be with you, Señora Yarborough."

✝   ✝   ✝

Just after hanging up with Brandon, Cam's TracFone rang. Eric Forsberg. "I miss you guys already," he joked.

Cam laughed. "We're just packing up. Going on another road trip."

"I'm calling because I just talked to Scott Wolter." Wolter was Forsberg's fellow researcher in Minnesota. "I told him about the triangular hole you found on the Tyngsboro Map Stone. He mentioned he found a reference once to a triangular hole in one of the boulders at America's Stonehenge also. He thinks there are probably others around. They're potentially important pieces to this puzzle. You're not by chance heading toward Maine are you?"

"As a matter of fact, yes. Machias Bay, way up north."

"Well, I think you should take a detour to Spirit Pond." He gave Cam the GPS coordinates for the exact location where the Spirit Pond Rune Stones were found. "My gut tells me you'll find a stone hole nearby."

Cam laughed. "Nothing would surprise me any more."

CHAPTER 11

Cam had been driving for almost five hours, the Subaru alone in the middle of the night in the middle lane of the Maine Turnpike sporting a license plate he had swiped from a rental car in the hotel lot. The NEARA conference would go through the weekend—by the time the rental car made it back to the rental lot and somebody noticed the missing plate he and Amanda would be long gone.

She slept peacefully in the passenger seat, an olive green fleece blanket draped over her. He studied her face for a second—even asleep it captivated him, somehow radiating both warmth and vivacity, heat and light. She sensed his eyes on her, shifted in her seat and turned toward him a bit and sighed contentedly. Her movement dislodged the blanket and he reached over and pulled the plush fabric gently back over her shoulders. He smiled. It probably wasn't practical to just drive around New England with Amanda in the passenger seat for the next ten years.

An SUV in the left lane closed on him quickly. Tensing, he slowed to allow it to pass. They seemed to have successfully evaded their pursuers for now but he needed to remain vigilant. These people, whoever they were, were not likely to just give up and go away. The SUV zipped past, a couple of young women smoking cigarettes in the front seat. He relaxed back into his seat.

Amanda breathed rhythmically, her mouth curved into a small smile. She seemed to trust his driving. Perhaps she had been observing him, assessing how he dealt with stress and pressure and adversity. Apparently he had passed this test. Not that it brought him any closer to solving this mystery. But it was nice to know nonetheless.

For the umpteenth time he mulled over Forsberg's Hooked X conclusions. A few days ago he and Amanda were working in the dark, the cover of the jigsaw box hidden from them, two puzzlers blind to the image they were trying to reconstruct. They had joined together the border sections of the puzzle and had even connected a few obvious pieces in the interior. But the knowledge that one tree is adjacent to another is a far cry from understanding life in the forest. With the Hooked X revelations, larger blocks of the puzzle were beginning to fall into place. There were still plenty of holes but they now discerned the gestalt, the overall pattern.

Amanda awoke, reached over and squeezed his hand. "How are you?"

"I'm fine. How'd you sleep?"

She rubbed her face. "Quite well, actually. Shall I drive for a bit?"

"Maybe later. I'm fine now—my mind is racing."

Her faced clouded. "I'm bothered that I cannot reach Beatrice."

"Why don't you try again?"

She looked at her watch. "It's five o'clock in the morning in London. I'll wait a bit."

She bit her lower lip, which he had learned meant she was deep in thought. "Cam, how does this all end?"

"What do you mean by *this?*" Was she referring to their relationship?

She read his thoughts, smiled and touched her fingers to his shoulder. "It's a tad early for *that* conversation. I was referring to this ... this quest of ours."

"When you say quest, I think of crazy old Don Quixote, riding off to joust with windmills."

She smiled. "Stone windmills, or wooden ones?"

"Very funny."

"In any event, I don't mean quest in that sense. But, to continue the Don Quixote analogy, we don't really know who our enemies are. We believe a fringe Vatican faction is involved but we're not even certain about that. Short of bringing down the Catholic Church, how does this end, how do we win?"

He didn't have a great answer. "I guess I'm hoping it ends when we reveal whatever secrets they're trying so hard to hide. They want certain things kept buried and they're willing to maim and kill people to get their way. But once everything is out in the open, what will they give a damn about you or me or Brandon or Eric Forsberg? I mean, they won't canonize us but it does them no good at that point to kill us. The truth is their enemy, not us."

"Then we simply go back to our lives and they leave us be?"

He reflected on the priest sex abuse case. The Church's lawyers—presumably acting pursuant to their client's instructions—ruthlessly attacked the accusers, planted false stories in the press, besmirched their reputations. All in an attempt to cover up the truth, to protect the Church. But once the case was settled, these same accusers were welcomed back into the flock. Organized crime groups and gangs punished informants and rats as a deterrent to others. And the radical Muslims called for the death of people like Salman Rushdie for the same reason. But the Church was different. It was almost as if it never expected to be in the wrong again and therefore saw no need to send a message of deterrence. He explained his theory to Amanda. "It's like they still think of themselves as this benevolent institution, the embodiment of Jesus' teachings. They can justify killing us for the greater good. But being vindictive? That's beneath them, that's the old medieval Church." He shrugged. "So, yes, hopefully they'll just leave us alone."

Amanda found a jazz station and then dozed off again, leaving Cam alone with his thoughts. One thing didn't make sense: How could a group of Scandinavians make their way to Minnesota in the 14th century? It was almost two in the morning; he dialed Eric Forsberg's number anyway.

"Shit, man, I just fell asleep. We closed the bar."

"Sorry. But I have a question. How did your guys make it all the way to Minnesota?"

"Probably up the St. Lawrence River. We're not sure why they weren't killed on the way. One possibility is they made friends with the natives. Maybe traded with them, maybe convinced them they were gods or something." He paused. "Hold on a sec. It's hot as hell in here — let me turn on the air."

Cam listened as Eric stumbled over to the controls and cursed as he stubbed his toe. A few seconds later a dull whir kicked on, humming over the phone lines.

"Eric, you there?"

Eric's phone made a thud as if it had fallen to the ground and bounced a couple of times. "Eric?"

The only response was a muffled cough and the sound of a metallic echo, as if someone were knocking against a piece of sheet metal. Was Eric banging against one of those climate-control units mounted below the windows of hotel rooms? A cold wave of fear passed over Cam.

"What's happening?" Amanda asked.

"I don't know. It's almost like Eric fell down or something."

"Is he unconscious?"

"I don't think so. I hear him knocking against something metal. Eric, can you hear me?" he shouted. "Eric?"

The whirring of the motor ceased, replaced by the scratchy noise of a phone being dragged across the ground. A muffled gasp and weak cough followed. "Poi-son," came the croaked, raspy response.

"Eric? Eric, can you hear me?" His heart pounding, Cam swerved into the breakdown lane. The two syllable reply, barely audible, assaulted him like a two-by-four. "Shit, Amanda, he's been poisoned!"

"What? What's going on?"

"I think something in the air conditioner."

"Hang up and call for help."

"Hang up?" It was like untying a lifeline. But Amanda was right — they only had one untraceable phone. "Eric, I need to hang up and get help. Hang in there."

Amanda was one step ahead of him. "The NEARA program will have the hotel phone number."

She unclipped her belt, leaned into the back seat and read the number out. Hands shaking, he jabbed the buttons. "This is an emergency." He tried to keep his voice calm. "Please listen to me. I just received a call from Eric Forsberg, a guest in your hotel. He's in room 332. Please call 911 and send someone up to check on him right away." He grimaced. "I believe he's been poisoned."

Not knowing what else to do, and feeling totally helpless, Cam put the Subaru back into gear and continued north. As he drove, he imagined Eric's ordeal, the images haunted by a Holocaust documentary he had once watched showing tortured gas chamber scenes: Eric stumbling toward the window and finding the controls to the heating and cooling system. Peering at the knobs in the dim light. Stabbing at the buttons. A motor whirring. A wet mist moistening his face. The taste of something bitter and almond-like filling his mouth. His breath catching in his throat. Feeling light-headed and weak. Falling to the ground....

But Eric was strong, healthy, vibrant. He would fight. Adrenaline would have kicked in. He would have clawed at the control panel's off button, torquing his body against the metal climate unit as the cold, deadly mist assaulted him. He would have tried to crawl away, keeping his nose and mouth low even as his lung muscles refused to constrict. Cam remembered stepping off a ski gondola once, recalled the feeling of panic and helplessness as an icy gale filled his airways and blocked the flow of air both in and out. Eric would be feeling that, fighting it, perhaps fumbling for his cell phone on the carpet of the darkened room in a final grasp at life. And if not life, at least defiance — somebody would know he had been poisoned, would alert the authorities, would perhaps even avenge his death.

Cam shook the visions of a writhing Eric from his head. Ten minutes had passed. A baleful voice in his head insisted that a trained paramilitary group would know enough to use a lethal, fast-working poison. He began to dial Forsberg's cell number. Amanda reached over, stopped him. "You can't, Cam. Surely the police are in the room. What shall you tell them when they answer? You can't give them your name; you're already wanted for questioning in the McLovick murder. You'd just be distracting them from searching for the culprits."

"I guess you're right."

He put the phone down and tried to focus on the road. But visions of Forsberg's face, purple and distorted and frothing at the mouth, filled his imagination. He pounded the steering wheel. "Damn it! This is my fault. Eric didn't deserve this. But I dragged him in, and now he's probably dead—"

The TracFone chirped, interrupting. Amanda grabbed it, looked at the display. "It's Eric's line."

Reaching for the phone, he took a deep breath. "Hello."

"Who is this?"

"You called me. Who is this?"

"Officer Reilly. Fitchburg Police."

"What can I do for you?"

"Do you know a Mr. Eric Forsberg?"

He hesitated. "Why do you ask?"

The policeman's tone turned aggressive. "Because he's dead. And because you called his cell about fifteen minutes ago. And because my guess is that you're the guy who called the hotel clerk. Now stop playing games."

Cam swallowed, trying to remove the knot from his throat. He described for the officer his conversation with Eric, the commotion on the line after Eric asked him to hold while he turned on the air conditioning. "When he came back on the line, all he said was, 'poison.' Then I called the hotel. I'm sorry, officer. I really am. But that's all I know." He paused. "One more thing. Contact Lieutenant Poulos from the Westford police. This is related to something he's working on." He ended the call and pulled into the breakdown lane again.

"He's dead." He leaned onto Amanda's shoulder and closed his eyes. He thought about Brandon, about Pegasus, about Eric Forsberg. Pain and sorrow, fed by fear and anger, built within him, suddenly erupting in a spewing torrent of fierce, violent sobs. Who were these animals who killed so thoughtlessly, so casually? And were he and Amanda next?

He had a vague sense of Amanda holding him, of stroking his head and humming into his ear, of removing Pegasus' collar from his pocket and forcing it into his clenched fist. But she knew better than to try to offer words of comfort.

✝   ✝   ✝

Standing on the periphery of the crowd inside the hotel lobby, Salazar watched as the paramedics wheeled Forsberg's body out the door and into the ambulance. The poison was quick-working; he suffered very little. And he left no children to grieve over his loss. His wife would be traumatized, no doubt. Salazar would pray for her soul to heal.

Moving away, he phoned Reichmann. "It's done."

"Excellent. What about Thorne and the girl?"

"Gone. They left before your men arrived." Another lie. Reichmann's back-up team made it in plenty of time but Salazar didn't want anyone else tracking his quarry.

"Do you have any idea where they are going?"

Salazar glanced at the screen on his tracking device showing them heading north into Maine again, relieved they hadn't run to the airport to catch a plane out of the country. "No."

✛   ✛   ✛

Beatrice Yarborough took the call on her satellite phone in her room at the Copley Plaza hotel in Boston as she watched the moon rise over Trinity Church. For some odd reason the church decorations included a number of Jewish stars. Nobody had been able to explain it to her.

"Mr. Forsberg has been eliminated."

Out of habit, she reached for Orkney, ready to stroke the cat's neck.

"I assume you questioned him first."

"You assume incorrectly." The man cleared his throat. "There was no time to develop an elaborate plan to abduct Mr. Forsberg. The danger of him disclosing the Hooked X secrets to others was too great." He had discussed the rune itself during his presentation, but it appeared only Amanda Spencer and her solicitor friend were privy to the rune's Jesus bloodline implications. "We chose to eliminate him immediately."

Beatrice ground her Gauloises cigarette into the bottom of a bar glass — not only did the damn American hotels ban smoking, they didn't even put ashtrays in the rooms. They were fortunate she didn't use the desktop.

"Are you planning to murder everyone with whom he might have shared his conclusions?" Presumably Forsberg had discussed his findings with his wife and fellow researchers as well.

Another sigh. "If necessary, yes. But we are hopeful that Forsberg's death will deter others. We have sent appropriate warnings to his confidantes."

The Hooked X revelation did not concern her — it did not impact directly on Prince Henry and Sir James. Her Argentine cohort could bump off Forsberg's friends and family or not. She cared only about Thorne and Spencer. "Your threats may deter others. They will not deter our young irritants in the Subaru."

"I agree. They, too, will have to be eliminated. Unfortunately, they remain ... elusive."

CHAPTER 12

[Thursday]

Amanda drove the rest of the way to Machias Bay. Cam had cried himself to sleep on her shoulder, his sobs fading to whimpers, his exhaustion finally overcoming his grief. He had allowed her to guide him, half-asleep, into the passenger seat, where she helped him test his blood sugar and held him until he nodded off again. She turned into a Dunkin Donuts parking lot on the outskirts of town at just after 4:00 A.M. and rang Beatrice on the satellite phone.

"Amanda, dear, I have been worried about you."

"I'm fine. But there's been another murder." She recounted Eric Forsberg's death.

"You and Mr. Thorne are in grave danger. You must end this silly quest of yours. Tell me where you are and I will arrange for someone to retrieve you."

Did the Consortium really possess the power to protect her from a Vatican fringe paramilitary group? "Did Mr. Babinaux consult with the council?"

"He did." Beatrice sighed. "I am sorry but they are not willing to violate the protocols. There is more at stake here than you know, my dear. Now please, tell me where you are."

The Consortium's position made no sense. Just like everything else. Cam's TracFone rang. "Sorry, Beatrice, I have to run. I'll ring you later."

She laid a reassuring hand on Cam's shoulder. "I'll answer. Go back to sleep." The embers of the eastern sky were just beginning to smolder. "Hello."

A halting greeting. "Is this Amanda?"

She recognized Marcotte's voice. "Yes, Monsignor. How are you?" It was well before dawn, he was calling on a phone designed for secrecy and Vatican cronies were trying to murder them. She might have skipped the pleasantries.

"Actually, I'm exhausted. I haven't slept since you left on Tuesday. But more importantly, how are you and Cameron holding up?"

She studied Cam, his fists clenched even as he slept. "Not exactly Sunday at Wimbledon but we're pushing on."

"Where are you?"

"Really, I'd rather not say. Please don't take offense."

"Of course, I'm sorry for asking. Again, I haven't slept." He took a deep breath. "I've been doing a lot of reading, a lot of research, speaking to a number of experts in the field—I just got off the phone with a colleague in Italy. I think I'm beginning to understand all this. It runs much deeper than I thought it did two days ago." She rolled her eyes. *You're telling me.* "I think you've stumbled into a real hornet's nest here. We need to get together so I can share what I've learned."

She nudged Cam awake, pointed to the phone and whispered, "Monsignor Marcotte."

He blinked a few times and rubbed his cheeks vigorously with his hands. "Please hold on one minute, Monsignor," she said before covering the mouthpiece. "He wants to meet with us, says he has important information to share." She smiled. "And, by the way, good morning." She leaned over, kissed him gently on the mouth. "I hope you feel better."

His lips moved in a smile but the sadness in his eyes remained. "I do feel better, thanks. Had a dream I was comforted by an angel. First she had blond hair, then it turned burgundy."

"Very funny. And it's good to have you back. But what should I tell the Monsignor? And while you are weighing our options, you should know I spoke with Beatrice: The Consortium is refusing to share its secrets with us."

"More good news." He stared out the window. "Are we in Machias?" She nodded. "Well, I think we can trust the Monsignor. He had us in his grasp once and let us go. Maybe there's a whole other layer to this we haven't figured out but he seems to be on our side."

"I agree." She glanced at a map of Maine, performed some rough calculations in her head. "We can get an early start and be finished with the petroglyphs by mid-morning."

"And I want to stop at Spirit Pond and look for a stone hole." He lowered his eyes. "It's on the way and it was the last thing Eric said to me, to look for a hole there. It could be an important clue."

"Very well. We'll make that detour early afternoon." She uncovered the mouthpiece. "Monsignor, is it possible for you to drive to Maine?"

"Of course."

She glanced again at the map, her eyes drawn to a Viking figurehead in a display advertisement. Appropriate. "Three o'clock then. The lobby of the Viking Motor Inn, just outside Bath, in Brunswick. And please be certain nobody follows you."

✞ ✞ ✞

After grabbing a couple of bagels and some coffee at the Dunkin Donuts, Cam and Amanda followed Route 1 to a local canoe and kayak rental shop, a flat-roofed, ramshackle structure that tilted toward the river behind it, as if straining at its foundation to join in the water activities it had witnessed for so many decades.

Amanda had driven — he felt numb, lethargic, as if waiting for the anesthesia to wear off post-surgery. At first he thought it was his blood sugar level but he checked it and it was fine. He had been going full tilt for almost a week, his adrenaline and anger and attraction to Amanda propelling him along. But Eric's death had been a brick wall in the night; he never even had a chance to take his foot off the accelerator, much less hit the brakes. It would take him a while to get going again. The breakfast helped, as did Amanda's energy.

Just before 6:00 a mud-covered, red pickup truck pulled into the dirt parking lot next to the Subaru.

"Howdy." A burly man in a gray sweatshirt and a paint-splattered pair of jeans ambled toward them. They stepped out of the Subaru to meet him.

"I'm Jed. You folks looking to do some fishing?" Jed spoke with a Down East Maine accent, the words nasaly and elongated and slow to leave his mouth. Single syllable words like 'here' became 'he-yah.' Cam glanced at Amanda — she probably wouldn't understand half of what Jed said.

"We're interested in seeing the petroglyphs." He explained they were only in town for the morning. "Especially any that depict ships or boats."

The man nodded. "Aiyuh. I can show you those myself. Take us about three or four hours." He glanced out toward the river. "You picked a good day. Calm. And not too hot."

Cam paid cash. While they donned life vests and grabbed some supplies from the car Jed dragged three kayaks onto a pier from a rack by the water. Unlike the building the pier was solid and fresh-looking. Similarly, unlike Jed's truck, the kayaks were spotless, gleaming in the morning sun. Apparently the man had his priorities straight.

They paddled along near the bank of the river, a handful of fishing boats staying in the deeper channel in the middle. Cam phoned Brandon as he paddled, the phone wedged between his chin and shoulder, and quickly detailed Eric Forsberg's death. "Call Poulos. He already knows. Maybe he has more info."

Jed turned and spoke over his shoulder. "The river goes out to the Machias Bay. The petroglyphs are on a rock ledge jutting into the harbor at Clark's Point."

After about 20 minutes the river dog-legged to the right. Jed pointed his paddle toward a spit of land in the distance. "About two miles away. That's where you'll see your petroglyphs."

He explained that the petroglyphs were dinted, or pecked, into the soft stone by Indian shamans using hard stone tools. Amanda peered from under the brim of a baseball cap she wore to shield her face from the sun. "We have some petroglyphs down in Massachusetts that are carved into schist and granite. You'd need iron tools to do that."

"Right," Jed nodded. "But like I said this is soft rock. They say some of these petroglyphs are 3,000 years old."

"How do you think they came to carve a European ship?" Cam asked.

"I've been around boats all my life and the ship I've seen is too old to be a Colonial vessel. So that means somebody must have been here before the Colonial era, seems to me." He bit a piece of skin off his thumb and spit it into the harbor. "I mean, they didn't just make it up, you know what I mean?"

They had moved into the open harbor and the sea, though calm, tossed them around a bit. Cam's shoulder throbbed from his encounter with Eric Forsberg, the injury doubly bothersome because every bark of pain reminded him of his tragic death. After about an hour, Jed guided them alongside a terra cotta-colored rock ledge protruding into the ocean. "At high tide, this ledge is under water." He pointed with his paddle. "There's your boat."

Paddling close, they inspected the weathered carving. It was smaller than Cam expected, about the size of his hand, the darkened subsurface of the rock ledge revealing the form of a single-masted ship. Amanda leaned out of her kayak, her face inches from the ledge; he held the edge of her boat so she didn't flip.

"Oh," she gasped. "It's an amazing carving. I've seen pictures before but they don't do it justice. Notice how careful they were with the curves on the stern and the sail."

MACHIAS BAY PETROGLYPH

"Brandon's right. It looks like the boat on the Boat Stone." He snapped some pictures.

"Yes, a knorr. I read a report that dates this type of ship between 1350 and 1450."

He stated the obvious. "Too early for the Colonists, too late for the Vikings."

She smiled. "The only thing missing is a Hooked X on its sail."

+ + +

They paddled back quickly, thanked their guide and were back on the road, heading south, by mid-morning. "Follow Route 1," Amanda said, peering at the map. "It's about three hours to Phippsburg. Then Spirit Pond and Popham Beach are down the road a bit from there."

Route 1 hugged the coast of Maine, much as it did the entire eastern seaboard. "You know," Cam said, "now that I'm here, I'm appreciating how long the Maine coastline is. For the Colonists to end up on Popham Beach as their first settlement, it couldn't be a coincidence. No way."

"I agree." She held up the map. "It says here there are over 3500 miles of coastline in Maine, 5000 if you include the islands. The Popham group was likely following an old map to Spirit Pond."

"Hey, do you think this is worth the detour?" He felt he owed it to Eric to look for stone holes at Spirit Pond. But that didn't mean it was a good use of their time.

"Yes. It's not far out of our way. Perhaps these stone holes are arranged in some kind of pattern, as they were at the Kensington site. If he thinks there's a stone hole nearby, that's quite good enough for me."

"Good." He squeezed her hand. "Thanks."

They exited Route 1 in Bath and followed the local roads south toward the coast, tracking the path of the Kennebec River as it emptied to the sea. A number of ponds and tributaries dotted the landscape. She directed him to a wooded area, part of the Popham Beach State Park. "Turn here. Spirit Pond is up on the right."

"How close are we to the Atlantic?" The area didn't have that marshy, tideland feel of the Maine coast.

"Not far, perhaps a mile. The pond connects to Popham Beach via a river. Six hundred years ago the area probably wasn't grown over so much and they could have sailed straight up. Or simply rowed up in smaller boats."

They pulled off on a dirt shoulder. She pointed across the pond. "That's the spot Walter Elliot found the rune stones." They found a path along the water's edge, their steps cushioned by a bed of pine needles. "I visited this site a year ago, when I first moved to the States. The woman who escorted me, an expert in local history who knew everyone and everything, recently passed on. She recounted a story about the archeological dig in the early seventies, during which they uncovered the planks from the sod house which they carbon dated to 1405. Apparently during the dig, one day, out of the blue, an official from the state shut down the dig. One of the archeologists leading the dig, a woman, screamed and hollered, arguing they had not completed their work. She was convinced the state was trying to cover something up."

"You know, a week ago I would have just laughed at that. Just another conspiracy theory. But now, well, it seems entirely possible."

They reached the far end of the pond and began to circle back to the left, still following the shore. "This is the spot they uncovered the two horseshoe-shaped sod houses."

They continued along the tip of the pond, again curving to the left, the Subaru visible on the opposite shore. Amanda stopped at a small clearing set back a few yards from the rocky shoreline of the pond. "Elliot found the rune stones here. He was seated on that rock, smoking a cigarette. He looked down and there they were, partially buried."

Cam hunched down and inspected the area. "Well, then, this is where the stone hole should be. According to Eric, it should be in a prominent location — on a large boulder, or maybe a uniquely-colored rock. Something that stands out."

They split up, Amanda wandering along the shoreline and Cam exploring the woods behind the Elliot discovery site. There were no particularly large or unique rocks. Nor was there a tall hill or ledge. He began to move back toward the pond when he heard Amanda yell.

"Cam, come here. I found something!"

He raced through the brush; she was kneeling on a stone outcropping about 20 feet off shore. *Of course.* The outcropping was by far the most noticeable feature in the area, a natural rock bridge protruding C-like into the pond, originating only a few yards from where the rune stones were buried.

"Look," she pointed. "It's triangular, just like the one on the Tyngsboro Map Stone."

He put his finger into the hole, felt the rough edges. Definitely not machine made. "I'll be damned. You found it. Just like Eric said." He looked toward the ocean. "So they sailed up the river to this pond, made an encampment, built the sod houses. Then they carved the rune stones, complete with a map of the area and a Hooked X."

"And they also drilled the stone hole, probably marked it with a flag."

"Right. Maybe they went up the Kennebec to explore, maybe they continued along the coastline." He tried to picture the medieval explorers. "Then, 200 years later, Popham came back to the same place and established his Popham Colony. Pretty freakin' neat."

She pulled him to his feet and kissed him, her soft lips firm on his. When she finally released him, she angled her mouth to his ear. "I think *you* are pretty freakin' neat."

Dizzy, he moved to kiss her again but she pulled away, taking his hand as she smiled. "Unfortunately, we have a date with a priest."

✝   ✝   ✝

As planned, Cam and Amanda met the Monsignor in the lobby of the Viking Hotel. After watching the cleric pull into the parking lot in a rental car, Cam had hiked through the woods a quarter mile up the road to make sure nobody tailed him. Fairly confident the Monsignor was alone, Cam instructed him to follow them to a deserted spot along the Bath harbor shoreline. He took a round-about route, doubling back a few times, reassuring himself they were not being followed.

They parked in the shadows of a massive, rusted steel crane once used to construct the destroyers and battleships of the nation's navy—the Bath Iron Works still built ships but on a much smaller scale than it used to. They walked across a muddy parking area and to an old picnic table set on a concrete slab perched overlooking the harbor. The Monsignor lowered his tall frame slowly onto the far bench, his back to the water. For decades iron workers had lunched at the table, complained about wages and wives, sweated out pink slips and Red Sox games. Today Cam had the feeling they were its first visitors in years.

The Monsignor rubbed his bloodshot eyes and breathed in the cool ocean air. He wore a pair of khakis and a green windbreaker and carried a blue duffel bag; he looked like a man on his way to the gym. "I'm glad to be outside. It's refreshing after spending so many hours in my library." Even without his robe and collar, and despite his fatigue and strands of gray hair falling haphazardly across his forehead, he possessed an air of serenity and peacefulness. But Cam sensed a turmoil in the man he had not noticed in their earlier meetings.

He liked the priest, trusted him despite the earlier abduction, appreciated his efforts to help them. "It's the one thing we've had going for us over the past week. The weather's been great." He tilted his head. "If I were religious, I might say God was smiling on us."

Marcotte grinned. "If you were religious, it's safe to say you wouldn't be on this quest." He leveled his tired blue eyes on Cam, his smile fading. "Actually, I believe you are doing God's work."

Cam held the Monsignor's eyes for a second. Here was a good man, trying to do the right thing, willing to question his devotion to an institution he had pledged his life to. "I appreciate you saying that. I know you're being pulled in a couple of different directions here."

Marcotte shrugged. "I have a simple rule: When in doubt, follow the truth. The path is often well-illuminated and it usually leads me in the right direction." He reached into his duffel bag, extracted a shoe box-size cylinder wrapped in newspaper. "Emily Gendron thought this might be important."

Cam pulled off the paper, revealing the ceramic lantern he had seen at the Gendrons' home. He handed it to Amanda who examined it, rotating it slowly. "Yes, it is a replica of the Tower," she said. "Eight arches, random windows, the correct proportions."

Cam re-wrapped the lantern, placed it carefully in his bag. "Thank you, Monsignor. I have a feeling this will turn out to be important."

Marcotte pulled a spiral notepad from his bag and flipped open the first page before closing it and sighing. "Amanda—I'm sorry, may I call you that?"

"Of course."

"Amanda, I'm sure you have recounted the history of the Knights Templar being excommunicated, tortured and even murdered in the early 14th century."

"Yes."

He turned to Cam. "Did Amanda tell you why the Church did this?"

"Well, the Church claimed it was because the Templars were heretics. But Amanda said it was because of financial reasons, to free the Church from debt to the Templars."

Marcotte pursed his lips tightly. "And historians generally agree with that conclusion. Accusing one's enemies of heresy was a common ploy in medieval times, during the Inquisition and the Crusades. There is a tragic story of the slaughter of an entire town in the Cathar-dominated region of southern France, in 1209. The Cathars were a Christian sect that failed to follow the orthodox teachings of the Church and were thus targeted by the Pope. A Crusader soldier asked a superior officer how they should distinguish the heretics from the true Catholics." The Monsignor shook his head sadly. "The officer replied: 'Kill them all. Surely the Lord will save those that are his.' As many as 20,000 Cathars were slaughtered that day. Clearly the Church was more interested in eliminating its enemies than in saving souls."

"So the Templars really weren't heretics?" Cam asked.

The Monsignor's eyes shifted from Cam to Amanda. "Actually, in this case I believe the claims of heresy were legitimate. I believe the Templars had rejected the teachings of the Church."

Amanda's brow furrowed. "But the Templars were the army of the Church, the protectors of Christianity."

Marcotte smiled sadly. "The protectors of Christianity, yes. But the protectors of the Church, no."

"Why? And what did they believe instead?" she asked.

"The why part goes back to the excavation of the Temple of Solomon two centuries earlier. I believe the Templars found ancient scrolls and writings that called into question the teachings of the Church. The Essenes, a monastic order living outside Israel, may have hidden many of their writings and archives in the Temple in 67 A.D., just before the Romans conquered the city. You may have heard of the Essenes — they were the authors of the Dead Sea Scrolls, which chronicled life during the time of Jesus Christ."

"What do you mean by called into question?" she asked.

The Monsignor raised his eyes to the sky, seemingly studying the clouds. "Bear with me, please, but to explain this thoroughly, I need to give you some more historical background. After Jesus died, a number of branches of Christianity emerged. Their teachings were often in conflict with each other, and with official Church doctrine, so much so that they were barely recognizable as the same religion."

"Are you referring to the Council of Nicea resolutions?" she interrupted.

"No, that was much later, in the early 4th Century. That was a rather trivial dispute, involving the question of whether Christ was *of* the Father or rather *from* the Father." He noticed Cam's quizzical look. "I agree. I find the whole issue rather pedantic."

The priest stood, pacing back and forth, silhouetted against the rusting hulk of a long-abandoned steel crane. "The dispute I am referring to goes to the question of the true roots and origins of

Christianity. After Jesus' death, some of his followers remained loyal to John the Baptist who, by the way, was a member of the Essenes. In fact, many believed Jesus was a disciple of John, rather than the other way around, and that John's religious teachings, based on his Essenic upbringing, were derived from the Egyptian worship of the goddess Isis. The similarities between the story of Jesus and Mary and the legend of Isis are striking: The husband of Isis, Osiris, was killed and then resurrected three days later to conceive their son, Horus. Many of the icons of Isis show her nurturing this son at her breast in much the same manner as the Virgin Mary is shown nurturing Jesus. And the teachings of the Isis religion emphasize repentance and confession." The Monsignor stopped, emphasizing his point. "Even the ritual of immersion into water as a purification rite has its roots in Egyptian legend."

He continued. "Isis in turn is based on the ancient religions that worshiped Venus, the first of which was practiced by the Grooved Ware people, so-named because of the pottery that was found at their settlements. They were the builders of Stonehenge."

"But Stonehenge is located in England," Amanda challenged. "Isis is in Egypt."

Marcotte nodded. "The Grooved Ware people traveled to the Middle East, trading. And they brought with them their Venus worship."

"But why would other cultures adopt these beliefs?" Cam asked.

"Simple. Because the Grooved Ware people had figured out how to use the rising of the planet Venus in the western sky as a kind of calendar. Venus travels in a five-pointed star-like pattern, repeating itself every 40 years. By studying this pattern, these Stonehenge builders were able to ascertain events like the summer and winter solstices and the spring and fall equinoxes. In ancient times, this was an incredibly important development; it told them when to plant crops, when to launch ships, when to slaughter livestock, when to hunker down for the winter. Often this knowledge was the difference between life and death."

"And so they came to worship Venus, believing it, or she, was the key to understanding the cycles of the earth," Amanda said.

"Exactly. Perhaps the best way to understand it is to say they worshiped Venus as the heavenly manifestation of Mother Earth. Many people call it worship of the Sacred Feminine."

"And this type of Venus worship is totally at odds with Church teachings," Amanda said.

"Church *teachings*, yes." The priest smiled. "But, actually, worship of the Sacred Feminine is totally consistent with Judeo-Christian *traditions*, though you will find few theologians or clergy who are aware of it. For example, have you ever heard of the Shekinah?"

Cam remembered hearing the term in synagogue a few times but didn't know what it meant. Marcotte explained. "It is a Hebrew word that refers to the feminine version of God. It is manifest throughout Jewish religious observances." He looked up. "How about the Holy Spirit?"

"As in the 'Father, Son and Holy Spirit'?" Amanda asked.

"Exactly. The Holy Spirit is one and the same as the Holy Sophia, goddess of wisdom in the Greek traditions. In the Apocrypha, the terms are used interchangeably." The Apocrypha was the section printed in the back of many Bibles, behind the Old and New Testaments due to its uncertain canonical legitimacy.

Despite his fatigue, the Monsignor was becoming more animated. "And here's another example. Remember the Venus 40-year cycle? Well, we see this 40 period repeated often in the Bible, as if the number is of mystical importance—the Jews wandered in the wilderness for 40 years; Noah's flood lasted 40 days and 40 nights; King Sol, King David and King Solomon all reigned for 40 years; Jesus fasted for 40 days and 40 nights; Lent lasts for 40 days; the period of postpartum rest and purification under Jewish law is 40 days; the list goes on and on. And speaking of King Solomon, some scholars believe that King Solomon's temple was a shrine not only to God but to Venus—it was built by Hiram Abiff, a Phoenician

Venus-worshiper, not by Jewish architects or craftsmen. The argument makes sense: Would you want non-believers building your most sacred shrine?"

Marcotte waited for his points to register before continuing. "The bottom line is that worship of the Sacred Feminine or the Goddess or Venus or Sophia or Isis or Mother Nature or whatever you want to call her is an integral part of the Judeo-Christian tradition. And these traditions remain in Christianity, despite the Church's attempt to whitewash them out and turn Christianity into a patriarchy." He took a deep breath. "I can give you a more graphic example: Just look at the design of most medieval churches and cathedrals."

Cam furrowed his brow. "I don't get it."

Marcotte slid a glossy photo across the table. The image showed a series of medieval churches featuring a pair of towers on either side of the doorway.

MEDIEVAL CHURCHES

He seemed a bit embarrassed. "I can explain best by reading directly from the reference material." He cleared his throat, read from a page he apparently copied from a book: "'If a woman lies on her back ... and then lifts her knees to be perpendicular to her body, her legs will obviously be elevated above her body as two projections. The genitalia will be given full view.'" The priest looked up. "This is the position, I believe, commonly assumed when giving birth." He continued reading. "'Transferring this posture to an architectural application in regard to building a sacred temple ... would reveal two elevated towers with an entrance to a temple between the towers at their base.... Such a scene is not unlike prime Gothic cathedrals having two spires on each side of an entrance leading into the sacred precincts.'"

"I see it," Amanda said excitedly. "That's precisely what they look like."

The Monsignor pulled another pair of photos from his bag and dropped them onto the picnic table. "These just happen to be the first two I found; there are many others. The first is a church in Lisbon, Portugal. The other is a church in Gotland, Sweden." Forsberg had said that the carvers of the Kensington, Spirit Pond and Narrangansett Rune Stones were probably Cistercian monks from Gotland. "Note the similarities between the doorway and the ... female genitalia," he mumbled.

CHURCH OF THE CONVENT OF CARMO, LISBON, PORTUGAL

LYE CHURCH, GOTLAND, SWEDEN

Amanda jumped all over it. "Yes, it's the vulva! The opening is the vagina itself and the arched ridges framing it are the folds of the labia." She pointed. "And the decorative point at the top—could that be the clitoris?" She looked up excitedly. "You said all church doors follow this pattern?"

"Not all but many. Far too many to be a coincidence."

"How fascinating," she said, still staring at the church images. "It's so symbolic. The church itself as the womb, the Sacred Feminine, the giver of life." She paused for a second and grinned. "The Templars were supposed to be celibate. Who would have guessed they were such experts on the vagina? They even included the clitoris—were you aware it is the only part of the human anatomy that serves no role other than giving pleasure?"

Cam rescued the Monsignor, who apparently wasn't sure whether Amanda's question was rhetorical or not. "The thing you read mentioned Gothic cathedrals in particular. That ties these doorways right to the Templars, doesn't it?"

"Exactly. The Gothic period coincides exactly with the rise of the Templars. They designed and built most of the stone Gothic cathedrals. Remember, when the Templars were later outlawed they morphed into the Masons, a stoneworkers' guild." Marcotte gathered the images, placed them back into his bag. "But we're getting off track. The key point is that the Church, even though it adopted many of these old Venus rituals, had a word for people who worshiped Venus or Isis or Mother Nature. It called them pagans. After all, the Church couldn't have peasants rutting in the woods every equinox."

"I'm sorry, peasants rutting?" Cam asked.

Marcotte nodded. "Yes. Easter is actually an old pagan fertility ritual, named after the fertility goddess 'Ishtar' and celebrated on the spring equinox. It really was little more than a mass orgy before the Church hijacked the holiday and turned it into the Jesus resurrection. But it still carries vestiges of its original meaning—the Easter egg and the rabbit are both signs of fertility and have nothing to do with Jesus or his resurrection. Same with Christmas—Jesus was born in September, not December. But the Church needed a way to convert the pagans. The sun was thought to be born on December 25th, the pagan winter solstice celebration. So the Church moved the birth of Jesus to the same date. And because the pagans worshiped the sun, the weekly day of worship was moved from the Sabbath, Saturday, to the day of the sun, Sunday."

"So is the Christmas tree a pagan symbol also?" Amanda asked.

"Yes, in fact. It's part of the pagan tradition of bringing an evergreen plant into the house to celebrate the rebirth of the sun after the winter solstice."

Amanda cocked her head. "Are you stating that many of Jesus' early followers were actually pagans?"

"I don't think they would have called themselves that but, yes, they believed in the Sacred Feminine, the power of the womb, the mystical powers of the planet Venus, what we would call Mother Nature. And they also believed in Jesus. The Church, as I said, tried to redirect these pagan beliefs and traditions and weave them into Christianity."

The priest took a deep breath before continuing. "Many early Christians also followed Mary Magdalene, believing her to be the wife of Jesus and the mother of Jesus' child, Sarah. I told you about how Mary and Sarah fled Jerusalem and went to France to live with some Jewish relatives and how their descendants, the Merovingians, ruled France and Germany during the end of the Dark Ages. Her followers, this cult of Mary Magdalene, were really just a continuation of the worship of the Sacred Feminine. The Church, of course, was based on a patriarchical theology, one that marginalized the role of women."

"Precious little has changed," Amanda observed.

The priest nodded. "To the Church's detriment, I fear. Despite the Church's efforts to demonize the Sacred Feminine, many sects worshiping the Goddess survived, drifting toward the more mystical side of the faith — the Gnostics for example. Gnosticism was based on ancient astrology and science, much of it, again, rooted in the old Venus worship. But it also incorporated some Christian teachings. Importantly, they believed Jesus was a prophet, not the son of God. And they did not believe in his resurrection." He raised an eye. "Remember the Cathars, tens of thousands of them slaughtered in Southern France in the 13th century?"

"The ones that God was supposed to protect if they were true Christians?" Cam said.

"Yes. Well, they were targeted because of their Gnostic beliefs and because they worshiped Mary Magdalene." The priest paused. "And this brings us back to the Templars. The Cathars were closely associated with the Templars, whose roots were in the region. The Templars shared many of their Gnostic beliefs."

The priest ran his hand through his hair. "I tell you all this to give you some historical context. In the early days of Christianity, in the first century or two, there were many different interpretations of the faith. Most of them were based on a concept of duality, of balance between the male and the female. As we just discussed, some believed that Mary and Jesus had a child, Sarah. Some doubted the resurrection story, believing it was recycled from the Egyptian religions. Many worshiped the Sacred Feminine. And all were based on historical sources — the Gospels of Mary and Judas and Thomas, gospels that have now been suppressed by the Church."

"Pardon me," Amanda interrupted. "There were more than just the four gospels?"

"Yes, there were dozens of accounts, or gospels, of Jesus' life. Many were in direct conflict with the official teachings of the Church; it is no surprise the Church suppressed them. As it suppressed the sects that followed them. Some groups were crushed violently, such as the Cathars. Others were merely marginalized. But all were eclipsed by the long shadow of the Church."

"The long shadow of the Church," Cam repeated. "That's a euphemism for the Crusades and the Inquisition and torture on the rack and burning at the stake, right?"

"Not to mention scores of other slaughters and atrocities and abominations that are mere footnotes in history." Apparently Marcotte had no delusions about the Church he served.

"Well," Amanda said, "how does all this tie in with the Templars?"

✝ ✝ ✝

Salazar edged around an abandoned warehouse, the barren waterfront making it difficult to get much closer without being seen. Thorne had picked his spot well. Just as he had wisely checked for anyone tailing the Monsignor's car. At some point he might even figure out the tracking device on the Subaru. But in the end he was an amateur, alive only because Salazar needed him to track the treasure.

Tucked behind a tree a hundred yards away, he could hear pretty much everything the Monsignor said using a parabolic listening device — a handheld, plate-size disk attached to a pair of head-phones. Fascinating information. But not nearly as interesting as what he had just seen through his binoculars. The model of the Tower was likely what McLovick had been searching for in the old couple's backyard, a crucial clue to finding the treasure. Too bad for him he hadn't bothered to look on their mantelpiece. As a treasure hunter, he probably wasn't used to finding valuables in plain view.

He adjusted the disk, focused on the Monsignor's explanation about Venus worship. Not altogether surprising. Many Native Americans cultures worshiped Venus or some other form of the Sacred Feminine. The Pawnee creation myth stated that Mars, the red morning star warrior, mated with Venus, the female evening star, to produce the first humans. And of course all tribes revered nature and the earth mother.

The Monsignor turned toward him for a second; the man looked terrible, like he hadn't slept in days. He was going to great lengths to share his information with Thorne and the girl, information that the Church was trying to suppress. More importantly for Salazar's purposes, the priest believed Thorne and the girl — Salazar's blood-hounds in his hunt for the treasure — were worthy recipients of this knowledge.

✟   ✟   ✟

The Monsignor stuffed his hands in his windbreaker pockets. Cam watched him intently, alert for any sign of deceit or dishonesty in the cleric. "Yes," Marcotte said, "how does this tie in with the Templars? That is the key question." He took a deep breath. "And here is the answer: I believe the Templars, while excavating beneath the old Temple of Solomon, uncovered ancient Essene documents and scrolls that called into question the core teachings of the Church. What they found emphasized instead the importance of both the

Sacred Feminine and other pagan practices including astrology, alchemy, magic and nature-worship."

"It sounds like witchcraft," Amanda said.

"Very much so. Another word for it is Kabbalism."

"You mean the Templars were Kabbalists? Like Madonna?" Cam blinked away an image of the vixen-like entertainer cavorting in the abbey with a legion of bearded, unwashed medieval warrior monks.

"The Hollywood version of Kabbalism has been dumbed-down but yes, like Madonna. Kabbalism has its roots in ancient Egypt and its sciences. Remember, a belief in astrology, alchemy and magic — what we might call witchcraft today — is really nothing more than a quest to understand the stars, chemistry and nature. Perfectly consistent with the Templar thirst for knowledge."

"And perfectly inconsistent with the Church's emphasis on blind faith over intellectual reasoning," Amanda said.

"Exactly. The Templars chose knowledge over faith, secretly rejecting the Church to which they had pledged their allegiance. The Templars — and their religious beliefs — directly conflicted with orthodox teachings of the Church."

Cam watched a squirrel snatch an acorn and scamper up a tree. "That would explain the whole Friday-the-13th roundup and massacre, what you said earlier about them being accused of heresy."

"Yes, especially if you look at the historical context. I believe that in the 12th and 13th centuries the Church and the Templars formed an uneasy alliance: The Church needed the Templar army and the Templars hoped to change the Church from within. And they both were willing to overlook differences with the other in order to expel the Muslims from Jerusalem. But the Holy Land was lost in the Siege of Acre in 1291, ending the Crusades and in essence making the Templars obsolete. So, by 1307, the Church was faced with an extraordinarily wealthy and powerful military wing that no longer served any useful military purpose and had lost much public support due to the loss of Jerusalem. Not to mention the small matter of the Templars practicing a secret, pagan religion. It is no surprise that the Church moved against the Order. Perhaps because they feared the Templars might preemptively move against the Church."

"Is there any evidence the Templars really were following pagan rituals?" It always came back to a question of evidence.

"There is. Of course, confessions made under torture are not reliable. But you know as a lawyer that when prisoners isolated from one another tell similar stories, even under torture, the evidence cannot be ignored."

"So one confession corroborated another?"

"Correct. The Templars admitted to worshiping a figurehead named Baphomet. Some people think Baphomet was a real skull—the preserved head of John the Baptist, maybe one of the things they found while digging in the ruins of Solomon's Temple."

Amanda crinkled her nose. "They worshiped an actual head?"

"It was actually quite common during medieval times. As I said, John, as an Essene, was a follower of the ancient Isis worship. It could be the Templars revered his skull as a link to the early Egyptian pagan beliefs."

Cam's own skull felt full, like it did before law school finals.

"The other possibility is that Baphomet wasn't a real head but rather a code word. Using an ancient Kabbalistic cipher, the word Baphomet translates into Greek as Sophia, which means wisdom. It's also a name for the ancient Goddess, the Holy Sophia. In fact, the Gnostic texts often equate Sophia with Mary Magdalene. In other words, by worshiping Baphomet the Templars were worshiping knowledge and science and learning as well as the Goddess and Mary Magdalene."

Interesting but probably not enough to sway a jury. "Any other evidence?"

"The Templars were a secret society so no records exist. But the circumstantial evidence is strong. For example, here is a picture of the floor pattern of the *Convento de Cristo* in Tomar, Portugal, a main Templar castle." He dropped another image onto the table. "The elliptical pattern on the floor is called a yoni, an ancient symbol of the Sacred Feminine, representative of the female vulva."

YONI PATTERN

Cam studied the picture. "Couldn't it just be some arbitrary pattern?" He thought about Freud for the second time in the last few days. "Isn't a cigar sometimes just a cigar?"

The Monsignor smiled. "With the Templars, nothing was arbitrary." He clasped his fingers together, rested his chin on them. "I spoke to a colleague in Lisbon. Apparently the entire *Convento de Christo* complex contains ancient pagan symbolism. Remember, the Templars were still 'in the closet,' as it were, when it was built. So the symbols are tucked away—carvings that are low to the ground or turned sideways or lost in a mish-mash of other carvings. But if you know what to look for you can't miss the signs."

Marcotte dropped his hands to the table. "Perhaps the strongest evidence of the true Templar beliefs comes from studying the life of Bernard de Clairvaux. Bernard, now known as Saint Bernard, was an extraordinarily powerful Cistercian monk in the early 1100s—I believe I mentioned him earlier as referring to Mary Magdalene as the bride of Christ. In fact, back to Amanda's question about preserving heads, Bernard's skull is preserved to this day at the Troyes Cathedral in France. Bernard came from an ancient Merovingian family, so we suspect right away he worshiped the Sacred Feminine. And these suspicions prove correct — Bernard was the driving force behind elevating the Virgin Mary to sacred importance in the Church. Before that, she was only a minor figure, barely recognized by the Church. It was also Bernard who convinced the Pope to accept the Templars as the army of the Church, and he who governed Templar religious practices. Bernard ordained that every Templar chapel be dedicated to the Virgin Mary and that every battle be fought in her name."

The Monsignor shifted uncomfortably. He slid another image onto the picnic table. "In fact, I came across a rather graphic medieval painting of Bernard lactating at the breast of the Virgin Mary. This is from a dream he had, in which the Virgin Mary cures him of an affliction with her breast milk. A disturbing image of a man later canonized as a saint but, again, his behavior and this image are more evidence of worship of the Sacred Feminine."

BERNARD De CLAIRVAUX LACTATING AT THE BREAST OF THE
VIRGIN MARY

Cam stared at the picture. No disputing it was the Virgin Mary holding the baby Jesus. Again Cam thought of Freud. But this time it had nothing to do with cigars; it had more to do with Saint Bernard's relationship with his mother. In any event the image made it impossible to dismiss Marcotte's assertion that Bernard revered the Sacred Feminine.

The Monsignor seemed eager to move on. "Two more interesting facts about the Cistercians." He explained that many of their practices — dress, lifestyle, vocations — were identical to those in the Essenes community. "Remember, it is the writings of the Essenes that the Templars may have found under Solomon's Temple." He also explained that, during Bernard's time, the order enlisted the assistance of Kabbalistic rabbis to help translate and study ancient Hebrew texts.

"Weren't the Jews being persecuted at that time as non-believers?" Amanda asked.

"Very much so. Which makes the collaboration between the Cistercians and the Kabbalists all the more strange."

Fair point. Why consult with the Kabbalists if you believe them heretics? And what exactly were they translating if not ancient Essene writings contemporaneous with the life of Jesus?

"Finally, we find more proof of Templar beliefs when we look at the Freemasons." Marcotte described how Venus worship and symbolism played a crucial part in Masonic ritual. "The Statue of Liberty is an example. It was a gift from the French Masons to the New York Masons. The original architect, Frederic Bartholdi, conceived the statue as an effigy to Isis, who of course herself is a representation of the Sacred Feminine."

The Monsignor stood. "I don't come to these conclusions easily. And I don't expect you to take just my word for it. Much of what I have told you is out there, written in books by scholars in Europe, some pieces here, some pieces there. It was just a question of pulling the threads of the tapestry together."

The Monsignor made a pretty compelling case. More importantly, the information was consistent with everything else Amanda and he had learned.

Amanda continued. "That helps explains the *Rex Deus* fixation. They pronounce they are the guardians of the true teachings of Jesus. But what are those secrets? Perhaps now we know." She looked at Cam. "And if *Rex Deus* families know the secrets, you can be bloody certain the Consortium knows them as well."

"I think that's a fair conclusion, Amanda," Marcotte said. "And it explains much of the Consortium's secretive behavior. This is not something they probably want to be associated with. At least not at this point in history."

Cam backtracked. "Let's go back to 1307 for a second. The Pope figures out the Templars are really a cabal that is, as the word itself suggests, practicing Kabbalism or some other pagan religion. And worshiping the Sacred Feminine. So with the French king's help he rounds them up, tortures them, puts them in prison, takes their land, burns a bunch of them at the stake. What happens next?"

"Well, whatever the truth of the allegations against the Templars, the result is not open for debate: As you said, the Order was decimated; those that weren't killed or imprisoned were forced to flee and go underground." Marcotte grimaced. "I can only imagine the pain this must have caused them. These are men who had sworn their lives to the Church, who had forsaken families and material wealth to serve their faith. And, importantly, probably had no idea they had somehow crossed the Church. To be suddenly excommunicated, ostracized, exiled...." He shook his head. "I can tell you what happens to priests today who are defrocked. The psychological impact is severe, their whole concept of who they are is shattered. And these are priests who have committed grave sins, who deserve to be cast aside by the Church. For the Templars, the blow must have been devastating."

"How could they have not known they were being ... heretical?" Amanda asked.

"Just as Cameron is *Rex Deus* yet had no idea of the true teachings of Jesus, so too the average Templar Knight, stationed in some abbey in Europe, knew nothing of Baphomet, knew nothing of the secret rituals performed by Templar leaders in France. Most of them couldn't even read. Like any soldiers, they were not privy to the inner secrets of their central command." Marcotte swallowed. "They worshipped Christ and the Virgin Mary just as other Christians did; in fact, they often gave their lives for them."

Cam didn't have much sympathy for defrocked priests, but Marcotte's anguish for the Templars was real.

Marcotte continued. "Do not underestimate the power of faith and religion. These men and their families — the remnants of the Templars — were not the type to just slink away. They were fighters. I would be very surprised if they did not play a large part in this mystery of yours."

✢ ✢ ✢

Salazar hesitated before placing the call to Reichmann. The Monsignor was, after all, a servant of God, no matter what his persuasion. The life of a holy man should not be taken lightly. But there was no choice — he needed to buy more time for Thorne and the girl.

"I am in Maine, following Monsignor Marcotte. I think he set up a meeting with Thorne."

"So you are back on their trail?"

"No. Something must have spooked them," he lied. "They didn't show. The Monsignor waited an hour; he's getting back in his car now."

"He might still lead you to them. Follow him. And keep me apprised of your location — I think it is time we had a little talk with this Judas."

CHAPTER 13

"By now they will have figured out you are not in Nova Scotia," Monsignor Marcotte had warned when he bid them farewell. "They will be getting more and more desperate to stop you."

Cam drummed on the Subaru's steering wheel; he didn't really have a destination in mind. Amanda now agreed it was almost certain that a Vatican fringe group, feeling threatened by their research, was intent on stopping them in any way possible. "It's like we talked about earlier. The only way this ends is if we figure out what the treasure is and where it's buried. Otherwise we're going to have to just keep driving around forever, running from this hit squad."

Amanda said, "Well it seems to me that if we want to locate this treasure, we need to begin thinking like medieval Templar Knights. After all, they're the chaps who buried it."

"Brandon told me they never took off their loincloths, even to bathe."

She crinkled her nose. "I said think like them, not act like them. Besides, they were celibate."

His face flushed; he tried to hide it by scratching his ear as he smiled back at her. Today was Thursday. They had been on the run since Monday. She had dyed her hair on Tuesday morning and the rash on her face, though largely faded, had been conspicuous since

Newport. It was as if the blond, aloof, cream-skinned Amanda of their initial meeting never existed. Only the accent remained.

She stared out the window a few seconds. "Among all the carvings at Roslyn Chapel, all the thousands of images, there exists only a single written inscription. It reads, 'Wine is strong, a king is stronger, women are stronger still but the truth conquers all.'"

The truth conquering all statement went against the concept of blind faith. As for the women comment, feminism wasn't exactly in vogue back then. "It's not what you'd expect to find in a medieval chapel."

"Unless the chapel was built by someone who worshiped the Sacred Feminine. And believed in truth over faith."

"A Templar. William Sinclair." Prince Henry's grandson.

She looked out the window again. "And there's another matter. The Monsignor spoke of the Grooved Ware folks, who evolved into the Druids, who were also Venus worshipers. Fancy this: The Druids always met in groves of oak trees." She looked at him knowingly.

"I'm not following you."

"Sorry. Sometimes I forget you're so new to all this. Almost every important site in America is associated with oak trees. The Oak Island Money Pit, for example—of the 300 islands in that area, it is the only one with oak trees. And we seem to always find oaks, sometimes red and sometimes white, near artifacts like the Westford Knight and the Newport Tower and the Boat Stone."

"You think the oak trees were planted on purpose? Maybe to help mark the spot?"

"Precisely. Recall that the Templar colors are red and white, like the oaks."

They rode in silence for a few minutes before Amanda spoke. "One more observation: If the Templars worshiped the Sacred Feminine, it stands to reason they also understood the importance of ley lines."

"Ley lines?"

"Ancient energy lines, believed to contain the psychic energy of the earth. The ancient megalithic peoples — the Grooved Ware people, for example — built most of their structures on or near them. Think of them as areas where the earth's energy is released — fault lines, mountain ranges, rivers, canyons."

"Wait. So you think Prince Henry would have been looking for these ley lines?"

"I do. It's part of the Mother Nature worship. They believed these sites were sacred."

"Do you know what Nashoba means?" he asked quickly. Nashoba was the Indian name for the Westford area.

"No."

"It means 'Hill that Shakes.' You know, like an earthquake. Westford sits on a geological fault line. That enough energy for you?"

"The Knight is on a bloody ley line." Amanda whistled. "I didn't know. Of course it makes sense — Prince Henry would have been looking to settle along an energy line."

"You know what else? This goes back to what Forsberg was telling us about where to find the stone holes — on top of the highest hills, along rivers, at the coastline."

"Yes. They'd all be considered energy line areas."

He pulled into the fast lane. "I think we should head back to Westford. Brandon mentioned Cowdry Hill. If that stone foundation in the Gendrons' backyard really is Prince Henry's encampment site, and if he really did mark it with the Boat Stone, there may be other clues up on that hill."

She smiled wryly. "Might we camp out again?"

The light was fading in the early evening but the sky remained clear. "I think it's too dangerous to get a hotel room, especially close to Westford. So I guess we get another night under the stars."

She took his hand, squeezed it, her voice suddenly serious. "Actually, please drop me at my flat. I'm sorry but I've had enough of this."

His head jerked around involuntarily. "What?" A cold knot tightened his chest.

She laughed, her eyes shining. "Just wanted to keep you on your toes. You might as well get used to it. You're stuck with me."

✛   ✛   ✛

Navigating a series of back roads into Westford, Cam followed an old railroad bed deep into the woods and hid the Subaru in the brush. As the daylight faded, he and Amanda set up camp in the same East Boston Camps site he had spent his first night on the run. They did so quickly, efficiently, a brisk wind again keeping most of the mosquitoes away. Cam ate an energy bar and an apple as he worked.

"I'm filthy," she announced. She pulled off her shirt and trousers and stood before Cam in a black bra and panties. "I'm going for a swim." She unceremoniously stepped out of her panties and unclasped her bra. "Join me, won't you?" she said, holding out her hand.

The scene was both a high school fantasy and the most natural thing in the world—there was nothing vulgar in her stance, nor anything contrived or pretentious. Just a woman offering herself as women had done for hundreds of generations.

He tried not to stare at her pale, lithe body. Tried to ignore the pink nipples erect on her breasts. Tried to look away from the golden, triangular tuft of hair between her legs. Then he gave up, allowing his eyes to feast for a few seconds. The term 'Sacred Feminine' echoed in his head and somehow everything Monsignor Marcotte said about Venus worship began to make sense. She stood with her arms at her sides, making no effort to cover herself, a woman without hesitation or shame. "Well, are you coming or not?"

He had cried on her shoulder while she comforted him like a scared child, which was in many ways more intimate than being naked together. It was time. He ripped off his jeans and t-shirt, his socks and boxers and insulin pump. Taking her hand, holding it gently, he joined her on the path leading down to the moonlit pond. "Can't think of anything else I'd rather do."

+   +   +

"The Monsignor is headed back to his church, I think," Salazar reported. "He should be there in under an hour."

"Any sign of Thorne and the girl?" Reichmann asked.

Salazar averted his eyes from the naked bodies in the pond down the slope. "No." Salazar didn't begrudge them time for a little romance. But hopefully they would consummate their relationship quickly and move on to the more important business of finding the treasure.

"Very well," Reichmann said. "I will handle it from here."

+   +   +

Cam and Amanda swam together in the pond for a few minutes, the water cool in the September night but not yet cold. Without any outward form of communication, they came together, each sensing the time was finally right. She wrapped her arms around his neck, opened her mouth to his. He spun her slowly in the shoulder-deep water, their bodies rotating as if in a high school slow dance, their music the sounds of the crickets and wind and frogs of the forest.

Their bodies intertwined like a pair of puzzle pieces, Cam slowly entered Amanda to complete their union. She gasped lightly before somehow pulling him even deeper inside her. Warmth enveloped him as if his entire body had descended into a heated cocoon. He dared not open his eyes, dared not release his grip, dared not do anything that might wake him from this rapturous fantasy.

He had no idea how long they moved together, slowly rotating in the water, their bodies as one. But when they finally had spent themselves, their flesh both flush from exertion and shivering from cold, the twilight had turned to darkness. He scooped Amanda in his arms and carried her like a bride to shore, her head nestled against his neck.

"Look," she said, her lips blue but her smile radiant in the moonlight. She pointed toward the western sky. "That bright star. That's Venus smiling down on us."

✝   ✝   ✝

Monsignor Marcotte checked the side view window. Nothing, surprisingly. He was one of the few links to Cam and Amanda. Which is why he had foregone his Crown Victoria and instead rented a car for his trip to Maine. But at some point the Legions of Jesus hounds would pick up his scent again.

He felt strangely at peace with his behavior. No doubt Church leaders—even the vast majority who knew nothing about the Legions of Jesus paramilitary team—would prefer Cam and Amanda fail in their quest. But he believed the Church would be the stronger if these secrets came out. Covering up a lie with more lies was not only morally wrong, it was also a policy doomed to fail. The world had changed; information was available with the click of a mouse—the days of keeping the populace ignorant by reciting masses in Latin were over. A Church built on lies and half-truths would in the end crumble beneath the weight of its own dishonesty, its good works and noble aspirations buried in the rubble.

He pulled into the driveway of the rectory, a large white Colonial structure abutting the church. After turning on some lights and feeding his tropical fish, he spent a few minutes in the rectory office checking messages and emails. But what he really wanted was to take a walk around the church's grounds. Most of his fellow clerics chose to think and reflect while inside the church edifice. But the church, though the house of God, was still erected by man. Nature, on the other hand, was God's creation — it was Bernard de Clairvaux, coincidentally, who first said God was more readily found in nature than in any church. A fellow priest once remarked he liked to think of nature as the clothing of God; Marcotte thought it was more akin to God's *skin*. He shook his head. Only the narrow-minded would try to suppress worship of the Sacred Feminine and Mother Nature, would fight efforts to reunite her with the Godhead. Just as the male and female united in nature to create life, so too did the Godhead require both a male and female aspect, a duality.

More than ever he believed in the teachings of Christ — compassion, generosity, forgiveness. But too often in history the Church had been hijacked by men who perverted Christ's teachings to their own ends. For better or worse, Cam and Amanda were about to force the Church to face its own history.

Marcotte flicked on the outside lights, slipped out the back door and took a couple of loping strides toward the garden. A pair of thick, black-clad men stepped out of the darkness and blocked his path, the air filled with a heavy cologne. "Monsignor Marcotte," the older of the two said in a Spanish-accented monotone. "A moment of your time, if you please."

Marcotte spun quickly, tried to retreat into the rectory. A strong hand gripped his shoulder, then a sharp object — a needle — penetrated his upper arm. He tried to struggle free, a sense of panic rising in his chest. "If you struggle, you risk the needle breaking off in your arm," the voice warned as he depressed the syringe.

A wave of dizziness splashed over him, reminding him of the time in college when he did shots of tequila at a frat party. His knees buckled and the two men supported him by his elbows and pushed him back into the rectory. Suddenly he felt light, almost giddy. He giggled, his soul cursing his brain for not being able to control his body. *Sodium pentothal*, his brain responded in defense.

"If you are smart, you will answer our questions quickly, before we are forced to administer a second shot of the truth serum." The man displayed a row of even, white teeth. "The second shot, unfortunately, is often lethal."

CHAPTER 14

[Friday]

Amanda and Cam spent the night wrapped together in a single sleeping bag, waking every couple hours to make love before falling back into a satiated sleep. She had experienced a normal number of lovers over the years — boyfriends, workmates, an occasional one-night fling — but had never felt so fulfilled afterwards. Not merely physically, but emotionally. Her body tingled at his touch and her heart raced beneath the warm gaze of his deep brown eyes.

She awoke at dawn, disentangled herself from Cam, threw on some clothes and walked down to the pond to wash. Despite her lack of sleep, she skipped and hummed her way along the path, stopped to watch a squirrel chew on a nut and listen to the birds chattering in the trees above her. A team of professional assassins was attempting to find and silence them. But today, right now, this minute, life was sublime.

Returning, she found Cam awake, boiling water for breakfast. He grinned as she approached; she skipped into his arms. "Good morning," she whispered, pulling him tight.

He kissed her ear, his beard tickling her scalp. "The best."

She held him a few more seconds before moving away to pack. As much as she would have preferred to spend the day in the woods, they needed to keep moving.

An hour later, they had eaten and packed their gear into the Subaru. They each shouldered a daypack. He pointed toward the northwest. "You up for a hike? It's about two miles, then we climb Cowdry Hill."

"I'd rather walk twenty miles than get back in that car. Just let me fetch a hat and some sunscreen so I don't turn into a swamp monster again."

They followed a path along the Stonybrook River. "You know," she said, "I've been considering what we discussed, about thinking like a medievalist. And I'm fairly certain we're on the right track with these energy lines. But it also struck me that the Templars favored chess. What do you think?"

"I'm in favor of chests also," he deadpanned.

She cuffed him. "I said chess, as in the game."

He smiled. "Sorry. Must be the accent."

"Chess was quite popular during medieval times, largely because of the thousands of Templars who learned the game in the Middle East and brought it with them back to Europe. Prior to the Templars making it so popular, chess was only played by royalty."

"How do you think it relates to all this?"

"It may not, but we have the Knight, of course. And it always struck me that the Newport Tower resembles the rook piece on a chessboard."

He nodded. "I had the same thought when I saw it. It may be a coincidence, but isn't the Templar flag black squares over white?"

"Yes." She hadn't considered that. "As a matter of fact, the flag is modeled after the floor of the Temple of Solomon, which featured alternating black and white tiles. The Masons copied the pattern — the floors of all Masonic temples and lodges are also in a chessboard pattern."

He pulled out his TracFone. "Another assignment for my cousin." After asking Brandon how he was feeling, Cam summarized

Amanda's ley line and chess theories. "So we need to figure out where Prince Henry and his gang might have buried their treasures, whatever they are. I think the stone holes play into it somehow, and also the ley lines and maybe even chess pieces in some way."

"Well, while you guys have been playing in the woods," Brandon said as Cam held the phone so she could hear, "I've been reading more about the Templars and the Masons. The Masons designed a lot of our cities, especially Washington. Even my dad agrees, right Dad?"

Peter grunted an affirmation in the background.

Brandon continued. "The Masons are big into this golden ratio thing—1.62 to 1. I don't think they invented it but they definitely used it a lot. Supposedly it repeats itself in nature over and over again, in plants and animals and stuff. The length and width of your face is in that ratio. Anyway, the Masons built D.C. using the same ratio. Maybe this Prince Henry used it also."

"Amanda, what are the dimensions of the Newport Tower?" Cam asked.

She was one step ahead of him. "The interior diameter is just over 18 feet. The height is 28 feet today but it was approximately 30 feet before the British troops blew the top off during your Revolutionary War." She smiled. "Sorry about that."

Cam dropped to a knee and did some calculations in the dirt with a stick. "Well, that's pretty damn close to 1.62 to 1."

"Come on, Cameron, that's just a coincidence," Peter said.

"Maybe. But I'm getting tired of people saying everything's just a coincidence. I don't buy some Colonial farmer just randomly building a windmill in this ratio."

"The arches stand just under 12 feet tall," Amanda said. "Does that ratio work as well?"

Cam scratched more numbers before smiling. "Bingo. Arch height compared to the height above the arch is just over 1.6 to 1. Another coincidence, Peter?"

"Could be."

Cam stood and tossed the stick away. "Whatever. Brandon, you said they used the Golden Ratio in Washington?"

"Yeah, it's like this: Using the Washington Monument as the point of the 'L,' the White House is 1 unit away and the Capitol building is 1.62 units away. The three points make a right triangle."

Amanda leaned into the mouthpiece. "Similar to the manner in which a knight moves in a chess game?"

"Just like that," Brandon said. "Some guy has a website and he shows all of Washington is this same Golden Ratio pattern repeated over and over again. Anyway, the Masons got this all from the Templars. All the old Templar churches and stuff were built using the same ratio. Including your Tower, I guess. These Templars were pretty sharp. Course, they had lots of free time because they swore off girls."

"Yes, we do hold you men back," Amanda teased. "No telling what our civilization would be like if you were left to your own devices."

Brandon laughed. "What, you have something against professional wrestling?"

"Actually, I fancy men who enjoy watching other people faking it. They make great lovers."

"Ouch. Cam, help me here."

Shaking his head and grinning, Cam changed the subject. "So, Forsberg thought the Newport Tower and all these other sites, along with the stone holes, were part of some mapping system. He called it mapping the New World. And we've got the golden ratio and chess pieces that might play into it also."

"I'll dig around more on this stuff. One other thing, on the Hooked X. This Forsberg guy may have been right. I've been reading a book about Mary Magdalene. It says, 'X is the common symbol of the alternative, underground version of Christianity that acknowledged Mary Magdalene as the lady of Christ.' Lady, as in bride."

"Great find, Brandon," Amanda said. If X was the symbol of Jesus and Mary Magdalene being married, it made perfect sense that a hook in the female portion of the X would symbolize their baby Sarah in Mary's womb.

"Wait until you hear what else I learned. My dad was skeptical that the Vatican — or even some fringe group — would care so much about all this — "

"Yes," Amanda interrupted, smiling. "Cameron and I had the same discussion. It does seem a bit like the elephant fearing the mouse."

"Well, it turns out the elephant has been afraid of the mouse for a long time. Did you know the Vatican still has an Inquisition office?"

"You mean thumb screws and stuff?" Cam answered.

"None of that anymore. But their job is still to suppress what they call 'false doctrine.' Well, guess who was in charge of the Inquisition in the eighties and nineties?"

Amanda and Cam exchanged shrugs.

"Pope Benedict, then know as Cardinal Ratzinger," Brandon said. "And check out what he said about the Masons: 'The faithful who enroll in Masonic associations are in a state of grave sin and may not receive Holy Communion.' And that's just one example. From what I read, the Church has been trying to squash Freemasonry for centuries."

"Grave sin? That's pretty strong language," Cam said. "Makes you wonder if they know the Masons have something on them. I mean, it's hard to see what's so threatening about a bunch of guys in funny hats organizing blood drives."

"Exactly. Like Amanda said, why else would they be so afraid of the mouse? I think the Masons have the goods on the Church."

"Good job, Brandon," Amanda said. If the Masons, as successors to the Templars, were the keepers of the Sarah secrets, that could explain why Vatican fanatics were so intent on suppressing research involving a preeminent Templar-Masonic family such as the Sinclairs.

"Thanks. Hey, Cam, give the phone to Amanda."

He did so and backed away.

"Hey. Not for nothing but my cousin can be a bit slow on this stuff. You may have to jump his bones, you know what I mean?"

That he was lying in a hospital bed without one leg softened the crassness of the comment. And she had already opened the door with her 'faking it' remark. "Done," she announced. "Four times."

He guffawed. "Good girl."

She hung up. "He's done some interesting research. And he seems in good spirits."

"I think he's focusing everything now on helping us, on getting his revenge. I'm worried about what happens after. He's got a long life ahead of him. It won't be easy."

Ten minutes further into their hike the Stonybrook River hairpinned to the left. They followed a tributary that continued straight, discussing Brandon's findings regarding the Vatican's antipathy toward the Masons. Brandon's research demonstrated a long-standing level of hostility on the part of certain Church factions toward the Masons and whatever secrets might be shrouded in Masonic and Templar symbolism and ritual. More to the point, his findings were consistent with the Monsignor's warnings that Vatican extremists were intent on suppressing research on Prince Henry and the Hooked X.

The stream slowed; they shifted their focus to their immediate surroundings. "If our theory about the encampment site is right," Cam said, "this is the river Prince Henry took to the Gendrons' back yard." It narrowed so much that in some stretches they could have leapt across it. "Not exactly the Mississippi."

"No, but 600 years ago, before all the mills and dams, it probably ran much wider and deeper. If you look closely, you can see the old river banks." In addition to the depression the river ran through today, a wider depression was apparent in the topography of the land, perhaps tripling the width of the river.

A few hundred yards before they reached the encampment site, the tributary slowed to a trickle. Cam turned to his left. "We want to cut through the woods over here, avoid being seen as much as we can."

They reached a main road, waited for the traffic to pass and crossed quickly. A long, freshly-paved drive snaked its way up a steep hill. "This is an access road for the new Westford Highway Department garage."

She smiled. "The one they refer to as the 'Garage Mahal'?"

"Yeah. They spent a few bucks on it, apparently." He led her into the woods to a path that paralleled the access road. It was a Friday and a steady stream of trucks moved in and out of the garage. "We're on Cowdry Hill. A lot of it has been quarried—they built the Bunker Hill Monument in Charlestown with the granite from here. But according to Brandon, there's an area at the top that hasn't been disturbed. It's the highest peak around other than where the Knight was found."

She glanced over her shoulder, down the road they just crossed. "It really is close to the encampment site and the Boat Stone."

The path climbed steeply, curving its way up the slope through the woods. "They brought the granite down on carts and sleds. That's why the path's so wide," he said. The trail ended at a round clearing about the size of a baseball infield. The entire ground was flat, smooth granite, almost as if the infield had been flooded and then frozen in a cement-colored ice. "Looks like they quarried the rock ledge right off the top."

"It's a beautiful spot, almost looks like an ancient amphitheater." Perhaps soon they could return and picnic. If they lived long enough.

They walked across the smooth granite, picked up the path on the far side of the quarried area and climbed another hundred feet. He checked his GPS device. "We're pretty much at the top. Let's look around."

She stepped off the path, wandered deeper into the woods and spotted a gray, car-size boulder split neatly down the middle. The two halves were almost equal in size, separated by a V-shaped gap. She beckoned Cam. "That's the largest rock in the area. And that split is remarkable. What could be stronger evidence of an energy line than a giant boulder split in half, seemingly for no reason?"

He nodded. "During medieval times, how else would you explain it?"

"If I were looking for a place to drill a hole for my mates to find later, I'd select this boulder."

Climbing on top, he began to examine the boulder. She squeezed into the gap and studied the surface for inscriptions or other signs of alteration, brushing away moss with a stick. Cam used his pocket knife to do the same. They worked for about ten minutes, slowly circling the boulder, brushing leaves and pine needles off the surface and crevices. Nothing.

She sighed. She had been certain they would find something.

"I'm going to look around," he said and began to walk away.

She took a few steps back and studied the boulder. They had cleared the entire surface and the stone was bare other than a small weed that had taken root in the rock's crevices like a lone acacia tree in the desert. *Taken root.* Of course. "May I use your knife?" He flipped it to her. She dug around the weed and loosened the soil. Yanking on the plant, she pulled it free, tossed it aside and probed into the root's crevice, extracting dirt. "Cam, look!" She triumphantly pointed to a silver dollar-size, triangular-shaped hole. "There it is. Just as we suspected."

Grinning, he squeezed her arm. "Good job. I totally missed it." He inserted his finger into the hole, rubbed the edge. "It's uneven, definitely not machine-made."

She inserted a stick into the hole. "Approximately three inches deep." Same size, same shape, same depth as the holes on the Tyngsboro Map Stone and the Spirit Pond outcropping. It was time to play Connect the Dots.

+ + +

"How are you on a bike?" Cam asked.

He and Amanda sat on the warm granite outcrop of the round amphitheater-like quarry clearing, sharing a bag of trail mix and a bottle of water. The sun had melted away the morning chill, promising another temperate day. The weather — tranquil and clear and comfortable — continued to stand in stark contrast to the storm swirling around them.

"As long as we stay off your mountain trails, I'll be fine. What's your plan?"

"I think we need to get to someplace with a lot of maps, where we can spread out and plot these points and try to figure out how everything fits together."

"Perhaps a library."

"Yes, but it's too risky to stay local. Someone might see us. And I really don't want to use the Subaru on the main roads."

"Well then, let's go buy me a bike." She smiled. "Something to match my new hair."

They followed the trail back down the hill, Cam mapping the path they would take through the woods to a nearby Wal-Mart. As they prepared to cross the main road, the sound of a siren broke the morning calm. He pulled Amanda behind a tree; a police car sped in the direction of Monsignor Marcotte's church just up the street. An ambulance followed quickly in its wake, its siren also blaring.

Cam resumed his mental mapping. "Do you hear that?"

"What?" She looked at him quizzically. "I don't hear anything."

"Exactly. The sirens didn't just fade away. They stopped. Which means the ambulance stopped."

Her chin dropped. "The Monsignor. You don't think...."

"I don't know what to think anymore." He phoned Brandon. "Can you find Poulos, ask him if knows anything?"

They walked in silence, hand in hand, waiting for Brandon to call back. "Really, it may be nothing," she said.

He frowned. "What's your gut tell you?"

"Unfortunately, the same thing yours tells you," she said, leaning against him.

Brandon called ten minutes later. "What?" Cam answered.

"It's bad. Monsignor Marcotte is dead."

"Damn it." A wave of thick, acrid bile rose in Cam's throat; he swallowed it down and spat to clear his mouth.

"Poulos is all over it. He's at the church right now. They think the Monsignor died of a drug overdose. Probably some kind of truth serum, sodium pentothal maybe. Poulos told me to tell you you should come in."

Cam steadied himself against a tree. "Listen. Tell Poulos to worry about catching the killers. Tell him that the Monsignor thinks it's some kind of extremist Catholic group called the Legions of Jesus doing all this. He's going to need some help—FBI, whatever."

He hung up. "The Monsignor was a good man. Just like Forsberg."

Her eyes wet with tears, Amanda slipped her arm over his shoulder. "I know."

"They must have figured out he was helping us." He retched again; again he swallowed his bile. The Vatican crazies had taken this to a whole new level. If they would kill a respected monsignor, they wouldn't hesitate to knock off a few more civilians. He pulled her deeper into the woods. "Brandon's not safe."

"Didn't Poulos post a cop at his door?"

"Yeah, but I don't think one cop has much of a chance against a paramilitary hit squad. And it's not like Brandon can just hit the road like we did." His mind raced. "It's only a matter of time before they get to him—he's the obvious link to us. We need to have a plan in place before they do. Something that Brandon can tell them that will buy him his life."

+   +   +

There was no time for caution, no time for buying bicycles and sticking to back roads. Forsberg was dead. Marcotte was dead. Brandon probably would be next. Cam swiped the branches off the Subaru, threw his pack in the back. "I have an idea but I need maps."

"Outside of Westford," Amanda said, "Groton's library is the closest."

"Anybody know you there?"

"No."

"Me neither."

Less than ten minutes later he pulled into the lot behind a yellow brick building near the town center. They found an oversized map of New England and eastern Canada at the reference desk. As Amanda spread it out on a heavy mahogany table, Cam found a stack of yellow Post-its at the reference desk and ripped a few of the sticky ends of the sheets into a dozen dice-size squares.

"Okay. Let's start marking important spots. If Forsberg was right, these artifacts and stone holes and carvings are part of some kind of elaborate mapping system."

"You do that," Amanda said. "There's a book I want to locate."

He worked quickly, sticking Post-it scraps to mark the Newport Tower, the Westford Knight, the original Boat Stone location, the

Tyngsboro Map Stone, Spirit Pond, the Narragansett Rune Stone site, America's Stonehenge, Lake Memphremagog in Quebec (where Templar artifacts were found and where Prince Henry may have sailed via the Merrimack River), Oak Island in Nova Scotia, and the stone hole they found on Cowdry Hill in Westford.

She returned, looked over his shoulder and studied the map. "Probably dozens of other artifacts and stone holes and petroglyphs were either destroyed or haven't been uncovered yet. When you think about it, it really is amazing that so much evidence still survives."

He only half heard her. He was looking for a pattern in the yellow scraps of paper. "Let's go back to this chess thing. And let's imagine that the Newport Tower really is a rook. It would move either vertically or horizontally." He traced the latitudinal line due east toward Europe: The line passed directly through Rome. Not a bad reference point for a prime meridian.

Focusing now on the north-south orientation, he dropped one end of his ruler on Newport. "Check this out, Amanda." He stood. "The Tower and America's Stonehenge are on the same longitudinal line. Maybe Forsberg was right — maybe the Tower is the key to some whole mapping system."

"And I wager that's what the lantern clue is trying to tell us also — the Tower is the key."

As they studied the map, a middle-aged man with thick glasses tapped Amanda on the shoulder and handed her an oversized, fabric-bound book entitled, *The History of Chess*. She waved it at Cam. "You continue working on the map. I'll work on the chess pieces."

"Okay." What about the Westford Knight itself? Did it fit into the mapping in any way? Brandon had said the Masons laid out Washington using a series of L-shaped patterns, similar to a chess knight's movement, with the two stems of the L in the golden ratio of 1:62 to 1. Cam marked the Knight on the map and maneuvered his ruler in different L-shaped combinations for a few minutes. He dropped his ruler as one of the L-shaped patterns in the 1:62 to 1 ratio landed his knight exactly on the America's Stonehenge site.

"What is it?" she asked.

He didn't want to overstate his case. Lives were at risk, including his and Amanda's. But this was a remarkable coincidence. Or it was more than that. "The knight passes through the America's Stonehenge site just like the rook—the Tower—does."

She set her book down and peered over his shoulder. "I suspected that might be the case."

"You did?"

She held up her book, waving it at him again. "A few interesting chess facts. First, as we knew already, the Templars played a large role in introducing chess to Europe from the Middle East."

"Makes sense. They were traveling back and forth a lot."

"But fancy this: The chess queen was originally a minor piece, only able to move one square at a time, similar to the king. The Templars were behind the change to make her the most powerful piece on the board."

"Venus worship strikes again."

"Precisely. And it gets better." Her eyes gleamed. "In medieval times there was no bishop on the board. They played with a ship piece instead. The Church was bothered because the game was becoming popular yet there was no Church player on the board. So the Church decreed that the ship piece—which moved diagonally, as would a boat tacking back and forth into the wind—be changed to a bishop."

Not only were the hairs on his neck standing, they were swaying in the wind. "Wait. So the bishop used to be a boat?"

"Yes. A medieval knorr. The same type of ship as is carved on the Boat Stone."

"Bloody amazing," he grinned. Turning back to his map, he drew a diagonal line through the Boat Stone, just as a bishop would move. The line passed through the Cowdry Hill stone hole to the southwest and the Tyngsboro Map Stone, which also had a stone hole, to the northeast. Extending it a bit further, his hands shaking as he moved the ruler, the line passed directly through the America's Stonehenge site, intersecting the L-shaped Knight and vertical Tower lines. Further north, the line bending to account for the curvature of the earth, the line would pass over the Spirit Pond stone hole as well.

"This is fascinating, Cam. You've got the knight, the rook and the bishop — or the ship — all intersecting in the same spot. America's Stonehenge."

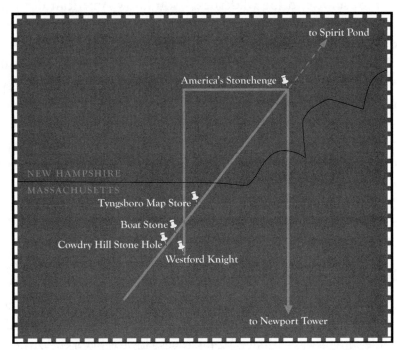

IMAGE SHOWING INTERSECTION OF ROOK, BISHOP AND KNIGHT
CHESS PIECE MOVEMENTS AT AMERICA'S STONEHENGE SITE

"It's like Eric Forsberg said. Everything the Templars did existed on multiple levels. So these artifacts were not only markers and signposts and memorials but also pieces to a whole secret map."

"Directing us to Mystery Hill, America's Stonehenge."

"But why? Why did Prince Henry devise a coded map using chess pieces to point to a bunch of ancient rock formations?"

She touched his shoulder, her face flushed in excitement. "You're not thinking like a medievalist, Cam. Don't you see? Finding America's Stonehenge would have been crucial to their survival in the New World. It was their calendar and their compass. In many ways it was just as important to them as Stonehenge in Britain was to the Grooved Ware culture. As the Monsignor said, it told them how to farm and manage their livestock and when to travel. Basically how to survive in the wilderness — you know American history, you know the Pilgrims almost perished that first year because they did not understand the climate here." She paused. "And it would also have told them when to celebrate religious holidays. Recall that, though they did not follow the dogma of the Church, they remained devout Christians."

She shifted in her seat, folding a leg beneath her. "And fancy this: It goes even further. It ties back all the way to Venus worship, to worship of Mother Earth. That's what the America's Stonehenge site is: It's the manifestation of man's understanding of Mother Earth. America's Stonehenge must certainly have been a sacred site; Prince Henry convinced the natives to share it with him, probably because they understood he worshiped nature just as they did."

She had made a compelling argument. And she wasn't done yet. "An ancient megalithic site called Maes Howe remains standing today in northern Scotland. Like Stonehenge, it was built by the Grooved Ware people and records the Venus cycles." She paused, made sure he was with her. "Cam, Maes Howe is in Orkney, where Prince Henry resided and ruled. He certainly knew about it, probably observed the Venus cycle himself. He would have immediately appreciated the importance of the America's Stonehenge site."

The more he thought about it from a medieval point of view, the more Amanda's conclusion seemed correct. Prince Henry traveled halfway around the world and what did he find? A series of stone structures — whether built by ancient Europeans or by Native Americans themselves — used by the natives to mark and measure celestial events in the same way his ancestors did in Orkney. It would be like going to another planet today and stumbling upon a Swiss watch. The discovery must have blown Prince Henry away. Could he have really hoped to find like-minded peoples amongst the 'savages' of the New World?

So it made sense he would consider the America's Stonehenge site a treasure of the New World. Just as his ancestors worshipped Sophia, the goddess of wisdom, so too would Prince Henry, in Templar fashion, understand that knowledge was the true Holy Grail. Knowledge of the seasons, knowledge of nature, knowledge of the stars, knowledge of the earth. Knowledge was the most valuable of all treasures. No wonder Prince Henry's coded maps led directly to the ancient stone structures that embodied this knowledge.

It was all perfectly consistent with Templar and Kabbalistic values and traditions. Yet he had the feeling that there was more to it, another layer to the onion they hadn't peeled away yet. As the Monsignor said, the Templars always operated on multiple levels....

But the onion-peeling would have to wait. For now they needed to save Brandon. He dialed his cousin's TracFone.

"Hey," Brandon said. "I just spoke to Poulos. They think they got one of the guys who killed the Monsignor."

Some good news, finally. "Is he talking?"

"No. He's got a bunch of high-priced lawyers, flown in from Miami."

Maybe not such good news. Probably just a low-level operative. No doubt there were dozens more Legions of Jesus soldiers waiting in the shadows to replace him. In some way they were like modern Templar Knights, willing to die for their religion. Looking back at the Templars and their fanaticism, perhaps the modern al-Qaeda movement and its seemingly endless supply of suicide bombers shouldn't surprise Western observers after all.

"Listen. I think we figured everything out." He recounted the chess movements, the intersection of all the pieces, the significance of the America's Stonehenge site as both a calendar and a link to ancient Templar spiritual beliefs.

"So that's it? No treasure?"

"Not a treasure in the traditional sense, no."

"Not even a genealogy or anything like that?"

"Nope. Like I said, nothing sexy. Just a coded map that points to America's Stonehenge."

"So the Vatican has nothing to worry about?"

Cam pictured the black sedans speeding toward Massachusetts General Hospital, the muscular goons, the long needle with truth serum dripping from its tip. He hated lying to his cousin. But he had no choice. "No, nothing. Prince Henry and his gang were just trying to stay alive. Just trying to figure out when to plant their crops and when to celebrate their holidays."

+   +   +

They only had a few hours, at most, before the Legions of Jesus operatives closed in on Brandon. But something Amanda had said resonated in Cam's mind, causing a bunch of otherwise irrelevant scraps of information to suddenly become not only relevant but potentially vital: *Somehow Prince Henry convinced the Indians to share the America's Stonehenge secret with him.* This was the key to peeling away the next layer of the onion.

Unfortunately, they didn't have time to pursue his theory now. "We need to move quickly. I have a feeling this all is going to come to a head today. My guess is they're going to abduct Brandon, use him to get us to come in and meet with them. I don't really see how we can stop them. Poulos has already posted a guard—we don't have enough evidence against the Legions of Jesus to convince him to put a whole SWAT team up there. And it's not like they can move him someplace safe; he needs to be in an ICU ward in a major hospital. These guys are trained paramilitary forces. Whether it's today or tomorrow or the next day, they're going to find him no matter what we do."

"I see your point."

"So we need to be ready."

Using the library's WIFI connection and his laptop, he typed a memo to Lieutenant Poulos, summarizing everything they had learned, including the Legions of Jesus' suspected involvement in the murders of McLovick, Eric Forsberg and Monsignor Marcotte. He emailed the memo to Poulos and also a copy to Uncle Peter and his parents, who had returned to North Carolina. "I will be checking in with Peter on his cell phone later this afternoon," he wrote, "and then every two hours after that until midnight, then again at 6:00 o'clock tomorrow morning. If anything happens to me, or if I fail to check in, you need to get this information to the press right away. They might not believe you at first but once they dig around they'll see it's all true."

He also took a chance and dialed Eric Forsberg's office number. He reached a secretary and asked to speak to Scott Wolter, Forsberg's boss and co-investigator.

"Can I ask who's calling?"

"My name is Cameron Thorne. Please tell him this is regarding Eric Forsberg's research." He wasn't sure Wolter would take his call.

Wolter surprised him by coming to the phone immediately. "Oh, man, I was hoping you'd call. Are you guys okay?"

Cam appreciated the stranger's concern. "Yeah. We're still on the run. Do you think this line is secure?"

"No, I don't. After they killed Eric, I'm sure they're keeping a close eye on me. So don't say anything incriminating. But there's an old pay phone in the lobby of my building. One of the last ones in the city." He gave Cam the number. "Call me back in two minutes."

They resumed their conversation. "Hey, I know Eric was a good friend of yours. He was a good man."

"The best. I still can't believe they killed him over *research*. It's like the friggin' Inquisition."

Cam summarized the events of the past week. "In case anything happens to us, I wanted someone who understands all this to know what we've been researching. I don't want the Vatican fanatics to succeed in keeping this all quiet."

"No way are they keeping me quiet. This is going public, big time. And check this out: I discovered another Hooked X."

Cam squeezed the phone. "Another rune stone?"

"No. It's part of Christopher Columbus' signature. If you're online, do a quick Google search using *Columbus* and *sigla*."

He did so and found the image. Sure enough, a Hooked X.

SIGLA (SIGNATURE) OF CHRISTOPHER COLUMBUS WITH 'HOOKED X' IN UPPER LEFT

"Why Columbus? I don't get it."

"I didn't either at first. But it turns out Columbus married into a prominent Templar family in Portugal, where they were called the Knights of Christ. Remember the sails on his ships, decorated with red Templar crosses? And he often wrote about having 'the royal blood of Jerusalem' in his veins. In fact, I'm reading a book now entitled, *Christopher Columbus, The Last Templar.*"

Another puzzle piece. But he couldn't see exactly where it fit. And he didn't have a ton of time to mull it over. Instead, he asked for Wolter's email address and sent him a copy of the memo he had sent to Poulos as they talked. "So, do you think we're on the right track with this Sacred Feminine stuff?"

"Definitely. The thing that convinces me is that whoever came over — and I happen to think it was a combination of Templars and Cistercian monks — must have forged some kind of friendship with the Native Americans. I mean, they didn't fight their way to Minnesota to carve the Kensington Rune Stone. And they would have needed help to build the Newport Tower."

"Good point."

"So they must have had some common ground. And I think that was their spiritualism, their worship of Mother Nature."

"Yeah, we thought the same thing about the America's Stonehenge site. The Native Americans wouldn't have shown it to them if they didn't have an appreciation for its importance."

"Exactly."

"All right. Thanks. It's good to talk to someone who doesn't think we're crazy."

"The people who are crazy are the ones who dismiss these artifacts. I mean, if you listen to them, North America must have been filled with Runic-speaking natives with iron tools and lots of free time on their hands."

He laughed. "Good point. Thanks again."

"Hey, I plan to be out your way in a couple of months. I'd love to buy you guys a beer. Eric said good things about you."

Cam hung up and checked on Amanda. She had photocopied the library's oversized map, taping nine sheets of paper together, and drawn the various artifact and stone hole sites around New England onto the map. Using a red pen, she superimposed onto the map the movements—vertical, diagonal and L-shaped—of the three chess pieces, the three bright red lines intersecting at the North Salem, N.H. site of America's Stonehenge.

She also had made photocopies of the relevant pages of the chess book discussing the ship/bishop piece and printed a handful of pictures of Masonic temples and lodges showing the chessboard-like floor tile pattern from the internet. "What's that?" he asked.

"The Church of the Holy Sepulchre in Jerusalem, built on the site Jesus was buried. Notice the chessboard pattern on the church floor."

"Nice." If they were going to sell this to the Vatican crazies they needed a good story. Good pictures always helped.

✛   ✛   ✛

Cam and Amanda grabbed some sandwiches and spread out on a bench outside the library. He forced himself to eat, his stomach fighting him at every swallow, his gut clenched as he imagined the Legions of Jesus henchmen closing in on Brandon. He ached to warn his cousin, to somehow arrange for Brandon to be wheeled to safety. But it just wasn't possible to hide an ICU patient from a trained paramilitary team. So instead he had come up with a plan.

"Cam, are you sure it's wise to put Brandon in danger again?"

"Like I said before, the reality is there's nothing we can do about it." Cam stared out at the hills gently rolling into the valley below. "Besides, I'm not sure Brandon would want it any other way. He's like an injured football player. He's stuck on the sidelines while his teammates are in the trenches. There's no worse feeling—he feels inadequate, powerless, gutted. If he could come in just for one play, make one key block or tackle to help win the game, he'd give up his other leg to do it. I know him. I know I'm right."

"Must be a guy thing."

"Not all guys. But definitely Brandon. If he finds out I babied him he'll never forgive me. It'll just eat away at him, knowing I didn't think he was up to it. But if we get through this and he knows he played a part in it...."

"You fancy it will help him recover."

"Exactly."

Putting aside his concern for Brandon's safety, Cam felt oddly confident and at ease, like a landlubber finally stepping ashore after a long ocean voyage. The solid, stable, motionless ground under his feet felt strangely alien but also, paradoxically, comfortable and familiar. Over the past week he had been playing the role of a Hollywood action hero — attacked by bombs and hurtling cars and black-clad henchmen, wooed by a beautiful woman, befuddled by an ancient mystery, opposed by a shadowy cabal of ruthless villains. Now he was back in his element: in a library, researching, strategizing, analyzing, problem-solving. He was a lawyer again. Preparing to argue the case of his life.

And, as often happened to lawyers he wasn't totally sold on the merits of his own case. The confluence of intersecting lines at America's Stonehenge was more than coincidence, more than a random occurrence. But he would have liked to have more data to support their theory. Unfortunately, time conspired against them — they were out of it now, and too many stone holes and artifacts had been lost to it. Even so, he could sell his case. Would sell it.

She studied him. "You seem different. More self-assured."

He nodded, motioning toward the library. "This is what I do, what I've been trained for. I build cases, make arguments." He smiled. "I know you think of me more as the James Bond type. But it's nice to get back to more familiar ground."

Amanda's smile was even more radiant in the sunlight. "Well, that makes me feel better. You'll win the argument. Then they'll shoot us in the head."

"Yeah, something like that. Actually, I don't think we'll be dealing with the same gorillas who've been chasing us. Based on what the Monsignor probably told them before he died, they know we've figured a lot of this out. They're going to want to know what we've learned so they'll need someone who is versant in all this Templar stuff. Probably a Vatican historian. Which is not to say the gorillas won't still be around. But at least they won't be calling the shots."

She stared out at the distant woods for a few seconds. "Really, one thing we might be able to use to our advantage is that we're not scholars, we're not experts." She smiled. "We're pretty much nothing."

"You think they might underestimate us?"

"Precisely. They may assume it would be impossible for us, in a week, to solve a mystery they haven't been able to decipher in decades of work."

"I see your point. Sort of like cognitive dissonance. Their egos won't let them accept that we solved the mystery when they couldn't." If they underestimated Amanda's intelligence, they did so at their peril. "But can we use this to our advantage? Remember, I want them to believe our theory. That's really the only way to get out of this mess."

Amanda sipped on her Diet Sprite. "Perhaps we need to make it appear as if we are not that bright, that we stumbled upon the solution by dumb luck. That way they can dismiss us as buffoons but still accept our conclusions." She smiled as she stood. "Follow me, I have an idea."

They walked back into the library, Amanda immediately running some Google searches. Within ten minutes she had printed out a stack of articles. One claimed that the *Rex Deus* line descended from a race of aliens. Another concluded that the Mormon Church was in possession of the Ark of the Covenant, having inherited it from the Prince Henry voyagers. A third discussed a 1990s plot by the *Rex Deus* leaders to marry Princess Diana to Bill Clinton (after killing off Hillary) in an effort to control the Western world. Yet another featured a guy in Seattle who believed he possessed the Biblical stone that symbolized the God-given power of the Davidic line of kings; he refrained from claiming the power as his own, instead waiting for Jesus' heir to claim it. A fifth claimed that the Shroud of Turin was actually a cloth used to keep a tortured Templar leader warm. The final article proclaimed that the Oak Island Money Pit was a portal to another dimension, allowing aliens to travel through time and space.

Cam perused them, taking strange comfort in the realization that there was a world of amateur researchers out there championing theories that made the conclusions he and Amanda reached seem downright pedestrian....

His TracFone rang; it was Brandon. He called Amanda over. "This is it." Taking a deep breath, trying to keep his voice normal even as his stomach clenched, he answered. "Hey, Cuz."

"I am not your cousin, Mr. Thorne." A sloppy, Spanish-accented voice.

They had Brandon. Cam had assumed it would happen, even planned on it. A single cop was no match for a paramilitary squad. But the reality filled him with fear and anger. He allowed his emotions to bubble to the surface. "Listen to me. You do anything to my cousin and I swear —"

"Your cousin is fine, Mr. Thorne. Other than his leg, of course." Probably the Latin American group, the Legions of Jesus, as the Monsignor had theorized.

"Let me talk to him."

"Very well. But only briefly."

A few seconds passed. "Hey, Cam." Brandon's voice was listless.

"You all right?"

"Not sure," he slurred. "They drugged me."

Probably the same truth serum they used on Monsignor Marcotte. It usually made people giddy, like a good buzz. But Brandon was already on medication; who knew how it would react in his system? "Listen carefully. Tell them everything. Don't try to lie or resist them. I'm serious!" Maybe they should have put him on a plane to Europe or something. Not that it could have been arranged in the two hours since the Monsignor's death.

The Spanish voice again. "Wise advice. In fact, he has been very informative already. Now, no further harm will come to him if you follow my directions."

Cam cut him off. "Let's get something straight right away: If he dies, I go public with all of this — all of Forsberg's research on the Hooked X, the Jesus bloodline, everything. Understand?"

"Obviously we are hoping to prevent such an occurrence. As I said, your cousin will not be harmed. We will release him if you cooperate with us. We understand that he is of no value to us if he is dead. However, you must act quickly; at some point the nurses will become suspicious." There was good news, at least — they hadn't been able to spirit Brandon out of the hospital. Probably figured it'd be easier to isolate him in his room. "In this chess game we are playing, Mr. Thorne, even a pawn must not be sacrificed to no purpose."

He and Amanda exchanged knowing glances — the chess reference likely was not a random one. Brandon must have told them about the chess pieces intersecting. Apparently they were intrigued by the theory. "Okay, so what do you want?"

"It is almost one o'clock. At three o'clock you will meet us at the America's Stonehenge site. Come alone, just the two of you. And please drive carefully."

The line went dead.

+ + +

Cam and Amanda made a quick detour on their way to America's Stonehenge. Paying cash, he bought a couple of decent-quality mountain bikes at Wal-Mart, took off the front wheels and tossed the bikes into the back of the Subaru. Meanwhile Amanda went next door to a Staples, made photocopies of all the documents they acquired at the Groton library and used a disposable camera to photograph the lantern from all sides. She also bought a cardboard box and some bubble wrap to protect the lantern, then packed that box into a slightly larger one filled with Styrofoam worms. After mailing the papers and the camera to the private box Peter maintained for his law practice they made it to Salem, New Hampshire with over an hour to spare.

Cam studied a map of the area and glanced at his watch. "Okay, we have to move fast." Following a series of side streets, he pulled into a cul-de-sac that backed onto the America's Stonehenge site. They parked the car, jumped onto the bikes and rode through some woods on a narrow trail. He checked his GPS and made a slight course adjustment, turning to make sure Amanda was keeping up. Not surprisingly, she rode well.

After a quarter-mile ride he jumped off his bike near a small creek. She did the same and he covered the bikes with some branches and leaves. "They're going to find the bikes, you know," she said, her breathing slow and easy as they jogged back to the car.

"Believe it or not, I have a plan—I'll explain it to you in the car."

He stopped by the edge of a slow-moving brook, reached through the water and pulled out a dripping pile of decayed leaves and muck.

She crinkled her nose. "It smells nasty."

He spread the muck over his clothes and into his hair. "I know. Sorry about that." He held his hand out to her. "Your turn."

"Why?"

"I want them to underestimate us, like we talked about before. It's human nature—if we're dirty and smelly and unkempt, they'll think less of us. I mean, when was the last time you asked a homeless man for directions?"

She reached out her hand. "Oh bloody hell. I was just getting over my swamp monster look. Now I'm going to smell like one."

+   +   +

A half-hour later Cam and Amanda pulled into the dirt parking area of the America's Stonehenge site. There were about a dozen other cars in the lot, which meant the site would be fairly crowded. Good. He didn't like the idea of going into the woods alone with these people.

He leaned over and kissed her gently, her lips opening to his. "The next few hours are going to be tough. I just wanted something to keep me going."

She exhaled slowly, her eyes still closed from the kiss. When she opened them the clover-colored orbs grew as her pupils shrank in the sunlight. She reached up and gently stroked his cheek. "Whatever happens, thanks for a wonderful adventure."

A caravan of three dark-colored sedans bounded into the parking lot. "Remember," he said as they hopped from the car. "Don't wow them with your intellect. We want them to underestimate us."

But Amanda was distracted. She squinted at the lead car. "Bloody hell! That's Beatrice Yarborough in the front seat. What is she—"

"I guess that explains how the Vatican got up to speed so quickly."

"I, I can't believe it, Cam. She was like a mother to me."

Before he could respond Amanda bounded across the parking lot. She reached the car just as the older woman rolled out, a long cigarette dangling from her left hand. Amanda didn't hesitate. She slapped her boss across the face, the sharp sound echoing off the surrounding trees and boulders. Staggering, Beatrice began to raise her hand in retaliation. "Just try it, you old frog," Amanda hissed. It happened so quickly that Cam had barely moved.

A barrel-chested man in a dark suit and blood-red tie slowly pulled himself from the back seat. He wedged himself between Amanda and Beatrice, moving with surprisingly agility. "That is enough," he crooned in the same wet, Spanish-accented baritone Cam had heard on the phone. Bowing his large body to Amanda, he offered a wide leer. "I see you two are already acquainted."

Beatrice raised her round chin. "I had the misfortune of being charged with training this tart. Apparently I neglected to teach her decorum." She sniffed at the air. "Or the importance of bathing. She smells like a loo." She sucked on her cigarette as if to clear her nostrils.

The man in the suit ignored her. "I am Ricardo Reichmann." No trace of any German accent. He bowed again. "You must be Miss Spencer."

Amanda glared at her boss, ignoring Reichmann. "You almost got us killed."

"Oh, stop behaving like a princess, Amanda. You are expendable. We are all expendable. This is what we do, this is who we are. We protect Prince Henry."

"Protect him from what? The truth?"

Beatrice turned, waved her away. "Grow up, Amanda. Stop being so naïve. There is no such thing as the truth. There are only shades of lies."

Amanda stared at her back for a few seconds before turning and marching back toward Cam, now most of the way across the parking lot himself.

She leaned into him, whispering. "I'm sorry. I had no idea the Consortium was involved in all of this."

"Is it the Consortium, or just Beatrice?"

"I don't know. I reckon Beatrice could be acting on her own, controlling what Babinaux and the council members know. She never allows me to speak privately with him."

"Either way, it makes no sense. Don't they want us to prove the Prince Henry legend is true?"

She gritted her teeth. "Apparently it's not that simple."

Reichmann cleared his throat impatiently. Cam returned to the Subaru and, carrying a large brown canvas messenger bag containing maps, the lantern packed in its box and the results of their research, he moved toward the dark sedans, feigning fatigue. In addition to Reichmann and Beatrice, the three sedans contained four black-clad henchman — one of whom Cam recognized as the muscular operative whose car they stole in Newport — and an angular, olive-skinned man with a long, thin face. Perhaps a decade older than Cam, he wore a black clerical shirt with a white collar, black pleated pants and a well-tailored Italian-cut blue blazer. Probably the Vatican scholar Cam had guessed they would employ, though he looked more like an international banker. The Newport operative edged closer, studying Cam. His face was pocked and his eyes steady and serene — other than his muscular build he looked like an overage alter boy with acne.

"You must be Mr. Thorne. I must say, you have been a thorn in our side," Reichmann grinned, his white teeth shining with saliva even as his steel blue eyes narrowed. "Unfortunately, this is no laughing matter." He motioned to the Newport operative. "Señor Salazar, *por favor*."

Salazar lunged at Cam, spun him around by the left shoulder and locked him in an arm bar before he even saw him coming. His shoulder, already injured from the Forsberg attack, screamed in pain as the messenger bag slid slowly down his arm to the ground. He began to resist but relaxed when Salazar tightened his grip and he felt the tendons begin to rip from the bone. "Okay, okay," he murmured, fighting to keep his eyes from watering. A second ruffian searched his pockets and patted him down. He removed Cam's TracFone and Swiss army knife, then nodded to Reichmann.

Cam sniffed. "What, you think I'm going to take you all down with a corkscrew?" He reached down with his free arm and grabbed the messenger bag.

Reichmann ignored him and turned to Beatrice. "Please lead the way."

As the group lumbered its way to the main building containing the gift shop and ticket office, the priest carefully stepping around the mud puddles, Salazar squeezed against Cam. "Your shoulder hurting?" he whispered not unkindly, his breath mint-scented.

Cam nodded slightly. Lightning-like, Salazar released Cam's left arm and twisted his right behind his back instead. "I hope that's better."

"Thanks." It came out automatically, before he could swallow it. The man was a killer, probably just playing the good cop to Reichmann's bad.

Beatrice must have made arrangements by telephone; she slid an envelope across the counter and the woman at the ticket desk quickly escorted them into a private room with eight folding chairs set around a rectangular banquet table. Two men guarded the door while Salazar and another stood in front of the room's two windows. Reichmann dropped into a chair at the head of the table, exhaled loudly through his mouth and dabbed his forehead with a handkerchief. Beatrice sat to his left, the unnamed priest to his right. Reichmann motioned for Cam and Amanda to sit; they did so at the far end of the table, Amanda at the foot.

Reichmann spoke, his thickly-accented words now accompanied by a soft rain pebbling against the roof. "We understand that you may have solved the Prince Henry puzzle." A statement, not a question. Cam did not respond. Amanda continued to glare at Beatrice. Reichmann continued. "As you know, Mrs. Yarborough is probably the leading authority on all things relating to Prince Henry

Sinclair." The Vatican scholar sat slouched in his chair, buffing his fingernails with an emery board, his body language conveying boredom and disdain. Cam didn't buy it—behind his drooping eyelids the scholar's gaze was alert and attentive. "Father Balducci has traveled here from Rome to add his considerable knowledge and experience to our group." Balducci sniffed an acknowledgement as Reichmann dropped both hands, palms down, onto the laminated wood table. "Now, please share with us what you have learned."

"First I want proof my cousin is okay."

Reichmann nodded. "I am a man of my word. Feel free to phone him. But quickly."

Cam dialed the TracFone. Brandon answered on the first ring. "You okay?"

"Yeah," he slurred. "I think so."

Cam exhaled. "Good. I'll call you later. We're with Reichmann and his men—"

"That is enough, Mr. Thorne," Reichmann interrupted, motioning for one of the henchman to end the call. "Now I expect you to honor your side of the agreement."

Cam placed the messenger bag on an empty chair and pulled out a roadmap of New England. He spun it so it faced Reichmann and took a deep breath. Reichmann, Balducci and Beatrice were the three-judge panel, the four henchmen the executioners. Not much pressure.

Using a red pen, he marked the important sites around New England. "Here's the Westford Knight, here's the Boat Stone, here's the Newport Tower, here's Spirit Pond, here's the Tyngsboro Map Stone...."

He addressed his presentation to Beatrice. The others would defer to her judgment as to whether the sites he chose were appropriate. She stared at the map, glowering but eventually huffed her assent. "Continue."

He turned to Father Balducci and detailed their conclusions regarding the Templars' rejection of Church dogma and worship of the Sacred Feminine. "But you know all this already. Just like you know Prince Henry is part of the Jesus bloodline."

Balducci shrugged, feigning continued boredom. But he had shifted forward in his seat and was pulling at his eyebrow rather than using the emery board. In his body language class in law school Cam had learned that self-touching was often an unconscious sign of discomfort or insecurity. The last thing the Church wanted was stories of the Jesus heir being persecuted by the Church, fleeing the continent to escape the Pope and his agents.

Cam continued. "They left lots of clues, most of them carved in stone. Some were clues revealing who they were and what they believed: the Hooked X, for example, symbolized the union of Jesus and Mary Magdalene and the resulting birth of the baby Sarah. Other carvings served multiple purposes: The Westford Knight was an effigy to a fallen knight but was also part of a larger mapping system. And, of course, the Newport Tower was their primary marker, their prime meridian, as well as being a baptistery and — "

Beatrice cut him off. "You are insulting us, Mr. Thorne. We have been studying these artifacts for decades. We have no need for a lecture from an amateur like you."

His ears burned; he took a deep breath, nodded and continued. "As I was saying, these sites served multiple purposes, were significant on multiple levels. That's the way the Templars operated." He turned to Reichmann — the Legions of Jesus operative, as a member of a quasi-secret society, would appreciate the clandestine methods of the Templars. His henchman Salazar also leaned in to listen. "So we also started looking for some kind of pattern, some kind of secret message embedded in the placement of all these sites." He paused for effect. "Some kind of coded map that might lead us to a buried treasure."

Though Beatrice remained impassive, Father Balducci studied Cam intently, his index finger now rubbing his cheek. The bloodline comment had hit a nerve. Reichmann, smelling treasure, hung on every word. "The problem, of course, is that so many of the sites have been destroyed over the years." He addressed Beatrice, knowing she would concur. "For every artifact or carving or rune stone that we've found," he said, gesturing toward the map, "there must be a dozen others that have faded away or been bulldozed or remain buried in the forests. It's like trying to do a crossword puzzle with most of the clues missing. That's why the stone holes became so important."

Beatrice did not want to reveal her ignorance but her curiosity won out. "Explain what you mean by stone holes."

Cam summarized the rounded, triangular-shaped holes found in boulders. "Usually these boulders are in prominent spots, at the tops of hills or at bends in rivers or along ridge lines. Places where they'd be easy to find again. We found a bunch of them." He picked up the red pen and marked them on the map.

Beatrice challenged him. "I've inspected the Tyngsboro Map Stone a half-dozen times. There's no such hole."

Amanda responded before Cam had a chance. "Perhaps it did not occur to you to examine the missing chunk of the boulder." She triumphantly slid a photo of the stone hole onto the table. "We have found that the secrets of Prince Henry and his expedition reveal themselves only to those worthy of possessing the knowledge. It is a self-selecting group."

Beatrice's round face blushed and her nostrils flared at the barb. She stared at the photo but resisted the urge to inspect it more carefully. Cam turned to hide his smile. He didn't begrudge Amanda her jab but there was no reason to further antagonize their captors. "We also found one at Spirit Pond, right near where the Rune Stones were found, and at the top of a big hill near where the Boat Stone was found." Amanda dropped two more photos on the table as he spoke. "There's probably hundreds of others out there, just waiting to be discovered. I bet there's one right here at America's Stonehenge, though we haven't had a chance to check it out yet."

"And these holes are part of this treasure map?" Reichmann asked, his lips and teeth wet with enthusiasm.

They were intrigued and Cam wanted to give them a little extra time to chew on the hook. "Again, when we first found them we didn't see any real pattern. Then Amanda suggested we needed to start thinking like medievalists. Or more accurately, medievalists in a cabal. One of the things we learned was that the Templars were the ones who brought the game of chess to Europe."

He paused while Beatrice and Reichmann turned to Father Balducci, who took a deep breath and lifted his chin slightly in a grudging sign of assent. Cam continued. "And the Newport Tower reminded me of a rook piece in a chess set."

Amanda pulled more photographic evidence from their bag as he spoke. "The Templars and the Masons have a long history of utilizing the black and white chessboard pattern, probably inspired by the floor design of the Temple of Solomon." Again Balducci tilted his chin.

"So, we had a knight and a rook and a chessboard." Cam waited for their full attention. "Then we learned that the bishop piece in chess used to be a medieval ship. The Church insisted on replacing the boat with the bishop when the game became popular in Europe."

This time Father Balducci cleared his throat. "I was not aware of this ... assertion."

Amanda, for the fourth time, dropped evidence on the table — a copy of a page from the history of chess book. Cam had learned early in his law career the importance of documentary evidence. There was something about seeing a point validated in writing that juries found overwhelmingly compelling.

Father Balducci pulled the page to him with a single finger, as if handling it might soil his soul. His eyes moved back and forth across the page. "I suppose it is possible," he sniffed, sitting back.

"And of course," Cam said, "we have a medieval sailing ship on the Boat Stone. So now we have three pieces on our chess board."

Cam pulled out the larger map Amanda had illustrated in the library. He unfolded it slowly, knowing all eyes were glued to it, smelling Beatrice's ashy breath as she leaned in closer. "So we started playing chess with these sites. The rook moves vertically, the knight moves in an L-shape, the bishop moves diagonally." Using a pencil, he traced the red lines Amanda had highlighted.

"They intersect right here," Reichmann breathed. "This must be where the treasure is buried, yes?"

Cam and Amanda exchanged a quick, knowing glance. This was the key moment. They had convinced Reichmann, but what about Beatrice and Father Balducci? In the end, Reichmann's opinion didn't really matter. Cam made an instant decision, guided by his gut. He smiled. "Wait, there's more."

✝   ✝   ✝

Beatrice Yarborough studied the young man as his finger traced the lines on the map. Handsome in that American boy-next-door type of way, despite the goatee. And obviously intelligent. His *Rex Deus* blood, though diluted by a series of ill-conceived marriages, coursed strong through his veins.

She had always known that it would take a person of the *Rex Deus* bloodline, the keepers of the true teachings of Jesus, to decipher the mysteries and puzzles left 600 years earlier by Prince Henry. Sinclair would have been careful to guard his secrets, to preserve them for his royal descendants rather than allow some commoner to ferret them out. The chess piece movement pattern was exactly the type of coded message a Templar leader would employ. Somehow

Thorne had deciphered it. And he was telling the truth—his chess movement theory matched exactly what his cousin Brandon had revealed under truth serum.

The problem, of course, was that Thorne's story was all too credible, all too believable; it was up to her to prevent it from being told. At her suggestion, Reichmann and his Legions of Jesus cohorts had arranged for a high-ranking Vatican official to contact Babinaux and inform him that Amanda and Thorne were engaged in a campaign to embarrass and undermine the Church. The message had been well-received, especially in light of Thorne's history as a rogue lawyer whose strong anti-Church sentiments had resulted in his suspension from the practice of law. Babinaux had been unwilling to abandon Amanda completely but he did refrain from sending a team out to assist her. Instead he ordered Beatrice to closely monitor the situation. Of course, he had no idea that she had already won Reichmann's confidence by feeding him information and was herself at the center of the Legions of Jesus' operation. So much for the Consortium's attempt to put her out to pasture.

But back to Thorne. Like his story, he himself was credible, his research solid, his conclusions reasonable and well-founded. But he hadn't followed the evidence to its inevitable ending point. She didn't give a damn if Thorne and Amanda destroyed the Catholic Church. But she would not allow them to besmirch the reputation of Prince Henry. The olive-skinned Father Balducci had turned ashen listening to Thorne, as if a dark cloud had seeped from his soul to his cheeks. He, too, knew Thorne was on the verge of discovering the true secret of Prince Henry's journey. Unless he was stopped.

Thorne's words, echoing inside her brain, brought her back to the present. "Wait, there's more," he had said.

She looked up; he was waiting for her attention before continuing.

"We were pretty sure we had solved the puzzle," he said. "Something was hidden at America's Stonehenge, something that Prince Henry wanted his followers to find. At first we thought the hidden secrets were ancient knowledge, knowledge of navigation and astronomy and geography and the seasons that would allow the explorers to survive in the New World. Then we realized the site also validated their Templar spiritual beliefs, ancient beliefs that focused on the Sacred Feminine and Venus worship."

She resisted the urge to nod. Thorne's theory made perfect sense — it would be just like Prince Henry, a Renaissance man centuries before his time, to have an appreciation of nature and the sciences and spirituality. He was not some glory seeker or treasure hunter; he and his knights were trying to improve the lot of his lieges. He would have wanted to lead his flock back to this important site. But she could not concede the point. Instead, she challenged the solicitor. "Your theory has a major flaw. There are no stones at America's Stonehenge aligned to identify or predict the Venus cycles."

Amanda responded. "That's not an accurate statement. Nobody has bothered to look for any Venus alignments. That doesn't mean there aren't any."

Beatrice dismissed the point with a sniff, even though the girl was correct — modern astronomers, not being attuned to the ancient Venus observations, were far more interested in lunar and solar cycles. It hadn't occurred to them to check for Venus alignments.

Thorne began to expound on the Venus worship history. She waved at him impatiently to continue. "Yes, we know all this. Get to the point."

"Well, as you know, we are in Salem, New Hampshire right now. Did you know that Salem is the Phoenician god of the evening, symbolized by Venus as the evening star? Could it be just a coincidence that the site that validated all the Templars' Venus worship beliefs is located in a place named after Venus?"

This was an interesting revelation. Fascinating, in fact. Place names often carried hidden, ancient meanings and clues. But, again, she resisted the urge to nod. "This is hardly compelling evidence, Mr. Thorne. There is also a Salem in the state of Oregon. Did Prince Henry travel to the Pacific Northwest as well?"

Thorne took a deep breath. "I agree, the evidence so far is not overwhelming. But when we saw this next thing, we knew for sure. We knew we had solved the puzzle. We knew that America's Stonehenge contained the true secret Prince Henry wanted his followers to learn." He nodded to Amanda, who slid another photo image across the table. "This is an aerial view of America's Stonehenge, taken from the Google Earth website."

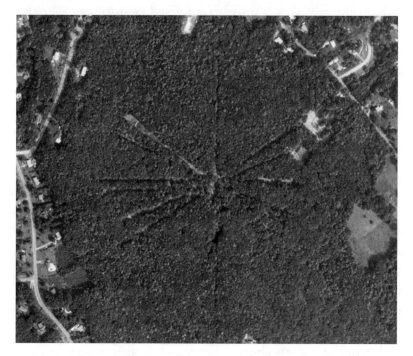

AERIAL VIEW OF AMERICA'S STONEHENGE SITE

Beatrice glanced down. A large starburst-like pattern dominated the image, superimposed on a dark green background. The dark green was clearly the forest as seen from the sky, the starburst pattern likely the clear cuts that had been made in the forest to allow for the celestial alignments to be viewed. Thorne continued, smiling. "When we saw this, we were just blown away. The center of the starburst is the center of America's Stonehenge. We think aliens must have seen the starburst from outer space and come down to investigate."

Aliens? Father Balducci and Reichmann both turned toward Beatrice. English was not their first language and they were not certain they heard correctly. "Did you say *aliens?* As in from another planet?" she asked.

Thorne nodded. "Sure. Just look at the picture. And imagine it without the roads, as it must have looked centuries ago. Pretend you're an alien. There you are, flying above the planet, and you see this vivid starburst pattern carved into the ground. Of course you'd come investigate."

"That is ridiculous," Beatrice said as Father Balducci rolled his eyes and exhaled slowly, the color returning to his cheeks. She had heard similar daft theories before — that the pyramids were designed by extra-terrestrials as intergalactic signposts meant to be viewed from above by alien visitors.

Thorne shrugged. "Look, you don't have to believe us. But we believe Prince Henry's secret is that he knew about the aliens, knew that they landed here. He and his men left with the aliens and went back to their planet with them. That's why there's no record of the expedition ever returning to Europe. And why nobody ever found Prince Henry's grave."

Amanda jumped in. "Or his treasures. The aliens probably kept them."

Beatrice stared at Thorne. She was mistaken — apparently his *Rex Deus* blood had been diluted too far. Her thoughts turned to

Orkney, the cat's Siamese breeding pure and regal and untarnished. "The whole *Rex Deus* line," he continued, "including King David and Jesus, is descended from aliens." He faced Father Balducci, continued in his matter-of-fact tone. "The Vatican knows all about it, ask Father Balducci. The aliens come back every couple of centuries and check on their descendants."

Balducci shook his head derisively but Amanda plowed ahead, too dense to notice. "We think the starburst is some kind of portal to another universe, just like the Money Pit at Oak Island." She pulled another document from her bag and dropped it on the table. "You can read about it here."

Beatrice ignored the girl and her paperwork and her loony assertions. She recalled an incident a year ago, an entry Amanda made in her log regarding aliens carving the Westford Knight. Perhaps the girl had convinced Thorne that ghosts and spirits were real as well. She ground her teeth. Why had she ever allowed the Consortium to transfer her out of Westford, to leave Prince Henry and Sir James in the hands of this simpleton?

"I think we've heard quite enough." She stood and turned to Reichmann. "Please ask your men to escort these two fools outside, with their ridiculous papers. We need to talk. In private."

✝   ✝   ✝

Cam swallowed a smile as Salazar stuffed their papers into Amanda's messenger bag. Salazar and another thug pushed them out the door and sat them at a freshly-painted picnic table, the now-steady rain soaking them. The four guards surrounded them like points on a compass, their arms folded across their chests, one of the men flexing his biceps for her benefit and glaring at Cam. Salazar studied them also, his eyes curious and questioning in the way a zoo animal sometimes looked out at his visitors. Cam kept his fingers away from the cage.

After a few minutes Reichmann, carrying a large black umbrella, marched to the picnic table and barked an order to his men in Spanish. Two cronies grabbed Cam, hoisting him off the bench. Salazar guided Amanda to her feet and handed her the messenger bag.

Reichmann walked along the path toward the main rock formations of the site, deep in the woods, the ruffians pushing Cam and Amanda along behind him. The other park visitors had departed, probably because of the rain; they were now alone at the site. "Where are we going?" Cam asked.

Reichmann ignored him, humming as he walked. He seemed happy even as his leather dress shoes became muddied. Maybe Beatrice had promised him the chance to try to extract more of the story from his prisoners. Or maybe even some time alone with Amanda.

Grinding his teeth at the thought of Reichmann atop Amanda, Cam stopped abruptly. He couldn't just let Reichmann march them deeper into the woods. One of the henchman gave him a sharp shove between the shoulder blades; Cam grunted and Reichmann turned at the sound. "I have something to say to Mrs. Yarborough and Father Balducci. Now."

Reichmann shrugged and motioned for the men to drag Cam along. Another shove, again jarring his injured shoulder. He took a deep breath and tried not to wince. "In seven minutes, if I don't make a phone call, this story goes public." Reichmann continued strolling but the humming stopped. "I'm not bluffing. Seven minutes. It'll be on your head if this story gets out." It wasn't much of a threat but it was all he had.

Amanda looked frightened, her arms encircling her body in a self-hug. Understandably so. They were alone in the woods with a group of sweating, muscle-bound thugs, two of whom were openly leering at her. The smell of the men's sweat, the sound of their labored breathing as they marched, the sight of their shoulders and chests tight against their shirts, all combined to drive home the immediacy and gravity of their predicament. Cam wanted to put a protective arm around her but feared it would only serve to titillate their already-lecherous escorts. He settled for a reassuring smile. She offered a brave wink in response.

They walked another few minutes, deeper into the woods, the rain ending but the air still thick with humidity. He studied Reichmann's back, tried to will him to stop this march. Any rational person would cover his ass by checking with his superiors. But these people were zealots and sometimes, by definition, zealots behaved in ways that defied logic. Reichmann had already wasted more than half of Cam's seven-minute countdown.

After another dozen strides Reichmann finally stopped and sighed, his face glistening with sweat. Cam again tried to reassure Amanda with a smile. Reichmann pulled his cell phone from his breast pocket, edged away from the group and held a hushed conversation with, Cam guessed, Beatrice.

"Give him his phone," Reichmann barked at Salazar, no longer any music in his voice.

Cam reached for Amanda's hand; as he dialed, he whispered to her. "Our bikes are only a few hundred yards away. Think you can outrun them?"

"Outrun them?" Amanda smiled. "I'm pretty sure I only have to outrun you."

Cam grinned. Newport was both less than a week and more than a lifetime ago. So much had changed. But not Amanda.

Uncle Peter answered on the third ring. "Cameron? Are you okay?"

"Yes, we're fine. But if I don't check in with you again in two hours, call Poulos and tell him we need help. Then call the press."

He hung up but kept the phone to his ear. Glancing toward Reichmann, he put his finger in one ear and called loudly into the phone. "Hello? Can you hear me?" Walking in a small circle, he removed the phone from his ear and examined it, pantomiming a man with poor cell connection. He edged a few yards away from Reichmann's ruffians. Amanda sensed his plan, moved toward a large tree near him and leaned against it, feigning fatigue.

They now had about a ten-yard head start. Reichmann's men continued to eye them, Salazar especially, but it didn't occur to them that Amanda — even with a head start — could outrun them. It was time. "Walk with me along the trail," Cam whispered. "But as soon as they take a step toward us, run."

He offered one last pantomime, cursed loudly. "Damn. There's too many trees around here."

He and Amanda gained another five yards before Reichmann's voice rang through the woods. "That is far enough, Mr. Thorne."

"Now!" Cam and Amanda broke into a sprint, tearing up the inclined trail deeper into the woods, their shoes digging deep into the soft, muddied ground. Reichmann immediately barked an order for his men to pursue, three of them charging up the trail, their fists pumping and their legs churning. Cam glanced over his shoulder. Salazar led the pack, his face serene and his stride strong.

They reached the top of a ridge near the cluster of rock structures that formed the center of the America's Stonehenge site. He called to Amanda, who was a few strides ahead of him still carrying the messenger bag. "Follow me." He glanced over his shoulder again — Salazar had gained on them, the operative's muscular legs well-suited to the muddy, uphill trail. The other two pursuers had fallen back.

Cam veered to the left, off trail now, zig-zagging around the trees and forest debris. Here, in the thick growth, he and Amanda had the advantage — their smaller bodies could squeeze between narrow gaps and duck under low-lying branches. They would need a big lead in order to have time to mount their bikes and get up to speed.

Amanda, displaying the balance and dexterity of a gymnast, darted through the woods like a rabbit, slowing only to turn so he could point her in the right direction. They were more than halfway to the bikes, perhaps a hundred yards away. Just as he began to scan for the creek where the bikes were hidden, a gunshot rang out, followed milliseconds later by the sound of tree bark splintering a few yards behind him. He instinctively changed course, yelled to Amanda to do the same.

Amanda turned, her eyes a fiery mix of fear and anger, and darted to the left.

His heart thumped in his ears, drowning out other sound. It was one thing to know, intellectually, that someone was trying to kill you. It was another thing entirely to hear the bullet explode into a tree near your head. A surge of adrenaline coursed through his body—an instinctive, ancient survival reaction. He crashed through the brush, oblivious to the branches and leaves and undergrowth, and sprinted toward the bikes. "Up there," he shouted, "near the clearing."

Amanda adjusted her course slightly; Cam, crouching, tried to angle himself so that he was continuously shielded from Salazar by a tree. Salazar was shooting while running at full speed. Not a high percentage shot. Then again, these were trained operatives.

As they approached the bikes he glanced over his shoulder again. Salazar was still in pursuit, maybe forty yards behind them. A fast runner could cover that distance in less than five seconds. Running uphill, through the woods, it might take Salazar eight or nine. Enough time for Cam to mount a bike and get to full speed. But not Amanda, who had little experience on a mountain bike and was burdened by the messenger bag. Salazar would chase her down. He made a split-second decision.

"Grab your bike and ride up the trail. I'll be right behind you." She turned, doubt in her eyes. "Trust me, Amanda."

He ducked behind a massive oak tree, finding a thick branch in the wet brush. Pressing his back against the tree, he snapped off the smaller limbs to make a club. Salazar crashed through the woods. Cam glanced up to see Amanda mounting her bike, wishing he could magically propel her along to safety. He lifted the oak club high, ignoring the pain in his shoulder. His body frozen, he waited — if he moved too quickly he would expose himself. He only had one shot at this.

Time slowed as he focused all his senses on the movements of his pursuer. Salazar would cross a pile of brush — moistened by the rain but likely dry underneath — about ten feet from his hiding spot. Ten feet, three strides. *There.* The crunch of shoe on twigs. Then the thump of a second stride. And finally the thud of a third impact. *Now!* He pivoted to his left, stepped away from the tree and swung the club like a baseball bat, his target a chest-high fastball.

He timed it perfectly. The blow struck Salazar across the chest before he had a chance to raise his arms to deflect the attack, the club recoiling from the impact. Salazar pinwheeled in the air, his feet continuing forward, his upper body propelled back by the force of the blow, his arms and leg flailing around him. He spun in almost a complete backward somersault, finally landing face down with a dull thud.

Cam raced over, kicked the gun from Salazar's hand and stuffed it into his waistband. As Salazar tried to push himself to his hands and knees and the other operatives crashed through the woods in pursuit, Cam sprinted for his bike.

The blow felt good, revenge for Brandon and Pegasus, for Eric Forsberg and Monsignor Marcotte. Salazar had shown him some kindness. But not nearly enough to offset his crimes.

✝ ✝ ✝

Amanda peddled hard through the subdivision and out to the main road, her eyes glued to Cam's back, her ears attuned to the early sounds of a vehicle in pursuit. He glanced down once in a while at his map; after about ten minutes he coasted to a stop and smiled at her.

"Shouldn't we continue?" Reichmann and his men could be just around the corner. She gulped air.

"No need," he grinned. "We got away."

"Are you certain?" She looked around. "Wasn't that too easy?"

"Exactly. The whole thing was too easy. They wanted us to escape."

"Pardon? Salazar looked bloody serious to me. Really, bullets and all?"

"Well, maybe he was off-script a bit. But the plan was to let us get away."

"Cameron, I'm not following you."

"Sorry. They believed our alien theory. Or, more accurately, believed that we believe it."

"Yes. That part I understand." Beatrice had suspected Amanda believed in aliens ever since the silly log entry. That was the plan — that Beatrice would convince Reichmann and Balducci to let them escape hoping they would go public with the alien story and discredit themselves. The strategy played perfectly into Beatrice's perception of herself as sneaky and cunning — as Napoleon once famously said, never interrupt your enemy when he's making a mistake. Beatrice must have reasoned that if word got out that Vatican affiliates were fighting to suppress the Prince Henry story — going so far as to murder both innocent civilians and Catholic priests — then the story must have real legs. In other words, why would the Vatican allies react so violently if the story was nothing more than another in the seemingly endless string of Templar myths bouncing around the internet? The more cunning strategy would be to let Cam and

Amanda publicize the story—personally and in all its resplendent absurdity—and have their conclusions sink under the weight of their wacky alien portal assertions. Never mind that 90% of their conclusions were valid—they would drown in the sensationalized alien headlines. "But what about the gunshots?"

"They had to make it look good so we wouldn't be suspicious."

It made sense. "Did you know this would happen from the beginning?"

He shook his head. "No, I thought they'd let us go when we threatened that the story would go public. They had me a little scared there for a few minutes. But then I remembered how Beatrice made sure we took our papers and photos with us before they dragged us out of the conference room. She tried to be subtle about it but why else would she want us to have them?"

"I see. She wanted to be certain we had pictures to provide to the press."

"Right. Once I realized that, I was pretty confident they would let us escape." He grimaced. "Though, again, I wasn't sure Salazar was going along with the plan. I think he might have had other ideas. The other guys were chasing us but he was flying—even with the head start they gave us, which I think they did on purpose, he almost caught us. So I started thinking maybe his plan was to just let *one* of us escape."

She grinned. "Just have to outrun the bear."

He leaned in, kissed her. "Well, I got away from the bear. So you're stuck with me for a while longer."

They stood together for a few seconds sipping some water, her head on his shoulder. "Really," she said, "I nearly started laughing in the conference room when you suggested that Beatrice pretend she's an alien."

"Actually, what I said was, 'Pretend you're an alien flying above the planet.' In my mind, I was picturing the Wicked Witch on her broom."

Amusing image, but the reality was more sobering. "Unfortunately the witch is not yet dead. We're free but what did we really gain?"

They remounted their bikes and rode at a leisurely pace, Cam riding no-handed. "A few days. They're expecting us to go to the press with the story, aliens and all. But they know it can't happen overnight. That'll give us time to get Brandon the proper protection, time to finish up our research, time to get the story out to the press in some kind of logical format. Without the aliens, of course."

She licked the sweat from her lips, tasted the mud she had spread on her face earlier in the day. "There better be time for a hot shower in there somewhere."

CHAPTER 15

After pedaling away from America's Stonehenge, Cam and Amanda followed the back roads into Massachusetts to the commuter rail station in Lawrence. They caught a train south to Boston's North Station then boarded another train heading north up the coastline to Salem, Massachusetts, losing themselves in the Friday evening rush hour. They had escaped but there was no guarantee they weren't still being followed.

"First Salem, New Hampshire, now Salem, Massachusetts," Amanda observed, raising her voice over the screeching of the train's wheels on the tracks.

"It's this Sacred Feminine thing. I'm hooked."

"I'm not surprised."

"Seriously, I think there's more to this mystery than just the America's Stonehenge site. That's part of it, and I still think the chess piece thing has some validity but we're missing something. Agreed?"

"Yes. There are a number of clues that have nothing to do with America's Stonehenge. Including this clay lantern we've been carrying around."

"Putting aside the lantern, there's been this bell ringing in the back of my head ever since you said that somehow Prince Henry convinced the Indians to share the America's Stonehenge secret with him. I couldn't put my finger on it until I was telling Beatrice that the Salem name is derived from Venus. Then it clicked. I did my senior thesis in college on the Salem witch trials so I read a lot about Judge Samuel Sewall, who presided over the trials. He used to talk about forming a 'New Jerusalem' here in America. And his big thing was that the Native Americans were essential to its formation."

"Didn't the early settlers consider the natives savages?"

"They did. That's why Sewall's position was so controversial. He thought the Indians were the lost tribe of Israel and they were key to any New Jerusalem."

She looked skeptical. "But he was a Puritan. And a fairly nasty one at that, based on what I've read about the witch trials. How could he be involved?"

"Later in life he had an epiphany and actually issued a public apology for his role in the trials." He lowered his voice. "And this is weird but his diary is full of comments and observations about his wife's menstrual cycles and her nipples and breast-feeding. He was obsessed with that stuff."

She crinkled her nose. "Are you thinking Sacred Feminine worship?"

Cam shrugged. "It always struck me as a really bizarre fascination for a Puritan judge, sort of like Bernard de Clairvaux lactating at the Virgin Mary's breast. Maybe there's some kind of connection." He turned in his seat. "Anyway, we need a place to hole up for a few days and I figured we could blend in pretty well with all the tourists in Salem."

"I trust you're not implying I have witch-like tendencies."

She closed her eyes and leaned her head on his shoulder while he phoned Uncle Peter. After confirming Brandon was okay, Cam convinced Peter to close the office for a week, fly to North Carolina with Aunt Peggy and take a long drive into the countryside with Cam's parents. "And no credit cards."

He hung up and phoned Brandon. Lieutenant Poulos answered. "I came to make sure Brandon is okay." He lowered his voice. "I'm sorry our guy didn't do the job."

"One guy doesn't have much of a chance against a team of paramilitary operatives."

"Well, we've got more than one guy here now. You going to bring these people down?" He was no longer insisting Cam come in for questioning.

"Planning to. Tell Brandon I'll call him tomorrow."

Once in Salem, they used the last of Cam' money for a room at a bed and breakfast in the historic part of town, then went out and bought food, toiletries and a change of clothes using a traveler's check Amanda had stuffed into her purse before leaving Westford; fortunately Cam had a few days worth of insulin in his fanny pack which hadn't gone bad yet. They grabbed a pizza and bottle of wine for their room and spent a couple of hours soaking together in a Jacuzzi. For a few hours, at least, they were just ordinary lovers, thankful to be alive.

✟   ✟   ✟

Salazar didn't need X-rays. He knew what broken ribs felt like and there wasn't much you could do about them other than kill the pain. He popped a couple of Advils — he didn't want anything stronger in his body — as he sat in a desk chair in a small office in the America's Stonehenge building, waiting for Reichmann to finish up with the nasty Englishwoman and the Vatican historian in the conference room.

He phoned Rosalita on his cell, reached her as Gloria was drawing her bedtime bath. "How are you, my little rosebud?"

"Hi Daddy! Grandma says I can take the kitty into the bath with me tonight."

"Really? But aren't cats afraid of water?"

"Well, how will we know unless we put her in and try?"

His laugh turned into a gasp as pain shot through his chest.

"What's wrong, Daddy?"

"I got hurt at work today, honey. But I'm okay."

"Did you fall down?"

"Yeah, yeah, I fell down."

"Well, you should be more careful."

Another laugh, another bolt of pain. He grabbed two more Advils. "I gotta go now, sweetheart. I just wanted to say goodnight and I love you."

"I love you more!" she shouted as she hung up.

A few minutes later Reichmann entered, shaking his head. "What were you doing? Your orders were to let them escape."

He coughed and winced as Reichmann eyed him. There was something to be said for taking one for the team, even a team accustomed to violence and death. It would preclude anyone questioning his commitment to the mission. "You said make it look good."

The truth was he needed to make sure the girl didn't drop the messenger bag. She and Thorne would need the papers in the bag, and probably also the lantern, to find the treasure. And he needed to ensure the homing device he tucked inside the bag stayed with them.

✛   ✛   ✛

[Saturday]

They woke early, Amanda curled into the crook of Cam's bent body. He stroked her hair gently as she stirred and snuggled closer against him. He had been attracted to many women in his life and even been involved in a few quasi-serious relationships, but inevitably he felt the need for some separation, some personal space, a few hours of alone time mixed in with all the intimacy. It was like ice cream, he used to tell himself: It tasted delicious but even so you couldn't eat it all day long. But Amanda was different, every kiss like the first bite of mint chocolate chip on a hot summer day. He was beginning to understand what all the poets and love songs made such a fuss about.

But in order to have a life with Amanda they had to survive the week first. He kissed her on the cheek, the rash and blisters pretty much gone. "We need to get moving, sweetheart." He swung his feet off the bed and headed for the shower.

In an effort to make themselves harder to track he shaved his beard and Amanda dyed her hair raven black. After blow-drying it she stepped out of the bathroom. His breath caught in his throat. With her porcelain skin and shamrock green eyes she looked like something off a fashion runway in Paris. "You look ... exotically beautiful," he stammered. "Wow."

She grinned. "I'm pleased you like it." She winked playfully. "It makes me feel naughty. A bit witch-like."

He felt a stirring in his groin but fought the urge to guide her to the bed, instead settling for the last two bites of his breakfast bar. Ignoring popular tourist sites like the Witch Museum and waterfront shops, they walked to the town library, a square-front, red-brick, Italianate-style structure. Other than the white-railed widow's walk capping the roof, the building looked like it belonged in Boston's Back Bay among the other Victorian structures, not in Colonial Salem. They were waiting at the front door when it opened at 9:00.

They plopped onto the carpeted floor among the stacks in the history section, surrounded by piles of dusty, yellowing books. "You're spot on," she observed. "It says here that Judge Sewall believed the American Indians were the lost tribe of Israel. He lists a number of similarities between the Jews and your Indians — the women move to a separate tent during menstruation, they don't eat pork and they practice circumcision." She read further, her black hair brushing against the book's pages. "Just as you said, he advocated that the Puritans join your Indians and form a New Jerusalem in America."

"You know, that's some pretty advanced, almost radical thinking. Most Puritans just wanted to be rid of the natives, wanted them cleared from the land."

A few minutes passed while they read. Amanda's curse broke the silence. "Bloody hell!"

"What?"

"You won't believe this." She pushed herself to her knees. "Do you remember I showed you a picture of the Bourne Stone, on Cape Cod?"

"Yeah." The stone featured the medieval ship that looked like the one on the Boat Stone in Westford.

She focused her eyes on his to make sure he was paying full attention. "The Bourne Stone was discovered in a church built in the 1600s on Cape Cod for the earliest Native American converts to Christianity. Well, it says here the local legend is that the stone wasn't carved by the Indians. Rather, it was given to them as a gift by Judge Samuel Sewall."

Blood rushed to Cam's face. *Judge Sewall?* How did a Puritan judge from Salem end up with an ancient petroglyph? And why would he gift it to an Indian tribe on Cape Cod, on the other end of the state?

She filled in a bit of the mystery. "Apparently he paid to have the church built as part of his plan to combine the Puritans and the natives and form a New Jerusalem."

Again with the New Jerusalem. But the mystery of how Sewall ended up with the stone, and why he gave it to the Indians, remained.

Amanda was back in her book before Cam could comment. After a few seconds she looked up. "I've also got him visiting Noman's Land, the island off of Martha's Vineyard, in 1702."

It was one thing to be on Cape Cod. But Noman's Land was an obscure, remote island. Especially 300 years ago. "What the hell was he doing there? Judge Sewall is like that Waldo character in the children's books. Every time you turn the page, there he is."

She raised an eyebrow. "The book doesn't say why he was there. I'm quite certain it had nothing to do with the Leif Eriksson Rune Stone," she said wryly, referring to the rune stone with Leif Eriksson's name and the year 1001 — and possibly the word Vinland — carved into it.

Cam smiled. "Nah. He was just picking grapes. Vinland, you know."

A few minutes later he looked up from his own book. "In 1689, Sewall traveled to England and visited Stonehenge. They called him America's first tourist."

"Stonehenge?" she laughed. "That's wonderful."

"And while he was there, he also visited a Jewish cemetery. Weird."

"Does it say why?"

"No. But he went alone. He left his other Puritan friends behind."

He kept reading. "And here's what I was talking about earlier; this is from his diary. He writes about how his wife was having trouble breastfeeding but the baby eventually took to the right nipple, the longer of the two, and then two days later finally took the shorter left one also."

She bit her lower lip. "I think I'd rather my husband not measure my nipples."

He kept his head down. "Here's something else interesting. Sewall befriended a Jewish guy named Joseph Frazon. When Frazon died, Sewall helped arrange for him to be buried in the Jewish Cemetery in Newport."

"Really, Newport? And once more with a Jewish cemetery, just like in London?"

"There are a lot of strange coincidences involving old Judge Sewall."

"Was he a Mason?"

"I don't know," he said. "Heck, I didn't even know my uncle Peter was. It wouldn't surprise me. But he would have had to keep it secret if he was." The Masons became prominent in American politics and society in the 18th century but their Templar-inspired ideals championing individual rights and liberties (including freedom of religion) would have seemed blasphemous to the rigid Puritans. Other than perhaps Judge Sewall.

Cam contemplated the latest revelations for a few minutes. Travel in the 17th century was extremely difficult and dangerous. But here was a man who sailed back and forth to England during a time of war between England and France, and who apparently made multiple trips from Salem to Cape Cod, and even further south to Noman's Land, a remote island, during a time when Native American raids were common. Curiously, none of these journeys seemed to have any commercial purpose. But they were anything but random. In fact, Judge Sewall's explorations struck him as eerily familiar. They followed the path of a man investigating unexplained artifacts, trying to educate himself on the very matters he and Amanda were immersing themselves in now.

He read for another 15 minutes but didn't find anything else of particular significance. He put his book down and switched gears. "I came across an interesting factoid yesterday at the Groton library. Did you know that a compass doesn't always point north?"

"Especially if you carry magnets in your pocket."

He met her smile. This was serious stuff—they had just yesterday been shot at in the woods—yet she always managed to be in good humor, always tried to wring a few drops of joy out of even the most parched circumstances. "Apparently the magnetic North Pole bounces around up there. So, especially if you're far north already, there might be quite a difference between due north and magnetic north. Today, magnetic north is about 450 miles southwest of the North Pole."

"That is quite a difference."

"Yeah, you can see how that would mess up navigation. That's why they used stars also—Polaris doesn't really move that much, it's always due north."

"I don't see the relevance."

"Well, I was thinking. We drew our chess piece line north-south, based on celestial north. And it ran right through America's Stonehenge. But if the Newport Tower really was meant to be a prime meridian, shouldn't it also be used as ground zero for magnetic north?"

"They would want to measure both?"

"Sure. There are weeks that go by when the stars aren't visible. And who's to say you'll always have a compass."

"Okay. But you said magnetic north is always shifting around. If we want to pursue this, don't we need to know where it was in the late 1300s?"

He smiled, flipped open a book to a page he had marked with a pencil. "In 1400, magnetic north was southwest of due north about 300 miles, not far from where it is today." He turned to another page. "Here's a map, with lines showing how a compass would point at different spots. For example, in far northern Maine, a compass reading north is actually pointing more west than north. Even in Boston, it has a significant westward tilt."

She grabbed the book. "What are we waiting for? Let's find a map and sketch some lines."

While she unfolded the map they had marked with the chess piece movements, he studied the magnetic declination patterns described in his book. On America's east coast, magnetic north angled to the west, the westward tilt becoming more pronounced the further north one went. On the west coast, the declination was the opposite, to the east. In the center of the country—on a line that passed, perhaps significantly, close to the site of the Kensington

Rune Stone in Minnesota—magnetic north and celestial north were identical.

She returned from borrowing a protractor from the reference desk. "One of the mysteries of the Tower is that the pillars do not sit precisely on the compass points. They're a few degrees off."

"Let me guess. The north pillar is rotated slightly to the west?"

She tilted her head. "Bingo."

Sitting on the floor with his laptop, he pulled up the Google Earth program, marked the Newport Tower and the location of magnetic north circa 1400. He turned the map so Amanda could see it. The back of his neck tingled. "Check out where our magnetic north line passes."

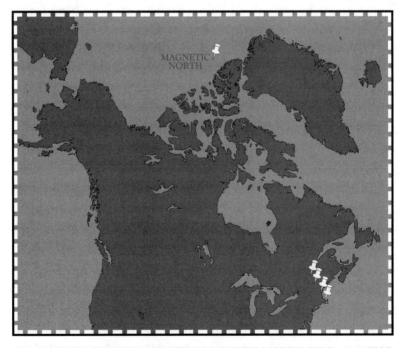

MAP WITH PLACEMARKS SHOWING MAGNETIC NORTH CIRCA 1400 (TOP OF IMAGE) AND (ON BOTTOM RIGHT OF IMAGE), MOVING SOUTHWARD IN SUCCESSION, TROIS RIVIERES, QUEBEC; LAKE MEMPHREMAGOG, QUEBEC; THE WESTFORD KNIGHT SITE; AND THE NEWPORT TOWER SITE

She leaned in. "Straight through Westford." She grinned. "I never saw that one coming. What's more, the Knight's sword points a bit west of north, just as the Tower does. We've always wondered why it didn't point precisely due north. You've answered the riddle now—the Tower and the Knight are oriented to magnetic north instead." She stared at the line. "If this is all a coincidence, it's a pretty damn unlikely one."

He was one step ahead of her. "Keep following the line north."

Her eyes moved up the page. "Straight through Lake Memphremagog." Many believed Prince Henry followed the river system north to Lake Memphremagog on the Vermont-Quebec border, a site where a number of Templar artifacts have been found.

He tapped the northern portion of the map. "The line crosses the St. Lawrence at a place called Trois Rivieres. I was sort of hoping it would go right through Montreal. But does Trois Rivieres have any significance?"

She chewed her lip. "There is something familiar about that name." She closed her eyes, then her lids flew open. "I recall. A coin and a ring were uncovered at an archeological dig there. Both artifacts featured Templar symbols on them."

"Okay. So that's four points." He marked them on the map and saved the image. He was beyond the stage of being surprised by any of this. In fact, he had reached the point where he would be surprised if the woods and mountains and river beds were *not* filled with more petroglyphs evidencing the Prince Henry expedition.

She studied the map. "You may be on to something here. They probably used the Tower as the prime meridian—you called it ground zero—for both celestial north and magnetic north. That's part of the 'mapping of the New World' Eric Forsberg believed these explorers were undertaking. But how does it help us?"

"What's that expression? You don't know where you're going until you know where you've been?"

Her green eyes narrowed. "What do you mean?"

"Well, we keep thinking about the petroglyphs and stone holes marking a journey beginning at the Newport Tower. But they had to come back, right? Maybe the Tower is an ending point also, not just a beginning."

"Very well. But I still don't see how Judge Sewall fits in."

He shrugged. "Maybe he doesn't. Maybe it's a dead end." He pondered it for a moment. "So far, the only connections between Judge Sewall and this mystery are the Bourne Stone, Sewall's travels to Stonehenge and Noman's Land, and this guy Frazon, Sewall's Jewish friend, buried in Newport."

"Don't forget Sewall's friendship with the natives—New Jerusalem and all that. His attitude toward the natives sounds much like Prince Henry's."

"Good point." He pulled out his TracFone. "Let's put Brandon on it. Maybe he can find something."

Brandon answered on the first ring. "I was just about to call you. I thought you might be hanging from your thumbs somewhere."

"No, we're okay. You feeling better?"

"Not bad. That stuff just took a while to flush through my system. Now I just feel like I have a monster hangover. They've got me up in this private suite, at the top of the hospital. Great views of the river. It's like glass, makes me want to ski."

"You know what? By next summer I have no doubt you'll be out there slaloming." Cam summarized the alien ruse and their escape. "Hopefully it'll buy us a couple of days." He also recounted Salazar's collision with an oak club. "I got him pretty good. He's gonna feel it for a while."

"Thanks." Brandon chuckled. "Good thing he was running straight ahead. You could never hit a curve."

"Tell me about it. My whole life is a curve right now."

"Well, I've got something interesting." Cam motioned for Amanda to lean in. "I was looking for some connection between the Newport Tower and the Sacred Feminine stuff, like you suggested. Do you know what the name Mary Magdalene means?"

"I believe it means Mary of Magdal, a town near the Sea of Galilee where she lived," Amanda said.

"True, but there's more to it than that. The word *magdal* comes from the Hebrew word *migdal*, meaning tower. So Mary Magdalene means 'Mary of the Tower.'"

Their eyes met and widened. "Blimey," she breathed. "The Tower could have been erected as a shrine to Mary Magdalene. That's quite an amazing discovery, Brandon."

"I thought you guys might like that."

Building the Tower as a shrine to Mary Magdalene was totally consistent with the message embedded in the Hooked X runes. And also consistent with the Sacred Feminine worship and the use of the Tower as a prime meridian in mapping the New World. "Think of it this way," Cam said. "We've got artifacts and stone holes lining up at both magnetic north and celestial north. And both lines converge at the Tower. The symbolism is perfect. Celestial north looks to the heavens. Magnetic north is earth-based. The Tower is the spot where celestial north and magnetic north meet and join together, the spiritual convergence of heaven and earth. Which makes the Tower an ideal shrine to Mary Magdalene." He smiled, the allegory almost too perfect. "She, as the wife of Jesus and mother of his line, is herself the living nexus of the heavenly and the earthly."

They remained silent for a few seconds, Amanda's eyes still wide as she studied Cam. Brandon broke the silence. "That's some pretty deep shit, Cam. And it doesn't even smell. I'm impressed."

"Thanks." The puzzle pieces were continuing to fall into place, the picture continuing to become clearer. But there were still unanswered questions. "Can you check on something for us?" He described for Brandon the relationship between Judge Sewall and Joseph Frazon, plus Sewall's eerie connection to the Bourne Stone and his travels to Stonehenge and Noman's Land. "Can you see if this guy Frazon fits in here at all? I mean, why did they send him all the way from Salem to Newport to be buried? And why was Judge Sewall involved at all?"

"I have an idea on the Sewall connection but I'm not sure it fits perfectly," Brandon said. "I just started looking through this book that talks about how a lot of the Pilgrim families descended from the Templars, how they were trying to bring the Templar ideals to America. I know the Pilgrims and the Puritans up in Salem were different groups but there might be a connection."

"You may be right. We know Sewall was an avid reader and pretty open-minded—he even issued a public apology after the witch trials. And we know he was traveling a lot down to the Cape Cod area, near where the Pilgrims were. Maybe he got clued in to the whole Sacred Feminine stuff by his Pilgrim friends." The theory, though hard to prove, was consistent with both Sewall's involvement with the Bourne Stone and Noman's Land and his interest in forming a New Jerusalem. "Can you keep looking?"

"Okay, chief. But it sounds to me like you love birds should get out of the sack and get your butts down to Newport."

Laughing, Cam hung up and looked up to see Amanda motioning excitedly. "Wait, I just recalled something. When I first viewed the Tyngsboro Map Stone, I did some research on the Merrimack River. Everything I read indicated the river was named after a native word meaning 'rapid water' or some such thing. But I know a woman who is an expert in Algonquin language—she laughed at that explanation. She said the Algonquin language doesn't even have the 'r' sound and beyond that the word doesn't resemble any word meaning water or river or rapids. She believed the name Merrimack was of European origin."

"Has it always been called the Merrimack?"

She nodded. "Since the very earliest Colonial times. Probably earlier." She raised her eyebrow, waiting for him to put the pieces together.

Of course. If it was a European name, and it predated the arrival of the earliest Colonists, and the Prince Henry expedition used it as their main thoroughfare....

She finished Cam's thought. "And the original spelling was 'M-A-R-R-Y-M-A-C-K.' Our friend Mary again. The Sacred Feminine."

"Wait. Take it one step further. 'Mac' means 'son of' in Scottish, right? So Marrymack means 'Son of Mary.' For a river, symbolically, it's a perfect name. The river flows, just like the Jesus bloodline."

Amanda repeated the words back to him. "The river flows like the Jesus bloodline." She grinned. "As Brandon said, that's some deep shit. But I think you're correct."

He shook his head. "This stuff just keeps coming together."

They had a river named after the son of the Virgin Mary in northern New England, a tower named after Mary Magdalene in southern New England and a bunch of fascinating artifacts in between. Plus a Puritan judge with a strange fixation on his wife's nipples and a series of curious connections to the locations and artifacts comprising this puzzle. Brandon was right: It was time to go to Newport to see if they could put the jigsaw together.

CHAPTER 16

Amanda snuck a look at Cam as they bounced along in a Bonanza bus bound for Newport. She liked him clean-shaven. Of course, she had also liked him with the goatee. She just liked him. Liked his competence, the way he always seemed to know what to do — how to solve a problem or make a plan or find his way. Liked the way he didn't complain, didn't lament his injured shoulder or his diabetes. Liked his loyalty and honor, the fact that he cried when Eric Forsberg died and refused to abandon his cousin or this fight or his ideals. And liked his easy smile, especially when it shined on her.

They had boarded the bus in Boston, stockpiled with a handful of newly-purchased books covering the history of Newport and early exploration of New England. She skimmed the accounts of Verrazzano, who explored the Atlantic Coast of America, including Rhode Island's Narragansett Bay, in 1524. "Listen to this. Verrazzano traveled up the coast from the Carolinas to Newfoundland — "

"Verrazzano. Isn't he the guy who explored Nova Scotia and named it Arcadia?" Cam interrupted.

"Precisely. Which is one of the reasons I'm reading his logs. He made a number of stops along his journey up the coastline, visiting the natives and describing the land. He describes the Native Americans as small and dark — he uses the term Ethiopian for the color of their skin. But have a listen at what he writes about your Indians in Narragansett Bay: 'This is the finest looking tribe … that we have found in our voyage. They exceed us in size, and they are of a very fair complexion; some of them incline more to a white….'" She looked up. "This is the first I've heard about white-skinned Indians."

"Not me, believe it or not. Roger Williams — you know, the guy who founded Rhode Island — lived with the Narragansett tribe for a few years and he said the babies were born with red hair and white skin. When I read it, it didn't mean anything to me. But now…." He stared out the window for a few seconds. "Maybe it explains something I haven't been able to figure out: What happened to Prince Henry?"

"I thought we agreed he left with the aliens," she deadpanned as Cam grinned. "Seriously, as I told you, there's no evidence in Scotland of his death. He may have remained in America and passed on here."

"That's my point. If he stayed here, probably with a few dozen other men, what happened to them, I mean before they died? There's really only two possibilities: The natives either killed them or befriended them. And we're already pretty sure the natives helped Prince Henry, served as his guides, showed him America's Stonehenge. It's a fair assumption Sinclair and his men would have become part of some tribe."

"The tall, fair-skinned natives."

"And the red-haired babies."

"Actually, there's an amusing story about a reunion in Nova Scotia between the Mi'kmaq tribe and the Sinclair descendants; Prince Henry wintered with the Mi'Kmaq his first winter in Nova Scotia, before sailing to Westford. The reunion commemorated the 600 year anniversary of the voyage so it would have been in 1998. The Mi'kmaq chief and the Sinclair clan leader looked like brothers. People couldn't stop commenting on it." She bit her lip.

"There was talk about doing DNA testing on the Mi'kmaq and Sinclairs. I wonder if it ever came to be."

"I'll ask Brandon to dig around. I'd love to hear the Rhonda Blanks of the world rebut a direct DNA link between the Sinclairs and the Mi'kmaq."

"It's similar to attempting to convince the Christian Fundamentalists we descend from apes. No amount of evidence will change their minds."

While Cam phoned Brandon, she explored the possibilities associated with Sinclair and his men living with the natives for an extended period. "This might explain another oddity: Verrazzano didn't mention the Tower in his log."

"Really?"

"I read it twice."

"Maybe he just didn't see it. It's a long coastline."

"I doubt it. He spent 15 days exploring the Newport area. One would think the Tower would be the type of thing the natives would show him. I suppose one possibility is he viewed the Tower but chose not to write about it lest the log fall into the wrong hands; he would tell the king in person. Recall that Marco Polo did not mention the Great Wall when he wrote about China."

"Maybe you have it backward. Maybe the Narragansetts purposely hid it from him."

She stared out the window for a few seconds, the trees flashing by in a blur. "Yes, that is a possibility. It had only been just over 100 years since Prince Henry's visit. Perhaps he warned the natives that other Europeans would come looking for him, for the Tower." She paused. "For his treasures."

"Yes, that makes perfect sense. Sinclair would have told them to be wary of other Europeans, to not share any secrets with them."

"And Verrazzano wasn't in on the secret, wasn't part of the Templar line, didn't know the password or code. So they kept him away."

Cam nodded slowly. "Or maybe it's just the opposite. Maybe he was in on the secret and wanted to keep it quiet. Remember, he's the guy who named Nova Scotia Arcadia. Maybe he was *Rex Deus* himself." His kind brown eyes settled on hers. "Either possibility is consistent with why the Tower is not in his report." He squeezed her hand. "Good job."

As the bus rolled down Route 95, they continued pouring through their stack of books. After twenty minutes Cam broke the silence. "Check this out. In 1622 somebody printed a journal recounting the early days of the Pilgrims. The journal talks about a group of settlers who went exploring in the woods and found an elaborate Indian burial site. They opened the grave and found crowns and knives and trinkets and jewelry — the typical stuff you'd find buried with a chief or king. When they got to the body, it had been embalmed; again, what you'd expect for a chief. But here's the interesting thing: Quoting from the journal, 'The skull had fine yellow hair still on it.'"

"Blond-haired natives to go with our tall, fair-skinned ones. And Plymouth is not so far from Newport."

Cam nodded. "Less than a hundred miles. That DNA testing may turn out to be pretty interesting."

✤   ✤   ✤

As the bus approached Newport, Cam's TracFone rang. He didn't recognize the number, looked to Amanda before picking it up.

"You really must answer it," she said.

He nodded. It was either a wrong number, in which case no harm would come from it, or somebody who somehow had tracked them down, in which case the harm would come whether he answered or not. "Hello."

"Is this Cameron Thorne?" A bit of a Midwestern twang but not a voice Cam recognized.

"Who's calling?"

He paused, cautious. "This is Scott Wolter."

Cam exhaled. "Hey, Scott. What's up?"

"I was getting worried about you guys. Are you all right?"

"We're still on the run, trying to put this all together."

"That's why I called. I've been digging around. I'm friendly with some Masons out here in Minnesota and they feed me information when I ask." He chuckled. "Actually, they're sworn to secrecy so sometimes they just sort of point at books and stuff with their elbow or chin. But eventually even a dunce like me figures it out."

The only experience Cam had with the Masons was being entertained by a group of smiling brothers with sock puppets when he gave blood a few years ago. It was hard to imagine these guys were the guardians of ancient secrets.

"So I asked them about your Prince Henry," Wolter continued. "Apparently your man Sinclair would have been a Masonic Grand Master himself."

Amanda, who was listening in, nodded.

"Here's the deal," Wolter explained, largely repeating Amanda's account of the Templars fleeing to Scotland with their treasures, where they were safeguarded in Roslyn by the Sinclair clan, a leading Templar family.

"Well, once they got to Scotland they reconstituted themselves as the Masons. Here's the interesting part: The Grand Master position was a hereditary one, held until the 18th century by the head of the Sinclair clan. So, like I said, your man Prince Henry would have been a Grand Master, as would his descendants. And you already know the Sinclair family was related to one of the original nine Knights Templar. So you've got a line of Sinclairs going from the early 1100s all the way to the mid-18th century being leaders of the Templar and Masonic orders."

Cam and Amanda exchanged glances. The Sinclair clan's leadership of the Masons into the 17th and 18th centuries potentially linked the family to events in Colonial America. Specifically, Newport.

Wolter continued. "This stuff definitely ties in with our Hooked X research. The Templars were in Scotland but they knew their time was limited — the English kings kept attacking Scottish lands, trying to bring them under Papal control. And trying to recapture the Templar treasures."

Cam saw where this story was going. "Then Prince Henry finds a map to the New World."

"Or maybe he had old Viking maps from his mother's family. Or maybe the Templars found an ancient map in Jerusalem — there's lots of evidence of the Phoenicians exploring North America. Either way, it was time. Time to take their treasures and their followers to a new land, the New World, where nobody could find them. You with me so far?"

"Totally."

"Look, I'm a scientist. This is really just a matter of logic. And the key to it all is the Cistercians. During medieval times the only people on the island of Gotland who had the ability to write were the Cistercian monks. And we know the Kensington Rune Stone was carved by people from Gotland because of the Dotted R rune, not to mention the unique grammar and dialect of the writing. Finally, we know the Spirit Pond Rune Stone and the Narragansett Rune Stone were carved by the same people who carved the Kensington Rune Stone."

"Right. Because of the Hooked X." It appeared on the three North American rune stones yet nowhere in Europe.

"Exactly. So we know a Cistercian monk must have carved all three rune stones. Now we just connect the dots. The Hooked X is a cipher, a symbol, that tells us the carvers believed in the Jesus bloodline. That tells us the Cistercians and the Templars knew the secrets of the Church, knew that Jesus and Mary Magdalene had a baby. That's not surprising — they knew all sorts of secrets. And your man Prince Henry not only descends from a long line of Templars, he's heir to the Jesus bloodline himself. And he's got a bunch of

Templars with him up in Scotland trying to escape the Pope. And he's got a map. So of course they'd get in their boats and — "

Wolter suddenly cut out, the cell connection broken as the bus pulled into the terminal in Newport.

Cam finished the narrative. "And sail to the New World."

✝   ✝   ✝

Cam and Amanda grabbed their backpacks and book bags, hopped off the bus and darted along the crowded America's Cup Avenue, the harborfront area lined with shops and restaurants and pubs. A few sailboats — yachts, actually — motored into the harbor after a day on the water, part of the dynamic panorama enjoyed by diners at outdoor tables and tourists lining the docks and children wrestling dripping ice cream cones. A warm Saturday afternoon late in September, a last chance to squeeze some summer out of the miserly New England climate.

"That stuff Scott Wolter told us fills in a lot of the missing pieces."

"Yes. It seems we're getting close." She sighed. "But where does it all end?"

The stress of the past few days was beginning to get to Amanda. As it was beginning to get to him. He took her hand. "I'd love to come back here with you and just hang out, walk around, tour the mansions, dinner and drinks, whatever."

She rallied quickly. "Dancing, too?"

"Only if you have two right feet to match my two left ones." They walked in silence a few strides. "Actually, one of the best things to do here is fly stunt kites."

"Stunt kites?"

"They have two lines and they're bigger than regular kites. You hold one line in each hand and you can make the kites dive and spin and do all sorts of tricks. There's a state park at the tip of

Newport; it's a great place to fly because it's always windy. Same reason it's such a good sailing area."

"Perhaps that's the real reason Prince Henry came. To fly a kite."

Cam laughed as they crossed the cobblestoned Thames Street and continued away from the harbor up a steep incline on Mill Street. "The Redwood Library has an amazing collection of Newport history. I think they're open until five today so I thought we could spend an hour there digging around." They were now in the oldest section of the town, centuries-old Federalist- and Colonial-style homes packed close together on narrow, crisscrossing streets. He pointed to his left. "That's where we ran away from Salazar."

Cam's TracFone rang. Amanda leaned closer; for the hundredth time he breathed in her floral scent as Brandon spoke. "That Frazon guy was buried at Touro Cemetery in Newport, just like you said. And like you said, it was arranged by Judge Sewall. That was in 1704. That's all I could find on him. But I've got some interesting DNA stuff. There's a web site run by some of the Sinclair descendants and they're having some symposium or something. They're hinting pretty strongly at a big announcement involving DNA matches between the Sinclair clan and the Mi'kmaq. I'll keep digging and call you guys later."

"Wow," he said. "A DNA match would be amazing."

"Yes, they've been discussing DNA testing since before I took the job." She paused. "Sorry to change the subject but what Brandon mentioned about Touro Cemetery also caught my ear. The Touro name comes up often."

"I noticed."

"Did you know the Touro family purchased the Tower land and donated it to the town of Newport in the 1800s, before a developer could demolish the Tower and build on the land? And now Mr. Frazon is buried in the Touro Cemetery. Perhaps it's just a coincidence."

"I don't believe in coincidences anymore, Amanda."

They approached the Redwood Library, a salmon-colored, pillared building that from the front looked a bit like the Supreme Court with a sunburn. Amanda requested materials covering the Newport Tower, while Cam focused on Joseph Frazon and the Touro Synagogue and Cemetery.

He found nothing more on Frazon. The absence of any apparent connection between Frazon and the Newport community only deepened the mystery—Frazon wasn't sent for burial in Newport because he had family or history here. As for Touro Cemetery itself, the land was purchased by the Jewish community in 1677, 19 years after the first Jewish settlers arrived in Newport. The decision to secure a burial ground for a growing Jewish population seemed perfectly sensible. But the history of the cemetery over the next 84 years was anything but. In fact, it was confounding.

"Amanda, listen to this. Other than Frazon, nobody was buried in the Touro Cemetery until 1761, 84 years after it was established."

"That's peculiar."

"Not just peculiar, downright weird. I mean, why have a cemetery if you're not going to use it?"

"Perhaps all the Jews left Newport before they passed on?"

He shook his head. "No. They died here; they just weren't buried at the Touro Cemetery. Our man Frazon was alone for generations."

"Where is the cemetery?"

He motioned with his chin. "Just up the hill from the synagogue, on Bellevue Avenue. Pretty much the highest point in Newport."

"That makes it only a couple of blocks from the Tower," she mused.

"There's a lot of material here on the Tower, mostly stuff I've seen before. But one thing I'm learning is how involved the Touro family was with the Tower. The sons moved to New Orleans during the Revolutionary War but even decades later they were still acting as custodians of the Tower, preserving the land and paying for its upkeep. They may even have helped perpetuate the myth that Benedict Arnold built the Tower as a colonial windmill — it would have been a good way to keep unwanted attention away."

"Good point."

He kept reading. "And check this out. The Touros also paid to preserve the Jewish Cemetery. At one point it had been aban- doned." The next step was obvious. "I'm going to do some research on the Touro family itself."

"You'd best hurry. The library closes in 20 minutes."

He dove back into his research, his eyes flying over the words, his hands flicking books open and closed. He was close: The pic- ture was coming into focus, the trees moving aside to allow a clear view of the forest. Over the past week they had visited a handful of sites, debated dozens of theories, examined scores of historical precedents. Each of these lines of inquiry was seemingly unrelated to the others, like spokes from a wagon wheel strewn by the side of the road after an accident. Now, finally, he may have found the hub of the wheel, the nucleus through which the knowledge they had acquired could be joined together in a coherent pattern. That hub, that nucleus, was the Touro family.

"Guess who were the first Masons in America? And guess who served as Grand Master in Rhode Island?" he asked as the librarian locked the door behind them.

"By the looks of your silly grin, I'd venture a guess it was the Touros and their Jewish friends in Newport." Cam waited for her to process the information. She did so within a few seconds. "Bloody hell!" she exclaimed, slapping him on the arm. "That just makes so much sense!"

He guided her north on Bellevue, toward the Touro Cemetery. "Here's what I think happened. You tell me if I'm crazy."

She smiled, her face flush. "Slim chance of me passing on that."

"Okay, here's my theory. All the stuff about the Jesus bloodline and escaping the Pope with the Templar treasures and mapping the New World — it all makes perfect sense. It never actually worked out the way Prince Henry hoped; war between Scotland and England, climate change, Black Plague, whatever — something messed up his plans for a full settlement. But a bunch of them stayed here, including Prince Henry, and intermarried with the natives. Others returned to Scotland, where Prince Henry's grandson memorialized the journey with cryptic carvings at Roslyn Chapel. But otherwise, for obvious reasons, they kept everything secret. Probably only the Sinclair family and trusted allies knew about their explorations. Plus the Native Americans who helped them. With me so far?"

"Completely."

"So these secrets get passed down through the Scottish Masons — probably Sinclair descendants — over the next couple of centuries, until colonization of North America really gets going. And then the American Masons, as caretakers of Prince Henry's secrets, take on the duty of preserving his legacy. Of course, I'm talking about only the highest-ranking Masons. Most members had no idea — that was the only way to keep the Church from finding out."

"When you say preserving his legacy, do you mean physically or spiritually?"

"Both, actually." This is where his knowledge of American history came in handy. "Spiritually, Masons such as George Washington, Benjamin Franklin, John Hancock and Paul Revere were leading proponents of the Bill of Rights and of separation of church and state, radical ideas at the time that were actually consistent with Templar beliefs and doctrine."

"I've heard people question whether Masonry really did influence your Founding Fathers."

"I had a history professor who did a lot of work on the Masons. She showed us something neat." Stopping and leaning against an iron railing in front of a real estate office, Cam pulled out a dollar bill from his wallet and a red pen from his pack. On the back of the bill he pointed out the pyramid with the all-seeing eye at its peek. He drew a triangle on the bill, following the lines of the pyramid, and then another triangle, this one upside down. "This is a Jewish star, of course."

"It's also the Seal of Solomon."

"Exactly. Whom the Masons revere. Which is why we see the star in Masonic imagery so often. Now, see this Latin writing ringing the pyramid? I'm going to circle the letters that fall on the points of the star." He handed Amanda the bill. "What are the letters?"

"A-S-M-O-N. I don't get it."

"It's an anagram."

Her eyes widened as she rearranged the letters. "*Mason*. How clever."

6-SIDED STAR SUPERIMPOSED OVER IMAGE ON U.S. DOLLAR BILL

"There's a whole bunch of this kind of Masonic imagery. You just have to look for it."

"Let's return to Prince Henry. Your theory is that the Masons were privy to his secrets and helped preserve his legacy."

"Right. The high-ranking ones, like the Touros here in Newport. They made sure sites like the Newport Tower were preserved."

"So where does Frazon being buried in the Jewish Cemetery fit in?"

"I have a theory about that also." They approached the edge of the Touro cemetery, opposite the Viking Hotel, and stood outside the wrought iron front gate framed by a granite arch. "We need to get in." A number of rose bushes climbed along the edge of the cemetery, partially blocking their view.

"It's locked," she said.

"Let's go around back. We can climb the fence." After what they'd been through, it hardly seemed like a major offense. They hoisted themselves over a stone wall in the rear of the cemetery and walked back toward the front gate, toward the roses. "This front section, along the street, was the original cemetery. They added to it later. But Frazon would be buried here."

Her eyes moved back and forth. "But there's no marker."

He smiled. "I know. That's part of my theory. There probably was a tombstone for him when he was first buried but once others were buried here later there was no reason to keep his marker out of disrepair."

"I'm not following you."

He took a deep breath. "I think Frazon was just a placeholder, a body to establish that this land was a burial ground and couldn't be disturbed."

"A placeholder? For what?"

On the one hand, he was sure he was right. On the other, he knew his theory was radical. "I think Judge Sewall — later in life, after he apologized for his role in the witch trials — became a Mason, or at least a Masonic sympathizer. I think the Masons knew the secrets of Newport, of who built the Newport Tower, of why Prince Henry was here in America. I think that's why the early Jewish settlers, who were Masonic leaders, bought this land and dedicated it as a cemetery. It wasn't because they needed it; they didn't bury any of their congregants here for 84 years. It was because they wanted to protect the land. You can't build over a cemetery — it's pretty much the only land guaranteed to resist development. So they buried Frazon here, the first Jew they could find." She nodded for him to continue. "They wanted to protect the land because they knew something was buried here. Either they had a map, or it was marked, or they knew how many paces from the Tower; somehow they knew this land was sacred, the secret passed down through the Masonic lodges." He studied the ground. "Whatever the secret is, it's probably right beneath our feet."

She edged toward him as if the ground beneath them might give way and swallow them up, like in some *Raiders of the Lost Ark* movie. "Yes. Yes, it all adds up nicely. This is the highest spot in Newport, near the Tower. The question is, what are we standing on?"

They both were thinking about the possible Templar treasures. Gold and silver? Religious artifacts? Ancient maps and formulas? The Jesus genealogy? All of the above?

She moved away, studying the ground from another angle. "It makes sense they didn't bury their treasures at the Tower — they would have chosen a less obvious location."

"And it also explains why the Masons have been so protective of this site."

She reached for his hand. "So," she asked teasingly, "when might we begin digging?"

✝   ✝   ✝

"Well, are there any loose ends?" Amanda asked, sipping a glass of wine at an outdoor café along Newport's waterfront.

"There is a small matter of the treasure. Whatever it is. With all these secrets, all these cabals, there just has to be a treasure."

She took Cam's hand. "I have no need for more treasure, thank you very much. What I meant was, is there anything else we need to learn?"

He picked at a piece of fried calamari and watched the sailboats motor into the harbor as daylight dimmed. A week. One week. That's how much time had passed since Brandon turned the key to a Bobcat and turned all of their lives into a tragic, stupefying rollercoaster ride.

He felt a strange combination of fatigue, satisfaction and anger. The fatigue he understood—they had been on the run non-stop for six days. And the satisfaction also—they had put the pieces together to a 600-year old puzzle, a solution that had befuddled historians and archeologists for centuries.

But there were still some things that didn't fit. "This whole New Jerusalem thing that Judge Sewall kept writing about still bothers me. Did he know something? Was New Jerusalem a code for something? It's a loose end." Just like Cam's anger.

"I've been wondering as well—is the New Jerusalem concept somehow related to Prince Henry?"

He linked his fingers around hers. "There's really only one way to find out."

She smiled. "Count me in."

They weren't done yet. Maybe he'd get a chance to deal with his anger after all. Someone needed to pay for what they did to Brandon, to Forsberg, to the Monsignor, to Pegasus. He couldn't let Beatrice and her Vatican friends just walk away.

He took a long swig from his Amstel bottle, his free hand finding Pegasus' collar tucked in his jeans pocket. He wasn't convinced the police would catch the culprits—the Legions of Jesus undoubtedly had access to fake passports and safe houses and transportation and whatever else they needed to escape detection. As for Beatrice, she could plausibly claim ignorance—she was an ocean away when most of the maiming and murders occurred. And Balducci, as a Vatican official, could claim diplomatic immunity.

As he gazed out into the bay and watched a couple of kids bounce along in an inflatable rubber tube, the seeds of a plan took root, a ploy that would allow them to both test their theory and also catch Beatrice and the Vatican extremists.

"Wasn't there some poem by Henry Wadsworth Longfellow about the Newport Tower?" he asked.

She looked at him quizzically. "Yes. It's entitled *Skeleton in Armor.* It concerns a Viking who sailed to America with his bride and built the Tower for her as a wedding gift."

"Well, when I was looking through the materials at the Redwood Library, I found another poem by Longfellow, this one called *The Jewish Cemetery in Newport.* Obviously, it's about the Touro Cemetery."

She tilted her head. "And?"

"Longfellow is related to Judge Sewall — the judge's sister is Longfellow's great-grandmother. And one other thing: The Longfellow Bridge, in Boston, is decorated with the prows of medieval Viking ships."

LONGFELLOW BRIDGE

"Do you believe Longfellow is a key to solving the Prince Henry mystery?"

He sipped his beer. "Actually, I don't." He was willing to connect dots, to follow clues, to draw conclusions supported by evidence. But sometimes a poem was just a poem and a decoration on a bridge nothing more than that. He smiled. "But it doesn't matter what I think, or what you think. What matters is what Beatrice and the Vatican extremists think."

CHAPTER 17

[Saturday Evening]

Normally Beatrice lodged at the Ritz Carlton while in Boston. But it had been sold so she took a room at the Copley Plaza in quarters designed to look like something out of a Dickens novel. It was one thing to decorate with authentic antiques. But the hotel furnishings were fakes, new pieces designed to look old. She reached for her smoldering Gauloises cigarette. This time she ground it into the desktop and watched it slowly discolor the mahogany veneer.

She lit another, inhaling the pungent, earthy smell. Food, wine, cigarettes. That's about all the French did well. But they did them very well.

More than 24 hours had passed since she had instructed her team of ruffians to allow Amanda and Thorne to escape. She had assumed they would run straight to the newspapers with their foolish alien portal story. But, according to Reichmann's Vatican sources, nobody had contacted the press—either in Boston or nationally—with any type of story involving Prince Henry or the Templars or the Sinclair bloodline. For what were they waiting? Had they begun to doubt their alien conclusions? Were they continuing their research, revising their story, eliminating the aliens from it entirely? Perhaps she had underestimated the young solicitor—he did after all descend from the *Rex Deus* blood line. And he had proven himself by besting Salazar, supposedly Reichmann's top man. Not to mention that he had, in a week, come closer to solving the Prince Henry mystery than anyone had in decades of work.

An hour of smoking and stewing passed, an interminable sixty minutes in a boxy hotel room in downtown Boston, more grains of sand in the hourglass of history lost without the glory of Prince Henry and his noble knight, James Gunn, having been revealed to the world. How many hours had been lost, wasted, frittered away in just such a manner? Now, finally, someone — all right, Thorne and the girl Amanda — had uncovered hard evidence of Prince Henry's journey, had tied the loose ends up enough to present a coherent story the public could comprehend and believe. But not embrace. Not with the ugly anti-Church details the two lovebirds would include in their narrative, which is why it was so imperative they discredit themselves with their ridiculous alien theory.

The ring of her mobile phone interrupted her musings. "This is Cameron Thorne."

She exhaled the smoke through her nose. "Mr. Thorne. At our last meeting you neglected to say goodbye."

"Sorry, we had to run."

She smiled. Royal blood, even diluted, shone through. "Well then, what can I do for you?"

"We've been rethinking our conclusions a bit. That whole alien portal thing may not be correct."

She ground her cigarette into the desktop again. "I see." Royal blood or not, he and Amanda had just shifted from the asset to liability side of the ledger. "And have you perchance moved on to a new theory?"

"As a matter of fact, we have. But we've hit a bit of a dead end. We need help from your Vatican expert. We need access to the Vatican archives."

"Very well. Tell me where you are and we'll come by and have a nice chat. I'm certain he'd be pleased to help you. Ultimately we're all working toward an identical goal: We want to learn the truth." She inhaled, covered the receiver to hide her cough. Truth was whatever the writers of history—the architects of coups and wars and, in this case, cover-ups—decided it would be.

He chuckled. "I'm afraid that after our last visit, we're not that comfortable with Reichmann and his posse." He paused. "We'll meet you on the Longfellow Bridge in Boston. Just you and Father Balducci. No goons."

That was fine. At close range she could fire a gun as well as anyone. And the consequences were irrelevant—as an old woman, her life was winding down anyway; she would gladly sacrifice a few years to save Prince Henry and Sir James. "Why the Longfellow Bridge?"

"Wait, I'm not finished with the conditions of our meeting. If we don't return, our story goes public."

Thorne's threat of the story being released to the media if he were found dead had kept her from killing them at America's Stonehenge. But now that they had abandoned their alien portal theory there was no benefit in keeping them alive—the story would come out whether she killed them or not. In fact, the story was one of those outlandish conspiracy theories that required a strong, articulate champion. With Cam and Amanda dead—not to mention Forsberg and the Monsignor—who would be bold enough, stupid enough, to grab the reins of this runaway stallion? The only likely candidate, ironically, would be the Consortium itself. Babinaux would not be pleased to learn of her involvement in the murders and cover-up but he would know enough to spin the story, to paint Prince Henry as a champion of Christianity rather than an enemy of the Pope. He would know which secrets to reveal and which to conceal. In retrospect, she may have played it too cute back at America's Stonehenge. Perhaps she should have just bumped them off and allowed Babinaux to finesse the story and clean up the mess.

She'd been given a second chance. "Again, why the Longfellow Bridge?"

"I'll explain it when we get there."

He was bluffing. "That's not good enough, Mr. Thorne. After your alien theory, you do not have a lot of credibility in my book."

"Okay," he sighed. "This is what we've found. First, Henry Wadsworth Longfellow, the poet for whom the bridge is named, is the grandson of Peleg Wadsworth. Peleg was a leading Freemason in the state of Maine. In fact, he settled a new town and named it Hiram. In Masonic lore, Hiram is—"

"I know full well who Hiram is, Mr. Thorne." He and the silly girl continued to insult her. Hiram Abiff, chief architect during the construction of King Solomon's Temple, was a paramount figure in Masonic tradition. She took a deep draw on her cigarette and exhaled slowly. "Continue."

"Well, Peleg's Masonic ties are the first link between Longfellow and Prince Henry."

"A rather tenuous connection. Many men other than Longfellow had Masonic grandparents at that time."

"Agreed. But did you also know Longfellow wrote a poem about the Newport Tower?"

"Something about armor, if I recall correctly."

"Yes. So that's the second connection. The third connection is the bridge itself. Prows of Viking ships are carved onto each of the four main bridge stanchions."

"Viking ships? Why?"

"Exactly our point. No Vikings came to Boston. Unless, of course, you count Prince Henry."

"Continue."

"The fourth connection is a direct link between Judge Samuel Sewall, a Puritan judge, and Longfellow." Thorne briefly explained Sewall's ties to the Bourne Stone and his visits both to Noman's Land and Stonehenge in England. "We think Sewall was somehow involved in keeping the Prince Henry secrets." Interesting. She had never heard of a Judge Sewall connection. Thorne continued. "Longfellow's great-grandmother was Sewall's sister."

Beatrice attempted to hide her surprise. Family links — secrets passed down through the generations — were of crucial importance in the Prince Henry history. Perhaps the young lawyer was on to something. He seemed to have an uncanny ability to ferret out random pieces of information and piece them together. "Why must we meet on the bridge itself?"

"Because we found some carvings we think are important. They're faint but they're clearly visible. If you know where to look."

As if she might attempt to locate the carvings herself. Why would she? He could save her the time while also giving her the chance finally to eliminate them. "How old is the bridge? The carvings can't be more than a century or two in age." She didn't want to appear over-eager.

"The bridge was built in 1906. But that doesn't mean the stones used to build it aren't centuries older."

"And you believe Father Balducci can help translate these carvings?"

"I don't know. We don't even know what they are. We've had a few people take a look and nobody can figure them out. They look like runes but not exactly. He's supposed to be the expert in all this stuff, right?"

"Yes. He is the Vatican expert on all things Templar." Time to reel him in. "The Templars utilized many codes that are unknown to all but a handful of Vatican scholars. The Vatican, you see, took custody of all Templar records in 1307. If it is a Templar code of some sort, Father Balducci will decipher it."

"Okay then. Meet us at eight o'clock tomorrow morning, on the bridge. Wait for us at the up-stream stanchion on the Boston side of the river."

+   +   +

[Sunday]

Beatrice Yarborough exited the taxi, dug in her purse for the exact fare and stepped to the curb on Charles Street, at the foot of Boston's Beacon Hill. The street was mostly empty on this Sunday morning. She tapped her foot impatiently, glanced at a window display of trinkets and attic junk that in America passed as antiquities. A pair of joggers ran by, more Americans fixated on buffing their bodies even as their brains shriveled from a nationwide dearth of intellectual curiosity and culture. Did no one in this country appreciate classical music or the arts or even fine conversation? She missed the Knight but she did not miss the States. When her work here was complete she would waste not a moment before boarding a plane to London.

That was, of course, assuming things went according to plan on the bridge. She patted the revolver in the breast pocket of her gray blazer. Cameron Thorne and Amanda Spencer would not leave the Longfellow bridge alive.

A black Cadillac pulled alongside the curb; a driver stepped out and opened the back door for Father Balducci. A whiff of expensive cologne wafted over Beatrice as the priest, well-dressed again in a herringbone blazer, climbed out of the car. She waited for him to apologize for being late; when he did not, she took a deep breath and addressed him as politely as she could. Just because his Italian manners were lacking did not mean hers should be as well. "Good morning, Father. Please follow me."

She led the angular scholar down Charles Street two blocks to a traffic rotary. They climbed a concrete stairway to the Longfellow Bridge, resting halfway to allow the Vatican emissary to dab his face with a handkerchief. They had discussed their plan last night by telephone but she reviewed it with him again once they reached the bridge itself. "Reichmann and his men will be in automobiles, circling back and forth across the bridge," she said. "Our goal is to obtain as much information from them as we can before we ... abduct them. We need to determine if they have spoken to the press yet. And, of course, we want to view these mysterious carvings."

Balducci stopped, his hands folded neatly in front of his genitals. "As you know, I take my orders only from my superiors at the Holy See." His dark, mousse-styled hair remained frozen in place even as the wind whipped down the river. "Fortunately, on this occasion, my orders and your instructions are in accord. We must not allow them to leave the bridge."

+ + +

Cam and Amanda stood on the Cambridge side of the Longfellow Bridge, a cool wind powering a lone sailboat as it darted across the river. Though the temperature was in the fifties, they both wore only biking shorts, tank tops and flip-flops. Cam pulled his fanny pack tight around his waist.

His TracFone rang. "I see them," Brandon reported. "An older woman and a tall guy in a blazer. They're on the bridge on the Boston side. Upriver."

"They alone?" Cam peered across the river at the Massachusetts General Hospital complex. Brandon sat somewhere at a window on an upper floor, a pair of binoculars trained on the bridge and river below.

"Yup. Nobody else with them. A couple of female joggers coming from the Cambridge side but I think they're legit."

"Any sign of Reichmann?"

"Oh yeah. I've seen four sedans, all black, circling back and forth across the bridge for the past half-hour."

"Black sedans again?" Amanda shook her head. "Don't they have any imagination?"

He smiled, no longer surprised by her irreverence but still amused by it. "What about Poulos?"

"I'm ready," the cop answered. "Brandon has me on a three-way call. I'm motoring upriver right now, just passing that condo complex in Cambridge that looks like a pyramid. You should be able to see me." Cam spotted the unmarked State Police pleasure boat, captained by a female officer in civilian clothes. "You should assume that once you start walking, the guys in the sedans will get out and move in on foot. They'll pinch you in the middle."

Cam wasn't sure he wanted to face Reichmann and his men again. Especially Salazar. They would be playing for keeps this time, no staged escape. That didn't give him and Amanda much time. He checked his watch. 7:51. "Okay. We're going to head across."

Poulos stopped him. "Check your transmitters first."

Cam shifted uncomfortably. "Actually, we took them off." Poulos' State Police buddies had fitted them each with small transmitters taped to their chests.

"You did what?"

"Too risky. You could see them every time the wind blew our shirts." Cam wasn't willing to assume Balducci wouldn't try to sneak a peek inside Amanda's blouse.

"Damn it, Cam. You can't go changing things last minute," Poulos said.

"Look, don't blame me for the wind. Anyway, I put one of the transmitters in my fanny pack. You should be able to hear everything still."

They began to walk along the 6-foot wide sidewalk on the upriver side of the bridge; only a green, wrought-iron pedestrian railing stood, chest-high, between them and a thirty-foot fall to the river below. Four stone obelisks—the so-called salt and pepper shakers that made the bridge famous—rose in a square-like pattern around the center of the bridge.

Within seconds they heard the rumble of a Red Line transit train approaching from the Cambridge side. The train rumbled past on the median portion of the bridge using tracks that divided the northbound and southbound lanes of traffic. Cam checked his watch again. 7:54. The trains ran at 20-minute intervals, each way, though Bostonians knew better than to set their watches by them.

Brandon's muffled voice echoed from inside Cam's fanny pack. "Beatrice and Balducci are at the first obelisk. They're still alone."

He took Amanda's hand and smiled. "Ready?"

"Quite."

+   +   +

Beatrice patted the revolver one last time for reassurance, forcing a smile as the two lovebirds sauntered toward her, barely dressed. They'd probably just rolled out of bed, the trollop no doubt distracting Thorne from the important work at hand.

"Now, Mr. Thorne, where is this carving of yours? Let's get on with it. I don't see anything other than graffiti." They met on a granite walkway that rimmed one of the salt-shaker obelisks, the walkway protruding over the river on the up-current, Boston side.

Amanda crossed her arms in front of her chest. "You can't believe we'd instruct you to meet us at the very spot of the carvings, can you?"

Feeling the cold presence of the revolver in the pocket of her jacket, Beatrice ignored the girl. "Mr. Thorne?"

He nodded. "Follow me." He began walking back toward the center of the bridge span. Turning casually to Father Balducci, he spoke. "You know, there's another reason I wanted to bring you out here. I wanted to get your opinion on something."

Aha. So there was more to this than merely some carvings.

+   +   +

Cam chose his words carefully as the scholar loped along, his hands in his jacket pockets. Cam would only get one chance to read

Balducci's face, to sense his reaction. Here, protected by trained operatives and with Cam at his mercy, Balducci would be candid, unguarded, his response an honest one. Which was why Cam was willing to risk the meeting on the bridge. The Vatican scholar's reaction would tell him whether he and Amanda had stumbled upon a hidden, shadow version of history that would change the way the Western world viewed itself.

He turned to face Balducci. He sensed he was about to learn something monumental, something that would make all the other earth-shaking discoveries of the past week seem like minor tremors. Amanda must have sensed it also; she reached over, took his hand and squeezed it tightly. Even Beatrice leaned closer to listen.

He took a deep breath. "The Church probably would have collapsed, wouldn't it?"

The scholar leaned against the ornate, green-iron pedestrian railing, adopting a casual pose. "You are a fool, Mr. Thorne, with foolish conclusions. The Church will never collapse."

Good. A witness that attacked was protecting something — usually a secret. "Prince Henry was going to start a whole new religion in America. A New Jerusalem. The Church might not have survived."

Balducci's patted his hair. "History is replete with misguided splinter groups breaking away from the Church. Martin Luther, for example." He sneered. "You do know who that is, don't you Thorne? Not Martin Luther King, but Martin Luther."

Cam ignored the question. After a few seconds Balducci continued, now rubbing the side of his mouth with his hand. "The Church has always survived. It always will." The self-touching told Cam the scholar was lying. Which meant it was true — Prince Henry wasn't just fleeing the Church, he was planning to oppose it. To create a New Jerusalem.

"But Prince Henry was not just some random village monk like Martin Luther," Cam countered. "He was religious royalty, the clan leader of a family that carried the blood of Jesus in its veins. He was Jesus' heir. How could the Pope compete with that?"

The priest straightened his back and rested his hands on his hips in an effort to appear authoritative. "Even if such an outlandish claim were true, there would have been hundreds of others so-called descendants of Jesus and the Magdalene at that time as well. Sinclair was only one man."

"You're wrong. And I think you know it. The Sinclair clan was the main branch of the Jesus bloodline tree. And the other branches of that tree, the other Merovingian dynasty families, fully supported him. The bloodline families had been fighting the Church for centuries, beginning back when Bernard de Clairvaux first convinced the Pope to embrace the Templars as the military wing of the Church. You know as well as I do that the Templars and the bloodline families were one and the same. Both were fighting to bring the Sacred Feminine back into Christianity, fighting to reestablish the duality of the godhead. And both were willing to undermine the Church if necessary to do so."

The scholar began to stammer a response but nothing coherent escaped his mouth. Finally he formed a tepid reply. "You have no proof of this." Balducci squeezed his bottom lip between his thumb and forefinger. Someday Cam would like to play high-stakes poker with him.

"We're here on this bridge, aren't we? Why else would you be here? What other true teachings of Jesus could the *Rex Deus* families be guarding all these centuries? And even if I don't have proof, Prince Henry sure did. He had a genealogy, records that showed the Sinclair and other Templar families carried the blood of Jesus in their veins. Not only that, he had documents—lost gospels—that showed the entire Church was built on lies and that the so-called pagan ways were the true path of Christ. So I'll ask you again: Do you think the Church could have survived the Jesus bloodline families calling for Christians to join them in rejecting the Church and forming a New Jerusalem? One to be led by the heir to Jesus?"

Balducci crossed his arms in front of his chest and angled his body away as Cam pushed on. "Prince Henry was going to bring down the Church. Not because he wanted power but because he was a believer in the true teachings of Christ, not the bastardized version of Christianity the Church had fabricated. Maybe the Plague or a shipwreck or simply old age stopped him. But I'm inclined to think the Church somehow found out about his plan and had a hand in stopping him. Not that I blame them — if his message had gotten out, the Church would have fallen. How could the Pope have prevented it? Spiritually, Prince Henry was a human Holy Grail, the carrier of Christ's blood. And strategically, he was protected by the Atlantic Ocean."

The cleric's normally olive complexion had turned completely pallid and lifeless, like the concrete sidewalk below them. Cam himself felt a bit unsteady. Balducci's reaction confirmed the unfathomable: Prince Henry Sinclair, with the support of the other Jesus bloodline families, had come to America to establish a New Jerusalem based on pagan beliefs and rituals. A religion in direct opposition to the Church, with ancient texts to support its claims for legitimacy.

It was impossible. Yet it was at the same time very possible.

Beatrice's voice cut through the wind on the bridge. "That is quite enough, Mr. Thorne."

She had overheard the conversation. And was now waving a revolver. Her hand, unlike the cleric's, did not shake. "You are sadly mistaken if you believe I'm going to allow you or anyone else to portray Prince Henry as a betrayer of the Church, a Judas." She motioned with the gun. "Keep moving."

He tried to ignore the gun, forced himself not to look at it as he positioned himself between it and Amanda. He was not surprised that Beatrice had a weapon. But it still scared the shit out of him.

He swallowed as a train approached from the distance. "That's why you don't want anyone digging around any of these sites — you're afraid of what they might find. Imagine the headlines: '*Jesus Heirs Reject Church.*'"

"There will be no such headlines, Mr. Thorne," Beatrice said icily.

Forcing his eyes away from the black hole at the end of the revolver, he baited her, stalling for time. The train edged closer. "I think a neat sub-headline would be something about how the Native Americans carry more Jesus blood in them than do most Europeans." Balducci's eyes widened at the possibility of Christ's blood coursing through a race of savages.

Cam glanced over his shoulder at Beatrice. It was time. "The carving is right up there." They were halfway between the obelisks, at the midpoint of the bridge itself. He slowed, the timing now crucial. "There," he said, pointing at the shaded side of one of the obelisks. "About eight feet high." The train was now 100 feet away, chugging along the median strip of the bridge, separated from the vehicle traffic on either side only by a pair of simple iron railings.

Beatrice quickened her pace, squinting toward the obelisk. "I don't see anything," she said, scampering past Cam toward the tower as Balducci shone a flashlight up toward the scratches.

The train closed to 50 feet. Cam took Amanda's hand and backed away a bit. He hadn't planned it this way but a line of graffiti caught his eye. It was too perfect. "There's also some here, on the walkway." He pointed to a red-painted splotch near Beatrice's feet. It read, *Screw You!*

As Beatrice crouched, he squeezed Amanda's hand. "Now," he whispered. He released her hand and together they took two running steps toward the green-iron railing. They planted their hands on the railing top and vaulted themselves over the barrier. He tightened, half-expecting a hot bullet to sear his body. But nothing. As they soared through the cool autumn air to safety, his eyes found Amanda's, her hair floating above her like a parachute, her mouth curved into a full smile.

He filled his lungs and braced for impact. Just before he hit, Beatrice's voice screeched over the sound of the approaching train. "Get them!"

He made himself small, allowing his body to knife deep into the tea-colored water of the Charles. Opening his eyes, he waited until he had stopped descending, turned his body and swam underwater beneath the bridge. They didn't need to swim to the other side but they did need to get far enough under so that Beatrice and the Reichmann posse could not lean over the railing and get a clear shot at them. After about seven or eight seconds underwater he spotted Amanda's form moving gracefully through the murkiness nearby; he angled upward toward her and grabbed her hand. Together they surfaced under the shadow of the bridge. The sound of the train crossing above them echoed, mocking Beatrice.

A few yards away a yellow and red water tube—the kind used for towing kids behind boats—bobbed on the surface. "Quick. Get on!" Poulos yelled from a nearby boat. Cam swam to the far side of the tube and he and Amanda linked arms across the top, using each other as resistance as they pulled themselves out of the water. Even before they were completely on the tube, the engine roared and the nose of the boat lifted into the air. A second later, the tow rope tightened and the tube leapt ahead, plowing through the water at first and then quickly reaching a plane and skimming across the surface as the boat accelerated. As they cleared the bridge Cam looked back. Beatrice and Reichmann and Balducci and the henchman were stuck on the far side of the bridge, blocked from pursuing them or taking a shot at them by a long, slow-moving Red Line train.

He playfully bounced the tube in the water. "I guess you would have mentioned if you didn't know how to swim, right?"

+   +   +

Salazar watched in his rearview mirror as Thorne and the girl leaped from the bridge and escaped on the tube. Pretty good plan for a couple of amateurs. But risky— Reichmann was under orders to eliminate them and Beatrice had grown so unstable that she might do so in broad daylight. There must have been something Thorne needed from the Vatican scholar, some key piece of information. Judging by the smile on Thorne's face as he bounced on the tube, he got it.

Salazar slowly accelerated away from the scene as police lights flashed and troopers rounded up Reichmann and the rest of his team. A couple of quick turns and he lost himself in the streets of Boston's Beacon Hill. He had smelled a trap right away— the pleasure boat cruising up and down the river was a dead giveaway. The woman captained the vessel with too much authority; most women were content to let their husbands drive— a sexist observation but true. And the man should have been reading the Sunday paper or casting a fishing line, not scanning the bridge deck.

Things had worked out perfectly. As far as Cam and the girl knew, Beatrice and Reichmann and his men were now out of action. They would let their guard down. And he didn't have to take orders from Reichmann anymore.

+   +   +

The boat slowed as it approached the Science Museum bridge, a half-mile from the Longfellow, Cam and Amanda still bouncing along in the tube behind. Poulos grinned at Cam as he pulled the tube toward the boat and handed Cam his phone and insulin pump. "Someone wants to talk to you."

"Fun ride?" Brandon asked over the sound of the engine.

"Best ever. How'd it look from up there?"

"It went perfect. For a second, I thought Beatrice was going to jump in after you. And you should have seen them jumping around and waving their arms when they realized the train was blocking them from getting to you."

He told Brandon about the graffiti, which elicited a whoop of joy. "What's the word from the bridge?" he asked Poulos.

"Went perfect. FBI and Staties moved in, arrested the whole lot of them."

"Did they resist?"

"Nah. Once they saw they lost you guys and were trapped on the bridge, they knew it was over. The Vatican guy is already claiming diplomatic immunity." Poulos shrugged. "We'll see what happens." He looked at Cam. "That was a pretty risky operation." Poulos and the Staties had been pushing for arresting Beatrice and Reichmann and his gang before he and Amanda even got on the bridge but Cam had insisted on the encounter on the Longfellow. "Did you learn what you needed to?"

Cam recalled Balducci touching his hair, his mouth, his lip. "Yeah, everything."

CHAPTER 18

After spending a few hours at the FBI headquarters in Boston answering questions, Amanda and Cam retrieved their bags from Poulos' car, showered in a health club in an office building next door and hailed a taxi for the short ride to Mass. General Hospital. Amanda felt unburdened; it was nice to not worry about being followed, to not have to scan the sidewalk for surveillance. But the thought of Beatrice spending the final years of her life in jail saddened her. Somehow her fixation on Prince Henry and the Westford Knight had consumed her, accentuating her obsessive-compulsive personality traits. Perhaps she'd be placed in a hospital rather than a penitentiary.

Her cell phone rang—Leopold Babinaux again. He had left two messages thus far, apologizing for Beatrice's behavior and for the Consortium's tepid efforts to assist Cam and her. "We believed Beatrice, believed she was telling the truth. We were mistaken, and I am sorry." She believed him, and she was glad he phoned, but calling him back was not high on her priority list at the moment.

A uniformed policeman escorted them into Brandon's room; presumably the officer would be reassigned soon now that the danger had passed. She lowered her eyes as Cam embraced his cousin. "You look good," Cam whispered. Even reclined in a hospital bed, Brandon was thick and rugged-looking with color in his cheeks and vibrancy in his eyes.

Brandon smiled. "Speaking of looking good, you going to introduce me to the pretty girl?"

"I don't need an introduction," she declared, stepping around Cam to hug Brandon. "After what we've gone through, we're practically family." The muscles in his back rippled as he embraced her even as he was careful not to press his body against her chest. "It's a pleasure to finally meet you, Brandon."

After a few minutes of small talk, Cam removed the lantern from his bag and handed it to Brandon. "Check this out." He explained its history and their theory that it was a clue to finding the treasure.

"Wait a second. Something about this looks ... wrong." Brandon studied the object for a few seconds. "Hand me that book over there, will you?" Cam did so; Brandon thumbed through until he found the page he was looking for. "This says there are seven windows in the Tower." He tossed the lantern to Cam. "Count them in your model."

She moved closer; together they rotated the replica slowly. "Eight," she exclaimed. "How did we miss that?"

"Probably because you haven't been lying in bed for a week trying to figure out who built the damn thing. I thought maybe the seven windows were significant—you know, seven days in the week, seven sacraments, seven deadly sins, seven dwarfs, something like that."

"Seven dwarfs?"

"Just ignore him, Amanda," Cam said, smiling. "But why does the lantern have eight windows?"

"Gee, Watson, you think it might be a clue?" Brandon turned to her. "It's amazing he didn't get you killed. Give me that thing again. Let's compare it to the original."

Using a diagram in one of Brandon's books they ascertained that seven of the windows were correctly placed and that the extra window was positioned on what would correspond to the north side of the Tower model, a few degrees east.

Cam pulled up Google Earth on his laptop. She peered in as he zoomed in on the Tower neighborhood. "Look," she said. "The window is pointing directly at the Touro Cemetery."

"That's not all, I bet." Brandon scribbled a diagram and a few lines on a piece of scrap paper. "Cam, how far away is this cemetery from the Tower?"

Cam used the ruler function. "About 250 yards."

Brandon consulted the Tower diagram in the book. "This is rough and dirty but it looks to me like a person standing on the second floor of the Tower, in the center, looking out that eighth window, would be staring right at the cemetery."

Cam grinned at her. "They buried their treasures in the Touro Cemetery. Just like we thought."

+   +   +

Cam appreciated the symbolism of the window clue. A window let in light, which was a metaphor for knowledge and understanding. It was exactly the type of clue Prince Henry and the Templars would leave. Subtle but clear.

"So what are you guys waiting for?" Brandon asked. "Get the hell out of here and go find out what's buried in that cemetery. If I could sneak past the nurses, I'd hop on out of here and come with you."

"But we can't simply go and start digging." Amanda said.

"Who said anything about digging?" He hoisted himself higher in the bed, grinning at the befuddled looks on their faces.

"Out with it Brandon," Cam said. "What's your plan?"

"Well, like I said, I've been reading all I can about the Tower. One thing leads to another and pretty soon I'm reading about these secret underground tunnels all around the old Newport neighborhoods. They were used in the 1600 and 1700s by smugglers and pirates. But who built them?"

"Benedict Arnold, after he finished the windmill?" Amanda deadpanned.

"Don't laugh. One of the tunnels runs beneath old Benedict's property. But here's the really interesting thing. Another tunnel begins under the Touro Synagogue. You access it through a trap door under the altar."

"Another coincidence involving the Touro family?" Cam asked.

"Not bloody likely." Amanda grabbed her bag. "They give tours of the synagogue every day. If we hurry we can make the last one." She turned. "Though I can't say I'm overjoyed about getting back in that Subaru."

✝   ✝   ✝

Amanda locked her green eyes on Cam as he navigated the Subaru, which Poulos had retrieved for them, south out of Boston. "So, based on Balducci's reaction, are you confident we got the story correct?" she asked.

"Maybe not every detail but the main gist of it. "

"The carvings at Roslyn Chapel point directly to the Sinclair family. It's either him or we're back to the aliens."

His phone rang. "You gotta call my dad," Brandon announced. "He's got some cool shit to share with you."

"Your dad? But he thinks we're chasing Elvis or something."

"He did. But once you guys convinced him about the Templar-Mason connection ... well, you know how he is — he's like a bulldog. Somehow he got permission to go through all the books and records at the Masonic Lodge in Washington, D.C.; he must have used a secret handshake or something. Anyway, call him. Now."

Peter answered on the first ring. Cam put him on speaker, glad to be using his higher-quality cell instead of the TracFone. "Cameron. Brandon says you're on the way to Newport to search for some tunnel."

"Beneath the Touro Synagogue."

"Answer one question: Do you think the Masons have anything to do with this tunnel?"

"Probably. If our theory is right, the guys who safeguarded the Tower and the cemetery all these centuries were a Masonic cabal."

Amanda leaned toward the microphone. "If the tunnel exists, and it leads to a secret treasure of some kind, somebody had to maintain it and keep it secret. It almost had to be the Masons. Who else could it be?"

"I agree. And you convinced me the Masons and the Templars are one and the same, right?"

"Right."

"And this Prince Henry was a Templar."

"Yup."

"Okay, then here's what you need to be on the lookout for: A symbol called the Delta of Enoch."

"The what?" Cam had never heard of it.

"You've probably seen the symbol—it's basically a golden triangle with Hebrew letters inside. If you go into any Masonic lodge or look at any Masonic artwork you'll see it. Hold on—if I can figure out how to work this thing, I'll email a picture to you."

Cam pulled into an office park off the highway and found a wireless connection for his laptop. A few seconds later the image appeared.

THE DELTA OF ENOCH

"I've seen that," Amanda said. "But what's Enoch?"

"Not what, but who. Enoch was Noah's great-grandfather, from the Bible. The ancient Book of Enoch says Enoch had a dream and in the dream he had two visions. First, he foresaw the great flood — I'll get to that later. Second, he saw a brilliant golden triangle. Inscribed on the triangle was God's name, which he was forbidden ever to speak. You may have seen the name written with the Hebrew letters Yud, Hey, Vov, Hey; it's pronounced 'Yahweh,' though religious Jews are not allowed to say it aloud."

"The tetragrammaton," she said.

"Correct — the Greek word meaning 'word of four letters.' In addition to the written name, during this dream Enoch also walked with God and saw God's face."

"They put you away for telling stories like that nowadays," Cam said.

"Don't joke. In Masonic ritual, Enoch is a very important figure."

"I'm sorry, it's just that you've been such a skeptic. Why the sudden conversion?" Cam merged back onto the highway.

"If you let me continue, you'll see."

"Fine. We're listening."

"According to Masonic legend, after his vision, Enoch took a triangular plate of gold and inlaid the name of God — the name that is not supposed to be spoken — on it with precious jewels. He then sank the gold plate into a cube of agate. That's the Delta of Enoch. Knowing the flood was coming, and wanting to preserve the name of God for future generations, he buried the Delta in a series of underground crypts. You with me so far?"

They exchanged glances. "Sure."

"Later, after the flood, King Solomon built his temple on the ruins of Enoch's crypts, at the base of Mount Moriah. During the construction his workmen found the Delta of Enoch, which Solomon placed on a marble pedestal and hid deep within the Temple of Solomon."

"The same temple the Templars excavated?" Now the relevance was becoming clearer.

"Yes. It may be one of the treasures they found and, if your theory is correct, brought to America. The reason this is significant to the Masons is that Enoch, in his crypt, also buried twin pillars engraved with mankind's accumulated secrets of science and the building trades so that these secrets would not be lost in the flood. These are the symbolic twin pillars upon which Freemasonry is built. I'm telling you this so you understand the connection between Enoch, King Solomon and the Masons."

"Other than the 12th-century excavations, do the Templars tie in?" he asked.

"Yes. Enoch was the father of astronomy. He and his followers tracked the movements of the sun and the planet Venus. I believe Monsignor Marcotte would have called Enoch an early worshiper of the Sacred Feminine."

Cam took his eyes off the road for a second, glancing first at the phone and then at Amanda. "But how could Enoch worship both God and the Sacred Feminine? Doesn't it have to be one or the other?"

"Does it?" She arched an eyebrow. "Think about it."

He was obviously missing something but Peter continued before he had a chance to figure it out. "In fact, many scholars believe Enochian tradition is the basis for Kabbalism, whose earliest practitioners were the Essenes."

The same groups, separated by the centuries, seemed to pop up again and again — Templars, Masons, Essenes, Kabbalists, Sinclairs.

"So, back to your Newport tunnel. As I said, Enoch buried the Delta under a series of nine underground crypts, each one progressively deeper. Each crypt had an arch. You had to pass through eight arches before you reached the treasure, which was buried under a ninth arch. Sound familiar?"

"Actually no."

Amanda shrugged. "I don't get it either."

Peter offered a small laugh. "All right, let's try this: After he buried the golden Delta, Enoch built a temple over the crypts. The structure is described as 'a modest temple ... of unhewn stones and roofless so as to view the celestial canopy that is the work of God.' Does that ring any bells?"

Amanda grabbed his arm. "The Tower, of course."

Cam steadied the wheel with his left hand. "Right. Unhewn stones and roofless."

She nodded. "And the Tower is an astronomical observatory, used to view the 'celestial canopy.' Ideal for a Venus worshiper."

Peter's voice, tinny but smug, continued. "Now let's go back to the arches. Remember what I said: Pass through eight arches; the treasure is under the ninth."

Amanda ran her hand through her hair. "The Tower has eight arches. But we don't think the treasure is buried there."

Cam slapped the wheel. "What if the ninth arch is someplace else?"

"Exactly," Peter said. "That's why I'm calling." He paused for effect. "The Tower accounts for the first eight arches. Find the ninth arch and I bet you'll find your treasure."

✝   ✝   ✝

Salazar had almost driven off the road when he heard the name 'Enoch.' Being able to listen in on their call was a lucky break—Thorne and the girl should have stuck to the TracFone. The mistake would cost them.

He switched lanes and pulled into a rest area as the Subaru disappeared down the highway. He could afford to let them go; he knew where they were headed, which was more than his bosses knew about him. Once the Legions of Jesus' mission imploded, standard operating procedure was to scatter and run; they probably assumed he was on a plane to South America. But standard operating procedure did not anticipate anything like this. He had a treasure to find and this Enoch thing was a key clue, a gift from the spirits.

From a thin leather portfolio he pulled prints of the digital photos he took of McLovick's files. Thumbing through the stack, he found a schematic drawing of the Oak Island Money Pit in Nova Scotia with the word 'Enoch' followed by a question mark scribbled in the margin. The word had meant nothing to him, even after Googling it. Until now.

Studying the diagram of the Pit, he began to understand why McLovick wondered about a connection to Enoch. The Pit, like Enoch's crypts, housed a treasure. And like Enoch's series of nine crypts the Pit was segmented into nine levels, or stories, by wooden platforms ten feet apart in depth. Beneath this ninth platform, according to an inscribed stone at the surface of the Pit, lay the treasure.

He scanned the other pictures. One displayed an Oak Island boulder with a large capital 'G' carved into its face; the 'G' was a common Masonic symbol connoting 'Geometry,' God being referred to in Masonry as 'the Great Geometrician.' Another contained a hand-drawn, bird's eye schematic showing three rocks in the shape of an equilateral triangle. The apex of the triangle pointed directly at the Pit. His chest tightened: Could the triangle represent this Delta of Enoch?

Closing his eyes, he rested his head against the seatback. The obvious symbolic connection hit him after a few seconds: The Templars employed the flood tunnels not only to safeguard the treasure but so that informed seekers would draw the parallel between the Money Pit treasure and the Delta of Enoch, also buried beneath floodwaters. The flood tunnels were both a clue to the wise and a booby-trap to the uninformed. The allegory was almost too perfect: The Money Pit — segmented into nine levels, inundated by floodwaters, marked by the perfect triangle and capital 'G' of

Masonic symbolism — was built by Masons to replicate the crypts built by Enoch, their patron.

He put the car into gear. He still didn't know how to get to the Money Pit treasure. But he had a clue that nobody ever had before. More answers lay in Newport, where Cam and the girl were about to learn more about both the ancient secrets of Enoch and the people who built the Money Pit.

+ + +

Cam and Amanda lingered at the tail of the tour group. The guide, a 60-something man wearing a maroon bow-tie with eyes magnified by thick glasses, explained that Touro Synagogue was the oldest in the country, built before the Revolutionary War. "George Washington once famously wrote a letter in support of the congregation, stating 'the Government of the United States ... gives to bigotry no sanction, to persecution no assistance.'" He pointed to the ionic columns supporting the gallery. "Twelve columns, representing the 12 tribes of Israel. And, of course, the women sat upstairs so as to not distract the men from their prayers." He shrugged. "In many congregations they still do." Probably not a bad idea — as a teenager Cam used to peer down the blouse of a girl sitting in the pew in front of him whenever she bent over in prayer. The guide led the group around a square platform in the center of the sanctuary. "It is a custom of Orthodox Jews to place the altar, called the *bimah*, in the center rather than at one end of the sanctuary."

He nudged Amanda. "Brandon said the trap door is under the altar." He pushed to the front of the group and motioned to get the guide's attention. "I'm sorry, we have to catch a flight. Thanks." He took Amanda's hand, guiding her toward the front door. Once out of sight of the guide, they ducked into a janitor's closet. He pulled a small triangle of wood from his daypack, which also contained flashlights, tools, a GPS device and some food along with the Tower replica. Using his army knife, he gently tapped the wood into the crack between the door and its jamb, wedging it tightly into place.

Amanda nestled against him. "What if they check the door before they lock up?"

"I put the jamb in by the knob so hopefully it'll feel like a dead-bolt. If he's just a guide, he probably won't know if the door has a lock or not."

She turned over a plastic bucket and sat on it. "Do you really reckon there is a secret tunnel?"

"Yeah. Back when they built this place they would have needed some kind of escape route. And apparently they used the tunnel as part of the Underground Railroad. If Brandon's right, they probably built the synagogue over an existing tunnel. A very old one."

The tour, the last of the day, ended fifteen minutes later. Ten minutes after that, the guide shuffled past them into the foyer area. They heard the beeping of an alarm system being enabled, then the guide closed and bolted the front door. "If there's a motion detector, we're screwed. Hopefully they just alarmed the doors and windows. That would be enough to keep kids out and there's nothing really worth stealing in here."

They waited a few minutes before Cam pried the jamb from the door. He pulled out a flashlight but Amanda covered his hand before he could flick it on. "There should be ample daylight. We don't want passersby to see the light."

He slowly pushed the door open. They entered the dark foyer; crouching, they found their way back into the sanctuary. After circling the *bimah* via the aisle opposite the street windows they climbed three carpeted stairs. He dropped to his knees. "Feel around for a gap in the floor. Or maybe a raised area."

"I have a better idea. Give me that torch." One ear against the carpet, she tapped the floor in a grid pattern with the hard end of the light. After a few passes, she smiled. "I found it. A hollow area."

He located a seam in the carpet and, using his knife, pulled the covering away. They stared at a rectangular wooden hatch. She took a deep breath. "Why am I certain there are rats down there?"

He fit his fingers along the rim of the hatch and folded it out. "Don't worry. You don't have to outrun them." He shone the light into a dirt-floored opening four feet below. "You just have to outrun me."

"We've already established my ability to do that, I believe."

Sitting on the edge of the trap door, he rolled his eyes and swung his legs into the hole. "I'll go down and help you from below. Unless the rats get me first."

"My hero," she said as he dropped into the hole. "Shall I cover the hatch?"

He shone his light into an arched tunnel extending beyond his light beam. "No, leave it open. It's creepy enough down here."

She landed soundlessly next to him, her gymnastics training evident. "Look, Cam. It runs back up the hill, straight toward the Jewish cemetery."

He took her hand. "This should be good." Pushing aside cobwebs with his flashlight, he pressed ahead. A shoebox-size ball of fur scurried away from the light beam. "I think that was a cat. At least I hope so."

The tunnel was narrow and arched; they moved single file, Cam needing to duck his head when not in exact center. The walls were cobbled together with rough stones pocked with grout and plaster patches. "Someone's been maintaining this." Otherwise there was no sign of human intrusion.

They continued upward, following the slope of the hill, walking the equivalent of a city block. He illuminated their path while she scanned the walls, in vain, for carvings or other markings. He stopped and examined a compass and street map. As he did so, the sound of something moving behind them echoed forward.

"Cam, what was that?"

He angled his light back toward the tunnel entrance, his ears and eyes straining in the dark for a few seconds until a faint meow sounded. "Must have been the cat. Or maybe a large rat. The tunnel magnifies sound."

He refocused on the map. "Assuming this leads to the cemetery, we're about halfway there." The air, already damp, turned dank and heavy. Rivulets of water ran down the tunnel walls, moistening the cobblestone floor. He illuminated the floor. "Careful, these stones are slippery."

"How does something like this remain secret?" she asked, her free hand braced against the wall.

"We're tracking the path of Touro Street. In Colonial times it was called Jew Street because, well, all the Jews lived there. My guess is that the Jewish community knew about the tunnel but also knew enough to keep their mouths shut. Remember, it was also an escape route for them."

The tunnel bent to the right. They followed the bend another twenty feet, the tunnel now flattening and straightening. He slowed as his light beam hit a void in the space ahead, diffusing and dimming. "That's weird. There's some kind of opening."

"An intersecting tunnel?"

"Could be."

She squeezed his hand. "Have we reached the cemetery yet?"

"No." He shook the compass. "Unless this thing doesn't work down here."

His beam bounced off a solid wall ahead. "Come on. We're here." Five steps later they stepped into a circular stone room, a rotunda. He aimed his light up. "We're in some kind of tower."

She focused on the walls. "Look, there are archways recessed into the walls." She raised her beam. "And window-like boxes recessed higher up." She faced him. "This looks like another Tower replica. Life-size."

"I agree. It's about 25 or 30 feet high, just like the Tower. The only difference is those stairs." He illuminated a narrow stone stairway spiraling upward along the interior tower walls.

"Actually, the Tower originally had a spiral stone staircase. You can see the marks on the inside surface." She smiled. "You may not be surprised to learn that the spiral is another symbol of the Goddess."

They spent a minute studying the rotunda, marveling at the effort and workmanship that went into constructing it. He paced off the diameter. "Eight paces, about 24 feet. What's the Tower?"

"Just over 23. As you said, this appears to be a replica." She ran her light along the circumference. "Eight arches. I was hoping for a ninth."

"Well, it must be here somewhere."

She took the pack from his shoulder and removed the lantern replica. "I wonder if the two models match up." She held the model, rotating it slowly and comparing the windows. "Have a look—all the windows are the same. Even the extra one that's not on the Tower itself."

"Really? Which one is it?"

She pointed her light to an indented square about halfway up the tower wall. "That one. It must be there for a reason."

"Only one way to find out." Pressing his body tight against the tower wall, he climbed the foot-wide spiral stairs. "Pretty cool to think that escaping slaves used this as part of the Underground Railroad."

"Pretty cool to think it was built 600 years ago."

He looked down. "I thought you Europeans didn't think something was old unless it predated the Romans."

"Obviously you Yanks have lowered my standards."

He continued slowly upward. The past week had been truly exhilarating; today's adventure was sweetened by the fact they were no longer being stalked by a team of hired killers. He reached the

indentation representing the extra window. "Here I am. The indentation is right beneath the step I'm on. What should I do now?"

"I don't know—what would Indiana Jones do? Can you reach
it? Press it or some such thing? Perhaps kill a few snakes?"

He dropped to his knees and bent over the cold, damp step.
Reaching down with one hand like a cat feeling for a mouse, he
pressed against the indentation. Nothing. Shifting forward, he
exerted more pressure. Still nothing. "Are you sure this is the right
window?"

She consulted the compass and the replica. "Yes."

"Well, any other ideas?"

She fixed her light on the indentation. "How about the window
ledge. Could that be a lever of some kind?"

He tried the bottom ledge, yanked up on one side. It budged
slightly so he braced himself against the wall and pulled harder. As
centuries of dirt and grime and settling gave way, the ledge pivoted
upward a few inches. A ball or some other round object rolled down
a track and the wall beneath the window slid back slightly.

"Cam, the wall moved!"

"I saw it."

She aimed her light on an area about five feet off the ground,
the beam muted by dust venting from the outlines of the wall
opening. "It's difficult to see but it seems the piece that moved is
about the size of a modern window."

"Let me guess. It's not a perfect square, is it?"

She waited a few seconds for the dust to settle before responding,
though neither doubted what she would see. "The ninth arch,"
she breathed.

A firm, low voice poured into the rotunda, carried along the
path of a fresh beam of light. "Good job. I knew you'd find it. Now,
Mr. Thorne, please get down from there."

+ + +

Salazar waved his Glock 22 in front of his flashlight, illuminating the polished steel. "Mr. Thorne, I'm not asking again."

Thorne turned to the girl. "I guess you were right. That sound we heard was a rat."

Actually, it was a cat. And it led Salazar right to his quarry. His ribs throbbed from the exertion of hiking the tunnel. "For the record, I'm sorry about your dog. That wasn't me who did that. Same with your cousin and the priest."

"What about Eric Forsberg? And McLovick?"

Thorne was stalling, probably trying to think of a plan. "No more talking. Time to see what's behind that arch."

Thorne descended the stairs slowly. Salazar moved his gun from Thorne to the girl and back to Thorne. "I don't want to kill you. But that doesn't mean I won't."

The girl glared at him. "We are aware you're working for the Legions of Jesus. Of course you plan to kill us. Your group will do anything to keep the truth from coming out."

He shook his head. "You're wrong. I'm working alone now. Like you, all I care about is what's hidden behind that ninth arch." He motioned for Thorne to stand next to the girl. "But unlike you, I happen to have a gun."

+ + +

Cam had never stared down the barrel of a gun before — on the bridge with Beatrice and Balducci he had managed to keep his eyes averted. It had an almost magic-wand-like ability to compel obedience. There was no way Salazar would shoot him if he refused to descend the staircase. He was sure of it. Yet his legs carried him downward nonetheless.

He took Amanda's hand, the sweat trickling down his armpits and into his waistband. Her fingers were cold.

"Put your bag and your lights down." As Salazar spoke, the tunnel cat rubbed against his leg. Salazar reached into the outer pocket of his pack, tore off a chunk of cheese and dropped it into the cat's mouth. Odd. "I'll shine my light on the wall. You two push."

Cam and Amanda pushed against the wall, shoulder high, rocking it from side to side to keep it flush in its track. It moved slowly, catching once in a while but after a few minutes they succeeded in forcing it back a couple of feet. The air behind it was stale and thick, even more so than the tunnel itself—the void had probably been sealed for 600 years. Cam reached in and felt an opening on either side of the slab and a floor beneath. "There's enough room for us to squeeze through."

"Good. The girl goes first."

Amanda spun. "Really, I have a name."

Salazar bowed. "I don't doubt it. Truth is, I never knew it."

She looked at him incredulously. "You've been tracking us for a week, you almost killed us a couple of times and you don't even know my name?"

Something in his eyes indicated he agreed that it sounded absurd. "No."

"Amanda."

"Okay, Amanda. You seem like a nice person. You both do. But now I need you to crawl through that hole."

The bottom edge of the opening was chest-high, a simple maneuver for an ex-gymnast. She hopped through and Cam handed her a flashlight. "What do you see?" he asked.

Crouching, she pushed aside some cobwebs and peered into the opening. "It's another tunnel, same direction as the first." Probably heading toward the cemetery.

"Your turn, Thorne."

Cam passed his flashlight and bag to Amanda and hoisted himself up.

"Now, both of you move back, away from the opening. I want you at least 10 feet away from me and I want you each to continue talking. If I hear either of your voices getting close as I climb through, I won't hesitate to shoot." They moved back as Salazar crawled in, gun raised. The cat jumped in after.

Cam was starting to get used to the gun. Salazar probably didn't want to kill them yet; he still might need their help finding the treasure. On the other hand, if he did decide to kill them, it might be another 600 years before anyone found their bodies. He crept ahead without waiting for Salazar's instructions; this tunnel was tighter than the first, about four feet high, and the stonework was rougher. A number of the stones had dislodged and fallen and the tunnel, in a few areas, bowed. There was no way to know for sure but it looked like this tunnel had been built first and the rotunda and synagogue passageway added later, probably by the Jewish Masons in the 1700s as a way to secretly access the older tunnel and whatever secrets it housed.

Feigning a slip Cam reached down and, using Amanda's body to shield Salazar's view, palmed an apple-size rock and slid it into his waistband. Salazar was probably four or five inches taller than him but in the low tunnel that might play to his advantage.

"Well done," Amanda breathed into his ear.

About twenty feet ahead his flashlight revealed another void. "That's right about where the cemetery would be," he whispered.

Amanda took his hand. "Your placeholder theory was correct."

"Yeah. Dead-on."

"Not the best choice of words."

The tunnel opened into a square crypt. Slabs of white and pink quartz covered the walls, ceiling and floor, giving the room a glowing, ethereal look. On the far wall an archway rose above a raised, recessed alcove. Cam shone his light inside: The niche housed a sandstone-colored tomb, its front face marked by a series of engravings.

Cam dropped to his knees and, starting at the top, brushed aside the dust from the carvings. Amanda quickly joined him, removing her water bottle, squirting the area with water and rubbing the tomb clean with her sleeve. Salazar was smart enough to let them work, watching intently.

It became quickly apparent that an engraving of a medieval knight, complete with helmet, sword and shield, dominated the front face of the tomb. Cam's heart raced as he peered through the particles of cave dust illuminated by his flashlight. "This looks a lot like the Westford Knight carving," he said.

"That was the custom at the time when burying a knight. The Temple Church in London is chock full of knight effigies."

"Yeah, but that's London. This is America." He focused on the top of the tomb face where a series of runic letters captioned the carving of the knight figure, presumably identifying the tomb's occupant. "I don't suppose you read runic?" he asked.

"Sorry, no," Amanda said distractedly as she rubbed at the knight's shield area. "But I do recognize this." She shone the light on an engrailed, or scalloped, cross in the center of the shield. "This is the Sinclair family crest." She squeezed his arm. "We found it, Cam. We found him. Prince Henry."

They stared at the effigy. So it was true. Beneath the crust and mold and sludge of history, they had found evidence of a remarkable expedition, led by a remarkable man, hoping to accomplish remarkable things in a new world. Cam barely cared that a gun was aimed at his back.

A number of other markings were inscribed near the bottom of the tomb face, beneath the Sinclair effigy. They rubbed at them, Salazar leaning in and even offering his water and a small towel. Three human-like figures appeared, one smaller than the other two. "Can you make anything out?" Cam asked.

"No," Amanda said. "But turn off your torch for a second."

"Wait," Salazar barked, grabbing Cam's arms and yanking them behind his back. "Just in case you have any stupid ideas."

As Cam winced, Salazar lessened his grip a bit. "Right," he sighed. "Your shoulder." He allowed Cam to shift his hands in front of his waist instead and quickly bound them in plastic cuffs. He also took Cam's heavy steel flashlight from him and handed him a small plastic one instead. "Okay now." Salazar flicked off his light.

Holding her flashlight off to the side, Amanda illuminated the carvings at a flat angle. The images practically jumped off the stone: A bearded man, a woman with long hair and a child also with long hair, all holding hands, the child in the middle. Amanda gulped a breath. "Look at the man's sharp, narrow features. I think it's Jesus. With Mary Magdalene and their daughter." If she was right, Prince Henry wasn't leaving much doubt he believed in the bloodline.

"How can you tell?" Salazar asked.

"It looks much like the carving in Royston Cave in England. I have a photograph the Monsignor gave us in my bag." Salazar nodded his assent and she removed the photo, explaining the cave was a secret 14th-century Templar meeting spot with walls covered with Templar carvings and imagery.

Cam leaned closer, comparing the carving with the Royston Cave image. "Look. These figures have crosses on their robes just like Royston Cave."

"I wonder what else we have," Amanda said as she continued to rub away at the carvings below the images. They were like kids on Christmas ripping through their presents. A series of shapes revealed themselves: a spiral, a rose, a five-sided star. Amanda squinted, turned her head. "These are all symbols of fertility."

"I don't get it," Salazar said, obviously wondering where the treasure was.

Amanda ignored him. "Bloody amazing! Here's a Hooked X. And this is the Sinclair family crest again."

"There's one more image below that," Cam said. "Jesus again?"

She angled the light toward the cave floor. "No, I think not. That's not hair."

Cam smelled the mint gum on Salazar's breath as the operative leaned in and spoke. "It's a headdress. Worn by a Native American chief or sachem." They looked at Salazar. "I'm a Narragansett Indian," he explained.

"I think he's correct, Cam. There's a similar image carved on one of the Spirit Pond stones."

She sat back, widening the light beam to focus on the entirety of the images. They studied the carvings in silence. Amanda spoke first, her voice little more than a whisper. "It's a genealogy."

"But there are no names." Cam said.

"No. But the pictures convey the information. Working down, below the effigy, the first thing we have are Jesus and Mary Magdalene and their daughter Sarah. Below them are symbols of fertility, telling us that their bloodline continued to procreate. Next is the Sinclair family crest and the Hooked X, indicating that the Sinclairs are carrying the bloodline and marking their journey to the New World with the Hooked X. And the Native American sachem, well, apparently this is telling us the bloodline flows through him, whomever he is."

"Probably Prince Henry's son," Cam said.

Salazar shifted and his eyes widened. "Wait a second. You're saying Native Americans are part of the Jesus bloodline?"

"*I'm* not saying it," Cam responded, "these pictures are saying it."

"But didn't Sinclair have other children?" Salazar's grip on Cam's shoulder relaxed.

"Yes. But apparently he wanted to make it clear that another branch of the bloodline flowed here in America. Probably with the Narragansett tribe, since that's who lived here."

Salazar whistled softly. "Holy shit."

+ + +

Cam, Amanda and Salazar sat quietly in the cave, studying the carvings on the tomb. For Salazar, the revelation that Jesus' blood flowed through his veins was oddly ... disturbing. His grandfather told him he descended from a long line of Narragansett chiefs. Which meant it was almost certain he had some of the Sinclair Jesus blood. But he had long ago rejected Catholicism, the religion of his mother, in favor of Narragansett spiritualism and its emphasis on nature. Was it possible he could unite the two beliefs, have the best of both worlds? And what about Rosalita, being raised Catholic by her grandmother? How do you tell a little girl that she descended from God? Perhaps that was a greater legacy than any treasure he could ever find. Not that it would pay for college.

Which brought him back to the present. What was the next step? He was ten feet underground with a secret that would change world history. Not to mention being a step or two away from some ancient treasure. And he was stuck here with a couple of people who knew he had committed murder.

Amanda solved the problem for him. She had rolled away and begun to examine the rest of the crypt. "My goodness, Cam, look." She focused her beam on an archway above the alcove. Salazar scrambled to his feet.

+ + +

Amanda reached up and rubbed at the arch's keystone with a wet cloth before refocusing her light beam on it. She forced herself to blink, just to be sure her eyes weren't playing a trick on her. The beam illuminated a multicolored slab of agate, its orange and pink and purple bands brilliant even in the dim light of the crypt. A triangular plate of gold, the size of a billiards rack and imbedded within the agate slab, glowed yellow in the dusty light. Dozens of gemstones were recessed into the gold, arranged to form four Hebrew letters — the tetragrammaton, the not-to-be-spoken name of God.

Cam brushed more of the dirt and grime away, fingering the jewels awkwardly, his hands still cuffed. "I can't believe we found the Delta of Enoch."

Her body tingled. "Do you realize that if this is authentic it predates Noah's flood? We're talking more than 5,000 years old. Older than the pyramids."

A quick glance at Salazar extinguished her excitement. He was studying the arch, probing the stonework with his hands. If he could manage to remove the keystone without the ceiling falling on his head, he would not hesitate to do so. If not, he'd make certain the keystone was here when he returned for it. In either event it was clear he valued the artifact for more than just its historical significance.

Cam hadn't yet deduced Salazar's intentions. He managed to extract his camera from his pack and snap a few pictures. "Who knows when we'll get back down here again," he said.

Salazar snatched the camera away. "Or if it will be here when you return," he said quietly.

✜   ✜   ✜

Amanda sat cross-legged on the stone floor in front of the niche. "Cam, what do you notice about that triangle?" She kept her voice low, hopeful that Salazar would be too focused on his treasure and the problem of extracting it to be bothered by anything she said.

Cam stood next to her. "It's equilateral."

"Anything else?"

"Not really."

"Men." She pulled him down. "Let's try this. Draw a triangle in the dirt." Squatting, he did so, his hands still cuffed. "Which way does it point?"

"Up."

"As do most triangles, correct?" She waited for him to figure it out.

He shifted forward. "I get it now. The Delta of Enoch triangle is pointing down. And the upside-down triangle is the womb, the pubic area — a symbol for the Sacred Feminine."

Just as the upward-pointing triangle symbolized the phallus, the blade, the male. "And why do you imagine the Delta might be pointing down?" She stood, urged him along with her hands. "Really, it was built by a chap who actually viewed the face of God." Sometimes our core values are so ingrained, so hard-wired, that they prevent us from reaching even the most obvious conclusions. "Don't you see, Cam? Enoch didn't choose a square or circle or oval. Or even a tablet like the Ten Commandments. He chose a feminine triangle, the Yoni Yantra, to proclaim and record God's true name."

His eyes widened. "Of course. That's the big secret, the mystery. The thing the Church was fighting so hard to suppress, is still trying to suppress. That's what the Templars and Prince Henry really believed, the reason for the big split with the Vatican." He shook his head. "They believed God is a woman."

She leaned down and kissed him. "Hallelujah."

✝   ✝   ✝

Salazar allowed himself to become distracted for a moment from the task of extricating the keystone. His eyes drank in the beauty of the agate and the jewels, the purity of the solid gold plate. He did some quick calculations: the plate itself probably weighed 50 pounds; at 900 dollars an ounce, that was almost a million dollars, not even including the diamonds and rubies and sapphires. But even as he completed his calculations, he realized the mistake he had made. And it wasn't a mistake of arithmetic.

+   +   +

Cam slid the rock from his waistband and edged around behind Salazar. Amanda nodded in agreement — Salazar was a killer. There was no way they could count on him letting them out of the cave alive.

He wished he had a bigger rock. Raising his cuffed hands high, ignoring the pain in his shoulder, he thrust the rock downward, aiming for a spot on the back of Salazar's skull.

He must have exhaled or grunted as he swung his arms, because Salazar turned and ducked at the last second. Cam adjusted his aim but the cuffs on his hands restricted him and the best he could do was deliver a glancing blow to the area above Salazar's ear. He tried to maintain his balance and follow up with another blow but the momentum of the attack propelled him sideways, out of range. Salazar groaned and staggered away, waving his gun unsteadily. He mumbled a couple of unintelligible syllables and blinked a few times, then dropped to his knees, swaying side to side. Before he could recover, Cam charged him again.

The Glock shrieked, flooding the crypt with the thunderclap of echoing gunfire. The bullet seared Cam's left upper arm as he flew through the air, pinwheeling him sideways. Amanda screamed and scrambled to the corner as he skidded across the floor. Salazar held the gun menacingly, tried again to speak. "Dumb. Move." Cam crawled away, a fire raging in his arm, and prayed Salazar would control his anger.

Salazar rubbed his head, examined the blood on his fingers and leaned against the crypt wall, blinking. Amanda edged over to Cam and held the light to his wound. "We must get him to a hospital. I can see shattered bone."

Salazar ignored her. The cat loped to him and licked the wound on his head. Eyeing them, he reached into his pocket and pulled out a piece of cheese. The act seemed to calm him; his eyes regained their focus and he took a deep breath. "Like I said, dumb move. Now, here's the deal. I'm not leaving this crypt until I get my treasure. That means you two aren't leaving either."

"Rubbish. We need a doctor." She ripped a strip from Cam's shirt and bandaged his arm. "He's bleeding quite badly." She lifted his arm as high as she could and rested it on his pack to try to reduce the bleeding.

Salazar ignored her again. "One choice is to try to get that keystone out of the arch. But I don't like our chances — the whole thing would probably fall on our heads."

"What's the other choice?" Cam forced the words out, his hands still cuffed. He had scalded his hand on a wood stove once; the pain had been excruciating for a few seconds. The pain from the bullet wound was just as bad. But it wasn't fading.

"We figure out the Money Pit mystery."

Amanda looked up. "What's to figure out. The treasure is here."

"I think there's more."

"What, a 5,000-year old slab of gold embedded with jewels is not enough treasure for you?"

"Actually, it is. But, as I said, it's stuck in that arch. Here's the thing: They didn't build that Money Pit for nothing. Something's buried there. And I think you two are the ones to help me figure out how to get to it. I have a theory."

"If we assist you, will you allow me to bring him to a hospital?" Amanda asked.

"Yes, as long as I believe you are putting forth your full efforts. I have no interest in seeing either of you suffer." Salazar summarized his conclusion that the Pit was meant to replicate Enoch's crypts, that the flood tunnels were actually a clue as well as a booby-trap. "But I can't put it all together."

Cam tried to focus but the pain made it difficult. Amanda stared at the crypt walls, obviously deep in thought. "When the Pit floods, how high does the water get?"

Salazar pulled a file from his bag and thumbed through some papers. "About 30 feet below the top."

She nodded. "That confirms it." She reached for her bag. "I'm going to remove the Tower model, okay? Not a weapon." Salazar nodded. She showed him the replica. "During your Revolutionary War, British troops blew a couple feet off the top of the Tower. It used to stand about 30 feet tall, the same depth as the Money Pit when filled with water."

"And?"

She pointed to the Delta of Enoch. "That's the key. The Sacred Feminine."

"I don't get it."

"Open your mind. Consider life and fertility and the womb. Here, I'll make it simple for you: What does the Pit represent, at its most base, symbolic level?"

Cam's head spun; Salazar looked at her blankly.

"Come on, guys. Even I've heard the old joke—the monument to Martha Washington is a 600 foot hole in the ground." She paused. "So what does the Pit represent?"

"The womb?" Cam said, the words coming out soft and weak.

"Precisely. And the most precious thing of all—life itself—is found in the womb."

"All right, I get that," Salazar said. "The treasure is in the Pit, in the womb. But how do I get it out?"

"Well, how would one extract life from a womb?"

He shifted from one foot to the other. "By seeding it."

"And just how does one do that?"

"I guess it starts by inserting a penis."

"You guess?"

He shifted. "All right, you put a dick in."

"Brilliant. You combine the male and the female. Just as with the Hooked X. And just as with the Jewish star, which happens to be a Masonic symbol—you combine the male triangle with the female triangle. So," she said, holding up the Tower replica, "do you know of any 30-foot phalluses?"

✛   ✛   ✛

Amanda was playing a dicey game here. Salazar was intrigued by her 30-foot phallus theory. But she was making it up as she went along.

"So you think this Tower model is the key to accessing the Money Pit?"

"Of course. Just as it was the key to locating the ninth arch."

"How?"

She glanced at Cam. His face was covered in sweat and he was shivering in the damp crypt. "If I tell you, you'll simply leave us here to die."

"Maybe. But if you don't, I definitely will." He pushed himself to his feet slowly, aiming the gun at Cam while eying her. He was wobbly from the blow to his head but still functional. Little chance of her overpowering him. "Give me the model. I'll figure it out myself."

She laughed. "Really, are you certain of that?" She needed a plan. One that satisfied Salazar but also ensured their escape from the cave. "I have an idea. We shall all leave the cave together. When we arrive at the synagogue, I'll give you the model and explain the clue."

He waved away her proposal, as she feared he would. "No deal. I've got the gun, I call the shots. But you're right—I'm not sure I can figure it out myself. Lucky for me I don't have to. We stay here until you tell me how the model gets me into the Money Pit."

Her mind raced. She needed a convincing story, plus a new plan. "The key to it all is the extra window. It got us through the rotunda and it will get you into the Pit."

"I'm listening."

She glanced at Cam, still shivering and moaning. He was running out of time. She ripped another strip from his shirt, this one about ten feet long. "First I need to change his dressing." Shielding him from Salazar with her body, she handed one end of the dressing to Cam. "Hold that tight," she whispered. "And sit up tall." Instead of tending to his wound, she passed the other end of the bandage through one of the windows in the Tower replica and wrapped it around her own wrist. Standing slowly so as not to alarm Salazar, she backed away from Cam and released the Tower model, allowing it to slide along the cloth strip like a dog on a leash run. The model hung between Cam and her, dangling a few feet off the ground, suspended by the thin ribbon of fabric. She turned to Salazar. "If either of us releases the fabric, the model will crash to the floor. And Cameron is beginning to lose consciousness."

Salazar smiled. "Nice try." He took a step toward the model.

She lowered her hand a few inches, sending the replica diving toward the stone floor. "Stop where you are. We have nothing to lose. And we have no need for the model anymore."

He stepped back. "Okay. Looks like we have a stalemate." He stared up at the Delta of Enoch. "How about this? You finish telling me about how to get into the Pit and I'll let you two walk out of here with that thing hanging between you. I only get it when we all get out. Okay?"

It gave them a chance, at least. "Very well. But we begin now. I see no reason for Cam to lie here bleeding in this crypt any longer."

✝   ✝   ✝

Cam staggered through the tunnel, head bowed, fighting to keep his feet. If he stumbled, the model — their ticket out of here — would fall and crash. He felt feeble, empty, out of fuel, similar to the way his body reacted when his sugar levels got too low. Who knew how a loss of a couple pints of blood affected blood sugar. And his arm seared. At least Salazar had cut his cuffs so he could brace himself against the walls with his right arm.

"Shall we rest?" Amanda walked behind him in the dark, the eight foot ribbon an invisible moat between them. Even if she wanted to help him, the tunnel was too narrow to walk side-by-side. He was on his own. Salazar brought up the rear.

"Doing okay. The rotunda is just ahead."

Amanda was still stalling, knowing the drop into the rotunda would be Salazar's best chance to grab the model. "So, as I said, the extra window is the key. You'll need to orient the model on the horizon, of course...."

Cam reached the rotunda opening, lowered his body into a sitting position. The model slid along the ribbon to him. Quickly, before Salazar could intervene, he dropped through the hole, hugging the model to his chest like a running back securing a football. His knees buckled as he landed but he somehow kept his balance. He raised his arm high in the air and the model slid back toward Amanda crouched in the passageway.

"Well done, Cam." She jumped through as well, landing soundlessly on the stone floor.

They moved away from the opening to allow Salazar room to climb through. The cat leapt down beside him. He turned and, using a couple of handholds expertly hidden in the panel's face, pulled the passageway door closed. "I haven't given up on that triangle of gold yet." He turned back to Cam and Amanda. "Because of that, you know I'm not going to kill you — at some point someone would track you to this rotunda and find your bodies. Then I'd never be able to get back to the crypt. But I still expect you to keep your end of the bargain. Keep talking."

Cam nodded. Whatever they could do to get rid of Salazar was worth it. And it wasn't like they had many bargaining chips — Salazar had the gun and time was running out on Cam. Amanda moved toward Cam, shortening the ribbon as she did so, and palmed the

Tower replica. Pulling her end of the ribbon through, she handed the model to Salazar. "From what I've read, the Money Pit flood tunnels are designed like the ones in the pyramids in Egypt. Which makes sense, since the Middle East is where the Templars learned most of their engineering tricks. There should be an alcove or niche in the Pit that matches up with the extra window on the model; I'm guessing it's about twenty feet beneath the surface, just like in the rotunda. That's your key. In the niche there should be a lever like the one that opened the ninth arch. Pull the lever and some kind of mechanism will release rocks and stones and debris that will seal the flood tunnel. That's how it works in the pyramids. Then you should be able to get to the treasure."

Cam steadied himself against the spiral staircase. True or not, it was a hell of a story. Better yet, Salazar bought it.

Salazar tucked the model into his bag and began to jog down the tunnel toward the synagogue. After a few strides, he stopped and turned. "I'm sorry about your dog, Thorne, I really am. And about your friends also." He ran his fingers through his hair as his eyes rested on Amanda. "I have a little girl, almost seven years old. I hope she turns out like you, Amanda."

CHAPTER 19

[Late September]

Amanda, blond again and clear-skinned, lounged in a chenille bathrobe at a bed and breakfast in Newport, picking at a corn muffin as she scanned the Sunday paper. She laughed quietly as she showed Cam a story headlined, *Da Vinci Code Comes to America.* "The irony is that this story wouldn't have been nearly so large if the Vatican fanatics hadn't gone around killing people willy-nilly to keep it quiet."

Cam had just returned from a long run along Newport's Cliff Walk. After a couple of days in the hospital and a few days rest, he was regaining strength. "It's almost always the cover-up, not the crime, that gets people in trouble."

A couple of weeks had passed since their jump from the Longfellow Bridge, which Amanda, in an accent he continued to find endearing, had renamed 'The Long *Fall* Bridge.' The press accounts, fueled by the arrests on the bridge, focused initially on the seedy activities of the Vatican extremists. But as the days passed a few outlets had begun to dig deeper into the story, to explore what it was that the Vatican was so intent on keeping secret. The Consortium, to its credit, did not attempt to finesse the story by downplaying either Prince Henry's opposition to the Church or the reality that the Narragansett Indians had as much claim to the title of heir to the Jesus bloodline as did the Consortium families. As Babinaux explained to Amanda, "Sometimes we forget the old Yiddish proverb, that a half truth is a whole lie. It is time to tell Prince Henry's entire story and allow the world to form its own opinions. If the Vatican is unhappy with us, so be it." Cam and Amanda were happy to stay out of the spotlight and allow the Consortium to speak for Prince Henry—it gave them time to recover, unwind and get to know each other in a less frenzied setting.

Despite the wisdom of Babinaux's Yiddish proverb, they had decided to keep their crypt discoveries—both the Delta of Enoch and the Prince Henry tomb and genealogy—secret for now. In a month or two, after the dust settled, they would contact the synagogue and cemetery trustees. Even without the crypt, the Prince Henry story was a monumental one: The account of the heir to the Jesus bloodline journeying to America 100 years before Columbus to establish a new Christianity based on ancient pagan ideology both altered American history and undermined many of the core teachings of the Catholic Church. But the millennia-old evidence in the crypt, showing that the earliest practitioners of the religion that spawned Judaism, Christianity and Islam believed God existed in a feminine form, would shake the world. The Christian fundamentalists and Orthodox Jews would go crazy; the hard-line Islamic clerics might go ballistic. "I have no interest in being the next Salman Rushdie," Amanda had noted. On a more practical level, they wanted to move carefully to avoid a Dead Sea Scrolls-like scenario—the Vatican somehow gained control of the scrolls in the 1960s and delayed release of any information for decades.

They did, however, phone Scott Wolter in Minnesota to share their crypt discovery and their conclusion about the femininity of God. Without his research they wouldn't have come close to solving the mystery. "Well, I guess now we know why Mona Lisa was smiling," he had chuckled.

Even without the crypt contents the Prince Henry saga filled newspapers, magazines and airwaves. Public opinion essentially fell into three different camps — some bought the story of Prince Henry, heir to the Jesus bloodline, coming to America to form a New Jerusalem in opposition to the Church; some believed he came but rejected the Jesus bloodline and any religious rationale for his journey; and a minority dismissed the evidence as circumstantial and questioned the events completely. Within this latter group, no doubt, existed racists who could not accept the notion that the blood of Jesus ran through a race of North American savages.

Amanda continued reading from the newspaper. "Even now, the Blinky Blanks of the world insist our entire version of events is hogwash. She's quoted in this story, still claiming the Newport Tower is a Colonial windmill." But she was in the minority. Even without the crypt, there was simply too much evidence, coupled with the Vatican fanatics' desperate desire to suppress it, for the public to dismiss the Prince Henry story.

"The press is clueless sometimes," Cam said. "Why are they interviewing professors and governmental officials? These are the people who couldn't figure it out in the first place."

"Yes. They should be interviewing the NEARA folks."

"In the end, it won't matter. I just ran by the Tower. There were about 50 people there, plus another tour bus arriving. Blinky Blank can say whatever she wants but people will make up their own minds."

Based on the talk shows and press accounts, most Americans, after the initial shock of having the name Jesus Christ linked with words like 'paganism' and 'Kabbalism' and even 'witchcraft,' seemed to be okay with Prince Henry's reported goal of reuniting the male and the female in the Godhead, of tempering Mars with some Venus, of respecting Mother Nature rather than merely conquering and exploiting her earth. Of course, most Americans didn't know that Prince Henry and his followers took it one step further and believed God existed in a female rather than male form.

The Masons, apparently, were in on the secret. Or at least a few of them were. Peter had done more research on the Delta of Enoch symbol. When portrayed in a Masonic lodge or on artwork, the triangle usually pointed up. But there was one special degree of Masonry called 'The Thirteenth Grade of the Ancient and Accepted Scottish Rite, the Royal Arch of Enoch.' During this ceremony a feminine, downward-pointing triangle was deployed. Apparently this degree, named after Enoch, signified that the Mason brother had reached an advanced level of understanding and enlightenment. "Once you reach it you're allowed to see the truth," Peter had said.

Cam gulped some water. "In retrospect, the idea of God being a woman isn't so outlandish. Like you said to Salazar, isn't life the most precious gift? I just had to get past my cultural bias."

"And swallow your male ego."

"That too."

"To be fair, I didn't see it either," she conceded. "Nobody saw it, other than perhaps a handful of high-level Masons. Not that the clues weren't there. The Cistercians were practically screaming it out to the world: They took the beehive as their symbol and they worshiped the Virgin Mary—they viewed themselves as a cluster of worker bees serving the queen. And the Templars dedicated everything to the Virgin Mary and made the queen the most powerful piece on the chess board. Why, if not to venerate the Sacred Feminine? It's not like medieval woman possessed any power."

Over the centuries, Judeo-Christian culture had flooded human consciousness with so many images of a male God that no other possibility seemed conceivable. It wasn't always so; Isis reigned supreme in ancient Egypt. But eventually the branches of the Isis tree—embodied in Templar, Cistercian, Masonic, Gnostic and Kabbalistic beliefs—became concealed beneath the smothering forest of patriarchal Christianity, Judaism and Islam. "It's just hard to believe nobody figured this out before. The clues are so obvious."

"More so than you know. Look what I stumbled upon." She handed him a printout from a webpage. "I was surfing the Web while you were on your run. How's your Hebrew?"

"I can do the blessing over the wine. That's about it." He glanced down at the paper. Some kind of Hebrew grammar lesson.

"A shame. It would have saved us a lot of time and work." She sat forward in her chair and explained. "In Hebrew, like Spanish and French, all words are either masculine or feminine, depending on their final letter. In Hebrew, words that end in the letter 'hey' are almost always feminine."

Blood rushed to his face as he grasped the importance of this information. "No way." The tetragrammaton, the ancient Hebrew name for God, was spelled Yud, Hey, Vov, Hey. Yahweh was a feminine word.

"Way. In fact, it should actually be pronounced 'Yahwah' instead of 'Yahweh,' which makes it even more clearly feminine. In some texts it's still written with the 'a.' Centuries ago somebody changed it to make it sound more masculine."

He smiled. "A man, no doubt."

"No doubt. The mainstream Jewish scholars perform all sorts of grammatical acrobatics to come to the conclusion that the word Yahweh is actually masculine or even gender-neutral, but I think that's more a reflection of cultural bias than anything else."

"What about other names for God?"

"Funny you should ask. Are you familiar with the word 'Elohim'?"

"Sure. It's the name for God in the Hebrew Bible."

"Correct. In fact it's the third word in the Book of Genesis. Well, the root word of 'Elohim' is 'Elowah.' And 'Elowah' is also a feminine word."

She leaned back. "So it seems that the ancient Israelites, both the ones who first named God and also the ones who wrote the Bible, may have believed God was a woman."

✝　✝　✝

Cam stepped out of the shower, his body still tingling over the revelation that Yahweh and Elohim, the ancient Israeli names for God, were feminine words. He had never been all that religious but felt strangely drawn to the spiritual side of Prince Henry and his worship of the Sacred Feminine. Or maybe they should rename her the Supreme Feminine.

Of course, that may have been because he himself was under the spell of Venus for the first time in his life. And happily so.

Amanda smiled at him, aware he was staring at her. She folded her newspaper as he dried himself and dressed. "Some of the newspapers are declaring Prince Henry rejected Christianity."

"Why would he do that? He was a descendant of Jesus. Of course he didn't reject him. He just wanted to bring Christianity back to its roots." The way it was before the orthodox Church fathers hijacked it. In many ways Prince Henry was the true Christian, the true messenger of Jesus Christ.

"I agree. I think that's what Roslyn Chapel is, an attempt to marry the Sacred Feminine with Christianity—Christ and Mother Nature, combined under one roof." She reopened the newspaper. "Fancy this quote from Niven Sinclair; remember, he's the current patriarch of the Sinclair clan: 'Roslyn Chapel is a story in stone—a story which tells us that God and Nature are One.'"

He smiled. "That's pretty good."

"Which is probably why Prince Henry got on so well with the North American natives. They shared a reverence of nature."

"Apparently that's not all they shared." Prince Henry's tomb made it clear he had merged his bloodline, and that of Jesus, with the Narragansetts.

"Good point. Speaking of which, did you see anyone at the Jewish Cemetery?"

"I ran right by but nobody was poking around." They had returned a few times to the cemetery, not surprised that no trees or plants, other than the rose bushes, grew in Frazon's corner of the cemetery — the roof of the crypt probably rose to just below the surface of the ground. Which was also probably why nobody was buried in this section of the cemetery other than Frazon.

"Do you really believe none of the synagogue officials know about the crypt?"

"I do." They had debated this question a few times already. "I think at one time people like the Touros knew. But when the Jews fled Newport after the Revolutionary War, the secret died. As far as they knew, the tunnel ended at the rotunda."

"I don't envy the synagogue leaders. They're going to have their hands full with this. And it won't help that they're Jewish — you know how people can be, especially when it comes to religion." She bit her lip. "They'd be wise to contact the Consortium for assistance. They're the experts on Prince Henry and they belong to powerful families in Europe."

"And they're Christian."

"Yes." She paused. "Whatever that means."

✝   ✝   ✝

"I have a poem I want to read you. I think you'll fancy it," Amanda said. Cam had finished dressing and they were walking hand-in-hand up the Touro Street hill, past the Touro Synagogue and toward the Jewish Cemetery a block away. The tunnels ran pretty much beneath them.

"Okay, shoot."

"It's a verse from Longfellow's poem, *The Jewish Cemetery in Newport.*" She pulled a piece of paper from her bag and read slowly.

"Gone are the living but the dead remain,
And not neglected, for a hand unseen,
Scattering its bounty, like a summer rain,
Still keeps their graves and their remembrance green."

She folded the paper slowly. "Sounds like Longfellow reckoned someone was secretly watching over the cemetery. Watching over a grave."

"A hand unseen," he repeated. "It's one of those things that once you know the mystery, you start seeing the clues all over the place."

"Speaking of clues, here's another we missed: Prince Henry was not just a prince, he was also part of the Davidic line of the Kings of Israel. As the Monsignor said, Jesus was a direct descendant of King David. And Mary Magdalene herself was from the House of Benjamin, another royal line. Therefore their heirs would have been Jewish kings. Kings of Jerusalem."

"I like it. Prince Henry, King of the New Jerusalem."

"Here's my point: In chess, where is the king positioned?"

"Right next to the queen." Then it hit him. "Oh, I get it. We didn't take the chess clues far enough. Sinclair is the king. He's buried next to the queen, Mary Magdalene, mother of the royal bloodline."

"We had it wrong. The Tower wasn't just a rook. It also symbolized Mary Magdalene, Mary-of-the-Tower. It was the queen."

Not wrong, just not completely right. The Tower was both rook and queen. "Just like you told me: With the Templars, always look at things on multiple levels."

As they walked he thought more about Prince Henry being buried at the Jewish Cemetery, just a few hundred yards from the Newport Tower. "That helps explain why the Touro family protected these sites. As Masons they were keeping the Templar secrets. And as Jews they were protecting Mary Magdalene and her sacred bloodline."

Amanda nodded. "Just as their ancestors did in France after she fled Jerusalem. She was Jewish royalty."

"Hey, here's a radical thought. Is there any chance Prince Henry and the Templars were protecting the Mary Magdalene bloodline, not the Jesus one? She was the female after all."

Amanda considered it for a few seconds. "Possibly, but I don't think so. They still believed Jesus was the son of God; they must have assumed a female God—the Sacred Feminine—could have impregnated the Virgin Mary as easily as could a male deity. It was Jesus' line that was paramount. They were still Christians; they still worshiped Christ."

They arrived at the front gate of the cemetery. Amanda reached between the wrought iron bars and snapped a red rose off its vine. Stretching forward, she dropped the flower onto a shaded rectangular area in the front quadrant of the cemetery, a few feet from where Frazon was buried. She bowed her head, took a deep breath. "Rest easy, Prince Henry."

Another tour bus cruised by, heading for the Tower. Cam grinned. "Yeah, rest up. It might get pretty crazy around here soon."

They stood silently for a few seconds, their fingers around the iron rails. She turned to him. "Did you realize the rose is the symbol for the Virgin Mary? And also for Venus? And also a pseudonym for Mary Magdalene?"

"No, no and no." He glanced at the rose vines. "But I'm not surprised."

"And Roslyn Chapel was so-named because it sits on an ancient European rose line, or prime meridian."

He nodded. "Just as the Newport Tower served as Prince Henry's prime meridian in the New World. It all fits together." He never would have figured this out without Amanda. "Roses. Another clue I missed."

"That's to be expected from a man with your last name," she deadpanned.

He laughed. "So you think these rose bushes have been here for 600 years?"

"Possibly. Just like the oak trees and the petroglyphs and the other clues they left." She stared at the grave site, her lips pursed. "Beatrice was spot on about one thing. Prince Henry really was a brilliant, special man." She stared at the patch of grass. "Years might pass before the crypt is opened. Perhaps we should give him a tombstone."

"Nice thought. What would you write on it?"

"Something that wouldn't reveal his identity, right? We can't have folks digging up his grave."

"Right. So it needs to be cryptic." He smiled. "And I think Prince Henry would prefer it that way."

The words popped into Cam's head as if carried to his ears by the rose-scented wind. "You know how the archeologists are always saying the ground doesn't lie?"

She nodded.

"Well I'd play off that theme using Niven Sinclair's own words." He took her hand. "It'd be a simple inscription: *The rocks don't lie: He was here, and he came because God and Nature are One.*"

EPILOGUE

[December 21]

There was one more thing they wanted to check out. Amanda stood huddled against Cam inside the Newport Tower, peering east toward the brightening morning sky. The temperature was in the teens and the wind howled across the park, swirling within the Tower.

Amanda grinned as she blew on her hands. "Perhaps the wind-mill theory is correct after all."

They had received special permission from the city of Newport to get inside the Tower for the winter solstice. If their theory was right, if the Tower really was a medieval calendar as well as a prime meridian and baptistery, it should mark the winter solstice in some kind of dramatic fashion. In ancient times the solstice was the most important day of the year, the day when the sun reversed its pattern of descent in the southern sky and offered the first promise of spring, of rebirth, of life renewing after a time of death and darkness.

Scott Wolter had noticed a tawny keystone above one of the eight arches on the interior of the Tower. He had done some calculations and theorized that, on the morning of the winter solstice, the sun's rays would pass through one of the seemingly-randomly placed windows of the Tower and illuminate the egg-shaped keystone.

His excitement on the phone a few nights earlier had been contagious. "The symbolism is perfect. If we believe the Tower is a shrine to the Sacred Feminine, then the egg-shaped keystone is what?"

"The egg within the womb," Amanda had immediately answered. It would have taken Cam a bit longer.

"Right. And in ancient times, the sun was believed to be the male to the Venus female. So the sun comes in and shines on the egg—"

"Fertilizing it," she had interjected.

"Exactly. It's an allegory. The egg is fertilized, marking the rebirth of life. Mother Nature, the Sacred Feminine, Mother Earth, gives life again."

Cam and Amanda had awoken at dawn, camera in hand, to test Scott Wolter's theory. From the looks of the angle of the sun and the height of the keystone it would be an hour or so—around 9:00—before the sun's rays hit their target.

Brandon had considered joining them but opted instead for a Caribbean cruise with one of the Mass. General nurses. He received his prosthetic leg in November; during Thanksgiving dinner someone asked for a drumstick and Brandon lifted his leg onto the table and made a show of removing the artificial section. Even Peter laughed. And he had already ordered a set of ski poles designed for one-legged skiers; no doubt he would re-master the sport before spring.

While they waited for the sun to rise, Cam took some measurements. "Hey, did you know the Tower isn't exactly round?"

"Really?"

"It's off by about six inches. Do you think that's on purpose?"

"I've come to the belief that everything they did was on purpose." She stared at the Tower walls for a few seconds. "It's another allegory, Cam. The earth itself isn't perfectly round. So why should a depiction of Mother Earth be? They built the Tower slightly ovular, just like the earth."

"I like it," he smiled. "And I would have figured it out myself. Eventually."

"Undoubtedly."

A blue sedan approached and rolled to a stop on Mill Street, near the Tower. After the driver spoke on a cell phone for a minute or so, a middle-age woman and a small girl stepped out. Hand-in-hand, huddled in thick parkas and mittens, they approached across the frozen park, buffeted by the wind. "I wonder what they want," Cam said.

"Probably curious. Normally the gate to the Tower is locked."

The woman and girl stopped a few feet away from the Tower as if waiting for permission to come closer. Cam's cell rang. "Thorne, this is Salazar."

The scar on Cam's arm burned. According to Lieutenant Poulos they hadn't been able to catch Salazar even though they knew he was probably headed to Nova Scotia. He motioned Amanda over and placed the call on speaker. "What do you want?"

"Believe it or not, I have a favor to ask. That little girl in front of you is my Rosalita. With her grandmother."

A pair of bold brown eyes stared out at Cam from behind a fur-lined hood. "What, do you want us to baby-sit?"

A short laugh. "Nothing like that. But if you're right about the Tower, about it being used to measure astronomical alignments, I figured something would happen this morning and you'd be there to check it out. My people also mark the winter solstice. I wanted Rosalita to see it."

Amanda squeezed Cam's hand. "He's not trying to make trouble. And it's never a bad thing to enlighten a child." She turned to the girl. "Is your name Rosalita?"

Rosalita's grandmother, her face made-up even at the early hour, guided her forward. "I'm seven," she announced, holding up two pink-gloved hands, one presumably shielding two raised fingers and the other five.

Amanda stepped forward. "Seven? You certainly are a big girl."

"Yes," Rosalita agreed. "Are you Daddy's friends from work?"

"In a way. Yes."

"Are you the ones who told Daddy that God is a woman? I told the nuns at school and they made me say ten Hail Marys."

Amanda laughed. "That's quite an interesting choice of penance." She smiled at Cam. "Did you also tell them Jesus was your great-great-great-great-grandfather?"

"Yes but they already knew that. They said I shouldn't brag about it."

"That's good advice." Amanda motioned her forward, into the Tower. "Your father wants us to show you something."

As Amanda took the girl's hand, Cam tried to reconcile the competing versions of Salazar as both doting father and trained killer. Perhaps it wasn't such a paradox—he just wanted what was best for his daughter like any other parent. "We have another friend, his name is Mr. Wolter," Amanda explained. "And he has a theory, an idea. Do you see this rock? It's called a keystone. If we pulled it out, the other stones would all fall on our heads. Do you see that?"

Rosalita backed away a couple of steps.

"No need to worry, honey, I won't touch it. Now look around at the other arches. Do you see any other stones similar to this one?"

Rosalita's little body rotated like a second hand on a clock. "No."

"Well, that made Mr. Wolter curious. And there's one other thing about this stone. Do you notice it's not exactly in the middle of the arch? That also made Mr. Wolter curious. The men who built this tower were very smart—they would not have put the stone off to the side unless they had a good reason."

"When I draw a picture of my friend, I put her nose right in the middle of her face."

Amanda laughed lightly. "As would I. To understand Mr. Wolter's theory, I need to tell you about the old days, before people had science to help them understand things. Well, in the fall, the people noticed the days were getting shorter and shorter. They were afraid the sun would never return, leaving them in permanent darkness and cold. They knew that without the sun the plants would die and they would starve."

"I can think of a plant that lives in the winter. A Christmas tree. Daddy and Grammy and I have one."

Cam smiled into the phone. So Salazar was in town. Did Poulos know?

"Correct." Amanda clapped her hands together. "In fact, in the old days, people used to place evergreen trees in their homes because they believed the trees were magic and would help bring the sun back." Which explained the Christmas tree custom. "Anyway, they would watch the sky very carefully to see when the days would stop getting shorter. When they were certain the sun was rising again in the sky they held a big celebration." Which explained the Christmas holiday itself—the Church took the date of the customary pagan rebirth-of-the-sun celebration and redefined it as Jesus' birthday.

She continued. "Well, Mr. Wolter believes that this tower was built to help tell the people when the days were going to start getting longer again."

"How will it do that?" Rosalita scanned the Tower walls. "Stones can't talk."

"Not in words. But they can still tell us things."

The sun had risen so that its light shone through the Tower's southeastern window and left a shoebox-size illumination high on the Tower's interior northwestern wall. As the sun slowly rose and moved along the horizon, the box of light crept down the Tower wall in a diagonal descent toward the keystone.

"Hey, Thorne. My mother-in-law has something for you," Salazar said over the phone.

Cam glanced up and the woman stepped forward, her dark eyes alert. She reached inside a canvas bag and, smiling tightly, handed him the Tower replica. "I made a mold and brought it up to Nova Scotia," Salazar said. "I met the guys who owned the land—you can't get near Oak Island they have so much security. Plus half the cops in Canada are looking for me. But I found the guys I needed, told them about the model, about Amanda's theory. They must've bought it—they gave me a hundred grand for the mold. Not bad. I put it into a college fund for Rosalita."

Cam took the replica. Hard to hate the guy until you remembered the blood in his wake. "It belongs to the Gendrons. I'll return it to them." He had no desire to chat further. Was it okay to hang up on a guy who shot you?

But Salazar wasn't finished. "One thing I was thinking about. Anybody you ask in Rhode Island will tell you: You need stonework done, hire a Narragansett Indian. My grandfather was a stonemason. I always thought they learned from the Colonists. But maybe it goes back further than that."

It made sense. Prince Henry would have needed help. He didn't have enough men with him to build the Tower. Or even the tunnel and crypt. Perhaps his stonemasons trained the Narragansetts.

Salazar continued. "Hey, thanks for letting Rosalita watch. She's getting all this Catholic stuff from her grandmother. I want her to understand her Native American side also. This Prince Henry stuff, worshiping Mother Nature, is pretty close to what my grandfather taught me."

"It wasn't just nature, Salazar. It was combining nature with Jesus' teachings—you know, the Golden Rule, love thy neighbor as thyself." Cam paused. "Maybe even some Commandment about murder being a bad thing."

"Yeah. I get that."

Cam ended the call and joined Amanda inside the Tower. "So, do we have a fertilized egg?"

She took his hand, her other remaining linked with Rosalita's. "Not yet. But it won't be long now." The light box was creeping, angling directly toward the keystone.

"I'd love to see Blinky Blank's face when she sees these pictures. A Colonial windmill that also just happens to mark the winter solstice."

As if on cue, the light beam kissed the edge of the egg. The corner of stone, normally tawny-colored, flushed golden. Rosalita gasped and pointed. "It's glowing."

Over the course of the next few minutes the box of light inched along until it illuminated the entire egg, the rectangle of light centered perfectly on the ovular stone. They stood and stared, transfixed. Normally adults were incapable of viewing the world through the eyes, wondrous and innocent, of children. Not this time. The egg-shaped stone radiated like an ember as the sun's rays, narrowed and focused by the window, fired against it. "This must have been truly spectacular 600 years ago," Amanda whispered. "They probably covered the other windows and the roof so that the Tower interior was dark. Then, every morning, probably commencing weeks ago, they'd watch as the light box approached the egg."

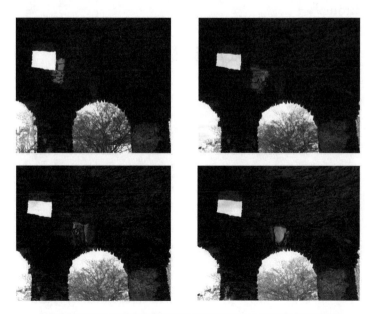

NEWPORT TOWER WINTER SOLSTICE ILLUMINATIONS

Cam stared at the egg. "You can see how the keystone had to be placed just off-center for the light to hit it. It probably had to be moved a few times to get it perfect."

"Yes. Whoever built the Tower was good. But not that good." Amanda sighed. "Originally I expected this to be a parable for the duality of God — the sun, representing the male, fertilizing the egg in the womb of the Tower, representing the Sacred Feminine and Mother Earth. But then I began thinking about the beehive again. The drones fertilize the queen bee, but that doesn't make them the king. They remain mere drones. It's the same with the sun. It plays an essential role, but that doesn't make it a king."

"You're probably right." Cam reflected on everything he had learned since the Bobcat first blew. "It's just like the Cistercians and Templars and Masons and Kabbalists have been trying to tell us all along." The message was both cryptic and clear, hidden and in plain view. He lifted her hand to his lips and kissed it gently. "They knew the truth. They knew the queen sits alone, high on her throne."

THE END

AFTERWORD

By far the most common question I get from readers is, "Are the sites and artifacts in this book authentic?" The answer is a resounding yes. With the exception of the crypt under the Jewish Cemetery in Newport (and its contents) and the clay replica of the Newport Tower, all the sites and artifacts described in these pages are real and genuine. Most, in fact, are on public property or in public custody, available for viewing. I invite readers interested in exploring these matters further to join the New England Antiquities Research Association (NEARA) or visit the NEARA website at NEARA.org. I also invite readers to check their television listings for a documentary by Committee Films that mirrors much of the research used in this book; the documentary is entitled *The Secret History of North America* and is scheduled to be released in the first half of 2008.

Readers interested in discussing any aspect of this book are invited to visit my blog site, westfordknight.blogspot.com.

NOTES

Page 56 — reference to British excavation of Solomon's Temple in the 1860s yielding Templar artifacts: http://www.robertlomas.com/Freemason/Origins.html

Page 59 — reference to Copper Scroll (of Dead Sea Scrolls) contents: http://www.usc.edu/dept/LAS/wsrp/educational_site/dead_sea_scrolls/copperscroll.shtml http://www.sdnhm.org/scrolls/description_cs.html; see also *The Mystery of the Copper Scroll of Qumran*, Robert Feather (Bear & Company 2003).

Page 63 — reference to Masonic activity as successors to Templars as early as 1390: *The Virgin and the Pentacle*, Alan Butler (O Books, 2003), at page 33.

Page 63 — reference to Templar involvement in 1391 Peasant's Revolt in England: *Born in Blood*, John J. Robinson (M. Evans, 1989).

Page 71 — reference to *Rex Deus* bloodline: http://en.wikipedia.org/wiki/Rex_Deus

Page 93-94 — reference to a general overview of the Prince Henry expedition: http://www.clansinclaircanada.ca/articles/beyond.htm; see also *The Lost Colony of the Templars*, Steven Sora (Destiny Books 2004).

Page 94 — reference to Mi'kmaq natives playing shinny prior to Colonial settlement: http://www.sonahhr.com/sonahhr/index.cfm?fuseaction=home.history&chapter=5

Page 116 — reference to Newport Tower architectural features and astronomical alignments: http://www.neara.org/CARLSON/newporttower.htm

Page 116 — reference to conclusion Newport Tower is not Colonial structure: http://www.chronognostic.org/over_touro_park.html

Page 116 — reference to Narragansett legend that Newport Tower was built by "fire-haired men with green eyes who sailed up river in a ship like a gull with a broken wing": http://sinclair.quarterman.org/newport_tower.html

Page 118 — reference to Westford town history publication rebutting legend that Fisher boys carved Westford Knight carving: *Gazetteer of the State of Massachusetts*, Elias Mason (B.B. Russell, 1874), at page 542

Page 131 — reference to Frank Glynn statement that Westford Knight "Encampment Site" had been plowed over: See "Westford Knight Collection" materials, J.V. Fletcher Library, Westford, Massachusetts, USA

Page 132 — reference to links between Robert Louis Stevenson and the Sinclair family: *New England's Ancient Mysteries*, Robert Ellis Cahill (Old Salt Box, 1993), at page 53; http://en.wikipedia.org/wiki/Robert_Louis_Stevenson

Page 134 — reference to outlawed Templars becoming pirates: http://www.greyfriars51.fsnet.co.uk/the_jolly_roger.htm

Page 142 — reference to dating of Spirit Pond Rune Stones to 1401-1402: "The Spirit Pond Rune Stones," Scott F. Wolter (unpublished paper), March 4, 2007

Page 143 — reference to the Noman's Land Rune Stone's original location high on a bluff: http://www.mvgazette.com/news/2007/07/06/rune_rock_credibility.php

Page 145 — reference to ancient maps being oriented with east at the top: http://www.strangehorizons.com/2002/20020610/medieval_maps.shtml

Page 147— reference to Popham Colony's founding in 1607: http://www.pophamcolony.org/new_page_1.htm

Page 148 — reference to America's Stonehenge site being built by either Phoenicians or ancient Europeans: http://unmuseum.mus.pa.us/mysthill.htm

Page 151 — reference to pre-earthquake river system in Lake Memphremagog area: *NEARA Journal*, Volume 40, Number 2, Winter, 2006, "The Knights Templar in Nouvelle-France," Gerard LeDuc, Ph.D, at pages 28-29.

Page 155 — reference to Tyngsboro mansions tunnel system: http://genforum.genealogy.com/farwell/messages/106.html

Page 161 — reference to "bloodline" families identified as Plantard and St. Clair in *The Da Vinci Code*: *The Da Vinci Code*, Dan Brown (Doubleday, 2003), at page 260

Page 163 — reference to Niven Sinclair quote regarding Sinclair family marriages: http://sinclair.quarterman.org/who/henry.html

Page 164 — reference to Bernard de Clairvaux referring to Mary Magdalene as the 'Bride of Christ': *The Magdalene Legacy: The Jesus and Mary Bloodline Conspiracy*, Lawrence Gardner (Weiser 2007), at page 160.

Page 192 — reference to original Templars being part of *Rex Deus* bloodline: *Templars in America*, Tim Wallace-Murphy and Marilyn Hopkins (Weiser Books, 2004), at pages 14–15.

Page 199 — reference to floorboards of longhouse near Spirit Pond Rune Stone site being carbon-dated to 1405: "The Spirit Pond Rune Stones," Scott F. Wolter (unpublished paper), March 4, 2007

Page 245 — reference to Holy Spirit and Holy Sophia being one and the same: *Mary Magdalene, Bride in Exile*, Margaret Starwood (Bear and Company 2005) at page 116; http://www.adishakti.org/text_files/holy_spirit.htm

Page 246-247 — reference to quote equating church architecture to female genitalia: http://www.askelm.com/doctrine/d980928.htm

Page 249 — reference to use of evergreen to celebrate winter solstice: *Mary Magdalene, Bride in Exile*, Margaret Starwood (Bear and Company 2005) at page 136

Page 255 — reference to yoni being ancient symbol of Sacred Feminine: *Mary Magdalene, Bride in Exile*, Margaret Starwood (Bear and Company 2005) at page 135

Page 256 — reference to Bernard de Clairvaux's skull being preserved: http://www.geocities.com/saintbernarddeclairvaux/history.html

Page 256 — reference to Bernard de Clairvaux's role in the veneration of the Virgin Mary: *The Knights Templar Revealed*, Alan Butler and Stephen Dafoe (Barnes and Noble, 2006), at page 202

Page 257 — reference to Bernard de Clairvaux's use of Kabbalistic rabbis: http://www.mystical-www.co.uk/mana.htm

Page 257 — reference to Statue of Liberty being modeled after Isis and Sacred Feminine: http://freemasonrywatch.org/statue_of_liberty.html

Page 261 — reference to Roslyn Chapel inscription: http://www.rosslyntemplars.org.uk/wine_is.htm

Page 262 — reference to Nashoba meaning "hill that shakes": http://170.63.97.68/dcr/stewardship/histland/reconReports/ westford.pdf, at page 24.

Page 270 — reference to the Golden Ratio: http://en.wikipedia.org/wiki/ Golden_ratio

Page 271 — reference to Masonic usage of the Golden Ratio in layout of Washington, DC: http://freemasonrywatch.org/washington.html

Page 271-272 — reference to 'X' as being symbol of underground religious movement that recognized Mary Magdalene as bride of Christ: *Mary Magdalene, Bride in Exile*, Margaret Starwood (Bear and Company 2005) at page 130

Page 272 — reference to Cardinal Ratzinger quote equating Masonry to grave sin: *The Virgin and the Pentacle*, Alan Butler (O Books, 2005), at page 142

Page 280 — reference to Templar influence in making queen most powerful chess piece: http://sinclair.quarterman.org/archive/2002/03/ msg00021.html

Page 280 — reference to Church changing ship piece on chess board to bishop: http://sinclair.quarterman.org/archive/2002/03/msg00021.html

Page 286-287 — reference to quote that Columbus had royal blood of Jerusalem in his veins: http://en.wikipedia.org/wiki/ Salvador_Fernandes_Zarco

Page 287 — reference to book, *Christopher Columbus, The Last Templar*: Ruggero Marino (Destiny Books, 2005)

Page 304 — reference to the name Salem's relation to the planet Venus: http://essenes.net/m44.htm

Page 317 — reference to Judge Sewall's belief that Native Americans were essential to creation of New Jerusalem in America: *Judge Sewall's Apology*, Richard Francis (Harper Perennial 2006), at page 37

Page 317 — reference to Judge Sewall's observations regarding his wife's breasts: *Judge Sewall's Apology*, Richard Francis (Harper Perennial 2006), at page 31

Page 321 — reference that Bourne Stone may have been gift to Native Americans from Judge Sewall: *Ancient Stone Sites of New England and the Debate Over Early European Exploration*, David Goudsward (McFarland & Company, 2006), at page 162

Page 321 — reference to Judge Sewall visiting Noman's Land in 1702: http://history.vineyard.net/dukes/bnk2c_71.htm

Page 322 — reference to Judge Sewall visiting Stonehenge in 1689: *Judge Sewall's Apology*, Richard Francis (Harper Perennial 2006), at page 60

Page 322 — reference to Judge Sewall visiting Jewish cemetery while in England in 1689: *Judge Sewall's Apology*, Richard Francis (Harper Perennial 2006), at page 60

Page 322 — reference that Judge Sewall helped arrange for Joseph Frazon's burial in Newport's Jewish cemetery: http://faculty.gordon.edu/hu/bi/Ted_Hildebrandt/NEReligiousHistory/Sewall-Diary1674-1729/Sewall-Vol2-1699-1714.htm

Page 323 — reference to location of today's Magnetic North: http://anthro.palomar.edu/time/time_4.htm

Page 324 — reference to location of Magnetic North in 1400: http://anthro.palomar.edu/time/time_4.htm

Page 324-325 — reference to Magnetic North declinations at various locations in America: http://geology.isu.edu/geostac/Field_Exercise/topomaps/mag_dec.htm

Page 328 — reference to Mary Magdalene meaning "Mary of the Tower": http://www.paralumun.com/marylife.htm

Page 329 — reference to relationship between Pilgrim families and Templars: *The Goddess, the Grail and the Lodge*," Alan Butler (O Books, 2004), at pages 295-97.

Page 329 — reference to the name Merrimack being of European origin: http://reel-time.com/forum/showthread.php?p=144741

Page 330 — reference to the original spelling of the name Merrimack: http://www.jstor.org/pss/1263431

Page 332 — reference to Verrazzano's log describing Native American appearance: http://content.wisconsinhistory.org/cdm4/document. php?CISOROOT=/aj&CISOPTR=115 at page 46.

Page 332 — reference to John Williams comments describing appearance of Narragansett babies: http://www.valhs.org/history/articles/society/ text/other_artifacts.htm ; Paul H. Chapman, "Norumbega: A Norse Colony In Rhode Island", *The Ancient American* 1994

Page 332 — reference to similarity in appearance between Mi'kmaq chief and Sinclair clan chief: *Templars in America*, Tim Wallace-Murphy and Marilyn Hopkins (Weiser Books 2004), at pages 116–17

Page 333 — reference to Mi'kmaq and Sinclair DNA testing: http://www. msthomas.com/spectator-articles/spec-spring06/spring06-pg3.htm

Page 334 — reference to possibility Verrazzano purposely withheld information on Newport Tower from his logs: *NEARA Journal*, Volume 39, No. 1 (Summer 2005), "Verrazzano's 1524 Visit to the Vicinity of Newport, RI," Terry J. Deveau, at page 30.

Page 334 — reference to 1622 Pilgrim journal: http://www.mayflowerhistory.com/History/explore4.php

Page 335 — reference to Masonic Grand Master position being hereditary one passed on to head of Sinclair clan: http://www.electricscotland.com/history/kt7-13.htm

Page 338 — reference to Touro family purchasing Newport Tower land: http://www.eyesofglory.com/mainframe.htm

Page 339 — reference to nobody except Joseph Frazon being buried in Touro Cemetery for 84 years: *The Old Jewish Cemetery of Newport*, Joshua L. Segal (Jewish Cemetery Publishing, LLC, 2004)

Page 340 — reference to Touro family and other Newport Jews as leading Masons: http://www.geocities.com/athens/Forum/9991/sephardic. html; http://www.eyesofglory.com/mainframe.htm

Page 341 — reference to many U.S. Founding Fathers being Masons:
The Goddess, the Grail and the Lodge," Alan Butler (O Books, 2004),
at pages 304–308

Page 346 — reference to Judge Sewall's sister being Longfellow's grandmother:
http://www.longfellowfamilytree.com/history.htm

Page 351 — reference to Peleg Wadsworth being leading Mason in Maine:
http://imaginemaine.com/mainestories/Wadsworth.html

Page 351 — reference to Hiram Abiff's role as architect of Solomon's Temple:
The Book of Hiram, Christopher Knight and Robert Lomas (Sterling
Publishing 2003), at pages 81–82

Page 370 — reference for Enochian tradition being the basis for Kabbalism:
The Book of Hiram, Christopher Knight and Robert Lomas (Sterling
Publishing 2003), at page 222

Page 371 — reference to Enoch's "modest temple": *The Book of Hiram,*
Christopher Knight and Robert Lomas (Sterling Publishing 2003),
at pages 349.

Page 399 — reference to words in Hebrew ending in letter 'hey' being
feminine: http://www.hebrew4christians.com/~hebrewfo/
Grammar/Unit_Four/Feminine_Nouns/feminine_nouns.html

Page 399 — reference to Yahweh as feminine word: http://www.helium.com/
items/133474-grammar-ancient-scripturebecomes

Page 399 — reference to change of spelling from 'Yahwah' to 'Yahweh':
http://209.85.165.104/search?q=cache:NwPiwEMap_IJ:www.seek-
god.ca/htname.htm+yahwah&hl=en&ct=clnk&cd=3&gl=us

Page 399 — reference to Elohim being feminine word:
http://occult-advances.org/nc-rel-elohim-allah.shtml

ACKNOWLEDGEMENTS

I hardly expected when I began this project that I would become a believer of the Westford Knight legend. But as I journeyed around New England — visiting related sites and inspecting related arti-facts — the lawyer in me became increasingly convinced that the sheer volume and weight of evidence supporting the legend of 14th-century European exploration in New England could not be ignored. But who was here, and why had they come? To unravel this mystery I relied on the generous assistance, patience, good will and knowledge of many scholars, researchers and experts in pre-Columbian history. Here are a number I especially wish to acknowledge, at the risk of no doubt omitting many others:

Niven Sinclair, the ultimate authority on all things, both European and American, involving the Westford Knight and Prince Henry Sinclair.

Virginia Kimball, Tom Paul and Norman Biggart, longtime members of the Westford Knight Committee and experts on its history.

Dan Lorraine and Rick Lynch, current and past Presidents of NEARA and experts on pre-Columbian sites and artifacts.

Penny and Dan Lacroix of the Westford Museum and Historical Society.

Sue Carlson and Roslyn Strong, longtime NEARA members and experts on the Spirit Pond Runestones, Newport Tower and countless other pre-Columbian sites and artifacts.

Janet and Ron Barstad of the Chronognostic Research Foundation, who conducted the 2006-07 archeological excava-tion at the Newport Tower.

Malcolm Pearson, longtime NEARA member who discovered, photographed and chronicled many of the sites and artifacts related to the Westford Knight.

Terry Deveau, NEARA researcher and expert on many sites and artifacts in New England and Maritime Canada.

Zena Halpern, NEARA member and expert on sites and artifacts related to Goddess worship in North America.

Judi Rudebusch, researcher and expert on stone holes and their alignments.

William Penhallow, Rhode Island Astronomy Professor who conducted astronomical sightings at and around the Newport Tower.

Anne Wirkkala, NEARA researcher and head librarian.

Lisa Long, of Newport, Rhode Island's Redwood Library.

Rabbi Shoshana Perry, for helping me explore some of the religious aspects of this story and for allowing me access to her library of Jewish source materials.

Elizabeth Lane, library volunteer who maintains the Westford Knight collection materials at the J.V. Fletcher Library in Westford.

Dan Kelly and Steve Voluckas, NEARA researchers.

Vance Tiede, expert on the Gungywamp site.

David Goudsward, historian and author of Ancient Stone Sites of New England and the Debate Over Early European Exploration (McFarland and Company, 2006).

I also wish to thank, as always, my wife, Kim, for the countless hours she spent reading, editing, revising and streamlining this story. Not to mention the dozens of day trips and family vacations I dragged her on to conduct research.

Thanks to my daughters, Allie and Renee, who heard so much about my research that they began to refer to me as the "rock nerd."

Many thanks to the readers of early drafts of the story — Richard Scott, Spencer Brody, Richard Meibers, Tom Coffey, Jeanne Scott, Jeff Brody, Janet Wolter, Scott Wolter, Dorothy Paine, Stan St. Clair, Lynn Brody Keltz, Donna Doherty, Elaine Jeffery, Richard Coleman, Susan M. Sinclair Green Grady, Romeo Hristov, Irene Gordon, Carolyn Metcalf and Audrey Desrochers — for their invaluable comments, insights and suggestions.

Many thanks also to the professionals that assisted me: John "Ike" Williams and Cara Krenn of the Kneerim & Williams literary agency for their advice on crafting the story and guiding me toward publication, and Amy Span Wergeles and David Scott Sloan for both their legal advice and friendship.

Finally, I offer a heartfelt acknowledgement to Scott and Janet Wolter for their invaluable assistance. Much of this story is based on research conducted by Scott, and he and Janet and I spent countless hours on the phone and via email exchanging notes, theories, ideas and information relating to this subject. We also spent many days together conducting field research. I am extraordinarily grateful for their assistance, and Kim and I have been enriched and blessed by their friendship.

PHOTO CREDIT

Photographs and images are provided courtesy of the following individuals:

WESTFORD KNIGHT SWORD – Scott Wolter

WESTFORD BOAT STONE – Kimberly Scott

TOMBSTONE OF SIR WILLIAM ST. CLAIR – Scott Wolter

ROSLYN CHAPEL "INITIATION CARVING" – Scott Wolter

SPIRIT POND RUNE STONES – Scott Wolter

RUBBING OF THE BOURNE STONE – Scott Wolter

THE SACRIFICIAL STONE AT AMERICA'S STONEHENGE – Dan Lorraine

TYNGSBORO MAP STONE – from *Bend in the River*, by John Pendergast (Merrimack River Press, 1992)

KILMORE CHURCH STAINED GLASS WINDOW, DERVAIG, ISLE OF MULL, SCOTLAND – Kathy Bragg

ROYSTON CAVE CARVING – Ben Hammott

KENSINGTON RUNE STONE (INCLUDING INDIVIDUAL RUNES) – Scott Wolter

NARRAGANSETT RUNE STONE – Richard Lynch and Dan Lorraine

MACHIAS BAY PETROGLYPH – Richard Lynch

CHURCH OF THE CONVENT OF CARMO, LISBON, PORTUGAL – Kimberly Scott

LYE CHURCH, GOTLAND, SWEDEN – Scott Wolter

YONI PATTERN, CONVENTO DE CRISTO, TOMAR, PORTUGAL – Kimberly Scott

BERNARD DE CLAIRVAUX LACTATING AT BREAST OF VIRGIN MARY – from *"Medieval Images of Saint Bernard of Clairvaux"*, James France (Cistercian Publications Inc., Kalamazoo, Michigan, 2007)

CHRISTOPHER COLUMBUS SIGLA – Scott Wolter

LONGFELLOW BRIDGE, BOSTON – Richard Scott

NEWPORT TOWER ILLUMINATIONS – Scott Wolter